Praise for
Candice Proctor's first novel,
Night in Eden . . .

"I haven't had a romance thrill me as much since I read Kathleen Woodiwiss's *The Flame and the Flower*, and I still have my *1972 copy*! This is a book I will definitely buy and read again."
—BRENDA ELLIOTT, Oxford, AL

"Candice Proctor will soon be an author everyone will be talking about. Her characters drive her story with an intensity that you can feel from the first page."
—JOSEPHINE MIRISOLA, Dedham, MA

"I began reading this book one evening, thinking I would read a chapter or two and pick it up the next day. Once I started, I could not put it down. Needless to say, I finished the whole book in the wee hours of the morning."
—ELLEN F. SMITH, Summersville, SC

"*Night in Eden* is really a page-turner. I felt like I was transported back to early 1800s Australia. Her characters and story were very believable and real. I sure hope a sequel is in the makings."
—KATHY BAKER, Fort Worth, TX

*Please turn the page
for more raves. . . .*

By Candice Proctor
Published by Ivy Books:

NIGHT IN EDEN
THE BEQUEST

THE
BEQUEST

Candice Proctor

IVY BOOKS • NEW YORK

An Ivy Book
Published by The Ballantine Publishing Group
Copyright © 1998 by Candice Proctor

www.randomhouse.com

Library of Congress Catalog Card Number: 98-92447

ISBN 0-8041-1827-2

Manufactured in the United States of America

First Edition: May 1998

10 9 8 7 6 5 4 3 2 1

For my mother, Bernadine Wegmann Proctor . . .
who has always been there for me

THE
BEQUEST

PROLOGUE

Central City, Colorado, February, 1874

An arctic wind gusted down the mountain, to fling icy snow crystals against the lamp-lit windowpanes of the gingerbread-trimmed mansion known as Celeste's Place. But inside the house's velvet- and brocade-draped rooms, firelight cast a warm glow over gleaming satin sheets and pale, naked flesh.

People said Celeste's Place was the grandest brothel between San Francisco and Chicago. Men sometimes rode the train up from Denver, just to visit the big white house at the top of Nevada Gulch. The whores were all young and beautiful, the wine cellar well stocked, and there was even a discreet gaming room where a fortune could be won. Or lost.

The woman who owned Celeste's Place knew all about winning and losing. Tonight, as she moved among the rich, powerful men who thronged her front rooms and ogled her whores, Celeste DuBois wore jewel-studded slippers, a blue satin evening gown, and a strand of real pearls around her neck. But there had been a time when Celeste had gone barefoot, and dressed in tattered hand-me-downs. There had been a time . . .

Celeste didn't waste energy dwelling on those memories, although she was careful not to allow herself to forget them, either. They reminded her never to become too complacent, never to take anything for granted. Not that she needed reminding tonight. Because if Doug Slaughter had his way, she would lose everything, including her life. Tonight.

She paused at the door to the gaming room, looking for her partner, Jordan Hays. Her gaze skimmed over the mine owners and bankers with bulging waistcoats and waxed mustaches, and settled on the poker table, where a hand of five-card stud was just ending. As she watched, the dark-haired, narrow-eyed gambler facing the front window raked in an impressive pile of chips.

Jordan glanced up, found her watching him, and flashed her a reckless grin that might have made her pulse quicken, if she'd still been susceptible to the lure of dark, dangerous men with charming smiles and wicked ways.

"Deal me out," he said in a slow, gentleman's drawl that was pure Virginia. Pushing back his chair, he came toward her with that unhurried, rolling gait of his that somehow managed to be both languid and menacing at the same time. He always dressed entirely in black, relieved only by the crisp white of his frilled shirt. Even the leather holster of the gun he wore strapped low on his hip was black.

And even a woman who knew men and their bodies as well as the devil knows sinners couldn't help but admire the grace of that young, hard physique. He was built long and lean, with an aristocrat's fine-boned face and hands. Beautiful, deadly hands, as skilled with a gun as with a deck of cards. It was because of those hands that Celeste had taken Jordan Hays on as her partner two months ago.

Most people assumed she'd taken him as her lover, too, but she hadn't.

"Any sign of trouble?" he asked, leaning in close so that only she would hear.

"No." She watched his gaze flick from the stained-glass surround of the front entrance, to the gaming room's bay window. Heavy green velvet drapes framed the graceful bow, and ecru lace panels screened the lower windows. But above, the anonymous blackness of the night showed through bare, frosted glass.

Put a marksman with a rifle on the hill out there, and he could pick you off, easy, Jordan had told her, when she'd insisted on circulating among her customers, as usual.

"I don't believe Slaughter hired someone to kill me." She turned her back on the uncovered windows. "I think he's just trying to put pressure on me, scare me into selling."

Hays shook his head, his gaze now scanning the crowd in the front parlor. "Slaughter knows you don't scare. You'd have sold this house to him months ago, if you were that easy to intimidate. Hell, look at you now. You won't even stay away from the front rooms."

"If I don't come out here and run this house, Slaughter won't need to shoot me. I'll put myself out of business."

"You can't run this house if you're dead."

"I'm not afraid of death," she said, her voice even. "If there's one thing I've learned in life, it's that dying isn't the worst that can happen to you in this world."

His gaze met hers, his green eyes flat with an absence of emotion that was a betrayal in itself. " 'The gods conceal from men the happiness of death, that they may endure life,' " he quoted softly.

And she nodded, because even though they'd never spoken of it, they both knew this was one thing they had in common, this living with pain and loss that went soul-deep.

Her hand crept up to finger the strand of pearls around her throat. It had been twenty years since she'd kissed the man who first clasped that necklace around her neck. Twenty years since she'd held him in her arms, felt his breath warm and soft against her cheek.

Twenty years . . .

Suddenly Celeste felt old, although she knew she wasn't, really. Her mirror told her she was still beautiful, still desirable—her waist still tiny, her breasts still firm, her face unlined, her pale blond hair still untouched by gray. But she felt old. Old and tired. And oddly calm.

She laid her hand on Jordan's arm, and leaned into him, because even though he was her partner and not her lover, he was still a man, and she was a woman who knew all of a woman's tricks and how to use them. "Promise me something, Jordan?"

He put his strong, tanned hand over hers, and smiled down at her, the creases in his cheeks deepening roguishly. "Anything I can, darlin'."

She laughed. She loved it when he called her darlin' and smiled at her like that. It always made her wish, for one wistful moment, that she was young again, and still had a heart to lose, just so that she could fall in love with him—even though she knew that any woman who made the mistake of falling in love with this man would end up with a broken heart. Because Jordan Hays was a drifter. A restless, death-haunted man with a hollow ache where his heart should have been.

But Celeste didn't want his heart. She wanted his fast

hands and his keen eyes, and his unswerving dedication to that noble code of honor that no Southern officer and gentleman could seem to walk away from, no matter how tragic his past, or how dissolute and debauched his present existence.

"Promise me you'll see Gabrielle gets my share of this place, if something does happen to me," she said.

Most men would have just shushed her, and told her not to worry her pretty little head, that nothing was going to happen to her. But Jordan had never patronized her. "She's your daughter, Celeste. I've already told you I'll see she gets everything she has coming to her. *And* I'll make sure she doesn't know where it came from, like you asked."

"Even though it means you'll probably end up having to sell this place to Slaughter?"

Jordan pursed his lips and blew out a bitter sigh. "I won't pretend I'd like doing it. But if it's what you want—"

"It's what I want. This place and the people in it are important to me, but not as important as my daughter. I want her to have that money."

He shifted his gaze, once again, to the cold, dark night beyond the bay window. She saw his eyes narrow, although she knew he couldn't possibly see anything out there. "I wish to hell someday you'd tell me how you ended up with a daughter who's a schoolteacher in a New Orleans convent," he said.

Even after all these years, the pain of her separation from Gabrielle could still thrust deep and sharp enough to take Celeste's breath away. "Gabrielle grew up in that convent," she said, her voice quavering. "I did think about bringing her out here, after the war. But a brothel is no place to raise a child. Especially a girl child."

" 'Keep thy foot out of brothels, thy hand out of plackets, thy pen from lenders' books, and defy the foul fiend,' " he quoted wryly.

"That sounds very biblical," she said.

He laughed. "It does, doesn't it? But it's from *King Lear*."

She started to laugh, too, just as the front window shattered behind her with a splintering tinkle of breaking glass. Something cold slammed into the center of her back, knocking the breath out of her.

She heard a woman scream. And a man's voice, shouting, "My God! She's been shot!"

Celeste pitched forward, trying to suck in air, but her chest ached and her legs buckled beneath her. She felt Jordan's arms come around her, cradling her, easing her down onto the plush carpet. She saw his face hovering over her, saw the glitter of his green eyes.

She wanted to say something, and he ducked his head, trying to hear. But she had no breath, so she moved her lips, mouthing a name, a prayer, a greeting.

Beau.

And then she smiled . . .

CHAPTER
ONE

New Orleans, Louisiana. Several weeks later.

Gabrielle Antoine pounded the last nail into the lid of the big wooden crate that stood on the convent's creeper-clad veranda. A mockingbird sang from the lowest branch of a magnolia in the corner of the mossy brick courtyard, his song sounding clear and sweet in the morning air. Gabrielle glanced up, searching the dense, leafy tree, just as the hammerhead came down, hard, on her thumb.

"Jesus, Mary, Joseph, and all the saints," she muttered, popping her sore thumb into her mouth.

"Swearing again, Gabrielle?" said Julia St. Etienne, coming up behind her with a swish of silk skirts.

Gabrielle swiveled her head to meet her friend's laughing black eyes. "I was not swearing, Julia." She grinned around her thumb. "I was praying."

"Of course you were, *mon amie*." Heedless of her elegant, dusky rose faille dress with its *tablier* of ivory damask and rows of flounces, Julia hopped up to sit on the edge of the packing case. "What were you praying for?"

"A better aim." Gabrielle swung the hammer again. Carefully. "And for the sudden, hideously painful death

7

of every blasted Yankee carpetbagger in the city of New Orleans."

"That doesn't sound very holy."

"I never claimed to be holy."

"No. Although I always thought the nuns were more successful with you than they were with me."

"They had me longer." Gabrielle swung the hammer one last time, then leaned her hip against the crate and gazed out over the lush green gardens, sunken brick paths, and mellow old buildings of the convent she had called home for most of her life. She felt as if something were shriveling and dying inside her. Something precious and vitally necessary to her sense of well-being and security. "I still can't believe the Sisters have to leave this place."

Julia grunted. "This may look like a convent to you and me, but to those Yankees, this is prime real estate in the hands of fifteen nuns who have dedicated themselves to poverty. No contest."

"It's just not fair."

Julia rolled her eyes and thrust the fingers of both hands through her thick dark hair. "Gabrielle, Gabrielle. How many times must I tell you, life is not fair?"

Gabrielle laughed sadly. "I know it's not. But it ought to be." She tossed the hammer onto the top of the crate and linked her arm through her friend's, pulling her along the brick-paved veranda and into one of the high-ceilinged classrooms. "Come on. I told Mother Superior I'd try to finish boxing up the primary school's books before lunch. Since you're here, you can help."

"I didn't come visit you today to help pack," said Julia, although she sank to her knees on the worn wooden floorboards and reached for a stack of faded old primers.

"I came here to talk you out of this ridiculous scheme to move to Mobile with the nuns."

"But I—"

"No, be silent for one moment and listen to me, please. There is absolutely no reason you can't come live with me at Beaulieu. You always enjoyed staying with me during the summer and Christmas holidays, didn't you?"

Gabrielle kept her gaze on the books she was carefully lining up along the bottom of one of the boxes. "That was different, Julia, and you know it. Those were visits. This would be permanent. I couldn't impose on your family that way."

"It would not be an imposition. And it wouldn't be permanent, either. You've been spending too much time behind these convent walls, *mon amie.*" She dumped her books into the box beside Gabrielle's, then spread her fingers before Gabrielle's eyes, like a magician doing a conjuring trick. "There are these mysterious, perplexing, and wildly fascinating creatures wandering around out in the real world called *men*. They wear trousers and waistcoats and differ from us females in strange but wonderful ways that cause them to fall in love with willing young women and marry them."

Gabrielle shook her head and set to work sorting out the mess Julia had just made of the box. "Not penniless young women."

"Gabrielle, you are not penniless. Not rich, perhaps, but then, the only people in New Orleans these days who are rich have Yankee accents and the instincts of sewer rats. Your trust fund—" She broke off as Gabrielle jerked involuntarily, then held herself too still. "Gabrielle? What haven't you told me?"

Gabrielle settled back on her heels and wiped her

hands on the apron that protected the front of her simple, high-necked gray serge dress. "You remember Monsieur Longchamps, the old lawyer who always handled the trust fund I was supposed to come into when I turned twenty-one?"

Julia nodded.

"Well, I told you he passed away after Christmas. It seems that after he died, his partner in the firm cleaned out as many of his clients' bank accounts as he had access to, and disappeared. My account was one of them. I've been to the bank, to the police. No one seems to be able to do anything about it."

"Mon Dieu," whispered Julia. "How can that be?"

"The world isn't a fair place, remember?" Gabrielle meant it to sound light and insouciant, only her voice trembled.

Julia scooted over to put her arm around Gabrielle's shoulders. "That settles it. You're not going to Mobile. If I let you go live with a bunch of nuns in Mobile, you'll never get married."

Gabrielle chuckled and clasped her friend's hand. "Oh, Julia. I am so glad you're my friend. But I could never burden your family by moving into their plantation house. And I'm not going to Mobile with the nuns, either."

"You're not?"

Gabrielle reached into the bodice of her dress and drew out a letter, worn from repeated readings and several days of being carried around next to her body while she helped to pack up all of the convent's sacred and profane possessions. "This came for me on Thursday. It's from a man called Mr. Jordan Hays. He lives in Central City, Colorado, and he has written to tell me I've inherited a house and a business there from some woman named Celeste DuBois."

"What?"

"I know it sounds incredible, but listen to this." Gabrielle unfolded the single sheet of paper. " 'Dear Miss Antoine,' " she read. " 'It is with regret that I must inform you of the recent death of my partner, Miss Celeste DuBois. While I understand Miss DuBois was unknown to you, she was nevertheless someone who always had your best interests at heart, and for this reason she has bequeathed to you her share of the house and business—' "

"Gabrielle!"

" '—located in Nevada Gulch, which we owned in common. As I am convinced you would have no interest in the property, I propose that it be sold and the proceeds divided between us. If you would kindly sign the enclosed papers, I will be able to move on the sale immediately, and will send your percentage of the proceeds to you, along with some personal mementos and items of jewelery I presume you would wish to keep. Yours faithfully, etc. Jordan Hays.' "

Gabrielle looked up from the page. She must have read that letter fifty times in the last few days, but the thrill of excitement, that feeling of hovering on the verge of a wonderful discovery, had never diminished. "What do you think?" she asked Julia.

"DuBois," said Julia slowly. "I've never heard of the family."

Gabrielle ducked her head to hide her smile. The St. Etiennes might be impoverished, and their River Road plantation falling into ruin, but they were still one of the oldest and best families in New Orleans, and to people like the St. Etiennes, names were everything. "No one has heard of the Antoines, either," she pointed out.

"Well, someone must have, or you'd never have been raised in this convent," said Julia. "The good Sisters of St. Agnes don't take charity cases into their academy."

"That's not nice."

"But it's true, and you know it." She reached down to rub at a smudge of dirt on the flounce of her rose-colored skirt. "You don't have any idea who this DuBois woman could be?"

"None. If Monsieur Longchamps were still alive, he might have been able to tell me, but as it is . . ." Gabrielle shrugged. "There's only one way to find out."

Julia stopped rubbing at her skirt. "You're not thinking about going out to Colorado yourself?" She shifted around until they faced each other, knee to knee, on the dusty floor. "Gabrielle? I don't like the look on your face. Give me that letter."

She snatched the sheet out of Gabrielle's hand and read through it herself, twisting sideways so that the light streaming in through the high French doors fell on the page. "Why doesn't he say what kind of business this is you've inherited? That's strange, isn't it? And what sort of a woman was this Miss DuBois, that she owned a house in common with a man who wasn't her husband? A business I could see, but a house?" Julia refolded the letter and held it out to her friend. "Gabrielle, tell me you're not going there."

Gabrielle took the letter and slipped it back inside her bodice. "I have to. Don't you see, Julia?" Gabrielle pushed off the floor and stood up to wander around the half-dismantled schoolroom. "All my life I've wondered about my parents. Who they were. Why no one seems to be able to tell me anything about them. I always suspected Sister Claire knew, because she was Mother Superior when I was first brought here. But she took whatever information she had to her grave with her."

"But, Gabrielle, whoever this Celeste DuBois was— whatever she knew— She's dead."

"I know. Which means that if I let this Jordan Hays go ahead and sell her house and business, and dispose of her things, I'll probably never find out what her connection to me was."

Julia let her breath out in a long sigh. "Did you ever think, Gabrielle, that there is probably a very good reason you've never been told anything about your parents? That someone obviously thought it would be better if you didn't know?"

Gabrielle stopped beside the open French doors to the courtyard. The gardenias and jasmine were in bloom, filling the warm, moist New Orleans air with their sweet, haunting fragrances. "Of course I've thought of it." She glanced over her shoulder at Julia, and smiled sadly. "I still remember my mother, you know. Vaguely. I remember her coming up a wide, polished staircase to kiss me good night. I remember the flicker of candlelight, and the laughing voices of men and women, and the sweet scent of potpourri. I remember how safe I felt when she held me. How I felt—oh, *surrounded* by her love. Whenever I think of her, she's always wearing a blue silk gown with silver lace." Gabrielle's voice caught. "Isn't it strange? I can remember that dress so well, but her face is a blur. All I can remember is that she had very pale blond hair, and that I thought she was beautiful. My father I don't remember at all."

"Because he was probably never there." Julia stood

and came to take her hand. "You know that's the most likely explanation for all this, don't you? That your mother was the daughter of a good New Orleans family who made the mistake of doing something she shouldn't have with a man who wouldn't or couldn't marry her. Her family must have let her keep you after you were born, but when she died, they sent you here. No mystery. Just . . . tragedy. And a twenty-year-old scandal everyone would rather forget."

Gabrielle shook her head. "Not me. I want to know. And it seems the only way I'm going to find out is to go to Central City myself."

Julia groaned and pushed past her to the veranda. *"Mon Dieu,"* she said, raising her hands to the sky as if asking for divine intervention. "Why don't you just write to this Mr. Jordan Hays and ask him what *he* knows?"

"He probably doesn't know anything. He would have said something, wouldn't he, if he did? I am going, Julia. I've made up my mind."

Julia wrapped one arm around the wrought-iron veranda support and swung about to look back at her. "There's nothing I can say to change your mind, is there?" she said after a moment.

Gabrielle grinned. "No."

"You do realize, *mon amie,* that you might not like what you find?"

"Yes."

"But when you find out whatever there is to find out, you will come back to New Orleans, won't you?"

"Of course." Gabrielle went to join her friend on the veranda. "I'm hoping there'll be enough money that I can start a school of my own. It's what I'd always planned to do with my trust fund."

Julia sighed. "When do you leave?"

"This Friday."

"Friday?" Julia let go of the veranda support. "Then, it's a good thing I'm spending the rest of the week in New Orleans with my sister. We have a lot of shopping to do if we're to get you ready by Friday." She caught Gabrielle's hand and tugged her out into the courtyard, toward the convent gates.

Gabrielle hung back, laughing. "Julia, wait a minute. The way I figure it, I have just enough money to pay for my tickets and a couple of weeks' stay in a hotel."

Julia stopped. "That's all?"

"That's all. I can't afford to buy anything."

Julia's brows drew together in a frown, then relaxed as she suddenly grinned. "Then, I know what to get you for a going-away present."

"What?"

Julia linked her arm through Gabrielle's, and nudged her toward the gate again. "A heavy coat."

Gabrielle laughed, conscious of a warm glow of affection for this beautiful, vibrant woman who had been her friend since childhood. The times Gabrielle had spent with the high-spirited, flamboyant St. Etiennes in their white-pillared plantation house overlooking the Mississippi had done much to ease the aching sense of aloneness Gabrielle had always carried within her.

Eased it, but never filled what remained a void in her life. Only a family and a home of her own would ever truly do that.

Gabrielle sucked in a deep breath of air so cold it hurt her lungs. Snowflakes hurtled down at her from out of the white sky, stinging her cheeks as she paused to gaze out over the town clinging to the scarce bottom land of Clear Creek Canyon, and the gashlike gullies that radiated out from it.

There were two towns, really, hidden away in these mountains high above Denver. Black Hawk, with its railway station and machine sheds and line of two- and three-story frame buildings, hugged what little level ground could be found along the creek. But Central City had been built on the side of the mountain itself, its steep, narrow streets crowded with an incongruent collection of buildings. Crude dugout cabins stood beside gingerbread-draped mansions, while raw, false-fronted dance halls rubbed shoulders with banks and legal offices boasting neoclassic facades, and expensive-looking stores with plate-glass windows. They all huddled together beneath a thick blanket of snow, as if seeking protection from the vast mountain range towering over them.

The wind gusted again, slamming into Gabrielle's back with enough force to make her stagger. She huddled deeper into her new Ulster coat and kept walking.

Nevada Street: that's what the gentleman who had driven her up the steep hill from the station in Black Hawk had called this snow-choked road. He'd been more than willing to drive her all the way to the top of the gulch, too. Except that once she specified exactly where she was going, both the carriage driver, and the station attendant who had agreed to keep her trunks for her, had started behaving in what the Sisters of St. Agnes would have called a *familiar manner*. She didn't understand it, and it made her so uncomfortable that in the end she'd insisted the driver set her down at the point where Nevada Street intersected the main thoroughfare.

Gabrielle's foot suddenly slipped sideways, and she

flung out both arms to keep from losing her balance. It wasn't easy walking through the three or four inches of snow that had piled up since the last time someone had swept the boardwalk. Her shoes had only thin soles, and moisture seeped through the seams, wetting her stockings. She would have to buy herself more suitable footwear, she decided, as soon as possible.

Hardly had the thought crossed her mind when both feet shot out from under her at the same time. She landed flat on her back with a jarring *thump* that took her breath away.

"Are you all right?"

Gabrielle blinked the snow out of her eyes and looked up to find a little girl with thick blond braids, and a thin-faced woman in an ugly black poke bonnet staring down at her. The woman eyed her with an expression that was half-concern, half-suspicion, but the little girl was smiling openly.

Gabrielle sucked the air back into her lungs with a painful gasp. "Yes. Thank you." She sat up. "I wonder if you could help me? I'm looking for the house that used to belong to Celeste DuBois."

The woman reeled back, drawing her breath in through her teeth with an audible hiss. *"Hussy,"* she spat. Snatching the child's hand, she whisked the little girl off down the hill as if Gabrielle had announced she had typhoid.

Gabrielle stood up, whacking her hands against her snow-caked skirts, and frowning in confusion as she watched the woman hurry away. The woman never looked back, but the little girl craned her neck around to stare at Gabrielle with wide-eyed interest. "Mama says naughty ladies live in that big white house. Are you a naughty lady?"

The woman shushed the child loudly, and yanked hard on her arm, jerking her down the hill.

Gabrielle turned to stare up at the only big white house in the gulch. It stood at the far end of the street, near the trees. She found it difficult to believe she'd actually inherited a share in a house this big. Including its gabled attics, the house rose three stories tall; a white frame mansion with a conically roofed turret and a wide, wrap-around porch dripping with gingerbread. Beyond it, she could see a variety of outbuildings: stables, a hay barn, some sheds, and, farther up the slope and built into the side of the steep hill, what looked like the remains of an old prospector's cabin.

She started climbing again, hobbled by the snow-dampened hems of her skirt and petticoats hanging sod-denly around her ankles. Ice from the fall coated her gloves, making her fingers stiff and aching with cold. But inside, she burned with confusion and something very much like apprehension. No matter how hard she thought about it, she could not come up with any explanation for the reactions she had encountered the few times she had mentioned Celeste DuBois in this town. It made no sense.

She reached the front of the white mansion and paused again, oddly reluctant to draw closer to it. She had to force herself to push open the gate in the picket fence that separated the snow-filled yard from the road. Hinges squealed as she let the gate swing shut behind her and walked up the freshly swept path to mount the wide wooden steps.

At the top of the steps, she stopped again, her heart racing with excitement and an unexpected flutter of nerves. There was no bell. She lifted the heavy brass knocker in the center of the paneled door, and let it drop.

It made a *bang* that seemed an intrusion into the almost unnatural silence of the surrounding, snow-covered hills. She heard no footsteps, but as she stared curiously at the red light displayed prominently in the front window, the door swung slowly inward perhaps two feet, then stopped.

A giant of a Chinese man wearing a long quilted shirt over loose, dull blue trousers appeared in the gap. At least Gabrielle thought he must be Chinese, since he had Oriental eyes and wore his black hair pulled back in a queue. But his hair was more curly than straight, and his skin unusually dark, and she didn't think she had ever seen an Oriental this big before. He stood at least six feet tall, with massive shoulders and arms like a blacksmith. "Missy has wrong house?" he suggested, his face impassive.

Gabrielle shook her head. "My name is Gabrielle Antoine. I've come to see Mr. Hays."

No ripple of recognition passed across the man's face, and it occurred to Gabrielle that she had probably acted impetuously in coming straight up to the house like this. She'd been too anxious. Too curious. She smiled ruefully. "I sent him a wire, so he should be expecting me. If he's not here now, may I come in and wait? I hadn't realized it was possible for a person to be this cold."

The doorman blinked, then nodded and opened the door wider. "Follow me, please."

Gabrielle stepped across the threshold, and caught her breath.

She stood in a wide entrance hall, wainscoted to waist height with paneling stained a deep burgundy. Flocked gold-and-burgundy-patterned wallpaper covered the rest of the wall, up to a molded plaster frieze picked out in burgundy and gilt paint. An enormous crystal and brass chandelier with burgundy silk tassels hung from an elaborate ceiling rose, and the walls on both sides of the hall were decorated with gilt-framed mirrors and dark oil paintings of naked women, their flesh showing pale and blue-veined against verdant backgrounds. The contrast between the cold, pristine whiteness of the snow-covered hills outside, and the rich, aggressive warmth of the house's interior could not have been more striking.

The sound of someone picking out a popular tune on a piano floated through the house as Gabrielle followed the big man down the plushly carpeted hall. Curious, she peered through the strings of crystal beads curtaining an archway on her right, and saw a pretty woman in a gaudy silk wrapper sitting at a bench in front of a black, burgundy, and gilt piano. Beside her stood an auburn-haired woman with pearly white skin, wearing only a thin chemise and a petticoat.

Gabrielle felt herself blush hotly with confused embarrassment, and looked quickly away.

"Wait here, please." The Chinese man opened a door farther down the hall, bowed her into what looked like an office, and left her.

She stood in the center of the room, her hands gripped together, her heart beating hard and fast. What kind of house was this? What kind of *person* was this Celeste DuBois, that she had associated with women who casually stood around in wrappers and petticoats and didn't even look up when strangers walked past?

The tick of a clock intruded on her consciousness, and she glanced toward the small Louis XVI clock on the mantel. It would be dark soon. Night seemed to come so early in the North in winter. She would wait another five minutes, she decided, then she would need to leave if she were to have time to find a hotel and arrange to have her trunks brought up from the station.

Feeling oddly restless, she stripped off her gloves and wandered around the office, studying the wide walnut partners desk, with its embossed green leather top and twin chairs, the glass-fronted bookcases, the mellow Brussels carpet beneath her feet. Unlike what she'd seen of the rest of the house, this was a room of blues and greens and exquisite good taste. A cool oasis in the midst of a burning heat.

Then she noticed an oil painting hanging on the far wall, beside the double-hung window. It was a portrait of a young woman. A beautiful young woman with pale blond hair, wearing a blue silk gown with silver lace.

Gabrielle stared at the painting. She did not recognize the woman. But the dress . . .

"I think Celeste must have been about your age when that picture was painted," drawled a deep male voice. "Maybe a bit younger."

CHAPTER
TWO

Gabrielle whirled around. A man stood in the doorway. A tall, lean man dressed all in black, like a devil; black evening jacket and trousers, black silk waistcoat, black tie. Only his shirt was white, with a discreet frill that did nothing to alleviate the faint aura of danger that hung about him. His gaze was intense, and decidedly unwelcoming.

She cleared her throat. It made her uncomfortable, being alone with such a man. She wished he would go away. "I was waiting to see Mr. Hays," she said. "If you could tell him I'm here—"

"I am Jordan Hays."

"*You?*" She stared at him in consternation. The Jordan Hays she'd imagined had been an elderly gentleman with graying side-whiskers and an avuncular manner. It had never occurred to her that he might be young. And intimidating.

Like his clothes, the man himself was dark. In the dim light of the snow-filled afternoon, his hair looked almost black. His skin was dark, too. She thought he must have spent years riding beneath the harsh western sun, to tan so deeply, except . . .

Except that she found it difficult to imagine him as a

cowboy. He certainly didn't look like any of the cowboys she'd seen on the covers of dime novels. Then a slight movement of his hand drew her eye to the gun strapped low on his hip, and it occurred to her that he might be a gunman. She could imagine him as a gunman. There was certainly something threatening and disturbing about him. He had such an arresting face, she thought: high-boned, with even features and deep-set eyes.

As she watched, a slow smile curled his lips. "I'm obviously not what you expected."

She realized how rude she was to be staring, how rude she must have sounded. "I'm sorry, it's just that I had assumed you were an older man."

He walked over to the small, spindle-legged table that stood beside the door, and picked up a crystal decanter. "You look cold. How about some brandy?"

"No, thank you."

He eased out the stopper and reached for a glass, the fine cloth of his coat pulling across his broad shoulders as he moved. "I hope you don't mind if I do?"

She shook her head, but he was already pouring himself a drink. The clear, ringing *clink* of the decanter hitting the side of the glass sounded unnaturally loud in the quiet room.

"Why did you come?" he asked, setting the decanter back on its silver tray.

Gabrielle hesitated. How could she possibly explain to this ominously dark stranger what had driven her halfway across the continent to this wild, frozen, frightening place? How could she tell him what it had been like to grow up comfortable and well cared for, and yet, essentially, lonely and bereft of a mother's special love?

She didn't even try. "I hadn't heard of Miss Celeste DuBois until I received your letter. I was curious to find out why she should have remembered me in her will."

"She didn't want you to come."

A log fell in the fire on the hearth, sending a shower of sparks shooting up the chimney. Gabrielle's collar felt tight, and she eased open the top three buttons of her coat. "Why wouldn't she want me to come?"

He lifted his glass to his lips and took a swallow. "Are you sure you're ready to hear the answer to that?"

His words reminded her of something Julia had said. Gabrielle felt the uneasiness twist her stomach and grow until it resembled something more like fear, but she managed to keep her voice steady. "I wouldn't have come here if I were not."

"Some things, a person is never ready to hear," he said, and she thought she caught the faint echo of some long buried pain in his voice. "Some things change your life, change you, so that afterward, you're never quite the same again. If you were smart, Miss Gabrielle Antoine, you'd walk out that door right now." He raised the hand that held his glass, and gestured toward the front of the house. "You'd catch the first train back to New Orleans, and you'd forget you ever heard of Celeste DuBois. Forget you ever saw this town, this house. Let me sell everything and simply send you the money the way I said I would." A tight smile she didn't like curled his lips. "Or is that the reason you came? Because you didn't think you could trust me?"

"No, it wasn't that at all," she said hastily. "It's just . . ." She didn't want to say these things to him, but she couldn't let him continue thinking she had questioned his honesty. "You see, my mother died when I was five. I was raised in a convent, where no one knew anything about her—or about the rest of my family. I thought if I came here, I might learn something. Anything would be better than nothing."

"You think so?" He sipped his brandy, his gaze traveling over her, assessing her in a way that made her uncomfortable. She wasn't used to a man looking at her so—so *openly*. It made her feel hot and uncomfortable.

"Then again," he said, drawling the words, "maybe the people who raised you knew something they thought you should never find out."

She ignored the ominous swelling of dread within her. "I don't like being kept ignorant. Whatever there is to know, I want to hear it. And I intend to keep asking until I find someone who will tell me."

He drained his glass with one practiced flick of his wrist. "All right, Miss Antoine. You wanted it, here it is." He twisted around to set his empty glass on the tabletop behind him. "Your mother didn't die when you were five, like you seem to think. She died just last month. Her name was Celeste DuBois, and that's a picture of her right over there, hanging on the wall."

Gabrielle's gaze followed his nod to the fair-haired woman in the portrait. There was a ringing in her ears, and she had the most peculiar sensation, as if she were free-falling through space, with no place to land.

Everything within her rose up to deny what she'd just heard. She looked pointedly away from the pale-haired woman. "No," Gabrielle said, shaking her head slowly from side to side. "I don't believe you. You're lying. I don't know why, but you're lying."

"Am I?" He pushed away from the table and moved

with two swift strides to close the distance between them. His hands fell on her shoulders, spinning her around to face the painting. "Look at her," he commanded, his voice harsh against her ear, his hands heavy on her body. "Even convents have mirrors, don't they? Tell me you haven't seen those same silver eyes staring back at you every time you've looked at yourself for the last twenty years."

"No."

"I'll admit you don't look enough like her for someone to recognize you at first glance. Your hair is gold instead of flaxen, and your nose isn't as straight as hers, or your face as perfect an oval. But I've only seen two women with a mouth like that. One is you. The other was your mother."

"No!" She wrenched out of his grasp and whirled to stare up into his high-boned stranger's face, into his chillingly hard green eyes. "No," she said again. She knew she was perilously close to screaming, but she couldn't seem to help it. "My mother is *dead*. They told me she was dead. Oh, God, don't you see? Why would she go off and leave me all alone if she wasn't dead?"

Her voice cracked, but he just stood there, watching her. She wondered how he could be so cruel, so uncaring.

"You haven't figured it out yet, have you?" His gaze flicked over her again, making her painfully aware of her youth, her inexperience, her ignorance.

Her breath was coming so hard and fast, her chest hurt. "Figured out what?" she asked warily.

"What this house is."

Naughty ladies live in that house. She shook her head.

"This isn't just a house, Miss Antoine. It's a business. A very successful, lucrative business that Celeste and I ran together. I took care of the gaming room. Your mother managed the whores."

"No." She backed away from him, shaking her head, denying him, denying his words, denying what she had seen, what she had sensed, what she didn't want to know. "No."

"Yes." He strolled after her, his body lithe and intimidatingly masculine, his face hard. "That's why she left you in New Orleans. Because she didn't want to bring you up in a whorehouse. And it's also the reason she didn't want you to come out here. She didn't want you to see this. She didn't want you to know that she was a whore."

Her hand flashed out, open palmed, catching him high on the cheekbone with a loud smack. His head jerked to one side with the impact.

She gasped and stepped back, her hands flying up to form a steeple before her nose and mouth. She could not believe what she had just done.

He turned his head, slowly, until he was looking at her again. "You did ask."

She spun away from him in consternation and confusion and a maelstrom of other emotions she didn't understand and couldn't begin to control. Her throat felt as if it were swelling shut. She wanted to tell him she was sorry for hitting him, but she knew she'd never get the words past the obstruction in her throat.

She was aware of him crossing the room and pouring another drink. She heard the swirl of liquid being poured into a glass, the solid *thunk* of the brandy decanter being set down on the table. He came to stand in front of her, close enough that she could feel the heat from his tall, male body.

"Here. Drink this." He held out a glass with an inch of sharp-smelling liquor in the bottom.

She shook her head. "No, I couldn't. I don't drink spirits."

"Sip it," he commanded. "You need it."

She stared at his long, tanned fingers curled around the expensive crystal glass. She felt oddly light-headed and disoriented, as if she'd wandered by mistake into someone else's life.

She took the glass and cautiously sipped some of the rich, amber-colored liquid into her mouth. It felt cool and pleasant on her tongue. Then she swallowed, and it was as if she had inhaled a bolt of fire that scorched a trail down her throat.

She gasped, opened her eyes wide, and fell to coughing so violently, the brandy sloshed back and forth dangerously.

"Here, give me that before you spill it." He plucked the glass from her hand. "Haven't you ever had a drink before?"

"No. Only wine."

"I should have known."

She was still coughing.

"Are you all right?" he asked, his straight, dark brows drawing together in a slight frown.

"Yes," she said hoarsely, wiping her stinging eyes. "I must admit, it does have definite shock-inducing properties."

"Almost as good as a slap."

Her hand stilled. She forced herself to look up and meet his gaze. "I owe you an apology for that. I asked you to tell me the truth. It wasn't fair to take my anger and distress out on you when I didn't like what you had to say."

"I understand." The words were unexpectedly compassionate, but the tone was still impersonal, flat.

She had never encountered anyone remotely like him. Disconcerted, she stared at him. At this coldly handsome man who wore his gun as if it were an integral part of his lean body. At this man who ran a gaming hall and lived in a house of ill repute. She found herself remembering a passage from *Richard III*; a disturbing passage that seemed to echo and reecho in her head, like a grim warning. *"Have not to do with him, beware of him. Sin, death and hell have set their marks on him . . ."*

She felt a frisson of fear, and a desperate need to get away from this house. To get away from him.

The front knocker banged loudly, startling her. It was followed by the tinkling of a little bell, and then a high-pitched feminine squeal.

They both turned toward the sound, and it was as if a peculiar bond of energy that had hummed between them suddenly broke. "You shouldn't be here," said Hays, moving toward the doorway, his tall body effectively blocking her view to the hall. "I'll get Wing Tsue to hitch up the sleigh so I can drive you down to the Teller House Hotel."

"But—" Gabrielle began, only to have her voice drowned out by a raucous male guffaw. "Come to Daddy, Jilly-baby," boomed a loud baritone. "You voracious, man-eating little whore, you."

Gabrielle heard herself let out a small, shocked mew.

"That'll be Jeff Hogan," said Hays, a faint smile of amusement touching his lips. "He always asks for Jilly when he comes to town. You had better wait here."

Gabrielle nodded. But as he disappeared through the door, she caught a glimpse of a massive, red-shirted man with a flowing, copper-colored beard and shoulder-length mane of hair. He was spinning around and around with a laughing slip of a girl with corn silk blond hair, who wore nothing but a black corset, red high heels, and a pair of stockings held up by red garters.

Gabrielle shrank back into the office, her gaze drawn irresistibly to the portrait on the wall. She realized suddenly that she was shaking. Shaking not with cold, but with a hot, all-consuming rage that swept through her as she stared at this woman. Celeste DuBois. Her mother. Her mother, who had apparently broken every rule young women like Gabrielle were brought up to respect and obey. This mother, who had once enveloped Gabrielle with a sense of security and love.

And then abandoned her, to grief, and to the care of strangers, in a comfortable but fundamentally lonely life.

The curving runners of the sleigh cut through the snow-filled road with a soft swish. The light was beginning to fade from the cloud-packed sky, the temperature plunging. Every time Gabrielle breathed, the exhalation of her breath showed white and frosty in the cold mountain air.

She glanced at the man sitting beside her on the padded leather seat of the shiny, plum-colored sleigh. He stared straight ahead, a low-crowned hat pulled low over his eyes, his lips pressed in a tight line. It was as if he had removed himself from her in some way, retreated to some barren inner place. Yet she remained painfully aware of his nearness, of the shocking intimacy and bluntness of the conversation that had passed between them in the house.

She supposed it hadn't been easy for him, telling her about her mother. But even though she knew it was unjust to blame him, all she could seem to feel toward him was anger. Anger, and revulsion.

Gripping the edge of the seat, she twisted around to look back at the big white house at the top of the gulch. Wispy, bluish-gray wood smoke curled from a half-dozen chimneys, and the windows blazed golden and welcoming in the cold and gloom of approaching evening. But the brightest light of all was red.

Gabrielle's vision blurred as she stared at that infamous red light. She'd thought herself prepared to face the worst. She'd thought herself strong enough to bear whatever she might discover. But that only went to show how naive, how blessedly ignorant she'd been. Because she had never imagined such a horrifying truth, never understood how quickly the pleasant, safe illusions of life as she'd always known it could be stripped away, leaving her face-to-face with a world of sin and depravity she barely even understood.

It was Julia St. Etienne who had first told Gabrielle about whorehouses. Julia, who at the age of thirteen had arrived at the convent like a breath of fresh air from the outside world, and quickly set about correcting what she considered some glaring deficiencies in Gabrielle's education.

"Those old nuns have kept you so shut away, I'll bet you don't even know what a hooker is," Julia said one hot August day as they sat side by side, dangling their bare feet in the muddy water of the river that rolled majestically past the St. Etienne plantation.

"Of course I do," Gabrielle answered, tossing her head. As much as she loved her newfound friend, Julia's worldly-wise attitude was sometimes a bit hard to take. "It's a man who catches fish."

Julia flopped back on the dock, her husky laughter floating above them on the moist, fragrant air. "No, silly. A hooker is a *lady*—a lady of the night." She rolled onto her stomach and rested her chin on her hands. "Louis told me all about them." Louis was Julia's brother, and sometimes he wasn't as careful as he should have been about the things he said around his little sister. "He says another name for them is whores. They live in places called whorehouses, and they sell their bodies to whatever men are able to pay for them."

"People aren't sold anymore," said Gabrielle, proud to know something Julia evidently did not. "The Yankees got rid of all that."

"They're not sold as slaves, silly. They just sell the use of their bodies to men. And it's not for keeps. It's for a night, or maybe just an hour, or however long it takes."

Gabrielle stretched out on her side, her head propped up on her elbow, and stared at her friend. "Why would a man want to buy a woman's body? To use for what?"

"You mean, you don't know?"

Gabrielle shook her head.

So Julia told her. In detail.

"That's the most disgusting thing I've ever heard," said Gabrielle with a gasp. She sat up and clenched her knees tightly together, as if the dreadful deed were about to be done to her. "I would never, ever let a man do that to me."

Julia had wrinkled her nose. "It does sound awful, doesn't it? Perhaps that's why whores are so despised.

Louis says they're degraded creatures, totally without shame. Very unrespectable."

A cold wind swept down the mountain, slamming into the drifts at the side of the road and kicking up swirls of snow. Gabrielle swung back around, her gaze falling to the gloved hands she held clasped together in her lap. What would Julia and the proud, genteel St. Etiennes think of her now, she wondered, if they discovered the truth about her? The St. Etiennes, with their reverence for family names and ancient lineages. She wanted to laugh, but the sound stuck in her throat and burned her chest, and she realized it wasn't a laugh at all.

Her gaze slid sideways, to the long-fingered, leather-encased hands of the man holding the reins beside her. They were the hands of a gambler, the hands of a gunman. She could not believe she was sitting in a sleigh with such a man, and she knew a moment of panic, as if she were slipping away from the life she'd always known, into something dangerous, something dark.

"Do you need me to come into the hotel with you?" he asked, breaking the long silence between them.

"No, thank you," she said, although she had never stayed at a hotel in her life before she left New Orleans.

"What did you do with your trunks?"

"I left them at the station. The attendant offered to watch them for me."

"I hope you didn't tell him where you were going."

Gabrielle felt her cheeks grow warm, remembering the way the station attendant had treated her, after she'd asked him how she could get to Celeste DuBois's house. "I'm afraid I did."

She saw the brackets around his mouth tighten, and it

occurred to her they were probably smile lines, although she had never seen him smile. "You know that made him think you're a whore, don't you?" he said.

She nodded, not trusting herself to speak. She had figured it all out as the long minutes ticked past while she waited in the office for him to come back from harnessing the sleigh. Two more customers had come, while she waited. She had shut the door, hiding from them, hiding from the raw, half-understood things they said, from the unfamiliar, frightening sounds they made.

Hiding from the truth.

"There are only two kinds of women who have anything to do with Celeste's Place," he went on, when she didn't say anything. "There are the older Oriental women who come up every day to do most of the cleaning and washing. And then there are the whores." She could feel the heat of his gaze on her, even though she had turned away from him. "You don't look like a cleanin' lady."

"Neither do I look like a—a—" She sucked in a deep breath, and pressed her lips together. She could not bring herself to say it.

"Not dressed like that, you don't. But you look enough like your mother that Wing Tsue saw the resemblance when you smiled."

She assumed Wing Tsue was the big, dark-skinned Oriental who had answered the door for her, but she didn't ask to find out for certain, because she didn't want to know. She didn't want to know any more than she already did about that house. "If I only look like her when I smile, then I doubt anyone in town is likely to recognize me," she said dryly. "I don't feel particularly inclined to smile at the moment." Given the way she felt, she found it difficult to believe she would ever smile again.

He laughed then, a short huff that surprised her into looking up at him. "No, I don't suppose you do." He glanced down at her, catching her gaze and holding it. She saw a flash of something in his eyes, something that was gone before she could define it. His lips twisted in a wry smile. "I suppose you realize now that you should have walked out that door when I told you to."

She shook her head. "I could not."

"No, probably not." They had reached the point at which Nevada Street emptied into the main road, and he turned his attention back to the milky-white mare between the traces, guiding her to the left. "If you want to know more about your mother," he said after a moment, not looking at her again, "I could—"

"No, thank you," she said hastily. She glanced away from him, at the twin rows of icicle-draped, false-fronted wooden buildings. She could see what must be the town's cemetery, high up on the side of the mountain, where the stark, snow-laden branches of a stand of aspen seemed to scrape the darkening sky. She only wanted to be gone from this place. From these towering mountains and this dangerous, disturbing man, and from the ugly, brutal truth with which he had confronted her. She felt smashed, bruised, hollowed out inside by what he had already told her. She didn't think she could bear to hear any more.

"No, thank you," she said again. "I plan to leave in the morning." It seemed so ironic, when she remembered how pathetically anxious she had been to get here; now she couldn't wait to be gone.

He reined up in front of a large brick hotel that seemed

to tower over its wooden neighbors. There were several sets of double doors, one of which stood open, revealing thick red carpets, the gleam of polished wood, and the unexpected leafy green of potted palms.

The Teller House Hotel looked expensive, Gabrielle thought, gazing up at its brocade- and lace-framed double-hung windows. It was a good thing she would only be staying here tonight. Tomorrow, she would be on her way back to New Orleans, and her uncertain future.

"I will need you to sign those papers on the sale of the house, before you go," he said, looping the reins over the sleigh's brass rail.

"Yes, of course. I brought them with me. I'll leave them at the front desk."

"I'll come pick them up in the morning. I can bring your mother's jewelery then, too, if you like. And if there's anything else you'd like to keep—"

"No, nothing," she said quickly.

He studied her tightly set face for a moment, then swung down and came around to help her alight. There was still some two or three inches of snow on the plank walkway, and she noticed he planted his polished black boots wide, for stability, as he reached up for her.

She placed her hand in his, and his fingers tightened around hers as she carefully stepped down. She felt the energy of his nearness, the strength in his grip, and for some reason, it frightened her. There was nothing at all exceptional about a gentleman helping a lady climb out of a sleigh. Yet it felt strangely intimate and inappropriate, perhaps because of the kind of man she knew he was. Because of the kinds of things she knew must go on in the house they had just left.

She was glad when he released her and turned to leave.

"I'll swing by the station for your trunks, and have them sent to your room," he said, climbing back into the sleigh and taking the reins in his hand.

"Thank you. You've been very kind."

His easy laugh brought the flash of a roguish smile to his lips. It made her think that this was a man who laughed often at life and the world around him. Although, looking at him, she thought perhaps it was the kind of laughter that came from the head, rather than from the heart.

Then the smile faded slowly from his lips, and he shook his head. "Kind? No, I haven't been kind."

He pulled off his left glove, and she couldn't imagine what he was about until he reached down to brush her lips, gently, with the pad of his thumb. "Leave here," he said, his voice soft, his face once again closed and unreadable. "Leave here as soon as you can. And don't ever come back."

She should have jerked her head away, but she didn't. She just stood there and watched him straighten up. She watched him spank the reins against the mare's rump, and watched the sleigh lurch forward. Then, realizing what she was doing, she glanced quickly around, afraid that someone had seen her with this man. This man who gambled a fortune at the turn of a card, and who lived with women who gave their bodies to strangers in exchange for coin; this man who obviously felt far too comfortable with the weight of a gun on his hip.

That disturbing passage from *Richard III* seemed to echo in her head. *"Sin, death and hell hath set their marks upon him."*

Sin and hell, she thought.

Sin, death, and hell.

Darkness came early to the Colorado Rockies in winter.

By the time Jordan retrieved Gabrielle Antoine's trunks from the station and drove away from the hotel, night had fallen, cold and cruel and beautiful.

"Get up there, Sugar," he called to the milky-white mare pulling the sleigh. "It's colder than charity out here." The mare snorted, wreathing her bobbing head in a white cloud of frozen vapor as she leaned more heavily into the collar, obviously anxious to get back to her own warm barn and feed bin. Jordan held the reins lightly through his fingers, letting the mare take them home.

Home. It surprised him when he realized that he'd casually thought of Celeste's Place as home. Surprised him, and disturbed him.

Some men drifted because they were looking for a place to put down roots. Not Jordan Hays. Jordan drifted to avoid staying in any one place long enough to start calling it home. Everything the word implied belonged to his past. A past that had ended some nine years ago, on that dreadful spring day in the wake of Appomattox, when he'd turned his back on the blackened, weed-choked ruins of the life he'd once loved, and ridden west.

A sweet sad ache bloomed within him, stopping his breath, ravaging his soul the way it always did when he thought of Sophie. His loving, beautiful wife, Sophie. He remembered the last time he'd seen her, standing at the base of the house steps, one hand raised to wave good-bye, the other hand resting on the swell of his baby in her belly . . .

His mind swerved away from the thought, and from other thoughts. Cherished, anguished images of Sophie laughing, Sophie reaching for him, Sophie lying beneath him, her lips falling open in a gasp as he drove into her. Memories too painful to visit, dreams too shattered to ever be resurrected.

Iced-over snow crunched beneath the sleigh's runners as the mare swung onto Nevada Street, jerking him back to the present. It wasn't late, but beneath the freezing temperatures the streets lay empty and quiet, the cold, crisp air heavy with the scent of wood smoke.

He glanced up at the ghostly glow of the snow-covered slopes towering over the town's tiny cluster of buildings, and found himself thinking about how strange and frightening it all must seem to a girl bred in the hot, flat delta land of New Orleans. Encountering the awesome majesty of the Colorado Rockies and the raw wildness of a mining town like Central City would have been difficult enough for a girl like Gabrielle Antoine, without her also having to face the uncomfortable truths he'd had to tell her.

Yet when he left her at the Teller House, she had appeared utterly composed and controlled, even though he knew that her cool, well-trained exterior must hide a riot of painful emotions and reactions.

Celeste would have been pleased, he thought; the Sisters of St. Agnes had raised her daughter well. It seemed, somehow, sadly ironic. Because he doubted that Gabrielle would ever be able to see her sheltered childhood and convent upbringing as the precious gifts they were. Jordan might know that Celeste had stayed away from

Gabrielle out of love. But he suspected that as far as Gabrielle was concerned, her mother had simply abandoned her. He remembered the hurt he'd seen glimmering in her luminous gray eyes, and it touched him in a way that surprised him. In a way he didn't like.

He didn't like how he'd reacted to her physically, either, but at least he could understand that. Gabrielle Antoine was a fine-looking woman, with hair the color of sunshine and the kind of wide, sensual mouth that made a man think of long, hot nights and the pleasures of the flesh. If she hadn't been a young, innocent virgin—and the daughter of a friend—he wouldn't have hesitated to act on those thoughts. As it was . . .

As it was, he decided it was probably a damned good thing she was leaving in the morning.

He heard a dog bark in the yard of one of the houses to his left, and noticed the dark shapes of two men, trudging through the snow up ahead. One of the men glanced over his shoulder at Jordan, and nudged his companion, who veered off the boardwalk and into the street close enough to make the mare shy. A hand shot out, seizing the reins just below the bit.

The mare tossed her head, snorting with fear. Jordan reached for his Colt. The gloves and heavy sheepskin coat he wore slowed him down, but he still managed to get his gun out of its holster and ready to fire in the time it took the man on the boardwalk to raise and cock his Winchester.

"You don't need that gun, Hays," said the man with the Winchester, a man Jordan recognized as Bart Tucker, one of the more dangerous of Doug Slaughter's hired thugs. "We're friends. See?" And he held the rifle aloft.

Jordan had met Bart Tucker before. The man was lean

and tough and fairly smart, but a bit on the short side. Being short had made him mean, Jordan thought. Mean to the point of being just a little crazy. And that made him unpredictable.

"Let's put it this way," Jordan said, easing the Colt back into place. "I know who you are. My *friends* don't usually point a Winchester at my chest."

"You've got yourself a reputation, Hays," said Tucker. "The Winchester was just to make sure we didn't get ourselves shot in the process of trying to say howdy." He slung the rifle over his shoulder with studied casualness.

"Now that you've said *howdy*, do you think you could ask your friend here to take his hand off my reins?"

"What? Don't you know Skeeter? This here is Skeeter McCoy. Say howdy, Skeeter."

"Slaughter wants to talk to ya," said Skeeter. "We was just on our way up to Celeste's Place to tell ya when Bart here see'd ya comin'."

Jordan's gaze shifted to the thug holding the mare's reins. He was a bull of a man with a thick, rawboned head planted almost directly on his massive, beefy shoulders. His fists were probably bigger than his brain, Jordan thought. But then, he looked like the kind of man who used his fists a whole lot more often than he used his brain.

It still rankled with Jordan, that no one had ever been held accountable for Celeste's death. An accident, the sheriff had decided. Someone slips in the snow, discharging his rifle into the night, then goes on his way, never knowing he's left a woman bleeding to death in a house high up on the hill. As for the rumor that Slaughter had recently hired himself a rifleman . . . well, said the sheriff, there was no law against a man of property trying to protect himself. Besides, some thirty men could testify they'd seen Bart Tucker and Slaughter standing together at the bar in the Silver Spur at exactly the time Celeste was shot. It was an accident.

But Jordan didn't believe much in convenient accidents.

He gathered his reins. "Tell Slaughter I'll be down to see him in the morning. Now, if you gentlemen will excuse me—"

Skeeter's hand tightened on the reins, making the mare snort and try to back up, the dry crusted snow crunching beneath her restless hooves.

"Slaughter says he wants to see ya *now*," said Skeeter.

"The thing is," explained Bart Tucker, one hand caressing the stock of his rifle, "Slaughter heard this nasty rumor that Celeste's daughter is in town. He got to thinkin' maybe you'd changed your mind about sellin' him the house. That worries him, you see. And Slaughter, he don't like to be worried. He said if you wouldn't come, we were to fetch the girl, so's he can ask her what the hell she's doing here."

Jordan considered a moment, then shrugged. "Well, we wouldn't want Slaughter to worry, would we?" He collected his reins again, then looked pointedly at Skeeter. "It would be easier for me to go relieve Mr. Slaughter of his anxiety if Skeeter here would remove his hand from my reins."

Skeeter threw a questioning look at Bart Tucker. Tucker nodded, and the big man stepped back.

Jordan turned the unwilling mare back toward Lawrence Street. "Sorry, Sugar," he crooned. "Dinner's going to be a bit late."

Golden lamplight and a discordant intermingling of music, laughter, and loud voices spilled out into the cold, snowy night as Jordan pulled up in front of the Silver Spur saloon on Lawrence Street, where Slaughter kept his offices. Reining in, he jumped down and went to stroke the mare's nose for a minute before climbing up onto the boardwalk.

A dark, bulky shape detached itself from the wall and stepped forward, blocking his path. "The hardware stays outside," said the man, filling the night air with a tobacco and whiskey-scented cloud of white exhalation.

Wordlessly Jordan reached down to untie the rawhide thigh strap of his holster, and unbuckle his gun belt. Peeling it off, he shoved it under the seat of the sleigh, then stripped off his heavy sheepskin coat and gloves and tossed them in, too, before turning to push open the saloon doors.

The Silver Spur was a cut above most of the saloons in the Rockies. The floorboards were polished oak, and crystal chandeliers glittered overhead, adding their sparkle to the gleam of brass and mirrors and varnish. There was even a stage framed with red velvet curtains, where a troop of traveling performers, dressed up like Tyroleans, were dancing and singing "Springtime in the Alps" to the accompaniment of a squeeze box.

Skirting the crowded tables, Jordan crossed to the long, ornate staircase leading to the second floor. His boots made not a sound on the thick, cabbage-rose strewn carpet as he slowly climbed the steps. But at the sight of him, the lanky man with a sallow face who had been loitering in the upstairs hall tossed away the match he had been using to pick his teeth, and stuck his head around the jamb of the partially open door beside him. "Hays is here, boss," he said to someone out of sight.

Jordan heard a chair scrape back, and the rasp of Slaughter's voice answering, "Send him in."

Jordan pushed the door open wider, and walked into the office. Straight into Doug Slaughter's fist.

CHAPTER
THREE

Doug Slaughter grunted with satisfaction as he watched the gambler fall.

He was a big man, Doug Slaughter. Two hundred and thirty pounds of muscle only just beginning to soften and run to fat. He still packed a hell of a punch, even if his handlebar mustache and the hair he kept swept back from his temples with Macassar oil were beginning to show touches of gray. He could still knock a man out cold with one blow, same as he'd done over and over again, when his name had been Danny O'Sullivan, and he'd earned his money the hard way, climbing into boxing rings.

It had been a long time since those days. A long time since anyone had called him Danny-Boy, a long time since anyone had dared to look down on this man, Doug Slaughter, into which he had made himself. The respect had been harder to earn than the money, but doubly precious.

The man on the floor lifted his head and shook it, as if to clear his senses. Slaughter might still be able to knock a man out when he wanted to, but it just so happened that in this instance, he hadn't wanted to. He'd learned early that force could be used to intimidate as well as to destroy.

Years of running saloons and gambling dens and whore-houses had left him with little but contempt for the people who'd made him rich. The drunks, the whores, the gamblers, they were all the same, as far as he was concerned. Easy to intimidate, easy to use. There was no reason to expect this one to be any different.

Only, Slaughter thought he saw the man's eyes narrow with anger as he rolled slowly into a sitting position and picked himself up off the floor. Then Hays lowered his gaze to pull a handkerchief from his pocket, and Slaughter decided he'd imagined it.

"What the hell was that for?" Hays asked, dabbing at the blood that trickled from a cut under his right eye.

"That was an example."

"Of your manners?"

"Of what I do to people who double-cross me. You obviously don't know who you're dealing with here," Slaughter growled. He was proud of his harsh, guttural voice. It hadn't been easy to eradicate all traces of his Irish homeland, those lilting cadences that marked him as a member of a nation of losers. But he'd done it. There wasn't anything Slaughter had ever set his mind to accomplish that he hadn't been able to achieve.

And the one thing he was determined to do now was to get his hands on that property up in Nevada Gulch.

"I'd say, 'Behold the ox-like Ajax' "—the gambler turned away to inspect his cut face in the small gilt mirror that hung near Slaughter's antique mahogany desk— "except that the epic allusion is misplaced. The problem is, at the moment I can't seem to think of an appropriate quotation from Aristophanes."

The fire on the hearth hissed and spat, filling the room

with golden light and leaping shadows. Slaughter frowned. He knew he was missing something; he just couldn't figure out what it was. "What the hell are you talking about?"

The gambler pivoted so that his back was to the wall. "Greek literature. Why? What would you like to discuss?"

"Celeste's Place, damn it." Slaughter rested one fist on his polished desktop, and leaned into it. He liked his desk. It was an eighteenth-century antique, brought all the way from England. Once this desk had graced the ancestral hall of the dukes of Northumbria. Now it belonged to him, Doug Slaughter, a man who had started life in a dirt-floored, thatched-roofed stone cotter's cottage.

Slaughter liked to think about that, liked shoving his success in other people's faces. He had fought, suffered, sweated, and bled to get to where he was today. He was proud of what he had accomplished, and he wasn't about to let some tin-horn gambler cheat him out of what he had already decided was rightfully his. He glowered at the man in his office. "We had a deal, Hays. I intend to hold you to it."

"I thought I made it pretty clear that my acceptance of your offer was contingent upon the approval of Miss DuBois's heir."

"Yeh? Well, what the hell is she doing showing up here?"

The man's face was a blank. "I don't know what you're talking about."

"Don't try to bluff me. I know all about Gabrielle Antoine. What is this? Some kinda scheme to get more money out of me?"

"Actually, I believe the young lady—"

"I'll go up to forty-five thousand dollars. No more."

Slaughter saw a muscle tick in the other man's jaw. "The business is worth more than that, and you know it."

"That house won't be worth nothing to either one of you, if you're dead. You tell her that. Forty-five thousand, or a one-way trip to the cemetery up Eureka Gulch. For you and your new lady friend. The choice is yours."

Hays leaned back against the wall, his hands resting negligently in the pockets of his black evening coat. "I don't like threats."

"No? Well, I don't like people who back out of a deal. I want that house. And I'm getting tired of listening to your mouth. Maybe I oughta call a couple of my boys in here. Convince you how serious I am about this."

"I wouldn't do that, if I were you." A small derringer appeared, as if by magic, in one of the gambler's fine hands, the barrel pointed straight and steady at Slaughter's chest. "Put your hands on top of your head, and do it nice and easy. You've made me real jumpy, Slaughter. Don't do anything that might make me leap to some nasty conclusion and decide to shoot you."

Slaughter stared in disbelief at the derringer. He might surround himself with men who used guns, but he never carried one himself. If he was personally going to intimidate or control a man, he liked to do it with his fists. It gave him a greater sense of satisfaction, of power. He liked power.

But looking down the barrel of a gun made him feel powerless, made him feel like the dirt-poor Irish tenant farmer he'd once been.

Murderous rage exploded someplace deep within him,

and spread in tingling waves through his body. When the rage was in him like that, Slaughter didn't usually think straight. It was the same rage that had filled him on that long-ago night, when the desperately hungry and fiercely resentful fifteen-year-old he'd once been had picked up a rock and used it to bash in the arrogant, sneering face of an English colonel he'd met on the high road to Dublin.

Slaughter took one unguarded step forward, and saw a chilling smile twist the gambler's lips. "Then again," said Hays, "shooting you does have its attractions."

It was the gambler's eyes that stopped him. They were the eyes of a gunman, a shootist, not a gambler: cold and hard and unforgiving, like a Colorado winter. It occurred to Slaughter that he should have paid more attention to those eyes before.

He laced his fingers together over his head and spread his elbows wide.

"Smart," said the gambler, waggling the gun sideways. "Move over by the fireplace. Now," he added when Slaughter hesitated.

Choking with impotent fury, Slaughter shifted to the side. He could feel the heat from the fire, flaring up beside his leg.

"Let me explain something to you," said the gambler, sauntering toward the front window. "I'm a patient man, and normally it takes a fair amount to make me lose my temper. But you've tried me tonight, Slaughter. You've tried me badly. I don't like being accosted by hirelings. I don't like people trying to rearrange my face. And I don't like being threatened with my own funeral."

Keeping the gun still trained on Slaughter, the gambler reached back with his left hand and flipped the window latch. "You're lucky, Slaughter. Luckier than you know, because it just so happens I find I don't particularly like running a whorehouse without a woman like Celeste as my partner. But don't push your luck too far. Piss me off like this again, and I might decide to stay in this business for the rest of my life. Just to keep you out of that house. Now, turn around so you're facing the fire."

"I'll get you for this, Hays," Slaughter murmured, doing what he was told. But even to his own ears, the threat sounded churlish.

"Not if you want that house," said the gambler. "And if you're smart, you'll stay away from Gabrielle Antoine, too."

A freezing blast of air hit Slaughter in the back. He spun around to find the window facing Lawrence Street gaping open, its elegant maroon silk curtains fluttering in the cold wind.

"Tucker! McCoy!" he bellowed, rushing to the open window. "Get your useless asses in here." He thrust his head out into the cold night.

The storm had begun to break up, revealing patches of star-strewn black sky through shifting clouds. In the intermittent moonlight, the ice-covered town glittered and sparkled, and the trail left by the gambler through the thick snow on the porch roof was clearly revealed.

But it took Slaughter a moment to locate the gambler himself, dangling off the roof's edge, high above the street. He hung suspended for just an instant, then dropped, graceful as a cat, into a plum-colored sleigh pulled up in front of the Silver Spur.

"Stop him, goddamn it," Slaughter hollered to the man who should have been waiting below.

But Hays had already whipped the reins free. "Get up there, Sugar," he called, slapping the reins against the haunches of the white horse harnessed between the traces. The horse bolted forward, jerking the sleigh so that it rattled and bounced around the street, its runners slicing through ice-encrusted, snowy ruts. Then the horse broke into a gallop, and the sleigh careened wildly around the corner as Hays swung up toward Nevada Gulch.

Even when it was out of sight, Slaughter could still hear the pounding of the horse's hooves on the frozen ground, carrying clearly in the cold night air.

Gabrielle stood beside the tall, satin-draped window of her room in the Teller House Hotel, and gazed at the snow-covered peaks that seemed to loom out of the darkness to hover menacingly over the town.

She felt disoriented, disconnected from the person she had always been. From the person she had thought herself to be. She had grown up knowing almost nothing about her family, about herself; now it seemed that even the little she'd been told had been a lie. Because her mother hadn't been dead, but alive, all these years. Alive, and the owner of a house of sin.

She should never have come. She knew that now. Better not to know, better never to know, surely, than to know . . . this.

She felt it again, that angry, overwhelming urge to be gone, to run away from this place, from the ugly, unbearable truth she had discovered here. But she knew now that she could never really run away. Oh, she could leave this town tomorrow, the way she had planned. But she wasn't the kind of person who could ever really hide from the truth, pretend it had never existed, go on with her life as if nothing had changed.

She had met people who could fool themselves like that, but she wasn't one of them. No matter what the cost, or how deep the pain, everything there was to know, Gabrielle wanted to know it—needed to know it. All of it.

All of it.

A whorehouse could be a damned sorry sight in the unforgiving light of morning, Jordan thought.

He paused in the doorway to the gaming room and let his gaze wander over the green baize-covered tables, the dirty liquor glasses, the spilled poker chips, the stinking porcelain cuspidors. Unlike other bawdy houses, Celeste's Place was too expensively fitted out, too well kept to ever look tawdry. The cruel light of day revealed no chipped gilt, no peeling paint, no worn carpets and stained wallpaper. But there was no denying that, stripped of evening's gentle light and murmuring voices, the place seemed more than just empty. More than just decadent. It looked ... lonesome. And maybe a bit sad.

Jordan yawned and stretched lazily toward the ceiling. He started to arch his back, then froze as something outside in the street caught his eye. Slowly lowering his arms, he moved to the graceful bay window that looked out onto the front porch, and pulled back the lace panel that hung between the heavy green velvet curtains.

The late-winter storm that had battered the area for the last three days had finally blown itself out, leaving the sky achingly clear and blue. Squinting into the glare of bright sunlight reflecting off snow-covered mountains, he studied the woman who stood on the boardwalk outside the gate. A slim, golden-haired woman wearing a gray Ulster coat and gloves too thin for the Rockies in winter.

"Son of a bitch," he swore under his breath. She was supposed to be getting ready to go back to New Orleans. What the hell was she doing here?

She had her head tilted to one side, staring up at Celeste's Place as if she could, by sheer force of concentration, will the house to tell her if what she'd heard about her mother were true. Or maybe what she sought was simply understanding. An explanation as to why Celeste had gone away, leaving her daughter to grow up alone.

He thought at first that this was all she had come for: to look at the house one more time, to make one last attempt to come to terms with what she'd been told, before she went away.

Then he saw her take a step forward and reach for the gate. Even from this distance, he could see her hand tremble. She touched the latch, then snatched her hand back, as if the cold metal had burned her. And it occurred to Jordan, watching her, that she was, in a very real sense, stretching her hand out to fire. Hellfire.

Up until now, the world Gabrielle Antoine had moved through was as pure, uncomplicated, and unsullied as the virgin snow on the mountain peaks around her. But on the other side of that gate . . .

On the other side lay a world whose existence she had, until now, only been told about, probably in hushed whispers and schoolgirl giggles. A world of decadence and depravity. Of sin.

Yesterday, she had glimpsed that world. Only briefly, and accidentally, and still it had subtly altered her. If she opened that gate and entered that world again, willingly, it would contaminate her. Slowly, surely, and inevitably.

He saw her step backward, and he was surprised when he realized he'd been holding his breath.

He was a man who cared about nothing, and no one. Everything this girl believed in, everything that was important to her, everything she undoubtedly wanted out of life—family, home, love—had died for him, long ago. Perhaps that was why it was suddenly so important to him that those things not die for her, too.

Go on, Gabrielle, he thought. *Turn around and walk back down that hill. Walk away from this house and its secrets—now, forever. Before it's too late.*

Only, she didn't do it. Instead she lifted the latch, and he knew by the determinedly stiff way she held herself that, this time, she wasn't going to back off.

He watched her push open the gate and march up the shoveled front path. And despite everything, he knew a moment of reluctant admiration for the sheer guts it must have taken this woman, raised as she had been, to do something she must surely realize had the potential to ruin her.

When she reached the top of the stairs, he was waiting for her in the open doorway. "New Orleans is that way," he drawled, gesturing toward where the sun was pulling away from a ragged, snow-covered peak behind her. "Didn't anyone tell you?"

She paused with one foot still on the last step, her head falling back as she gazed up at him. She looked painfully white, the features of her face drawn, pinched. He watched the muscles in her slim throat work as she swallowed. "I've come to find out more about Celeste DuBois. About . . . my mother."

He'd just finished shaving, and he wore only his black trousers and a white shirt open halfway down the front, with his suspenders flapping down around his hips. He could tell by the way her gaze skittered over him that his state of undress made her uncomfortable, but he made no move to pull his suspenders up, or to button his shirt. "You know what this house is."

"I know." She took the final step up onto the porch. "It is a house of sin. But it is where she lived."

He met her eyes, those strange silver-colored eyes she'd inherited from her mother, and pushed his breath out in a long sigh. He suspected it was probably beyond him to imagine why she'd come, why she'd felt the need to put herself through this. The loss of Jordan's own family had left a cold, empty ache in his heart. But, before that, they had been his life. His mother, his father, his brothers. Loving, laughing, fighting, *caring* about each other, through all his growing-up years. Whatever the needs that had driven Gabrielle up that hill and into this house, whatever her particular pain, he had never known it.

He stood back, and let her walk into the house.

He shut the door behind her, and watched her throw one, quick glance at the gaming room on the left, then another, equally furtive look through the beaded, arched entrance to the front parlor, where the ornately carved banister curved invitingly upstairs.

"Like a tour?" he suggested.

She shook her head, high color flooding her pale cheeks. The morning sun streaming in through the leaded glass window of the door fell full on her young, open face. She might not be the classic beauty her mother had been, but there was an appealing warmth and vitality about this young woman, an inner joy, that Celeste had lacked. Or maybe Celeste had been like that once, he thought. Perhaps it was simply that the life she'd led had obliterated any soft, vulnerable characteristics she might once have had, leaving only the cold, calculating woman he had known.

It disturbed him to realize that the same thing could happen to Celeste's daughter. But it bothered him even more to realize that this woman was touching some sensitive place, deep within him, that he had thought long dead.

He turned away from her. "No tour? Then, you'd better come out to the kitchen with me while I get something to eat. If we stay here, you're liable to run across a few stray customers, and learn more about your mother and her life than you bargained for."

She didn't say anything, just followed him down the long, wainscoted hall, with its carefully polished floorboards and imported Persian runner and rows of lurid oil paintings. He never looked back at her, but he was aware of her behind him. Aware of the stiff way she held herself, staring straight ahead, as if those two swift glances into the front rooms had already shown her more of the house than she wanted to see.

He knew another unwelcome surge of emotion that was part pity—and part anger. She seemed to think she could just come in here, ask a few questions, hear a few stories, then walk away, turning her back, once and for all, on an aspect of her life she never should have known about, never should have seen. But Jordan knew better. Whether she realized it or not, he thought, with every decision she made, with every step she took, she was moving farther and farther away from the sheltered world of innocence and piety and safety in which she'd grown up. Inexorably, inevitably, she was drawing closer to the complicated, sinful, dangerous life from which her mother had struggled so valiantly to save her.

So valiantly, yet so futilely.

CHAPTER FOUR

"Hungry?" Jordan Hays tore a chunk off one of the loaves of bread cooling on the pine kitchen dresser near the sink, and held it out to her, his dark, fine-boned fingers curling around the golden crust.

Gabrielle gazed down at his outstretched hand, and shook her head. She hadn't had any breakfast, but she couldn't bear the thought of eating at the moment.

She didn't understand what was wrong with her. She was desperate to hear more about this woman who had been her mother, and yet . . . And yet she was afraid, too. The fear was like a tight band around her throat, making it almost impossible even to breathe.

He shrugged and turned to the counter, his fine white linen shirt pulling tightly over the muscles of his back as he worked cutting a slice of cheese, and pouring himself a glass of milk from the pitcher cooling near the window. She realized she was staring at him, tensely waiting for whatever he was going to tell her. She yanked her gaze away, and looked at the kitchen instead.

It could have been a kitchen in any big house, Gabrielle thought, noticing the pretty yellow muslin curtains hanging at the windows, the well-scrubbed pine table in the middle of the floor, the orange tabby cat curled up on the caned seat of a slat-backed rocker in front of the fire. The air was rich with the yeasty scent of freshly baked bread and the tangy pine of the fire crackling on the hearth. It could have been a kitchen in any big house.

But it was not.

"Sit down," he said, motioning to the spindle-backed chairs that flanked the long kitchen table.

She jerked off her gloves and unbuttoned her coat, hanging it along with her hat on one of the hooks near the back door. She turned to find him watching her intently, a strange heat glittering in his eyes. She wore a plain gray serge dress with a high collar and modest lines. But there was something about the way he was looking at her body that made her feel oddly exposed. She found herself wishing she hadn't taken off her coat, and she pulled out a seat at the end of the table nearest the fire and quickly sat down, hugging herself.

"Here. This will help, if you're chilled." He set a mug of steaming cider in front of her.

The sweet scent of apples tickled her nostrils. "Thank you." She wrapped her hands around the warm mug and watched him fold his long, lean frame into the chair opposite her. The movement pulled at his half-buttoned shirt, revealing a slice of tanned, bare chest. She lowered her eyes.

"I only met your mother a few months ago," he said, taking a bite of cheese. "So I can't say I knew her all that well." He took another bite, and she found herself watching him again. Watching the movement of his strong jaw as he chewed. Watching the muscles work in his throat when he swallowed.

Simply by agreeing to talk to her, he was being kind. She knew that. And yet she sensed no real kindness in him, no compassion. It was as if he were a hard, empty shell of a man. As if everything gentle, everything vulnerable and caring within him, had died. She wished she didn't have to talk to him, but there was no one else.

"I'll try to answer whatever questions you have," he said.

She took a sip of her cider. It was sweet, but too hot, and she scalded her tongue. More than anything else, she wanted to know why her mother had abandoned her. But she couldn't bring herself to ask something so personal, so revealing. So instead she said, "Do you know why she left New Orleans?"

"Not exactly. I know she had a house there, before the war." He reached for his glass of milk, and drank deeply before continuing. "I think she ran into trouble, either with the authorities, or with someone powerful enough to cause her problems."

Gabrielle's hand jerked, almost spilling the cider. "You mean, she ran a house like this? In New Orleans?" She thought of the mother of her memory, the beautiful, pale-haired woman, dressed in satin and lace and delicately scented with expensive perfume. The woman who had always come to kiss her good night. She tried to imagine that woman—she tried to imagine her own, five-year-old *self*—living in a house like this one, a house of sin. And it was as if something tore loose inside her, as if something vitally important were slipping away from her.

"That's right," Hays said, calmly eating his bread and cheese. "She had a brothel on Prytania Street." His gaze fastened on her face, and she turned to stare at the fire, hiding her shock, hiding everything she felt and didn't want him to see. She kept telling herself it wasn't right to resent him for telling her these things. But she did.

"After she left New Orleans," he continued in that same, emotionless voice, "Celeste went out to California and worked the mining towns out there. Then about ten or twelve years ago, she came up here, not long after the first strikes were made. She had a house down on Eureka Street, in the early days. Of course, it was nothing like this. Mostly canvas and logs, from what I understand."

He paused again. She still couldn't look at him. She just sat there, staring at the flickering flames, not knowing whether she wanted him to go on or not. His words seemed to echo in her head. *Celeste worked the mining towns.* Celeste DuBois, this woman who had given her life, her *mother*, had worked as a— But Gabrielle could not bring herself even to think the word. She tried to imagine the life such a woman must have lived, the things she must have done, only she could not.

"Did Celeste DuBois even know who my father was?" Gabrielle asked, her voice a tearing whisper.

"If she did, she never said."

"But my name is different," Gabrielle insisted almost desperately. "Antoine, not DuBois." It was as if the last visages of the person she'd always believed herself to be, were slipping away from her.

He shook his head. "She gave you the name she was born with herself. A lot of women change their names when they go into this business." He shoved back his chair, twisting sideways so he could thrust out his long legs and cross them at the ankles. She knew he was looking at her again, knew it even without glancing toward him. It was something she could *feel*. Something she'd never experienced before. She kept her gaze fixed on the fire, and those crossed boots.

"None of this is easy to hear, is it?" he said, his tone suddenly, unexpectedly gentle.

For some unaccountable reason, his gentleness almost undid her, and she had to blink quickly to stem the sudden burning of tears in her eyes. This was what she had asked for, this information. This was what she had wanted, what she had come here for. But she felt no thrill of discovery, none of the sense of accomplishment she had anticipated that learning more about her mother would bring. She knew only a profound and totally unexpected impression of loss. The image of her mother as she had built her up over the years in her dreams was disintegrating. And she wasn't certain she could cope with the reality forming in its place.

"I noticed you haven't asked why she left you behind in New Orleans."

She raised her gaze to his fine-boned face, and felt the thrumming of her blood through her veins, the easing of her breath, in and out of her lungs as they stared at each other. The moment stretched out in a taut, aware silence filled only with the crackling pop of the fire.

She did not like this man. He had become, for her, a symbol of the debauched, depraved world that had claimed her mother. Yet in some way she did not understand, in some way she did not want, a bond was forming between them. Coming to this town, to this house, learning these things about her mother, about herself, was proving to be the most profound, the most difficult experience of Gabrielle's life. And whether she liked it or not, she was going through that experience with this man. This dark, dangerous, sinful man, who knew truths about her that no one else did. And who seemed, in some ways, to understand her—perhaps better even than she understood herself.

He stood up to carry his plate and glass over to the stone sink. "The night Celeste died, I asked her that. I don't know why she didn't take you to California with her in the first place, but I do know she almost went back for you when the war was over. Only, she decided against it. She didn't want you to grow up in a whorehouse."

"I wish," Gabrielle said softly, "I wish she had come for me."

"Do you?" He turned, and his unsentimental gaze seemed to slam into her. "That's only because you never lived in a whorehouse."

There was a rattle and clink of glass, and Gabrielle glanced around to see a woman carrying a heavy tray come bustling through the doorway from the hall. She was a pretty young woman in her twenties, with golden-brown hair and eyes. She was also, Gabrielle realized with a sense of shock, heavy with child.

"Lord love us," said the woman in a lilting Texas accent as she dumped the tray full of glasses down beside the sink. "I wish this baby would hurry up and get itself born. I ain't worked this hard in years."

Gabrielle watched as a roguish smile curled Jordan Hays's lips and creased his lean cheeks. This was a side of him she hadn't seen before: a dangerously charming side. "What?" he said, his voice as light and teasing as his smile. "Pickin' up glasses and makin' beds? 'If all the year were playing holidays, to sport would be as tedious as to work.' "

Gabrielle recognized the quote immediately. It was from *Henry IV*. She stared at the gambler in stunned silence, trying to reconcile this unexpected ability to quote Shakespeare with the image of the man she'd had before.

"Yeh?" said the woman, her eyes narrowing with confusion she obviously didn't want to admit. "Well, I'm a sportin' gal all right, and I'll be glad enough when I can get back to it."

She turned to leave, but her gaze fell on Gabrielle, still sitting by the fire, and she paused, one hand balanced on her swollen belly. "So who might you be?" she asked with undisguised curiosity. "I didn't know we was gettin' a new whore."

Gabrielle wanted to shrink back into her chair. "I am not— That is, I am—" She floundered helplessly.

"She's Celeste's daughter," said Hays. "And she's not a whore, Crystal."

"Celeste's daughter? From New Orleans?" Crystal swung back to Hays and startled Gabrielle by throwing her arms around him and kissing him full on the mouth. "Aw, Jordan, bless your little heart! I knew you weren't really gonna sell out to Doug Slaughter. I just knew it. Wait till I tell the girls." She disentangled her arms from his neck and spun around, as if to rush from the room.

Hays snagged her by the arm, pulling her up short. "Hang on there. She's just here to finalize the sale."

"The sale?" The word ended on a kind of wail, and Crystal collapsed against him. Then, as Gabrielle watched, the woman's pretty face hardened in some way. Her smile remained sweet, but a calculating gleam crept into her soft brown eyes, and she slipped her hand through Jordan Hays's open shirt to run her palm over his bare chest in a way that made Gabrielle feel so uncomfortable she had to look away. "I cain't believe you're plannin' to sell out to that ol' son of a bitch." Crystal's voice was as much of a caress as what she was doing with her hand. "You know none of us girls wants to work for him. He treats his whores like shit."

Gabrielle's head snapped back around. She had assumed that this pretty, pregnant young woman must work in the house as a cleaner. Now she wasn't so sure.

Hays shrugged. "Then, you'll have to find a new house."

"He owns just about every other house in this town."

"Then, find a new town."

Crystal laid her palms flat against the gambler's chest and pushed away from him. "You're a mean bastard, Jordan Hays." And with that, she flounced out of the kitchen.

Gabrielle stared after the departing woman. "I had the impression from something you said yesterday that the women who clean the house are Chinese," she said slowly.

"They are," he said. "Crystal is a chippy." He reached out to select an apple from the fruit basket on the end of the counter. She watched his lips curl away from his straight white teeth as he bit into the shiny red fruit.

She shook her head. "I don't understand."

He took another bite of the apple. "When the girls can't work the upstairs rooms, they help with the cooking and cleaning. They don't like it, but Celeste didn't believe in letting anyone eat for free. Otherwise, she said, some of the girls would be claiming to have their monthly flow every week, and maybe not be as careful as they ought to be about using their female preventatives."

Gabrielle felt her entire body tingle with hot embarrassment. In the convent the nuns used to shut the doors and drop their voices to a whisper if for some reason they had to refer to something as intimate as a woman's petticoat or drawers. A woman's monthly flow was never mentioned at all, let alone in mixed company. Whereas the state of being with child . . .

From upstairs came the sound of a woman's voice, raised in excitement. Hays nodded his head toward the back stairs. "Thanks to Crystal," he said, chucking the apple core into the pail under the sink, and beginning to fasten his open shirt. "In a few minutes half the whores in this house are going to descend on this kitchen, wanting to take a look at Celeste's daughter."

Gabrielle had never watched a man button his shirt. It seemed a shockingly intimate thing to do, but she couldn't seem to tear her gaze away.

"If you're smart," he continued, easing his suspenders up over his shoulders, "You'll get your coat and hat, and let me drive you back down to the hotel now."

She stood up and was reaching for her coat when the kitchen door banged open and two children burst into the room, bringing with them a sprinkling of snow and the crisp, fresh air of the mountains.

One of the children, a dark-haired, pretty girl of about ten, lost her footing on the slippery kitchen tiles and went down with a thud. The scrawny, sandy-haired boy who'd been chasing her, jumped on her stomach and ground the fistful of snow he carried into her face. "You take that back, Arabella!" he yelled. "You take it back right now."

Arabella kicked and thrashed her head back and forth, but she kept her mouth fiercely screwed shut.

Jordan Hays reached down to close his fist around the boy's collar and lift him into the air. "Benjamin Franklin," he said, setting the boy down on his feet and letting go of his coat. "You must be real good at muckin' out stalls, son, to get finished this quick."

Benjamin Franklin hung his head. "I ain't finished, sir." He shot a ferocious sideways glare at the girl, who had scrambled to her feet and now stood smirking at him. "She said my mother—"

Something the boy must have seen in Hays's expression closed him off. Benjamin Franklin wiped his nose on his sleeve and turned, dragging his feet to the door. "I'll go finish, sir."

Out of the corner of her eye, Gabrielle noticed the dark-haired girl sidling toward the stairs. But Hays's deceptively silky voice stopped Arabella in her tracks. "Should I have Wing Tsue dredge the well for George?" he asked quietly.

He wasn't looking at Arabella when he said it, so it took Gabrielle a moment to realize that the remark had been addressed to the girl. Arabella turned slowly to face him. "Sir?"

He lifted his chin, buttoning his collar, while the girl waited nervously. "I saw Jeff Hogan in this house last night," he said, smoothing his shirt. "And it was my understanding he always buys Jilly for the night."

"Yes, sir."

"It was also my understanding that it's your job to watch George while his mother is busy."

"Yes, sir. Only, Mr. Hogan, he left early today, and Jilly came and got the baby from me more'n an hour ago. Honest."

"Then, you should be upstairs, helping your mama with the beds. And, Arabella," he added, as she started to leave, "don't let me catch you botherin' Benjamin Franklin again. You hear?"

"Yes, sir." She turned and pelted up the stairs, her skinny, black stocking-clad legs kicking up the flounce of her dress as she ran.

Gabrielle stared after her. "What are those children doing here?"

"They live here," said Hays, letting his breath out in a huff of laughter at the look of horror Gabrielle couldn't keep off her face. "Most brothels have children in them. When men and women do the things that men and women do together in bawdy houses, the result is children, no matter how careful the girls are. Or didn't they teach you about that in the convent?"

Gabrielle felt her cheeks burn fiery red, but she was beginning to realize that he deliberately tried to shock her with the things he said, and she refused to be provoked. "How many children are there in this house?"

"Five, at the moment. Although technically I'm not sure you can count Benjamin Franklin, since his mother ran off with one of her customers about eighteen months ago and simply left the boy behind."

Gabrielle swallowed hard. "But, do they know what goes on here? I mean . . ." She glanced toward the stairs. "That little girl said—"

He snorted and pushed away from the counter. Before she could stop herself, Gabrielle stepped back. "Of course they know," he said. "How could they help but know, living here? Arabella herself will probably be working here in another few years."

Gabrielle shook her head, in revulsion, in denial. "Oh, no— Surely her mother—"

"Her mother is Crystal. And Crystal was born in a bawdy house herself down El Paso way. Whoring is the only life she's ever known." He advanced on her, his face blank, his eyes cold and hard. "Still wish your mother had brought you here when you were Arabella's age? Would you like to have been her?"

Gabrielle shuddered. It was an effort to meet his gaze, but she made herself do it. She didn't know what she wanted, what she wished, anymore. Except that she wanted to get away from this house. Away from this man.

"Take me back to the hotel now," she said. "Please."

He didn't take her directly to the hotel, after they left the house. Instead he drove her up Eureka Gulch, to Central City's graveyard.

She hadn't known she had this need within her, this yearning to see her mother's grave, until he suggested it. From anyone else, she would have thought the suggestion sprang from kindness. Only, he had made the offer in that remote way of his that could make even the most considerate gesture seem somehow cruel. As if he had some other motive entirely that she couldn't even guess at.

They left the sleigh beside the road and entered on foot through the cemetery's iron gates. "Celeste's grave is over there," he said, nodding toward the far side of the hill.

She glanced at him. The cold seemed to have sharpened the clear, strong bones of his face in a way she thought made him look almost sinister. He wore his thick sheepskin coat, and had his black hat pulled low over his eyes. The hat had a peculiar band, she noticed; a thin strip of hammered silver, that looked as if it might be Mexican. She found herself wondering how he'd come by it, and why he wore it. She knew so little about him.

"The ground in here is uneven beneath the snow," he

said, reaching out unexpectedly to touch her arm. "So watch your step."

It was the lightest of all possible touches, just a simple brushing of his fingers against her elbow. Yet it sent a shudder through her, a reaction so intense she almost gasped. She told herself it was revulsion, and she was careful to put some distance between them as they tramped through the thick snow that lay between the rows of wooden crosses, rusting iron rails, and granite headstones. She did not want to risk accidentally touching him again.

She felt a cold wind kick up, moaning mournfully through the pines and thrashing the bare branches of the aspen trees that stood out, pale, against the darkening sky. She glanced up, surprised at how quickly the brilliant blue sky of that morning was disappearing beneath the rushing clouds.

"Looks like it's going to snow again," he said, following her gaze. "We'd better not stay too long."

He had stopped beside a white marble pillar topped with a neoclassical figure of a weeping woman. Coming up beside him, Gabrielle silently read the inscription.

Celeste DuBois
née Gabrielle Marie Antoine
born, 16 November 1833
died, 20 February 1874
May she rest in peace.

Gabrielle realized she'd been holding her breath, and let it out in a long sigh. "She was only forty years old. Forty is young to die."

"She didn't even look thirty," said Hays, his voice dispassionate. "I don't think I've ever known a more beautiful woman."

Gabrielle stared down at the snow-covered, freshly dug grave, and swallowed the knot of emotion in her throat. "When I was a little girl," she said quietly, "the nuns told me that my mother had gone to heaven, to live with Jesus Christ. That's exactly the way they put it. I suppose they thought I'd understand what they were trying to say, but I didn't. I thought she was simply living someplace else. They also used to tell me that one day she would be waiting for me, at the Pearly Gates." Gabrielle's voice trembled, and she found she had to swallow again. "The convent had these big, wrought-iron gates, painted white, you see, and I thought those must be the Pearly Gates. So I used to stand by them for hours, waiting for my mother to come. It took me a long time to realize that she was never going to come back. That what the nuns were trying to tell me was that my mother was dead."

He didn't say anything. Just stood beside her, looking out over the houses strung along the gully below, his hands jammed into the pockets of his thick coat.

"Only she wasn't dead," said Gabrielle, feeling again that helpless welling of fury toward this beautiful, beloved woman who had walked away from the five-year-old girl Gabrielle had once been, and stayed away from her, through all those lonely, growing-up years. "Until now."

She realized she was clenching her fists, and forced herself to open them. It didn't seem right to be so furious with a dead woman, but she didn't think she could remember ever having so much anger within her. She was even, she realized suddenly, angry with her mother simply for having died. For dying now, without ever seeing her daughter again. Without ever explaining to her why it had all happened.

"How did she die?" Gabrielle asked, glancing at the man beside her.

He swiveled his head to look at her, his long, lean frame standing out stark against the white-covered hill. "Someone shot her in the back."

Gabrielle felt as if she'd been punched between the juncture of her ribs. "Sh-shot?" she stammered, staring at Jordan Hays.

"A rifle bullet came through one of the front windows of the house."

Gabrielle sucked in a deep breath of freezing air. "But—*who?* Who shot her? And why?"

He shook his head, his eyes hooded, unreadable. "The sheriff decided it was an accident."

She expected him to say more, but he didn't. He turned away from her, lifting the collar of his coat against the growing wind, and she realized he was giving her time alone.

She made a hasty sign of the cross and began to pray. Her lips silently formed the right words, but as she stared down at that snow-covered mound, all she could seem to think was, *Why, Mama? Why didn't you want me anymore? Didn't you love me?* She felt the tears begin to well in her eyes, and angrily dashed at them with the heel of her gloved hand.

"She didn't abandon you, you know."

His words followed so disconcertingly upon her thoughts that at first it seemed she had imagined them. Only he followed them up by saying, "It would have been easy for her to bring you out here, let you grow up at Celeste's Place, like Arabella. The hard thing was missing you all those years, sending the money to keep you in the academy even when things were tight for her."

The cold wind gusted between them, flapping the hem of her coat, tugging stray tendrils of hair from her chignon and sending them flying across her face. She wanted to believe what he was saying, wanted desperately to believe that Celeste's leaving her at the academy had been a sacrifice born out of all that was noble and unselfish and giving in a mother's love. But wanting to believe, and believing, were two different things.

She hugged her coat against the cold, and turned into the wind so that it blew the loose wisps of hair out of her face. Then the full implications of what he'd just said slammed into her, and the fingers clutching her coat curled into something like claws.

"Do you mean," she said, her words coming out slow and halting, "do you mean to tell me that the money I've been living on all these years . . . the money that was in my trust fund . . . It all came from what those women in the house earned, selling their bodies to men?"

He tilted his head sideways, squinting up at her from beneath the brim of his hat. "The thought bothers you, does it?"

"Yes. Yes, it does."

"It was hardly your fault, and there's nothing that can be done to remedy it now, in any case. So why let it ride your conscience?"

She shook her head, unable to explain. She became aware of the cold seeping up through the thin soles of her shoes, and the heavy white clouds, scuttling overhead. A shiver coursed through her. "I'm ready to leave."

They walked toward the cemetery gates, neither of them speaking. She was acutely conscious of the crunch of the snow beneath her feet, of the cold, wood-smoke-scented air she drew into her lungs, of the lonely, sighing sound made by the branches of the pine trees along the ridge as a sharp gust of wind blew up the gulch.

"Do you really think my mother was killed by accident?" she asked at last when the silence between them became unbearable.

"Either that, or someone was very good with a rifle." He stared out over the treetops, and she knew she wouldn't get anything else out of him.

"You brought me here to tell me this, didn't you?" she said, realizing intuitively that it was true.

"Yes." They had reached the road outside the cemetery, not far from where he had left the sleigh.

"Why?" She stopped, her breath billowing white around her in the falling temperature.

He swung to face her. "I think it's time you left here."

"I plan to leave."

"When?"

"Soon." She felt suddenly uncomfortable beneath his scrutiny, and turned to look back at the lonely, grave-filled hillside behind them. "I want to leave. It's just that I know if I left now, without learning everything I could, I would regret it. Don't you see? It would be like . . ." She paused, searching for the right words.

"Running away?" he suggested quietly.

Her head snapped around, to find him still regarding her with that cool, calculated stare. She had expected to find his expression as gentle as his voice, but she could see no sign of compassion in that fine-boned face. He must be a very good gambler, she thought. Nothing ever showed on his face.

"Yes," she said. "It would be like running away. And I don't believe in running away. At least not from the truth."

And then she realized that she'd been wrong, that sometimes his face wasn't remote and closed, at all. Because there was a definite warmth in the depths of his eyes that hadn't been there before, and a faint, attractive curving of his lips.

"Some truths, it's all right to walk away from," he said softly. "You've already learned more than Celeste wanted you to know, and you've seen more than a woman like you should ever be exposed to. Innocence is a precious thing, easily corrupted." He stretched out his hand, and she thought he was going to touch her face, the way he had once before. "Go away from here, Gabrielle. Before it's too late."

And then he did touch her, his fingertips tracing the line of her jaw, before falling away.

She felt a frisson of excitement tingle through her. And she knew, suddenly, that what his touch aroused in her was not revulsion, as she'd thought, but something else entirely. Something that heated her blood, something sinful and shameful. She dropped her gaze, afraid that he might see the effect his touch had on her, written clearly in her eyes.

She didn't understand her reaction to this man. He was a wicked sinner, a man whose entire way of life was surely an abomination to God. Everything about him frightened and disturbed her. And yet . . . And yet, oddly, he fascinated her, too.

And she thought it was probably the way he fascinated her that frightened her most of all.

"Please," she said, her voice little more than a whisper. "Take me back to the hotel now."

She climbed quickly into the sleigh, before he could make a move to help her. All the way down the hill, she sat stiffly beside him, careful not to glance at him, especially careful not to brush against him. The only time she did allow herself to look at him was right before he drove away, when she thanked him. And then she found his face so closed, so distant, she might almost have believed that she had imagined that moment of unsettling affinity, of intimacy, that had passed between them outside the cemetery gates. Except . . .

Except that he had called her Gabrielle.

She stood on the boardwalk in front of the Teller House Hotel, and tilted back her head to watch the snowflakes fall gently from the sky. He had used her first name, and it had seemed so natural, so right, that she hadn't even thought to protest at the familiarity. And then he'd touched her face, and she hadn't moved, hadn't complained about that, either.

Because the truth was, she had wanted him to do it. The thought came to her, in a flash of guilt and shame, as she turned to enter the hotel and climb the wide, red-carpeted stairs to her room. She had wanted him to touch her. She had wanted to experience again those strange, exhilarating, sinful feelings that swept through her when he touched her . . . and even, sometimes, when she simply looked at him.

Tormented by mortification and self-reproach, she fumbled with the lock on her door, trying several times to turn the key before she realized it was already unlocked. Puzzled, she twisted the handle, and pushed the door in.

Her room was large and airy, with a four-poster bed draped with a white crocheted coverlet, and two slipper chairs upholstered in rose satin that stood beneath the long, double-hung window overlooking the street.

At first Gabrielle thought she must have the wrong room, because a woman lay sprawled across the bottom of her bed. A beautiful woman, wearing a vivid emerald-and-white-striped silk dress with lace-trimmed puff sleeves and a scoop neckline that showed off a startling percentage of her white shoulders and swelling bosom. Two ostrich feathers, dyed a matching green, nodded from the thick, titian-colored hair dressed half on top of her head, half cascading in loose ringlets around those bare shoulders.

Another woman, a tall, graceful woman with straight black hair, bronze-touched skin, and knifelike cheekbones that hinted at Indian ancestry, occupied one of the slipper chairs. And in the chair beside her lolled a woman with golden-brown hair, a pretty smile, and a round, bulging stomach that showed clearly beneath her gown of violet grosgrain trimmed with contrasting vivid pink velvet ribbon. Crystal, from Celeste's Place.

"Howdy," said Crystal, her bright smile belied by the nervous shifting of her golden-brown eyes. "We come to have a chat with ya."

CHAPTER
FIVE

Gabrielle stood in the doorway and stared at the three painted women filling her room with their ostrich feathers, their gaudily colored silks and satins, and their expanses of naked flesh.

They were harlots, jezebels. The church had many names to describe these fallen women, these women of sin, and none of the names were nice. They were the handmaidens of the devil, these women who flaunted their carnality, who engaged in lewd, unspeakable, unthinkable practices with men in exchange for a few sordid coins. They were the daughters of Eve: instruments of evil, temptresses, who lured men into vice and damnation. These were the women who wove the winding-sheets of souls, and laid them in the urn of everlasting death.

Her mother had been one of these women.

Gabrielle whisked herself inside and quickly closed the door behind her with a snap, before anyone could come down the hall and see these women in her room. See *her* with these women.

"What do you want?" she demanded. Her voice didn't sound like her own. It was husky, roughened by fear. She realized that these women frightened her, although she couldn't quite understand why.

"Like I said," explained Crystal, resting one languid arm along the back of the chair. "We jist wanna chat. About the house. This here's Tierney." The woman on the bed nodded. "And Sirena." The dark-haired woman simply stared at Gabrielle with fierce self-possession. "And I'm Crystal." She gave Gabrielle a wide, sultry smile. Even six months with child, there was a lush, overripe sensuality about the woman that reminded Gabrielle of a hot, steamy New Orleans night, when the air was close and it was hard to breathe and the skin felt tight and uncomfortable.

She turned away to strip off her ecru kid gloves. She needed warmer gloves, she thought; her fingers felt stiff and awkward with cold. "How did you get in here?" she asked, setting her gloves on the edge of the marble-topped washstand.

Crystal nodded toward the woman on the bed. "Tierney there's real good with locks."

"My da taught me how to do lots of things," said Tierney, stretching her arms over her head. "Before they hanged him, back in London." The way she sprawled across the bed with one knee casually drawn up and apart, had hiked up the ruched frill of her striped dress, revealing a green satin petticoat and delicate white silk stockings encasing long, shapely calves.

Gabrielle wanted to look away, but she couldn't. She found herself trying to imagine what it must be like for this woman, to lie like that for a man, for a stranger. She wondered what this woman thought about, when she felt his weight, pressing her down into the mattress. What it felt like, when he shoved his man's part inside her secret woman's flesh. How she survived it.

Sinful, forbidden thoughts. Gabrielle felt her cheeks grow warm, and turned away to take off her coat and hat and hang them on the hook beside the door. "Why are you here?"

"Because you're Celeste's daughter," said Sirena, the tall, dark-haired woman sitting near the window. Gabrielle looked at her with interest. Her speech sounded surprisingly cultured, despite the strange, guttural undertone that went with those fiercely high cheekbones and the darkness of her skin. She wore a dress of blue-gray foulard, trimmed with yak lace, that was no less revealing than the gowns of the other two women, yet still managed to look not quite so vulgar.

Gabrielle crossed her arms against the prim, tucked front of her own simple gray dress. "That still doesn't explain why you are here."

Crystal leaned forward, displaying a shocking swath of cleavage. "We're here because Jordan is selling the house to Doug Slaughter to pay you off, and we don't want to see that happen."

Gabrielle shook her head. "Why?"

"Because none of us wants to work for Slaughter, that's why," said Crystal. Her eyes narrowed speculatively. "And I think someone ought to let you know that your mama fought with just about her last breath to keep that man from gettin' his hands on her house. He tried for months to talk her into selling to him, and when she wouldn't do it, he got real mean and tried to scare her into doin' it. Only she wouldn't scare, your mama. So instead, she ended up dead."

Gabrielle felt a chill that had nothing to do with her frozen fingers or the snow-encrusted hem of her petticoat, lying wet and heavy against her ankles. "I thought my mother's death was an accident."

Tierney swung her legs over the side of the bed and sat up to cast a swift, sharp glance at the other woman. "There now, Crystal, why you want to be bringing up all that talk? You know as well as I do the sheriff decided it was an accident." She stood with a swirl of silk skirts and ruched frills, and wandered over to fiddle with the glass bottles on Gabrielle's dressing table.

"Yeh? Well, it was a real convenient accident for Slaughter, wasn't it?" said Crystal. "He wanted Miss Celeste to sell, and she wouldn't do it. So someone *accidentally* shoots her, and he gets the house."

Tierney shrugged one bare, beautiful shoulder, making her copper-colored ringlets bounce provocatively. "Sure then, just because an accident makes things turn out the way somebody wanted them to, doesn't mean it wasn't an accident." She picked up the rosary that had been the nuns' parting gift to Gabrielle, and studied it curiously.

Sirena reached over to pluck the rosary from Tierney's grasp and set it back down. An almost palpable frisson of animosity passed between the two women, although neither said a word.

Gabrielle's gaze drifted from one woman to the next, trying to see past their painted mouths and cheeks, past their artfully dressed hair ornamented with nodding ostrich plums and bunches of artificial flowers. She couldn't stop thinking about the things these women must do with the men who were their customers in that big white house at the top of the gulch. It seemed to her that those things should have marked the women in some way more visible than the boldness of their eyes and the defiant tilt of their chins.

She realized they were all staring at her expectantly. She cleared her throat. "I'm sorry, I don't see how I can help you."

"You could tell Jordan he don't need to sell the house," said Crystal, her smile sweet, her gaze level and determined. "He's only sellin' to pay you off—*and* because he never did like dealin' with anything other than the gamin' room. So if you was to stay here and take over running the other parts of the house for him—"

Gabrielle gasped. *"Me?"*

Crystal raised her arched, carefully plucked eyebrows. "Well, why not? What you got in New Orleans that's better than Celeste's Place?"

"But you don't understand," floundered Gabrielle, looking from one woman to the other. "I simply couldn't. I'm not—I'm not a—"

"I think what she's trying to say is that she's not a whore," said Tierney, walking up to Gabrielle with a swish of striped silk. "Look at her. Did you ever see a chippy wearing a gray serge dress with a collar high enough to choke a priest?" Her gaze swept Gabrielle contemptuously, from the sedate French knot at the nape of her neck to the conservative shoes peaking out from beneath the hem of her modest gown. "Take a real close look at her. Why, she's so innocent and pure you can practically smell the incense and holy water."

"A *virgin*?" Crystal threw back her head and laughed. "Sakes alive, Tierney. The ideas you do get."

Gabrielle opened her mouth to insist hotly that *of course* she was a virgin, but something she saw in Sirena's face stopped her. The warning was there in the quiet woman's quickly lifted chin, in the flash of her dark eyes. Sirena knew all about the convent, Gabrielle realized. And for some reason, Sirena thought it best that Gabrielle keep the truth about her past to herself.

Gabrielle swallowed everything she'd been about to say. She supposed that as far as these women were concerned, virginity was a weakness, a sign of vulnerability. And Gabrielle knew she couldn't afford to appear either weak or vulnerable to them.

"I'm sorry," she said, jerking open the door. "I must ask you to leave now."

Crystal stretched slowly to her feet. "All right." She picked up the fur-trimmed violet velvet cloak she'd thrown over the back of the chair. "We'll leave fer now. Come on, girls."

The other women collected their cloaks and fur muffs and gloves, and trailed out into the hall.

"But you think about it, honey," Crystal said, pausing on her way out the door. "You think about everything I said." She swirled the fur and velvet cloak around her shoulders. Even through the heavy folds of the fabric, Gabrielle could still see her hips swirling provocatively back and forth as she walked away.

Gabrielle shut the door behind them, shutting them out of her room. But the uneasiness they had engendered within her lingered, like the ineradicable scent of their expensive perfume. And it was an uneasiness that went beyond the alarm any decent woman might experience after a confrontation with such women.

She heard a peculiar, ragged noise, and realized it was the sound of her own breath, soughing in and out. She was almost gasping with reaction, with fear. *Some truths, it's all right to walk away from,* Jordan Hays had said. The problem was, she hadn't walked away soon enough. And the truth . . . the truth was shattering the confines of the protective cocoon in which she had been raised.

She had thought of herself as a grown, mature woman. But she realized now just how sheltered, how ignorant she had been. The last two days had opened up before her horrified, fascinated eyes an entire world she had known almost nothing about. A world where women were bold and forward, rather than modest and unassuming. Where flesh was something to be exploited rather than hidden. Where physical pleasures were not condemned, but deliberately, actively pursued and exalted.

She pressed her shoulder blades against the closed door, as if she were barricading her room, barricading herself against the forces of darkness. She felt as if she were being sucked into the dangerous, frightening, yet undeniably fascinating world that had opened up before her. She remembered the way she had trembled that afternoon when Jordan Hays touched her face, and the fear was there again, curling low in her belly, spreading through her body like something warm and aching. Something that was more than fear. Something powerfully seductive. Something sinful.

She could not stay in her room.

She finally drew on her coat and went out again. The clouds still hung heavy over the mountains, but only a few light snowflakes floated down from the white sky.

She wandered aimlessly along the boardwalks, feeling alone and out of place. It was more than the effect of the strange, snow-covered buildings she passed, more than the cold, pine-scented air she drew into her lungs, more than the unfamiliar sight of rough, bearded men in red wool shirts and grease-splattered gray trousers. It was as if she had been so profoundly affected, so altered by what she had seen and learned in the past two days, that she didn't fit *in herself* anymore.

There were so few women on the streets, that when she passed a stern-faced, middle-aged matron in a sturdy black coat and plain sarcenet bonnet, the unknown woman unbent enough to nod her head and smile at Gabrielle. Gabrielle smiled back, but all she could think was, *If she only knew the truth.* If she knew Gabrielle had just spent the last half hour in the company of three painted harlots; if she knew Gabrielle had developed an inexplicable fascination with a man who was not only a gambler and a gunman, but who consorted regularly with fallen women; if she knew of Gabrielle's association with the white house at the top of Nevada Gulch; if she knew the truth, how would this uncompromising-looking woman react then?

Gabrielle's fist closed around the rosary she had thrust into her coat pocket at the last minute before leaving her room. The edge of the crucifix bit through the thin leather of her glove, pressed into her palm, but Gabrielle clutched it anyway. It was as if by so doing she could hold onto her past, hold onto the woman she had once been.

A bell rattled as someone nearby drew a door closed. Gabrielle looked up to find that she had paused beside a café window with red-checked curtains and a hand-lettered sign propped up in one corner that read, FRESH APPLE PIE TODAY. A hollow grumbling in Gabrielle's stomach reminded her it was almost supper time, and she'd eaten nothing all day. Pushing open the heavy café door, she went inside.

It was there that Doug Slaughter found her.

* * *

She was pouring tea from a squat brown earthenware pot into a rose-strewn china cup when a man stopped beside her table.

"Miss Antoine?" he said, his voice guttural, his accent oddly clipped.

Gabrielle looked up, startled to hear herself addressed by name. She had never met this man. He was big, with intimidatingly broad shoulders and a not unattractive face sporting a neatly trimmed brown mustache, and side-whiskers. He had the appearance of being self-consciously prosperous, with his well-cut coat, brocade vest, and a diamond the size of a black-eyed pea glistening in the folds of his silk tie. But his eyes were hard and glittering and the color of topaz. Gabrielle had seen animals with eyes like that, but never a man.

"Excuse me, sir." She kept her voice polite, but unencouraging. "Do I know you?"

"Not exactly." Those peculiar yellow eyes stared down at her, assessing her in a way that made her feel uncomfortable. "I'm Doug Slaughter. Mind if I sit down?" Without waiting for her reply, he pulled out the pressed-back oak chair on the far side of the table and lowered his enormous frame into the seat. Even sitting down, he was so large she had to resist the urge to scoot back in her seat and put some distance between them.

"I don't know if you've heard of me, but I'm the man who's buying the house."

"Yes," said Gabrielle, slowly stirring her tea. "I have heard of you."

He tapped his fingertips on the red-checked tablecloth. "I must confess, I hadn't expected to see you out here in Colorado."

"No," she said noncommittally, and saw his mouth

tighten with swift annoyance. He was not, obviously, an even-tempered man.

"I hope your coming here doesn't mean you're reconsidering selling the house." *Tap-tap-tap, tap-tap-tap* went his thick fingers.

Gabrielle took refuge in her tea. It would have been so easy simply to smile and say, *No, of course not.* Except that there was something she didn't like about this man. Something that had nothing to do with what those three painted women from the house had said to her that afternoon. She had seen much that was impure and ungodly in the last two days, much that reeked of sin and debauchery. But there was something distinctly different about this man. This man was evil.

The teacup rattled in its saucer as she set it down. She felt a queer flutter of fear, deep in her stomach, but somehow she managed to push the words out. "Actually, I never agreed to sell the house."

His fingers stopped their drumming and splayed out as he shoved his hand, flat, against the table. He had large, powerful-looking hands, thickly covered with coarse, wiry brown hair. "What the hell does that mean?" he growled, his brows lowering, his unpleasant eyes narrowing as he leaned forward in a way that made Gabrielle, in spite of herself, edge backward in her chair.

"I offered your partner forty-five thousand dollars for that house," said Slaughter. "Now, it's a big, fancy house, I'll grant you that. But we both know it's not worth that kind of money, so if you're angling to raise the price, forget it."

Gabrielle wasn't even consciously aware of having made a decision. She simply looked at the evil, yellow-eyed man across from her, and said, "I am sorry, Mr. Slaughter. The house is not for sale."

"*What?*" The word exploded out of him, whipping through her as he came half out of his chair and loomed over her. She had no experience with this. No experience dealing with the way a man could use the primitive, deep rumble of his voice and the potential menace of his great size and strength to threaten and frighten and intimidate.

"Let me tell you something, girl," he said, sinking back down into his chair. "My father, he was a tenant farmer back in Ireland. When he died, we were turned off the land—all seven of us. Me, my mother, my three brothers, and two sisters. And you know what? They all died. From the hunger. From the cold. All died. All except for me." A muscle in his cheek bunched as he tightened his jaw. "I don't give up."

"Mr. Slaughter," she repeated, her voice scratchy with fear. "The house is not for sale."

He leaned forward. "Everything's for sale in this world. Everything, and everyone. Including you. It's just a matter of finding the right price."

Gabrielle felt the blood drain from her face. "Not all women are for sale."

"No?" He sneered, his thick lips curling until she could see the moisture glistening on the dark pink inner flesh. "Let me tell you something else, girl. You may have been raised in some expensive New Orleans convent— That's right," he said when she jerked in surprise. "I know all about you. But it doesn't matter where you were brought up, because when it comes down to it, you're still Celeste's daughter. And your mother was nothing but a goddamn, high-priced whore."

His words sounded all the more frightening for being

uttered in a voice that was low-pitched and chillingly calm. Even the middle-aged couple at the table beside them couldn't possibly hear what he was saying. "I own half-a-dozen houses full of women like you," he continued, his hot, tobacco-tainted breath washing over her. "I can make those women do anything I want them to do. Do you understand what I mean? Anything."

She suddenly, desperately needed to get away from him. She shoved back her chair, but he reached out and captured her wrist, pinning her arm flat to the table so that she couldn't stand up. "You'll sell, girl. You'll sell. Or before I'm through with you, I'll see you naked and whimpering at my feet." Then he flung her arm away from him, thrust back his own chair, and pushed up from the table.

She refused to watch him leave. She reached out a hand that was not quite steady, and with a show of serenity she was far from feeling, poured herself some more tea. Only her hand shook so badly, that some of the hot liquid splashed onto the bright red-and-white-checked cloth. She dabbed at it absently with her napkin.

She felt a frigid gust of air lift the tendrils from her forehead as the café door opened to the night, but she didn't look up. Even when the door shut again, her gaze remained fixed, intently, on the disfiguring brown stain on the cloth before her.

The night air was cold and sharp, stinging Gabrielle's nostrils and burning her lungs with every breath. Sunset had sent the temperature plunging, glazing the snow with a thin, icy crust that broke beneath her with every step, making walking difficult.

Only Gabrielle wasn't walking, she was running. Running through the night, heedless of the startled faces that stared after her, heedless of everything but the need to reach the white house at the top of the gulch. She couldn't have said if it was the house that drew her, or the man she knew she would find there. She only knew she had no place else to turn.

Away from the crowded streets of the town, the wind seemed stronger. It rustled the bare branches of the aspen trees and moaned through the pines with a low, mournful sound that echoed the sound of her soul. Except for the wind, and the noise of her own breath sobbing in and out of her throat, the night was quiet. The thick covering of snow that blanketed the buildings and hillsides silenced all movement, absorbed all sound. It was something she had never experienced before coming here, that unearthly quiet that a fall of snow brings to the world. When she had first arrived, she had found it peaceful and soothing; tonight, it seemed somehow sinister.

She quickened her step up the hill, one hand hugging her coat close to her, the other fisted over the crucifix in her pocket. She clung to the rosary as if it were a talisman. As if it could provide her now with the same comfort and sense of stability she had known in the convent. If she concentrated, she could conjure up images of the familiar, sequestered gardens and high, creeper-covered brick walls. But no matter how hard she tried, she could not recapture the peace of the innocent young woman those walls had once protected. That woman was gone.

I wish . . . I wish she had come back for me.

That's because you've never lived in a whorehouse.

Jordan Hays's harsh voice echoed cruelly in her head. And as she pushed on through the white-shrouded darkness, it occurred to Gabrielle that tonight, in Doug Slaughter's terrible yellow eyes, she had finally glimpsed the truth of what Hays had been trying to say to her.

Gabrielle's childhood had been the greatest gift her mother could have given her. A childhood sheltered by high walls and gentle nuns as innocent as the children they cared for. A childhood far away from this raw world of sin and debauchery, of painted women and lusting men.

Your mother was nothing but a high-priced whore.

A whore. She thought about the three women who had invaded her hotel room that afternoon, and she realized she had no concept of what their lives were like, what *they* were like. They were three very different women, linked by their common occupation, but hardly defined by it.

Yet her occupation was essentially all Gabrielle had managed to learn so far about Celeste DuBois. A picture hanging on a wall and a tombstone in a snow-covered cemetery. What did they tell her of Celeste DuBois, of Celeste's life, of her world? It was a world that repelled Gabrielle, yet it exercised a terrible fascination, too, if for no reason other than because it *was* Celeste DuBois's world. And Celeste DuBois had given Gabrielle life.

The big white house loomed out of the shadows, almost a part of the snow-covered hill behind it—except for the red light, that glowed like an evil eye in the night.

The hinges of the gate shrieked when Gabrielle shoved it open, then let it bang shut behind her. *She didn't want you to come.* Jordan Hays's cold voice echoed in her mind again, joined to another voice, the voice of Julia St. Etienne, saying, *You do realize that you may not like what you find.*

Gabrielle paused at the top of the wide, white steps.

Golden light spilled out from between the heavy velvet curtains, bringing with it the clink of glasses and the sound of voices and laughter. Someone was playing a sprightly but slightly inaccurate tune on the piano, accompanying a woman singing in a low, husky contralto.

Gabrielle started to grasp the brass knocker, then changed her mind. This was her mother's house. Her house. She reached for the faceted knob, and pushed the door open.

She hesitated just inside the wide, carpeted hall. The vast expanses of gilt-framed mirrors reflected the golden, flickering light from the great crystal chandelier overhead, and from the double rows of wall-mounted oil lamps. The atmosphere was thick with the scent of candles and expensive liqueurs, and hazy with the smoke of fine cigars. From the darkly paneled room on the left came a low murmur of voices and the discreet shuffle of a deck of cards. Gabrielle saw a whirling wheel of darkly stained wood slowly spin to a halt, revealing a face painted in a peculiar striped pattern of red, white, and black. "Thirty-six red, gentlemen," said the lanky man with thin blond hair who stood beside it. "Place your bets."

A loud burst of laughter jerked her attention to the front parlor on the far side of the crystal-beaded archway. The room was crowded with a peculiar mixture of men; rough, red-shirted miners rubbed shoulders with men in elegant evening jackets and silk ties, and ranchers in fancy-stitched boots and leather vests. There were women, too; beautiful women. Some half naked, some gorgeously dressed in silks and satins, velvets and lace, with jewels glistening around their bare white necks, and ostrich plumes nodding from the coils of their gleaming hair.

Gabrielle recognized the elegantly tall, dark-haired

woman who had come to visit her that afternoon. Sirena leaned forward and whispered something into the ear of the man beside her, something that made him laugh. On a velvet-covered chair beyond her, British-born Tierney sat in the lap of a middle-aged businessman. He was kissing her neck, and had one of his hands pressed down the front of her low-cut, lace-trimmed yellow velvet bodice. As Gabrielle watched, the man shoved the bodice lower, exposing one of the woman's naked, cinnamon-tipped breasts.

Lean, strong fingers closed on Gabrielle's arm, yanking her around. "What the hell are you doing here?"

She stared up into Jordan Hays's dark face, and sucked in a peculiar, popping kind of breath.

There was a glitter in his green eyes as his gaze raked her. She could imagine what she must look like, with her hair tumbling down, her face clammy and cold. She tried to say something, but the words seemed trapped by a tight band of emotion, squeezing her throat.

He seemed to sense it was beyond her to answer. Wordlessly, he spun around, striding down the hall, dragging her behind him.

Pulling her away from the narrow-eyed men and spinning wheels and laughing, bare-breasted women of the front rooms.

A fire burned brightly on the hearth, filling the office with its crackling, golden warmth. Jordan watched Gabrielle Antoine wander over to hold her trembling hands out to the dancing flames. Whatever had driven her up the gully through the cold and the darkness had obviously shocked her badly.

"Here," he said, coming up behind her to lay his hands on her shoulders. "Give me your coat."

His breath disturbed a loose tendril lying beside her ear. He saw her shiver, but she made no move to unfasten her coat. He reached down to flick open the first button, then the second. His fingers brushed her throat as they moved lower, seeking the third button, and the shock of his touch seemed to jolt her. Her hand flew up to close over his, stopping him. Her startled gaze met his for one, intense moment before sliding away. "I'll do it," she said hoarsely.

He turned away, although the urge to stay close to her, to keep touching her was damnably strong. He'd intended to pour her a brandy, to help her warm up, but he poured himself one instead, and downed it with a flick of his wrist as he watched her strip off her coat and hat.

She still wore the same modest gown she'd had on that morning. It was made high at the neck with a discreet white lace ruffle and frill, and she'd swept her beautiful golden hair back into a loose crimped chignon at the nape of her neck. She looked exactly like what she was: a maiden schoolteacher, convent-bred and earnestly devout. And yet . . .

And yet she was Celeste's daughter, and the simplicity of her dress seemed only to emphasize the tiny waist separating the swell of her breasts and hips. He could imagine all too clearly what she would look like naked. How she would feel sprawled beneath him in bed. Like her mother, Gabrielle moved with a seductive kind of fluidity and nubile grace. Except that in Gabrielle's case, it was all the more alluring for being totally unconscious.

She draped her coat over the chair beside the fire, and half turned to cast him a nervous glance over her shoulder, as if she'd somehow surmised the dangerous direction of his thoughts. But then, perhaps she had. She might have spent most of her life in a convent, but she was still a woman.

"Like a brandy?" he offered, his voice roughened by his unwilling arousal.

He expected her to refuse. She surprised him by saying, "Yes, please."

He poured a couple of fingers' worth of the rich, amber-colored liquor into the bottom of a glass, and silently held it out as she walked over. He noticed she was careful not to let her hand brush his when she took the glass.

"Some of the women from the house came to see me this afternoon," she said. He watched her lips pucker as she took a small, cautious sip. Her eyes widened, and she sucked in a quick breath of air, but she did not cough.

He was so absorbed in watching her that it was a moment before her words registered. "Some of the girls?" He turned away to pour himself another drink. "Why would they do that?"

"They don't want you to sell the house to Doug Slaughter."

He eased the top out of the decanter. "I know. I don't want to sell it to him myself."

"Then, why him?" she asked, taking another sip of brandy.

Jordan shrugged. "There is no other buyer. He's let it be known he wants it. No one will stand against a man like him."

"Except, apparently, Celeste DuBois." She frowned down at her glass. "Crystal seems to think Slaughter arranged my mother's death."

Jordan paused in the act of pouring his own drink to cast her a quick, assessing glance. He could tell she was keeping something back from him; he just wasn't sure what it was. "The sheriff decided it was an accident," he said.

"But you don't think so."

He didn't answer. Just raised his glass to his lips and took a long, slow swallow.

Her eyes sparkled with unexpected anger. "How could you even think of selling this house to that man, if he was responsible for my mother being shot?"

He met her gaze with a cool, tense stare. "There is no proof that Slaughter killed your mother. Believe me, if there were, I'd have done something about it before now. And as far as letting him have the house goes, Celeste specifically told me that if anything happened to her, she wanted me to sell the place, even if it meant selling to Slaughter. The most important thing to her was that you have the money—without ever finding out the truth about this house."

Gabrielle walked over to sink into one of the blue-and-green-brocade wing chairs beside the fire. "I don't see how I could in all conscience accept the money from the sale of this house," she said after a moment, staring into the flames. "Not now."

"Oh, really?" he said dryly. "Why the hell not?"

She twisted her head to look at him, her eyes solemn, her hands clenched tightly around the brandy glass she held in her lap. "How can I take it now, knowing how it was acquired?" She gestured toward the front of the house. "From women selling their bodies. And men wagering their hard-earned wealth."

"An honorable sentiment." He raised his glass in a

mock toast. "But is it worth thirty thousand dollars? That's right," he said when she gave a small start of surprise. "I own a third of this place. The rest is yours. Can you really afford to walk away from that kind of money?"

She shook her head. "As a matter of fact, I barely have enough to pay for my room at the hotel."

That surprised him. As far as he knew, Celeste had been funneling money into an account for her daughter for years. He wondered what had happened to it. But all he said was, "Then, it doesn't sound like a good idea."

"Doesn't it? I suppose it depends on how important honor is to you. It happens to be very important to me." She tilted her head against the back of the chair and quoted softly, " 'If I lose mine honor, I lose myself.' "

He stared at her, both startled and oddly disconcerted to discover that they shared this. This love of Shakespearean poetry. *"Antony and Cleopatra,"* he said slowly.

She nodded.

"Unusual reading, surely, in a convent?"

A delicious smile curled her lips. "I didn't read that one at the academy." The smile faded, and her delicate brows drew together in a worried frown. "I want you to tell me exactly why the women in this house don't want to work for Mr. Slaughter."

Jordan went to take the chair opposite her. He leaned back, and stretched his boots out to the fire before answering her. "I understand he used to be a boxer. That's how he first made his money—and his reputation. He's in business now, but he still has a bad reputation."

"For what?"

He wasn't about to tell this woman the kind of things a

man like Slaughter did. "Well . . . he doctors his whiskey, for one thing."

Her forehead puckered in puzzlement. "What does that mean?"

"It's a way of stretching your profits. You take a cheap keg of alcohol and mix it with water, burned sugar, and whatever chemical it takes to make it taste like bourbon or cognac. And then that's what you sell it as."

"He owns a saloon?"

"Honky-tonks, gambling halls, cribs. A regular captain of vice."

"What's a crib?"

He looked into her wide, innocent eyes. "You don't want to know."

Her gaze shifted to the brandy glass she still held. He watched the muscles of her slim throat work as she raised the glass to her mouth and swallowed. A virgin school-teacher had no business with a mouth like that, he decided. Wide and full-lipped and tempting, it was a mouth made for sinning.

Annoyed with himself for the thought, he shoved up out of the chair again, and almost missed hearing her say, "I met him today."

Jordan spun around. "Who?"

"Mr. Slaughter," she said. Her voice was calm, but he noticed that two tight lines had appeared, bracketing her pretty mouth, and her face was as white as it had been when he'd come upon her in the front hall earlier. He knew now what had scared her enough to send her up here through the snow at this time of night.

"He wanted reassurance that my decision to come out here to Colorado wasn't going to interfere with the sale of the house," she explained.

"And you told him ... what?" He looked down at her, knowing even before she said it what the answer would be.

She met his gaze with level determination. "I told him I'd decided not to sell the house."

CHAPTER
SIX

Gabrielle wasn't certain when she decided what she had to do. She didn't know if she could manage it, and she certainly had no idea if Jordan Hays would agree to it.

She only knew what she wanted.

She watched him drain his glass and walk away from her. "Let me explain something to you," he said, setting his empty glass beside the brandy decanter. "Celeste and I might have been partners, but the whores were her part of the business. I'm a gambler, not a pimp. And while living in a house with a dozen sportin' gals might be a lot of men's fantasy, believe me, the reality can be a sore trial. I *want* to sell this house."

She didn't know what a pimp was, or a sporting girl, but she decided it would be more prudent not to ask. She leaned forward and said earnestly, "Then, if I could come up with fifteen thousand dollars, would you allow me to buy you out?"

He glanced at her over his shoulder. "What in God's name do you want with a brothel?"

She shook her head, feeling the discomfort she always did whenever anyone put a name on exactly what this house was. "I don't want it as a—a house of sin. I want the house itself. I want to help the people who work here to find other jobs—preferably other *respectable* jobs. And then I'd like to turn the house into a school."

She was unprepared for his reaction. He stared at her for several seconds. Then he tipped back his head and laughed.

"It is not funny," she said. "I am utterly serious."

He lowered his head. "I know you are. Although, leaving aside everything else for the moment, I'm a bit curious here. You just finished saying that you're virtually penniless. So how the hell do you plan to get your hands on enough money to buy me out?"

"I've been thinking about that." She plucked at the fabric of her skirt where it tightened over her knees. "I could use the money from my share of the profits of this house. I don't like doing it, but in this case it seems justified." She had to force herself to look up at him again. "How long would it take me to save the fifteen thousand dollars I need to buy you out?"

"About ten months."

She knew a sinking, hollow feeling in the pit of her stomach. "That long?"

He nodded. She searched his dark, handsome face, but with the exception of that faint touch of amusement, it was unreadable. She could not begin to tell what he was thinking.

He wandered over to hitch one hip on the edge of the big, leather-topped partners desk. "There is another way," he said after a moment, crossing his arms at his chest and eyeing her thoughtfully. "I told you Celeste left you some jewelery. If you wanted to, you could use that. There isn't as much as there used to be, because she sold some of it herself recently. She'd been workin' some old claims in the area, grubstaking prospectors. That takes money."

"You mean, my mother was interested in mining?"

"In a sense. But never mind that now. Let's put it this way. You let me have, say, Celeste's diamond bracelet, and a sapphire necklace I know she kept, along with all the house profits for the next three months, and the place is yours."

She felt a surge of hope, but tried to dampen it down with caution. "Is that a good deal?" she asked, then realized it was a stupid question, since of course he would say it was.

He grinned. "Yes. But don't take my word for it. Get the jewelery appraised. And take a look at the books."

"I will." She met his mocking gaze squarely. "And I kept the books for the convent after Sister Claire's eyesight began to fail, so don't think I won't know what I'm looking at."

"Well, you oughta do just fine, then," he said with a slow, sarcastic drawl. "There can't be that much difference between a convent and a whorehouse, after all."

She sucked in a quick, shocked breath. "There is no need to be crude, Mr. Hays."

"Miss Antoine, I'm not being crude. I'm being realistic. This crazy scheme you've come up with might satisfy your conscience, and I'm sure it appeals to what you consider your sense of holy obligation and Christian duty and God knows what else, *but it's not going to work.* It's as simple as that. First of all, even if you could manage to find someone to hire them, the women in this house don't *want* respectable jobs."

"But . . . why not?"

He gave a short, mirthless laugh. "For the simple

reason that nothing these women can do that's respectable will earn them anywhere near the kind of money they're already making now, just by lying flat on their backs and remembering to moan at the right times."

She felt her cheeks heat with embarrassment, but she knew he was deliberately trying to disconcert her, and she refused to be deterred. "I can only try."

"And pray?"

"Yes," she said with quiet dignity.

He shifted his weight, thrusting both legs out in front of him. "All right, let's say for the sake of argument that by some miracle all the chippies in the house are suddenly struck by a desire to reform their ways and give up their lucrative profession. Do you honestly believe the people in this town are going to send their children to school in a converted bawdy house being run by a schoolmistress everyone thinks is an ex-prostitute?"

She sat up straighter in her chair. "I might have inherited this house, but that hardly means I work here!"

"It doesn't make any difference. The day you first set foot inside that door, you became a whore as far as most people in this town are concerned."

She became aware of the sound of the wind, howling around the house, and gusting down the chimney to make the fire flare. Here was one aspect of the scheme that hadn't occurred to her. She was simply too ignorant of the ways of the world. Woefully, dangerously ignorant. "I will explain the situation to the townspeople. But if they don't believe me, and it becomes obvious that you are right and they will not patronize my school"—she shrugged—"I suppose I could always sell the house, and go back to New Orleans to open a school there."

He sighed. "Wouldn't it be a lot easier just to sell the

house to Slaughter and go open a school in New Orleans now?"

"Easier, yes. But not morally acceptable."

"Oh, I see. If you sell the house as a failed school rather than as a brothel, *then* you can take the money in all conscience."

There was enough truth in that statement to make it sting. "I am not a hypocrite, Mr. Hays. I genuinely intend to try to make a success of this school."

He grunted. "And exactly where are you planning to live for the next three months until you do buy me out?"

She shifted to look at the fire again, trying to escape those probing green eyes that seemed to see right through her. "I thought I would use my mother's room," she said with a show of serenity and confidence she was far from feeling. "Here, in the house."

In the sudden quiet she could hear a burst of song from the front rooms. The fire beside her crackled and danced. She had expected him to meet her statement with a startled exclamation, not silence. She raised her gaze to find him staring at her intently. All traces of amusement had vanished from his face.

"Why?"

The word whipped through the air to hang between them, demanding an answer she wasn't sure she could give. She sucked in a quick gasp of air. "I beg your pardon?"

He rested his fist on the top of the desk and leaned into it, his eyes narrowed, his jaw held tight. "And don't even think about pretending it's because you can't afford to stay at the hotel. There are ways around that, and you and I both know it. You could buy me out in four months instead of three, and use the difference to pay for a room someplace."

"That would be living on the proceeds of sin," she said quietly. "I couldn't do that."

"Oh? And you won't be living on the *proceeds of sin* if you stay in the house?"

The fire danced up, casting harsh shadows across the planes of his face. "In a sense, I suppose I would be," she said quietly.

"I see. It's like using the *proceeds of sin* to buy out my share of the house. It's justified."

"Yes."

"Then, it seems to me you ought to feel more than justified using the *proceeds of sin* to stay in a hotel for the next few months."

Anger flared within her, and she leaned forward, meeting his gaze unflinchingly. "You mean, hold myself aloof from this establishment, like a Pharisee, refusing to consort with Samaritans? The Son of God did not disdain to befriend Mary Magdalen, remember? Who am I to scorn these women and their children? After all," she said, the anger draining out of her, her voice dropping almost to a whisper. "There but for the grace of God go I."

He stared at her, steadily enough that she had to resist the urge to shift uncomfortably in her seat. "There's more to it than simply finding a place to live, isn't there?" he said after a moment.

She lifted her chin and tried to look cool. "I don't owe you any explanations."

"No," he said evenly. "You don't. But if you want to buy my share of the house, you're going to tell me."

She had known him for only a few days, but it was long enough for her to be convinced that he meant what he said. Suddenly restless, she stood up and went to set her virtually untouched glass on the mantelpiece. "It has to do with my mother," she said, not looking at him. "I don't know if I can explain it, though. I don't entirely understand it myself."

"Try."

She drifted over to stand with one hand gripping the high back of the chair. She still could not look at him. "When I was a little girl, I used to make up fantasies about my mother and father. I imagined they were like, oh, Romeo and Juliet, or Robin Hood and Maid Marian. But as I grew older, the fantasies weren't enough anymore. I wanted to *know* who my parents were, what they were like. I used to try as hard as I could to remember my life before the convent."

Her fingers drifted over the chair's brocade upholstery, tracing the intricate blue and green pattern. "I couldn't remember much. I knew I had lived in a house with a grand staircase and big rooms, and I remembered my mother wearing silk gowns and jewels. I thought none of that would have been possible if I hadn't come from a good family, like the other girls I went to school with. St. Agnes Academy is considered the best girls' school in New Orleans—or rather, it was. I knew someone was paying to keep me there, someone who could afford to set up the trust fund administered by Monsieur Longchamps."

She fell silent for a moment, remembering the small, plump lawyer, with his shuffling walk and enormous, bushy eyebrows and shiny bald pate surrounded by a graying fringe of hair. When she was little, she used to think he must be a disgraced monk, because that graying fringe looked exactly like the tonsure worn by St. Francis of Assisi in the holy picture of the gentle friar feeding the birds that hung in a simple frame above her bed. But as she grew older, she realized Monsieur Longchamps wasn't a monk, just a gruff-natured, cantankerous old bachelor whose infuriating, enigmatic silence had always frustrated her many attempts through the years to get him to tell her something about her parents.

"So you built up a picture of your mother in your mind," he said softly. "And in that picture, she was like the mothers of your friends?"

Gabrielle nodded. "Coming here destroyed that picture. But it hasn't replaced it with anything else. You see, in a sense, I know less about my mother now than I thought I did before. I know her name, and I know what she looked like, but I know nothing else about her. Nothing except that she kept this house. And I realized today that I don't really know what that means."

She came around to sit on the edge of her seat again, her hands clasped together in her lap, her gaze fastened on her white, entwined fingers. "I was brought up to think that women who sold their bodies to men were . . . vile, obscene, degraded. Strange creatures we whispered about, and condemned. They weren't anyone we needed to try to understand. Only now . . ."

She looked up at him, even though she knew she couldn't keep the confusion and pain she felt inside from showing on her face, where he could see it. "Now, I do need to understand. And the only real way to do that is to live here myself."

His eyes flicked over her, seeing the aching need within her, yet remaining unmoved by it. "You don't know what you're saying. You have no idea what goes on in this house."

She met his gaze squarely, although inside she was quaking. "Then, I will learn."

"Why? To punish yourself?" He came to stand in front of her. "That's what this is all about, you do realize that, don't you? This whole idea is just some crazy, self-imposed penance for what you imagine as your sin of having lived all those years in the comfort and safety of the convent, while your mother and these women degraded themselves by living and working here."

"No."

"Yes." He rested his hands on the arms of the chair, and leaned into her, pressing her back into the seat. He was so close she could see the fine lines that splayed out from the corners of his eyes, and the faint beginning shadow of his dark beard beneath the smoothly shaven skin of his cheeks. "You want to know what goes on in a whorehouse? I'll tell you. A man comes to the front door, he pays his three dollars and picks out his whore, and then she takes him upstairs with her. Next to her bed, she keeps an egg timer, and she turns it over the minute she walks into the room. So that man, he drops his pants and hops on her as fast as he can, because he knows that when the sand runs out, his time is up and she's going to push him out and wash away whatever mess he's left between her legs so she'll be ready for her next customer."

Gabrielle felt the blood drain from her face and the bile rise in her throat, practically choking her. She looked up at that cold, almost cruel face looming above her, and wished she could tell him to stop. Only she couldn't, because if she didn't keep her lips pressed tightly together, she was afraid she might be sick.

His uncaring voice rolled on. "Your mama, though,

she set up a real, high-class establishment here. Any man who walks through this front door after five o'clock pays ten dollars, just for the privilege of being here. For his money, he gets a drink on the house, and all he can eat from the hors d'oeuvres spread out in the dining room. He can gamble, or he can stand around with his friends, smoking cigars and listening to music and talking for as long as he likes."

Gabrielle found herself watching his lips move as he spoke. If she concentrated on his mouth, then maybe she wouldn't have to listen to the words his mouth was forming.

"But when that man is ready, he selects the girl he fancies and he takes her upstairs, and what happens up there isn't any different from what happens in the filthiest crib or back room. She still spreads her legs, and he still shoves his cock inside her, and he grunts and she moans until he comes or his time is up."

He was being brutal, deliberately cruel. She knew that. But she could not stop herself from trembling, could not stop herself from sucking in quick, frantic gulps of air.

His empty eyes flicked over her, seeing her horror and revulsion, seeing her fear. His lips curled back in a smile that showed his teeth. "Still think you want to move in here? Still think you *can* move in here?"

She looked at him, really looked at him, and saw the hardness of his heart and the bleakness of his soul. "Yes," she said, putting into that one word all the hatred and revulsion this man and his way of life aroused in her.

With a smothered exclamation, he pushed against the arms of the chair and flung away from her to go stand before the fireplace, his hands on his gun-slung hips, his shoulders taut.

She looked at his profile. At the arrogant, aristocratic line of his nose, at his fine, high cheekbones, at the firm line of his lips. "I know what you are trying to do," she said, keeping her voice level with difficulty. "But I am determined. I am determined not to sell this house to that vile man. I am determined not to take money accrued in ways sinful in the sight of God. I am determined to do everything within my power to help these women find a better life, and to see this house serve a useful purpose."

"You move in here, and everyone in this goddamn town is going to be convinced you're a whore," he said, gazing down at the dancing yellow flames.

"A moment ago, you said that anyone who knows of my association with the house thinks that already."

He tilted his head to glance at her sideways. "And what exactly are you planning to do while you're in this house? Set up prayer meetings and Bible readings in the parlor? That wouldn't exactly be good for business."

"I am not an Evangelical preacher, Mr. Hays. My beliefs are personal. I promise to do nothing that might interfere with your profits until the house is completely mine."

"Oh, yeah? You doing nothin' except skulking around wearing that dying-on-the-cross, a-martyr-for-the-cause look is bound to be bad for everyone's morale, mine included." He propped one elbow on the mantelpiece, next to the Louis XVI clock. "It occurs to me that, not only are you going to be living and eating in this house on the *proceeds of sin*, but it's going to be cutting into my profits. Don't you think you ought to be doing *something* to earn your keep?"

Gabrielle felt a stirring of interest. It would certainly square better with her conscience, if she knew she were supporting herself with her own honest labor, even if the setting were sordid. "I can cook," she said hopefully. "I haven't had much practice, I admit, but the nuns believed all girls—"

"I already have a cook," he said. "A very temperamental French chef your mother brought out here from New Orleans. But I do need a piano player. The fellow I used to have ran off with one of the girls a few weeks back. And while Vanessa can pick out a tune, she's not all that good, and it's a waste of talents that can be used more profitably elsewhere."

When she didn't say anything, he looked at her with one raised eyebrow. "I presume they taught you how to play the piano in that convent of yours?"

Gabrielle stared at him. "You want me to go out there in the evening and publicly play the piano in a—a—"

"Brothel." He enunciated the word carefully. "It's a brothel. You can call it a bagnio, a stew, a cathouse, or a bawdy house. There's lots of names for places like this. But you'd better learn to say one of them, if you're going to live here."

She stood up abruptly and walked across the room, as far away from him as she could get. In the corner near the window, a curtained archway led to another room. The dusky blue velvet curtain was swept to one side and held back behind a brass hook made in the shape of a naked woman. Through the arch she could see a bedroom. Her mother's bedroom.

"Can you play?" demanded the fierce, relentless voice behind her.

Could she do it? Gabrielle wondered wildly. Could she? "I know how to play the piano," she said slowly.

"But I honestly do not know if I can do what you ask of me."

"Then, the whole deal is off."

She spun around to face him. He stood before the fire, looking dark and dangerous and faintly smug. And she knew. She *knew* that he hadn't really wanted her to play the piano at all, that he had come up with the suggestion simply as a way of getting her to back away from the entire scheme. She lifted her head, sucked in a deep breath, and said, "I'll do it."

She saw his eyes narrow and his lips tighten. He was annoyed, and he wasn't making any attempt to disguise it, the way he normally did.

"I told you, Mr. Hays, that I am determined. I'll do whatever is necessary, within reason, to achieve my purpose."

"Oh?"

He could put more mockery into one syllable, she thought, than any person she had ever met. A violent tide of dislike for this man spread through her, almost choking her.

"And what are you going to do when one of those men out there decides he wants to go up the stairs with *you*?" he asked, tipping forward slightly on the balls of his feet.

She felt again that queasy twist of her insides, and glanced toward the curtained bedroom doorway. Whatever she might have done at one time, surely Celeste DuBois had no longer entertained gentlemen upstairs in this house? "What did my mother do in such circumstances?"

"Your mother could handle men better than anyone I've ever met. She knew exactly what she was doing. You don't."

"I can learn."

"Can you?" He came at her with that lean-hipped stalk she found so intimidatingly masculine. "What are you going to do the first time a man walks up to you and puts his hand on your breast? Like this." Even as he spoke, he reached out, ever so casually, and splayed his hand over her left breast.

She went rigid with shock and sucked in an audible gasp of air, her gaze flying to his face. There was still the faintest suggestion of a smile on his face, but it was a mean smile, and his eyes held a definite challenge.

He raised his eyebrows mockingly. "Nothing? What if he backs you up against a wall?" His hand left her breast and closed on her hair, hard enough to jerk her chin up as he pressed her back, pinning her against the soft velvet of the door curtain.

"You have made your point, Mr. Hays."

"Not quite." His warm breath rustled the hair at her temple.

She tried to twist away, but he leaned into her, his fist tightening in her hair, his face so close to hers she could see the sudden flaring of heat in his eyes, see the faint creases left by long-ago smiles beside his fiercely determined mouth.

"What are you going to do, Miss Antoine, if he kisses you?"

He's going to do it, she thought, her heart pounding against her ribs in panic. *He's going to kiss me.*

And his mouth slammed down on hers.

She made a strange whimpering sound in her throat. Her hands fisted, digging into the rigidity of his enormous shoulders, trying to shove him away. But he was big and powerful, and his weight held her fast, the solid muscles of his chest crushing her breasts, trapping her against the wall.

Her senses swam with the scent of him. The scent of expensive tobacco and brandy and hot, aggressive male. She made herself go still, to suffer his kiss. Only then his mouth pressed down harder, slanting against her lips, forcing them open in a raw, naked invasion of her mouth. Somehow he had managed to insinuate one of his hard thighs between her legs, pressing intimately, shockingly, against her. She felt overwhelmed, possessed, ruthlessly dominated. She could think of nothing except the moist heat of his mouth and the hard pressure of his body and the fierce pounding of her own heart.

Then his lips left hers with an abruptness as shocking, in its own way, as that kiss. Her entire body felt shaken and violated, her lips swollen, bruised. Wet. She was conscious of a strange, hollow ache, somewhere inside her deepest self. If his body hadn't still pinned her to the wall, she thought she might have fallen.

"If you hoped to make me hysterical by what you just did," she said, her voice sounding calm but oddly husky, "then I am sorry to disappoint you. I was brought up to behave like a lady in all circumstances, no matter how trying."

He still hadn't let her go. She splayed her hands against his upper arms, trying to put some distance between them. She looked up into his lean, dark face, to find it as unreadable as ever. But the kiss hadn't left him entirely unaffected, she noticed; his breath came short and fast, and there was a peculiar, taut look about his features that hadn't been there before.

"You try acting like a lady out there," he said, nodding

toward the front room, "and you're likely to find yourself raped."

She shook her head. "The lesson you obviously intended to teach me by your calculated act of brutality, Mr. Hays, is well-taken. I will arm myself as quickly as possible with whatever strategies are necessary to fend off such unwelcome advances."

She put extra emphasis on the words *unwelcome advances*. To her surprise, he laughed. And let her go. "You really are determined, aren't you?" he said, turning away.

"Yes."

He reached for the brandy decanter and poured a healthy measure into one glass, a thimbleful into another. "Shall we drink to our agreement, then?" He held the smaller glass out to her and, after the briefest of hesitations, she took it.

One eyebrow cocked questioningly, almost tauntingly, he lifted his glass in a toast. "Deal?"

She raised her glass to his, and knew again that odd sense of dislocation, as if she were a separate person, looking down on this strange woman inhabiting her body, drinking brandy and making an ominous pact with a dark, dangerous man.

The two glasses clinked together.

"Deal," said Gabrielle. But when she lifted her glass to her lips, what she tasted was him.

He sat in the burgundy leather wing chair beside his bedroom window. Cold came in waves off the bare glass, but he made no move to draw the heavy brocade drapes across the frosted panes. Outside, the blackness of the night almost obscured the pale, snow-covered slopes and the ghostly shadows of the pines, moving restlessly in the harsh wind.

Around him, the house settled into stillness. It was late. Far down the hill, in her room at the Teller House Hotel, he had no doubt that, by now, Gabrielle Antoine lay safely wrapped in the sleep of innocence. Only that innocence was about to end, he thought. Tomorrow morning she would be moving into her mother's house, into a way of life he knew she could not begin to envision or understand. She might think she could live in the midst of corruption and sin, and still maintain her innocence, her purity. Jordan knew better.

He lifted the glass chimney of the brass oil lamp that stood on the scarf-covered table beside him. Striking a match, he lit the burner, then paused, staring into the flame. It had been her decision, her choice, he thought. He could even, to a certain extent, understand why she felt the need to do what she was doing.

What she had learned about her mother had shattered her equilibrium, altered her perception of who and what she was, and filled her with seemingly more guilt than shame. He could understand that. What he could not understand was why he was sitting here, in the middle of the night, thinking about her, and about the life-altering step she was about to take.

The last few days had awakened within him feelings he had thought long dead. Feelings he had no desire ever to experience again. He eased the lamp's chimney back into place, and reached for the slim volume of poems, bound in tooled leather, which lay beside the base of the lamp. The book was well-worn and charred at one edge—a legacy of the long-ago night that had ended everything that had any meaning in Jordan's life. He opened the book, resting it on one knee. But instead of reading it, his eyes lifted again to the dark, wintry landscape outside the window. His head fell back against the smooth leather of the chair. After a moment his lids drooped, and he felt himself sliding away into sleep.

He slept. And in his sleep, the sun rose golden and warm, and the grass grew green and lush in the wet heat of a Virginia summer. A cavalry saber clanked against his gray-clad thigh as he walked toward the familiar red brick house that rose proud and gracious before him. In the shade of its wide veranda, a woman waited for him, a beautiful woman with hair the color of polished mahogany. She smiled, but it was a sad smile that didn't touch her gentle brown eyes.

She reached out to take his hand, and pressed it against her belly, where he had planted his child. "Come home to us, Jordan," she said softly. "Whatever happens, just make certain you come home to us."

He wanted to take her in his arms and kiss her, but although he could still see her, it was as if he were no longer there and the dream changed, as it always did. The sky became overcast and cold. He heard coarse laughter. Blue-coated soldiers staggered drunkenly against walls, stumbled down garden steps, dragged the woman away.

Jordan moaned. *Sophie. God in heaven, no. Sophie.* He tried to raise his sword hand, tried to stop it. But he could not. He never could.

He heard her screams. She screamed and fought. But there were so many of them. Too many of them. It seemed to Jordan as if he could feel their rough, dirty hands pulling her down. Feel the hot, sour breath that washed over her face as impatient, sweaty fingers tore at her clothes, fumbled with buckles and buttons, curled into a fist that slammed into the gentle mound of her belly when she kicked out at the men who loomed over her. More hands seized her legs, forcing them apart.

No. A tall, white-haired man staggered onto the veranda. Blood trickled from the gash on his forehead as he pulled himself down the shallow steps, across the shell drive. *No*, called Hannibal Hays. *Stop.*

One of the soldiers waiting his turn at the woman looked up. A pistol cracked. Jordan's father crumpled. Twitched. Lay still.

Noise and movement faded into darkness. The woman lay alone, unmoving, her blood and that of her unborn child forming a pool to reflect the glow of the flames that licked at the walls of the burning house.

Slowly Jordan opened his eyes, then squeezed them shut again. The dream had, mercifully, ended. Only it wasn't just a dream. And he was so tired of living with the memory.

He thrust out his hand, twisting off the lamp, plunging the room, again, into darkness. Outside, somewhere up on the snow-cloaked mountain, a wolf howled. The lonely, mournful cry echoed down the gulch, mingling with the rush of the wind through the pines and the heavy pounding of Jordan's heart.

He couldn't control his dreams, but he could control his thoughts, and it wasn't often he allowed himself to remember, to dwell on what was past, to torment himself with useless longings for what was still precious and loved, even though long ago lost forever.

Yet every once in a while, he couldn't resist. And as his fingers gently traced the tooled pattern of the book's leather cover, Jordan held the image of his beloved, dead wife in his mind. Beautiful, gentle Sophie, with her shining brown eyes and hair the color of polished mahogany. Her hair . . .

Jordan's breath caught, his hand tightening around the book's slim spine, his eyes widening with a sudden, startling realization. Because this time the dream, the dream he'd had night after night, year after year . . . This time the dream had been different.

Oh, it had begun the same, with Sophie on the veranda, her eyes sad, her smile trying so hard to be brave. But then . . . Then, somehow, it had altered.

Because the woman struggling beneath the grunting, rutting men in his dream . . . That woman had been fair, with hair the color of sunshine, not mahogany. And the face he'd watched contract with terror and pain, that face hadn't been Sophie's, either. Those glittering, brutalized eyes had been a rare silver-gray, not light brown. And the woman whose life had slowly bled out of her hadn't been Sophie. It had been Gabrielle.

Gabrielle Antoine.

CHAPTER
SEVEN

Weak, fitful sunlight filtered through the lace panels at the double-hung window, throwing a delicate pattern of shadows across the Belgian carpet. A faint, exotic scent hung in the room. The scent of jasmine. Her mother's scent.

Gabrielle stood at the foot of her mother's big tester bed, her hand curled around one of the carved rosewood posts. All morning she had moved with a peculiar sense of unreality, a blessed disassociation from the ominous, far-reaching implications of what she was doing. But standing here now, in this room, her trunks at her feet, her coat thrown across the dusky blue satin coverlet, she could no longer shut her eyes to the possible repercussions of the fateful step she had just taken.

Everything that was important to her, everything that she'd always wanted—marriage, a family, a home of her own—all had been thrown into jeopardy by her decision to move into this house. She might succeed in helping at least some of these women to leave this life of sin for a more secure and decent future. She might even, somehow, manage to turn the house into a school. But she suspected it was doubtful that the people of this town would ever accept her as a schoolteacher. Not now.

Gabrielle sighed. By moving into this house, by trying to repay the obligation she believed she owed these ladies of the night, she had effectively branded herself as one of **them**. Yet she could not regret it. She knew she could not have lived with herself otherwise.

Stooping down beside one of her trunks, she lifted the latch and threw back the lid. She tried to tell herself that if the people here refused to accept her as the virtuous woman she was, then she could always go back home, to New Orleans. In New Orleans no one had ever heard of Celeste's Place, no one would know that she had spent three months living in a house of ill repute. No one would know . . .

She picked up a gray foulard dress with black velvet trim. Shaking out the creases, she rose to lay it across the bed, then reached for a brown alpaca.

"If that's what all your dresses look like," said a lazy male drawl, "we're going to have to find something more appropriate for you to wear tonight. That is, if you're still planning on playing the piano."

Gabrielle whirled around, clutching the simple gown to her.

Jordan Hays stood in the arched doorway from the office. He wore a silver and black brocade vest with his usual black coat and trousers. He had one hand braced against the door frame, and she had the impression he had been there for a while.

"I still plan on it," she said, color flooding her face as she remembered the way he had touched her, the way he had kissed her the night before. He had done it to make a point, she knew that. But no man had ever handled her in such a way, and she could not seem to stop thinking about it.

He dropped his arm and came forward to throw open one of the three doors of the massive rosewood wardrobe with a serpentine front and carved cabriole legs. "You look about your mother's size." He ran his hand along the row of brightly colored silks, satins, and velvets hanging from the central rod. "Why don't you try on one of hers?"

"I could not," she said, still clutching her plain brown alpaca.

His hand paused at a gown of cream-colored faille, then moved on to the next. In the convent they'd still hung their clothes from hooks, or folded them neatly on shelves. But all Celeste DuBois's dresses hung from their own wooden hangers. It seemed an incredibly self-indulgent luxury.

"This one," he said.

He held up a wine-red velvet dress with a fitted bodice and satin-trimmed strappy sleeves. Gabrielle stared at the gown, and felt an unanticipated stirring of interest, of longing even. She had expected something gaudy, something blatantly, provocatively sensual, something like what the women who had come to her hotel room yesterday had worn. This dress certainly looked as if it would display far more skin than she was used to showing, but there was nothing vulgar or ill-bred about it. Any lady would be proud to be seen in such a gown. Gabrielle had dreamed of some day owning a dress like this, but she had never worn one.

"Oh," she breathed, taking a hesitant step forward to touch the luscious red velvet. "It is lovely." She took the gown from him, holding it away from her, careful not to crush it as she spread it tenderly across the bed, admiring the tiny satin roses at the neckline and waist.

She glanced back at the man who still stood beside the mirrored wardrobe door, an enigmatic expression on his face. "You should not be in my room, Mr. Hays. It is most improper."

"You mean, you'll wear that dress?" he asked, as if he had expected her to balk at the suggestion.

"Why, yes, of course. It's lovely."

His lips tightened, then curled up into an unexpected smile she did not understand. He shut the wardrobe door. "It occurs to me I haven't heard you at the piano yet. Maybe you're not good enough to play in public."

Gabrielle's chin jerked up at the challenge. "I can assure you, Mr. Hays, that my playing is more than adequate. But if you require a demonstration, by all means. Please come with me."

Her back held straight, she marched down the hall to the front parlor. She had not been in either of the front rooms yet. At the crystal beads she hesitated for an instant, then determinedly pushed them to one side and passed through.

She heard the crystals rustle as he entered behind her, then clatter and sway into place again. She allowed herself one, swift glance around the room, with its richly upholstered burgundy furniture and lurid paintings and faint, lingering scent of expensive perfume and expensive cigars. Then she pulled out the bench before the piano, and sat down.

She skimmed her fingers lightly across the keys, running scales, assessing the instrument. It was a Steinway, and someone who knew what they were doing had recently tuned it.

Almost of their own accord, her hands moved first into a solo from a Mozart concerto in D Minor, then a Haydn sonata. Beside her Mr. Hays leaned against the wall, his arms crossed at his chest, his intense stare never wavering from her.

She had just finished an early piece of Beethoven's when he said, "That's all quite lovely, Miss Antoine, and I can see those nuns made you practice diligently as a little girl. But we're not holding a piano recital here, and most of our customers wouldn't know the difference between a fugue and a sonata. How are you at something like 'Campdown Races'?"

Holding his gaze, she launched into "Buffalo Gals," followed by "Little Brown Jug," "Silver Threads Among the Gold," and, finally, maliciously, "You Naughty, Naughty Men." She ended with a flourish, and smiled up at the man beside her. "Satisfied, Mr. Hays?"

He didn't answer her smile. Instead he reached out to close his beautiful, fine-boned hand over her right wrist, his fingers clenching almost tight enough to hurt. "Enough is enough. I don't want you to do this, Gabrielle."

"I know you don't." Trembling slightly, she eased her hand from beneath his, closed the lid over the keys, and stood up to put some distance between them. "Nevertheless," she said, absently rubbing the wrist he'd touched, "playing the piano is an inherently respectable practice. And while, under ideal circumstances, I would not do so in public, these are not ideal circumstances. I am determined to pay my own way as long as I am here, and providing music seems to be the only way for me to do so. I may have, unknowingly, lived off the disreputable traffic of this house in the past. I have no intention of deliberately doing so today."

"Playing the piano in a place like this is *not* respectable. My God, lady. Take a look at this."

He grabbed her by the shoulders and spun her around to face a long, prominently displayed board. It said *"Menu"* at the top, painted in a fancy scrolled copperplate. But what was written beneath it was not a description of the culinary delicacies prepared nightly by Celeste's Place's famous French chef.

"When a man pays his ten dollars at the door, he gets two tokens. A yellow one he can trade for a glass of the house bourbon or a brandy or a turn at the roulette wheel, and a red token he'll give to the chippy he eventually takes upstairs. If he wants the French Trick, or a three-some, or anything else unusual or slightly perverted, he can get it here. Only it costs extra, and this is the menu. Take a good look at it, Miss Antoine. *This* is what will be going on upstairs, while you're sitting here playing the piano."

Against her will she scanned the list of obscenities, spelled out in that same precise copperplate. She didn't understand half of it, but the images conjured up by what she did grasp were graphic enough to send a shudder through her. He stood behind her, his hands still resting heavily on her shoulders. She knew he felt her body quiver. Only she couldn't stop it.

He brought his head down until his mouth was close to her ear, close enough that his warm breath tickled her neck. "I've gone along with you this far because I thought when it came to the sticking point, you'd balk. But believe me, you don't want to be in this house, and you certainly don't want to be out here, even if all you're doing is playing the piano."

She drew in a deep, shuddering breath. "I told you, Mr. Hays. I am determined to see this through."

"Then, before it's too late to back out, I think you

ought to take a look upstairs. See exactly what you're getting yourself into."

"Upstairs?" Her voice ended in a disquieting squeak.

"Upstairs," he said.

She'd been afraid he meant to show her the upstairs himself. But he said curtly, "Wait here," and disappeared up the wide staircase, taking the steps two at a time.

Left alone in the front parlor, Gabrielle glanced around nervously, eyeing the scattered, overstuffed chairs with their whorled feet and balloon backs, the cartouche-shaped marble tabletops with their fringed scarfs, the heavy brocade drapes that shut out most of the light. She knew the house was closed. She knew no men would be banging the front knocker, looking for a woman to ease that strange, mysterious pressure that seemed to obsess men to such an extraordinary degree. Yet even in the daylight, she felt uncomfortable being in this public room, as if someone could suddenly come in and force her up that ominously curving staircase, force her into an act, into a profession the very thought of which was a sin.

The sibilant whisper of fine cloth brought her head around, and Gabrielle found herself being coolly regarded by one of the women who had come to her hotel room yesterday. Sirena, the tall, elegant woman with straight black hair and fiercely chiseled cheekbones.

"So you decided to stay," she said in that husky contralto that carried just the hint of a guttural accent. She showed no sign of approval, or even surprise. She simply stated a fact, reaffirmed Gabrielle's choice.

She had come from the back of the house, through the dining room and the wide doorway joining the front and back parlors; now she moved forward, her turquoise satin skirt shimmering gracefully as she walked. Of all the women Gabrielle had seen in this house, Sirena seemed the least like what Gabrielle had imagined a harlot to be, although her satin dress was cut so low that it left virtually all of the woman's small, rounded breasts exposed. As she drew closer, Gabrielle could see that, like the others, she painted her face, but the lines of kohl around her eyes were more finely drawn, the vermilion staining her lips more subtly applied.

"Jordan asked me to show you around," said Sirena without smiling. It wasn't that she was being unfriendly, exactly. She was simply disinterested. She turned toward the stairs, leaving Gabrielle to follow if she wanted, or not.

Gabrielle clutched the cannonball-shaped newel post and watched Sirena's straight back as she mounted the stairs. Gabrielle did not want to go up there. She knew that, in her naivety, she could not even begin to imagine what she was going to see up there. She only knew that this was another challenge that Jordan Hays had thrown at her, the same as he had done with the gown and the music. He didn't think she had what it took to carry through this obligation she had set upon herself.

He was wrong.

Slowly, her heart pounding, Gabrielle climbed toward the second floor. Like the central hall and front parlor, the staircase was wainscoted to hip level with intricate paneling stained a deep brick red. Here, as in the hall, mirrors in heavy gold frames alternated with lurid paintings and tasseled lamps, although these lamps were crystal instead of brass. She glanced at the first oil, and saw it was of two nude women entwined on a low, red-tasseled divan beside a red-and-white-striped marble Turkish bath. Gabrielle stared at the painting. It looked as if the women were—she could not *believe* what they were doing to each other.

She dropped her gaze to the swirling blue, red, and gold carpet at her feet, her heart thumping louder, her cheeks heating with color. Then, realizing what she was doing, she forced herself to lift her head, forced herself to look at each painting as she passed it. By the time they reached the wide central hall that bisected the upstairs, she felt almost dizzy from the impact of what she'd seen.

"Most of the rooms are empty now," said Sirena, stopping before a half-opened door at the top of the stairs. "Our personal rooms are on the third floor. These rooms are all for entertaining customers. We use the same room for a week, then we change, although of course we all have our favorites. This is called the Lido room."

She gave the half-opened door a push, sending it swinging open wide. Someone had obviously been in this room, cleaning. A bucket, a small broom, and a shovel rested beside the fireplace, where the ashes had been swept from the grate. The windows had been thrown open, letting in a blast of freezing mountain air.

Gabrielle shivered. She didn't know what she had expected. Something decadent, surely—perhaps even sinister and frightening. Instead she found herself confronting a beautiful room filled with delicate Louis XV-style furniture, dominated by an enormous canopy bed. The walls had been painted a pale, robin's egg blue, with a plaster frieze, picked out in white, running around the ceiling. When she studied it, she realized the frieze depicted a naked woman doing unnatural things with a swan.

Gabrielle's stunned gaze dropped back to the bed. The ice-blue satin coverlet had been rumpled, but not pulled back. Whatever had been done in this room had taken place on top of, not beneath, the covers.

"You were wise not to admit to the others that you are a virgin," said Sirena quietly. "Tierney might suspect it, but she can't be sure."

Gabrielle didn't know what to say. Her shocked reaction to the paintings, to the plaster frieze, to the rumpled bed, must be written clearly on her face. Yet she didn't know this woman, and certainly had no reason to trust her with the truth. In the end she didn't say anything.

A faint smile curled the other woman's lips. "Silence is probably your best option," she said. "Although not many people in this business tell the truth about themselves. You'll find most chippies make up their own past, their own excuse for being where they are, doing what they're doing."

Gabrielle glanced at the elegant young woman beside her. She wanted to ask Sirena what her story was, why she was . . . doing what she was doing. But she could never be that forward, that rude; so she stared at the wrinkled satin coverlet and said, "What excuse do most of the women give?"

Sirena shrugged. "Usually they blame some handsome, sweet-talking man, who got them to drop their drawers by promising them a wedding ring, then disappeared. Sometimes, I suppose, it's even true. Most often, though, the truth is that their daddy started poking them as soon as they started growing tits, if not before then. Sometimes it was a brother, or a grandfather, or maybe all three. But whoever it was, the effect is the same. Lying under a man getting poked is about the only thing they think they're good for, the only life they know."

Gabrielle had never heard of, never even imagined

such a thing happening—a man forcing himself on a child. Yet there was something about the casual, matter-of-fact way Sirena had said it that convinced her it was all too horribly true. She had a sudden, vivid image of Tierney, stretching languidly across Gabrielle's bed at the hotel and saying, "My da taught me how to do lots of things, before they hanged him, back in London." Was *that* what the girl had meant?

Sirena turned then, as a tiny Oriental woman with iron-gray hair, a face like crumpled parchment, and a stooped back came shuffling down the hall toward them. She clutched a china bowl and pitcher in a pretty flowing blue pattern against the front of her chang-fu, her slippers rubbing together with a soft hiss as she walked.

"Good morning, Xin-Huey," said Sirena.

Xin-Huey ducked her head and chattered something unintelligible in a singsong voice, then hurried into the blue room. As Gabrielle watched, she placed the china pitcher on the marble-topped washstand. But the basin she put on the floor, near the door. Gabrielle found it curious, but she wasn't about to ask Sirena to explain it to her.

With a few swift, efficient strokes, the woman smoothed the coverlet, picked up a bundle of what looked like flannel pads, retrieved her bucket and broom from the hearth, and hurried out into the hall again. As she passed, an intense, musky odor arose from the bundle of dirty laundry in her arms. It was the same, unfamiliar smell that seemed to linger in the air up here, despite the open windows, despite the exotic fragrance from the Oriental incense cones Gabrielle saw smoking everywhere, despite the bowls of rose and lavender potpourri on the marble-topped, cabriole-legged gilt tables in the hall. She thought it must have something to do with what went on up here, but she wasn't about to ask.

"Come, I'll show you some of the other rooms," said Sirena.

"There's no lock on the door," Gabrielle said as they turned to leave.

"None of these rooms have locks. Sometimes a customer can turn mean, and none of us wants to find herself locked in a room with a lunatic on a rampage."

Gabrielle pressed her lips together and told herself to keep them shut.

The next room was a deep bloodred, with heavy Jacobean oak furniture. Beyond that lay a room decorated in a pale pink, the color of the first blush of dawn on a summer's day. In mood and style each room was different. Yet in some aspects they were all the same: the beds were all massive, the curtains, coverlets, and bed hangings all of silk, satin, brocade, or velvet. And virtually every wall was covered with mirrors. There were even, Gabrielle realized with a sense of confused shock, mirrors *over* the beds.

Gabrielle stared at the pink silk draped half tester. "Why would anyone want a mirror over a bed?" she asked, the words tumbling out of her mouth before she could stop them.

Again, that hint of a smile touched Sirena's lips. "Some men like to watch while they're doing it."

The words conjured up sinful images in Gabrielle's mind, images of a man and a woman entwined naked on that pink coverlet, the woman pale and soft, the man hard and dark, his hands moving possessively over the woman's flesh, his glittering eyes watching, watching . . .

Gabrielle felt a tide of mortification sweep to her

cheeks as she jerked her gaze away from that stage set of decadence and depravity. It seemed to her that she must have blushed more in the last forty-eight hours than she had in the rest of her life altogether. She felt a sudden, desperate need to be alone.

"I think I've seen enough," she said.

Sirena shrugged and turned to lead the way down the back stairs to the kitchen.

But as she followed the other woman, Gabrielle wondered why, out of all the women in the house, Jordan Hays had sent Sirena to show her around. "Why did Mr. Hays ask you to take me upstairs?"

For a moment she didn't think Sirena was going to answer. Then she said, "Probably because I don't talk very much."

"And because you already knew about me, didn't you?"

The other woman didn't say anything, but Gabrielle felt certain it was the truth.

"Why do you know," she asked, "when the others do not?"

Sirena paused with one hand on the simple wooden railing that ran alongside the steep back steps, and glanced over her shoulder at Gabrielle. "Sometimes, when you don't talk very much, other people talk to you. My people have a saying, 'The silent mountains hear more than the babbling brook.' "

"Your people?" repeated Gabrielle.

Sirena's face remained expressionless, but Gabrielle caught the flash of pride in her eyes. Pride, and something else that might have been pain. "My father was an Apache warrior."

"And your mother?"

"My mother was not Apache."

It explained much about this woman, Gabrielle thought as she followed her down the steps. The coal-black hair, the chiseled cheekbones, the fiercely quiet self-possession. But it didn't explain what she was doing here, in this house.

And it didn't explain the pain in her eyes.

For Gabrielle, evening came far too quickly.

She had meant to spend the afternoon putting away her clothes, sorting through her mother's things, learning more about the house, about her mother, about the women she considered in some part her responsibility. Instead she sat in the dusky blue velvet chair by the window and watched the wind tear at the heavy bank of clouds hovering over the mountains. Sometimes she could see the jagged, snowcapped peaks; then the clouds would shift, swirling in misty wisps that thickened until she could see only white snow-covered fields and white clouds. But the mountains were always there, even when she couldn't see them.

It was like the rooms upstairs. In her mind she kept seeing them, over and over again, those sinfully wide, satin-draped beds, the mirrored walls, the lockless doors. But that wasn't all she saw. Her wayward mind created other images, images of men and women in those beds. Images pulled from the lurid paintings in gilt frames she'd forced herself to look at, and now couldn't forget.

She tried to imagine what it must be like for a woman to join her body to a man's, only she could not. Yet the women in this house did just that, night after night, with dozens of men. *Dozens of men.* The thought echoed with horror as she tried to grasp what it meant. Sirena, Crystal,

Tierney—all of them, letting strangers touch their bodies, invade them. Some of the men might be young and handsome, but many, surely, were not. Many must be coarse or old or ugly. Gabrielle could not imagine letting someone like that anywhere near her.

How could these women do it? How could they *enjoy* it? And they must enjoy it, surely, otherwise they wouldn't be here. After all, it was their excessive carnality, their insatiable lust for the sins of the flesh that drew them to this life.

And tonight she was going to have to sit in the front room and play the piano while it happened.

Gabrielle jerked, realizing suddenly that the clouds outside her window had taken on a rosy hue spread by the unseen setting sun. It was late.

She thrust herself up out of the chair, a flutter of nerves unsettling her stomach. Before she had time to think about it, before she had time to change her mind, she walked over to yank open the door of Celeste DuBois's enormous wardrobe . . . And sighed.

This was the stuff a young woman's dreams were made of—even a modest young woman raised behind convent walls. Gabrielle's reason for wearing one of these dresses was forgotten as she let her hand trail over the luxurious silks and satins, the velvets and brocades, her breath catching in little gasps of delight as she studied the intricately worked tucks, the fine embroideries. She finally selected a rose-colored faille evening dress with an overskirt of Valenciennes lace. Its chatelaine bodice was made far more modestly than the wine-colored velvet Mr. Hays had selected for her that morning, but the gown was still exquisite.

She stripped off her simple wool dress and washed

quickly, the ordeal of the evening ahead of her temporarily submerged beneath the thrill of anticipating what she would look like in such a beautiful dress. She held her breath as she pulled the rose silk over her head, afraid it might not fit. But as she shook the luxurious folds of material into place and fumbled with the hooks at the back, she felt a thrill of excitement, because it did fit, hugging the curve of her waist, the swell of her breasts as if it had been made for her. She smiled quietly to herself, imagining what Jordan Hays would think, when he saw her in this dress.

Her fingers stilled at their work with the hooks, as she realized the direction her careless thoughts had wandered. Vanity wasn't a sin she succumbed to often, and it was disturbing to find herself indulging in it at such a time, and in such a place.

Her pleasure in the dress became like ashes in her mouth, bitter and shameful. She quickly finished doing up the hooks, and refused even to look at her reflection as she reached for her brush and began to jerk it through her hair.

She was pinning up her hair in a cluster of curls when someone knocked at her bedroom door.

"Who is it?" she called.

The door opened, and she spun about in surprise to see a man silhouetted against the lamplight in the entrance to the hall. A fire crackled and danced on the hearth beside her, but she had lit only the crystal oil lamp on the dressing table, leaving the edges of the room in shadow. Yet she knew it was Jordan Hays, even before he moved forward into the golden lamplight, knew it by the way he stood, by the way he walked. By the way the air seemed to hum with energy when he was around her.

He stopped some five feet from her, his gaze flicking over her. But if she had been expecting him to comment on her appearance, she was disappointed. He looked more annoyed than pleased. "So you're really going to do it, are you?"

She lifted her head proudly, meeting his hard stare. "Yes."

She saw his lips tighten and something that might have been anger flash in his dark green eyes. But then he let his gaze wander over her again, more slowly this time, and she realized the light in his eyes wasn't anger at all, but something far more dangerous.

"I brought you this." He reached inside his coat, and brought out a single strand of exquisite pearls, fastened with a diamond clasp. "It was your mother's."

She stared at the pearls, glowing softly in the palm of his hand, but she made no move to pick up the necklace. She didn't want to touch him.

"I don't know exactly who gave it to her, but I do know it meant a great deal to her. Turn around. I'll put it on for you."

She didn't move. His hands closed gently on her shoulders, spinning her around to face the mirror. The lamplight caught the rose silk of her dress, causing it to shimmer. She tried to see his face in the glass, behind her, but it was only a dark shadow. So she watched his hands as he settled the necklace around the base of her neck.

The pearls felt cool against her throat. But the touch of his fingers was warm and gentle and terrifying in the way it brought every nerve in her body leaping to life. His hands looked so dark and strong against the fragile white of her bare skin. She found herself imagining what it would be like to feel those hands ease down the curve of her neck. To watch in the mirror as he—

To watch in the mirror.

He dropped his hands. "There," he said softly. "You're beautiful." He nodded to her in the mirror. "Look."

For the first time she lowered her gaze from the disturbing image of the man behind her, and concentrated on her own reflection. She felt her cheeks grow pink with pleasure as she stared and stared. It was vain and sinful, she knew. And yet . . . He was right, she *was* beautiful— or, at least, as close to being beautiful as she had ever been. She'd never imagined she could look so elegant, so mature, so . . . different.

"I think perhaps I should have had you wear the brown alpaca after all," he said. She thought at first he was serious, until she caught the light, teasing note in his voice. "Or at least the gray serge with the high lace collar."

She laughed, sucking her lower lip between her teeth. She watched in the mirror as his gaze fastened on her mouth, and stayed there. She saw the teasing light fade from his eyes. And still he stared at her mouth.

She felt her skin grow warm and tingle beneath his gaze, so that she had to resist the urge to wet her dry lips. She remembered with sudden clarity how his hard mouth had felt on hers last night, remembered that punishing kiss. Remembered it not with the revulsion she should have experienced but with an unexpected rush of excitement. It was sinful, but she couldn't help it. Any more than she could help being painfully aware of the fact that she was once more alone with this man. In her bedroom.

He jerked away from her, disappearing out of the mirror, breaking the spell, snapping her back to her senses. She turned away from the dressing table and smoothed her hand down over the shimmering rose gown, her pleasure in the beautiful dress once more destroyed.

"I'm ready," she said, although it was a lie. She would never be ready for what she was about to do.

He stood beside the door, waiting for her, his face, once again, unreadable. "It's not too late to back out of this, Gabrielle," he said. "I'll understand."

She shook her head. "We have a bargain, Mr. Hays. I intend to keep it." Brave words, but she didn't feel brave. Inside, she was shaking like one of those quaking aspens out there.

She walked out of her bedroom, into the lamp-lit hall. She was painfully conscious of the man beside her, painfully conscious of the urge to steady herself by grasping his strong arm. She forced herself to walk rigidly ahead. From the front room came the low-pitched rumble of a man's laugh, followed by a woman's husky Southern drawl.

Through the crystal curtain, Gabrielle could see several men and some four or five women, none of whom she recognized. One of the women, a plump, pretty woman with reddish-blond hair, was sitting on the lap of a lanky, silver-haired rancher with a beaver-skin vest. She wore only an orange silk wrapper, lace drawers, and a corset so low it exposed her enormous breasts. She had her legs wrapped around the man's waist, facing him. As Gabrielle watched, he jiggled his knees so that the blond woman's naked breasts bounced up and down, slapping him in the face. "Atta girl, Amy," he roared. "Ride 'em cowboy!"

Gabrielle paused with one hand poised to part the bead curtain. Jordan Hays's fingers closed around her wrist, stopping her. For one pregnant moment her gaze met his. She shook her head, and he let her go.

Squaring her shoulders, Gabrielle pushed aside the bead curtain, and walked into the front parlor.

CHAPTER
EIGHT

Upstairs, in her room on the third floor, Sirena slowly dressed for the evening.

Her name, Sirena, meant enchantress. Her mother had told her that once, as they sat together outside their tepee. Her mother had been braiding Sirena's hair at the time while Sirena played with her baby brother. Sirena remembered listening to the sound of her mother's voice as the wind rippled through the buffalo grass, and the wild ducks called from the blue sky above.

Most of the girls in the house had changed their names when they went into the business. But Sirena kept hers. It was the only thing she did keep. Her name, and the knife she wore strapped to her calf.

People usually thought Sirena must be an Indian name, an Apache name, but it wasn't. According to Sirena's mother, it was from a language that had already been old when Jesus was born. Sirena's mother knew that because her father had been a scholar, back in Boston, where Sirena's mother had been raised. Far from tepees and war parties and the endless, rolling plains.

Sirena ran a comb through her straight black hair and stared at her face in the mirror of her dressing table. Leaning forward, she searched her image for the legacy of that long-boned, fair-haired New Englander who had been her mother. Sometimes she saw her. But at other times, such as now, she saw a stranger's face, remote and alien to the little girl who had once sat outside her father's tepee, and watched the clouds float free across the wide-open sky.

The front-door knocker sounded below, followed a moment later by Wing Tsue's little brass bell. She was running late.

Pushing away from her dressing table, Sirena stripped off her fine linen chemise and drawers, with their delicate, handmade lace, and buttoned on another set. These were also made of fine cloth and trimmed with red satin ribbon run through eyelet, but they were not her best. Sirena never wore her best for entertaining, the way the other girls did. Sirena kept the best for herself.

Reaching for her red satin corset, she tightened her stomach so that she could do up the front buttons without having to unlace the back. Sirena never resorted to tight lacing. She hadn't worn a corset as a young girl growing up, and she didn't think she would ever get used to one now. The baleen supports dug into her ribs, and the jean lining chafed her skin, even over the fine batiste of her chemise. The corset was one of the concessions she made to her profession. There was something about the sight of a woman in a corset that made a man all hot and anxious.

Humming a half-forgotten tune, she sat on the edge of the pristine white cotton spread that covered the single bed in her private room, and rolled on her red-and-white-striped stockings. Smoothing the silk up over her knees, she tied on red garters, then held up one leg to admire the effect. Stockings and garters were like corsets: they drove men wild.

Standing up, she selected a black silk kimono embroidered all over with red fire-breathing dragons. Often she wore a dress downstairs, and played cool and alluring by turns, sometimes teasing, sometimes tantalizing. The men who visited her loved that, loved what they saw as the challenge of taming her, winning her.

They didn't know that they never won her, that she took them. They never took her. And they never dreamed, as she smiled and fondled and exclaimed over them, just how much she hated them. Hated and despised them. They were like overgrown children, so vaingloriously proud of what they had between their legs, as if every other man alive didn't have the same equipment, as if it were as much a marvel and delight to women as it was to the men themselves. They thought she loved them, that she couldn't get enough of that special organ of theirs, that she was always hot for it.

But she never got hot, and that was the secret they never guessed. What Sirena loved was the power her sex gave her over them, the power to make them desire her, to make them rut and sweat and thrill, while she remained scornful and detached and untouched. Thousands of men might have groped at her breasts and poked at her with their cocks and spewed their seed inside her. But Sirena remained untouched.

She was strapping her knife to her calf when she heard the piano begin to play. She tilted her head, listening to the thumping chorus of "Camptown Races," and knew that it was Celeste's daughter who played. Celeste's convent-bred, virgin daughter, playing the piano in her dead mother's whorehouse.

An unexpected and not entirely understood emotion welled up within Sirena, a sensation that was part sadness, part admiration, and part something else that felt strangely like hope, although that made no sense. She couldn't begin to comprehend the guilt and sense of obligation that drove Gabrielle Antoine to do what she was doing. But that didn't keep Sirena from recognizing the girl's strength and courage, and her dedication to an ideal that was good and right and noble, even if it was doomed.

The problem was, Gabrielle didn't know it was doomed. She had lived such a sheltered, protected life, and she knew so little of human nature—she knew so little of her *own* nature. She thought she could live in this house, even play the piano in the front room, and remain unaffected.

But Sirena knew better, which was why she was sad. For Gabrielle, and for herself.

Sirena had the Jacobean room that week. She stopped by there on her way down to the parlor, to make certain a bowl of butter sat waiting on the dresser beside the oil lamp and the egg timer. She checked that a fresh pad lay on the bed, and that a stack of clean ones waited in the bottom drawer. She filled the pitcher on the washstand with hot water from the tin reservoir in the hall. Then she went downstairs.

As she reached the landing on the steps, she swung into the languid rolling strut that was as much the mark of a chippy as face paint and a come-hither smile. The front parlor was already crowded, and as she came down the last few steps she noticed one of her regulars, a middle-aged mine owner named Sam Cox. He was wearing a dark green suit, a purple and green brocade vest, and a purple silk tie. When he saw her, he sucked in his stomach and thrust out his chest, reminding her of a peacock, unfurling his gaudy tail to the presumed admiration and delight of all females in the area.

She strolled up to him and ran her hand, caressingly, across his shoulder and down one arm. "Hi, handsome," she purred, although he was far from handsome, and had probably never been handsome, even ten or fifteen years ago, before lack of exercise and too many bourbons had sagged the flesh on his face and added a loose roll of fat around his middle. "Looking for a good time?"

"I was looking for *you*, Sirena," he said, a smile twitching the ends of his brown handlebar mustache as he reached down to rub her buttocks, familiarly, with his splayed hand.

She leaned into him and laughed breathily, letting her half-exposed breasts rub suggestively against his chest. She wasn't in the mood to dally tonight. She just wanted to get it over with.

Behind her, the piano fell silent as Gabrielle finished playing "Listen to the Mockingbird." Sirena could feel the girl's eyes on her, feel her shock and disapproval. *Well, hell,* Sirena thought. *What in God's name had she expected?* Just to show she didn't care, Sirena turned to give the girl a wide, brilliant smile. Then, holding Gabrielle's gaze, Sirena deliberately cupped her hand over Cox's bulging hard crotch.

Hot air came whistling out of Sam Cox's pursed lips, his eyes widening with shocked delight. But Gabrielle's face went white, and she snapped back around to send her fingers flying over the keys in some song that didn't sound like any honky-tonk tune Sirena had ever heard. As soon as he got his wind back, Cox smiled and said, "Ah, Beethoven's 'Fur Elise.' I like your new piano player."

By one o'clock Sirena had made the trip up the stairs a dozen times with a dozen different men. As the night wore on, the men got drunker and rowdier, and the whores came downstairs with fewer and fewer clothes on. Tierney was naked beneath her thin wrapper; and Jilly wore nothing but her black corset, black stockings, and red high-heeled shoes. Only Youngmi remained precisely dressed in the red silk *chang-fu* she always wore buttoned up tight to her throat. But then, Youngmi hated being a whore. Sirena could never understand why the little Chinese girl stayed in the business. It had something to do with shame and destiny, but Sirena didn't understand it, any more than she understood what kept a virgin like Gabrielle playing the piano in the midst of all this debauchery.

Sirena had expected Gabrielle to last ten minutes in the front parlor, maybe half an hour at the most. Yet here it was, almost closing time, and she was still there. Oh, she'd taken a few breaks, but she always came back.

Snagging a glass of champagne off a silver tray, Sirena glanced at Jordan, and felt a rare smile of genuine amusement curl her lips.

He usually spent the evenings in the gaming room, keeping an eye on his dealers, making sure they weren't cheating either the house or the customers, because while the play at Celeste's Place could be deep, it was never supposed to be dirty. But tonight, he couldn't have done much more than cast a few, swift glances into the room across the hall, because every time she'd seen him, he'd been standing just like he was now, his shoulders propped against the wall beside the piano, his long legs thrust out in front, the tips of his fingers tucked into the waistband of his black trousers.

And if Gabrielle's painfully straight back and cold, reserved manner weren't enough to keep the men from doing more than casting the pretty new woman interested glances, the scowl on Jordan's face, and the pointed way he kept the tail of his coat folded back from the gun on his hip, was enough to scare away anyone who wasn't either drunk or stupid.

Sirena took a slow sip of her champagne, ignoring for the moment the big miner with the flowing black beard and ruddy cheeks who was trying to catch her attention. She knew Jordan wasn't happy about Celeste's daughter moving into the house, or about her plans to play the piano in the front room every night. He and Celeste had been friends, maybe as good of friends as two loners can be, without becoming lovers, too.

Only, watching Jordan now, Sirena saw something in his face that she suspected had nothing to do with the fact that Gabrielle was Celeste's daughter, and everything to do with the fact that Gabrielle was a beautiful, intelligent young woman. Innocent and beautiful, and—to a man as jaded as Jordan—all the more desirable for being so totally unaware of it.

The clicking of the bead curtain drew Sirena's attention to a new customer, who came in bringing the cold, wood-smoke-scented air of the mountains with him. He was a wealthy young man, judging by the cut of his dark suit, and the quality of his white shirt and tie. Good-looking, too, in a polished, pretty boy kind of way, with his wavy blond hair and blue eyes and even features. And from the moment he walked through the beaded archway, he had eyes only for Gabrielle.

He accepted a glass of brandy from one of the girls,

then stood watching Gabrielle while he sipped his drink and she played another one of those tunes Sirena had never heard before.

He stood that way for a few minutes, listening and watching. Then he polished off his brandy with a flick of his elbow and set his glass on a table with barley-sugar turned legs. Gabrielle was just finishing the last bar of her piece when he walked up behind her, cupped the nape of her neck with his hand, and leaned in close.

"Hey, lady," he said with a brilliant smile as Gabrielle jumped and whirled to face him. "How'd you like to take a break from playin' with those little ivory keys, and go upstairs and play with somethin' a whole lot bigger and more interestin'?"

Even Sirena was surprised at how fast Jordan came away from the wall, his hands hovering suggestively loose and relaxed over his hips. "The *lady* is here to play the piano," he said in a voice that was low and calm and decidedly lethal. "Take your hand off her. Now."

The pretty boy jumped back, lifting his hands high and wide in a gesture of surrender. "No offense meant, mister. No offense at all."

"Margot?" Jordan said over his shoulder, without shifting his intense gaze from Gabrielle's admirer.

Margot, a tall black woman with long legs and firm, high breasts, sashayed forward. "Man, oh, man," she said, licking her lips with relish as she ran her eyes up and down the pretty boy. "Ain't you a treat?" She slipped her hand through his arm. "You like t' have a good time with ol' Margot here?"

The young man inserted one finger between his neck and shirt collar, as if he were having trouble sucking enough air into his lungs. But he managed to summon up a ghost of his flashy smile and say, "You look like my kind of woman, Margot."

"Oooh, honey, you're a real sweet one," cooed Margot, snuggling up to him, and wiggling her naked tits beneath his nose. "Come on, then, handsome. I'm agonna do you good."

Margot didn't have her new customer halfway to the staircase before Gabrielle shot up off the piano bench. Sirena expected the girl to burst into tears and run from the room. Instead she turned to Jordan and said quietly, "Thank you, Mr. Hays, for your assistance. However, I thought we agreed that if I am to play the piano in this house for the next three months, I need to learn how to handle these situations myself."

The girl was so visibly shaken by what had just happened that her face was white, and her pupils had dilated until her eyes looked black. But she'd managed to keep her voice calm, and Sirena felt an unwanted stirring of admiration for the sheer, raw guts this girl must have, to move into this house and come out here and play that piano, having been raised the way she'd been raised, and thinking the way she did.

Sirena glanced at Jordan, and saw her own thoughts reflected in the wry smile that twisted his lips as he stared at the girl. But Sirena saw something else, too—something hot and unholy that flared in his dark green eyes.

Oh, hell, thought Sirena. *Someone really ought to warn this sweet little thing to keep her drawers buttoned, because Jordan Hays is a handsome, sweet-talking devil if ever I saw one.*

But of course she didn't say it. She just sauntered up to

Jordan and linked her arm through his, giving him a saucy smile because he knew her well enough not to take it seriously. "She's got a point, Jordan. You can't exactly guard her every minute of every night, now, can you? What she needs is someone to teach her . . ." Her voice trailed off as she noticed Jordan's attention shift to something behind her. Something that made his eyes narrow, and his face grow so still and cold it sent a chill of apprehension up her spine. Slowly, she turned.

And saw Doug Slaughter, brushing aside the swaying curtain of Austrian crystals.

Doug Slaughter paused just inside the parlor and listened to the bead curtain *click-clacking* shut behind him as he surveyed the room. They had a sizable crowd for a Thursday night, he thought, shoving back the brim of his beaver hat. But then, Celeste's Place usually did do a damn good business.

His gaze settled on Celeste's daughter, standing beside the piano with Hays and that breed whore, Sirena. He'd been told Gabrielle Antoine had moved in here and was filling in as piano player, but he'd be damned if he'd believe it without seeing it with his own eyes.

Now he'd seen it, and he felt the rage pumping through him, swelling his muscles, hardening his fists. He hadn't paid much attention to her yesterday, when she'd told him the house wasn't for sale. But she had his attention now, and in a way he swore she was going to regret. He didn't like people who went against him. Didn't like people who weren't afraid of him. It was the reason he didn't like gunmen, unless they were on his payroll. A man confident in his ability to handle a gun wasn't intimidated by Slaughter's size and strength, the way most men were.

He watched Jordan Hays detach himself from the group near the piano and saunter forward. He had his thumbs hooked in his cartridge belt, an easy smile on his lips, and a cold light in his eyes.

"You want somethin', Slaughter?" he said.

Slaughter let his gaze drift significantly over the crowd. "This house is full of men looking for nothing more than whiskey and a woman, Hays. What makes you think I'm any different?"

"Maybe because I can't think of any reason why a man who owns half a dozen tonks of his own would need to walk up a steep hill in the cold night air, just to have a drink and get laid."

Slaughter showed his teeth in a smile. "I heard you got yourself a new piano player."

Hays didn't blink, didn't move a muscle in that enviably blank face of his. But there was an almost visible concentration of the lethal energy that radiated out from him, until it became like a hum. "That's right."

Slaughter's smile broadened. "I always did like piano music."

Glass shattered, the sudden, unexpected sound startling the room into silence. Hays spun around, his hand going to the Colt on his hip in a reflex action. But it was just one of the whores, a little Chinese girl who didn't look much over sixteen, who had dropped a glass. She stood near the double doors joining the front and back parlors, her frightened dark eyes riveted on Doug Slaughter as if she were oblivious to the broken glass at her feet.

It was that breed, Sirena, who went and put her arm

around the girl. "It's all right, Youngmi," she murmured in a voice unexpectedly gentle for a woman they said always kept a knife strapped to her calf, even when she took a man between her legs. For a woman they said had killed a couple of men once, down in Fort Collins.

With his gaze fastened on the two women, he didn't realize Gabrielle Antoine had left the piano and come up to them, until she ranged herself alongside the gambler.

"What's the matter with that girl?" she asked him quietly.

Hays nodded toward Slaughter. "Youngmi used to work in one of his cribs."

Slaughter shrugged. "All Chinks look alike to me."

Gabrielle turned her big silver-gray eyes on him, and he took a good look at her, a really good look, for the first time since he'd come in here tonight. And he knew an awakening that was more than interest.

She'd been pretty enough the first time he'd seen her, in that modest gray dress of hers, with her hair pulled back primly at the nape of her neck. But now, with her hair in curls and the white flesh of her shoulders peeking above shimmering pink silk, he saw the woman she could be, the woman he supposed she had been before, simply hidden beneath her convent-bred ways and schoolteacher demeanor.

She was Celeste's daughter, a woman with a body made by God to tempt a man, to drive him wild, to satisfy his darkest primeval urges. Her hair was brighter than Celeste's, the hot golden color of the sun, rather than the pale glimmer of moonlight. Her features were different from Celeste's, too, all except for her mouth . . . God, he could make a fortune off a whore with a mouth like that.

Something of his thoughts must have showed on his face, because he noticed she edged closer to Hays. It was an instinctive movement; he doubted she even knew she'd made it.

He gave her a wide smile. "I came to let you know that my offer to buy the house still stands."

It was Hays who answered. "I thought the lady made it pretty clear yesterday that she's not selling."

"A lady can change her mind," said Slaughter, his gaze never leaving Miss Antoine's face.

"I won't," she said.

He shrugged. "You know where to find me if you do." He held her gaze while he settled his hat more firmly on his head, then nodded to the gambler, standing quiet and watchful at her side. "Hays," he said, and turned to slap the bead curtain open so he could pass through it.

Behind him, the crystals swayed and clattered and clicked, but not so loudly that he couldn't hear her say again, "I won't." He didn't know if she said it to the gambler, or to herself. But then he heard her say it again, and he knew she was saying it to herself, trying to convince herself.

Slaughter walked out of the warm, perfume-scented atmosphere of the house, into the cold mountain night, and smiled. He would have the house, all right. Have it before summer. And he'd have Miss Gabrielle Antoine, too.

Even if he had to kill Jordan Hays to do it.

Gabrielle sat in one of the brocade wing chairs beside the office fire. Around her the house settled into the stillness of the night, the only sounds were the crackling pop of the log on the fire and the sighing of the wind outside.

Obscene images of the evening kept playing and replaying in her head, images of taut-faced men and laughing women whose naked flesh gleamed pale in the lamplight. She drew in a deep breath, and let it out slow and soft.

"It was worse than you expected it to be, wasn't it?" said Jordan Hays from across the room.

She nodded her head, but she didn't look up from the fire, and she didn't say anything. She was afraid if she tried, the self-control she had managed to preserve this far, would crack.

"Had enough?"

The words were harsh, but his gentle tone surprised her into looking up at him. He stood beside the table, a glass of brandy in one hand, an unreadable expression on his face. She glanced away again. She didn't know why she was here with him now. Except that she didn't think she could bear to be alone yet, and he seemed to sense it.

He came at her, leaving his drink on the table behind him. She expected him to take the other chair. Instead he hunkered down in front of her, and gathered her hands in his. "We can still sell," he said.

She watched the firelight play over his dark, handsome face, accentuating the sharp line of his cheekbone, the shadows of the hollows beneath. He was not exactly, she realized, the man she'd thought him at first. She'd thought him mean and cold and callous, and he was. But there was more to him than that. She had discovered he could be kind. Kind and caring. He might act as if he didn't care; perhaps he honestly believed he *didn't* care. But she knew now that he did. She was starting to see him as a person, she realized, rather than as a personification of darkness and sin. She wasn't sure she liked that.

She dropped her gaze to his lean, tanned fingers,

curled around her small white hands. She could feel his
warmth and strength flowing through his fingers, flowing
into her. "I'm ashamed to admit it," she said, her voice
rough with emotion, "but I am tempted to sell."

"I know."

Her hand twisted beneath his, gripped it. There was
something she had to ask him, something she needed to
know. But her throat felt so raw, it hurt to push the words
out. "Tell me about the Chinese girl. About Youngmi.
Why just the sight of Slaughter should have such an
effect on her."

He pursed his lips and blew out a long sigh. "It's not a
pretty tale."

"Tell me anyway." Her gaze caught his, and held it. "I
think I need to hear it."

"All right." He dropped her hands and straightened up,
going to prop one elbow on the edge of the mantel. He
stood, staring silently down at the flames for a moment,
before blowing his breath out in a long sigh.

"You might think this house is decadent and sinful,"
he said, and it was as if he spoke to the flames, not to
her. "But at least it's clean and well kept and, largely
because of that, the women who live here have managed
to retain a certain amount of self-respect. You don't see
that in other whorehouses. Or in the honky-tonks, where
girls charge three dollars for a five-minute lay, and take
on any drunken cowboy or stinking mule skinner who
has the price of admission to some sordid, miserable
back room."

He paused, and she thought he was probably visual-
izing those rooms. She knew instinctively that he had
seen them, and paid his three dollars for a five-minute

lay. "And a crib is another name for one of these places?" she asked, her voice little more than a whisper.

"Of a sort. Only it's the lowest sort. They look . . . not unlike a line of stables, really. Each one is that small. From the outside they're just a string of doors opening into narrow rooms barely wide enough to hold a bed. Slaughter owns a couple rows of them, down near Dostal Alley. The conditions in them are so bad, the only women who'll work them are either opium addicts, or else Chinese slave girls, brought in from San Francisco."

Gabrielle felt the shock of his words like a jolt, slamming into her. *"Slave girls?"*

He swiveled his head and looked at her, and she wondered how she could ever have imagined there was anything gentle or caring about this man. It was as if he had withdrawn to some cold, barren place within him, where no one could touch him. "That's what Youngmi was," he said flatly. "After her parents died back in China, Youngmi's aunt sold her to a Shanghai trader. It's not unusual. She's just one of hundreds—maybe thousands—of Chinese women shipped over here every year. Slaughter had her brought in last year, and he locked her in one of his cribs and made her whore for him, until she got so sick from the cold and the filth and the way she was treated that he thought she was going to die. So he had her dumped in one of the shafts up on Quartz Hill and left her there."

Gabrielle stared up at him. Her throat worked, but nothing came out.

His voice rolled on. "Some miner just happened to find her, and brought her down to Doc Collins. The doc did what he could, but what she really needed was someone to look after her while she rested and got some decent food in her. Problem was, whatever she might have been when she left China, by that time she was a whore, and none of the good women of this town would have anything to do with nursing a whore. So your mother took her in."

Gabrielle stretched out her hand, as if she would touch him, then curled her fingers into a fist and drew it back. "But how can this man get away with such a thing? You're talking about *slavery*. And what amounts almost to murder."

He looked at her long and hard. "If you're going to live out here, even for a short time, there's something you need to understand about Western mining towns. Youngmi and most of the other girls like her are Chinese, and the man who brought her and the others like her in here from the coast and sold them to Slaughter was Chinese. As far as most people are concerned, none of it is any of their business."

"Isn't it? 'How shalt thou hope for mercy, rendering none?' " she said indignantly.

A gleam of unexpected amusement lit up his eyes. "Maybe they've never read *The Merchant of Venice*. Or maybe they reckon they live such lives of holy rectitude that they don't need any mercy."

"Huh." She jerked her gaze away from his sparkling green eyes. "What I don't understand is why Youngmi is still here." Gabrielle remembered the girl's high-necked *chang-fu*, and the blank look on her pretty young face as the evening's procession of men ogled her and fondled her and walked her up the stairs.

He shrugged and turned his back to the fire. "It's her own choice."

"Is it?"

"Most people's choices in life are fairly narrowly defined. Or at least, that's the way they see them. Most people would say you have no choice but to sell this house to Doug Slaughter, simply because the consequences of keeping it are so severe."

"But you don't want to sell to Slaughter, either."

"No. But I'll do it. I made your mother a promise."

"For my sake. Only my mother didn't know me."

"No, which is sad. She thought of you as the child she remembered, someone young, someone who still needed to be protected, to be taken care of." He reached out and touched her, a gentle brushing of his fingertips across her cheek. "She would have been very proud of the woman you grew up to become."

It was nothing more than the whisper of a caress. Yet, long after his hand fell back to his side, she could feel his touch on her face, and she had to resist the urge to press her palm to her burning cheek. Her chest rose and fell with her breath, and for one aching moment, their gazes held. It seemed to her, looking at him, as if all the skin on his face had suddenly been drawn taut, sharpening the flare of his cheek, making his eyes blaze with a strange heat.

She saw a slight shudder ripple through him, and he spun away. "I think you'll be all right alone now," he said. And then he left her, still sitting by the fire.

She felt something swell within her, something warm and aching and frightening. And because he was no longer there to see her do it, she raised her palm and pressed it to the cheek he had touched.

She didn't know what was wrong with her, why she reacted to this man the way she did. She only knew that, in some way she didn't entirely comprehend, he was far more of a threat to her, to who and what she was, than living in this house ever could be.

The next day Gabrielle awoke to a noonday sun that filtered in around the heavy velvet drapes to fill the bedroom with a snow-brightened glow.

She yawned and stretched her hands up over her head, her fingertips brushing the flocked blue and green paper covering the wall behind the bed. Never in her life had she slept so late. But instead of getting up, she crossed her arms behind her neck and stared up at the dusky blue satin lining of Celeste's rosewood canopy bed. No mirror here.

All the shocking, sinful things she had seen and heard and learned these last few days threatened to crowd in on her, weighing her down, oppressing her. She drew in a deep, cleansing breath, and pushed them away.

Her gaze drifted around the room—her *mother*'s room—and an unexpected thrill of excitement thrummed through her at the thought. Somehow, in the course of the last few days, she had lost that heady sense of impending discovery she had known when she left New Orleans. Now, alone in Celeste's room, with a whole day stretching ahead of her, she felt it again, quickening her heartbeat, filling her with energy.

She threw back the covers and swung her legs to the cold floor. The fire had burned down long ago, and she quickly reached for her dressing sacque and thrust her feet into her slippers before going over to stir up the coals on the hearth. She added enough kindling to coax a small flame, then went to throw open the heavy drapes before returning to toss a couple of pine logs on the strengthening blaze.

Impatiently she turned to the inlaid mother-of-pearl and rosewood chest of drawers, then paused with her hands on the intricately turned knobs. What she was about to do seemed an intrusion, in invasion of privacy. Necessary, perhaps, but unutterably sad, nevertheless. It didn't seem right that the living, breathing woman who had once owned all these things should be gone from the world, while her material possessions lingered on.

Easing the drawer open, Gabrielle lightly ran her fingertips over the rows of neatly folded chemises, camisoles, and stockings. All were beautifully made of the finest materials, meticulously maintained. The next drawer contained rows of bags, fans, and gloves, then fichus and scarves. All carefully categorized and arranged, they spoke of a wealthy woman with good taste and a nearly ruthless penchant for organization. There was nothing of a sentimental nature here. No pressed roses, no treasured trinkets that had obviously outlived their usefulness, but been kept anyway.

Sighing, Gabrielle sank back on her heels, and gently closed the last drawer, conscious of a sense of failure, of disappointment. She wasn't sure what she'd been looking for—surely nothing as obvious as an ancient Bible with her entire family tree carefully penned in the back leaf, or even her own birth certificate. But whatever she had been seeking had eluded her. And she had this terrible fear that it always would.

She glanced at the big wardrobe, and decided to get dressed and find something to eat before she started on that. Although she already knew what she would find. Rows of beautiful, well-kept dresses and mantles and dolmans, but nothing personal, nothing sentimental, nothing *graspable*.

She spent most of the afternoon working in her mother's bedroom. Many items she packed away, making space for her own clothes. But some things, like the exquisitely hand-painted fans, the carved glove boxes, the silver fili-gree bouquet holder, she kept, to remind her of this mother she had never known.

The sun was already sinking low in the sky, heading for the wild, jagged peaks to the west, when she extended her explorations to the office. She stoked the fire and lit the oil lamps and the brace of candles near the mantel-piece, then moved to the big partners desk.

Pulling out the top drawer on the side facing the window, she stared down at a deck of cards, a man's boodle book, and a silver whiskey flask, among other miscella-neous items. The scents of leather and expensive tobacco wafted up to her, and she closed the drawer quickly.

She went around to the other side of the desk and sat down, conscious of a peculiar feeling in the pit of her stomach. She'd had no idea that Jordan Hays used this desk, used this office, too. She stared at the painting of Celeste DuBois on the far wall, and the echo of Jordan Hays's voice came to her, saying, *I don't think I've ever known a more beautiful woman.*

It was something she hadn't thought about before, her mother and Jordan Hays. She suspected it was probably a measure of her innocence, that she had blithely assumed their relationship to have been limited to that of business partners. But now that it had occurred to her, she sat there in the gathering gloom, trying to decide if she had been naive before, or if she were being overly suspicious now.

And trying to figure out why the idea of her mother and Jordan Hays bothered her so much.

A light tapping on the door brought her head around. "Come in," she called.

It was Sirena. She stood in the doorway, her gown of champagne satin shimmering in the lamplight.

Gabrielle jumped up, her gaze flying to the Louis XVI clock on the mantel. "Goodness, I had no idea it was this late."

Sirena came in and closed the door behind her. "I thought you'd like to talk to me, before you went out there again."

Gabrielle surprised herself by laughing softly. "About handling the unwanted advances of men?"

"That's right." Sirena walked over to the brandy decanter on the side table, and helped herself to a drink. "You see, I think it's mainly a matter of deciding ahead of time how you're going to deal with a situation when it arises. And despite what happened last night, I don't think the occasion will arise all that often."

Gabrielle leaned back against the desk and watched Sirena pour herself a large measure of brandy. She was intrigued by this woman, with her strange combination of quiet pride and bold, shameless ways, with her educated syntax and faintly guttural accent. Intrigued, but intimidated, too. She kept her voice light with difficulty. "I'll try not to take that statement as a comment on my appearance and charms."

A soft smile of amusement curled Sirena's lips. "It wasn't. The thing is, you see, that for all their brag and bluster, when it comes right down to it, most men are terrified of women. Especially smart, gently bred woman. They like their females light and easy and willing."

Gabrielle cupped her elbows in her palms, holding her forearms close to her midriff. "Well, I don't know about the light and easy part, but I would think the mere fact of my being in this house would make me seem willing enough."

Sirena shrugged and took a long pull on her drink. "Normally I suppose it would. But you watched the way the girls worked the front room last night. There's a certain look a woman gets in her eyes that lets a man know she's interested. She catches his gaze, gives him a come-hither kind of smile, plays with her hair—there's lots of little signals we use, without even thinking about most of them. But a nice girl like you doesn't send out those signals."

"I must have done something last night."

Sirena drained her glass. "No, it wasn't you. Some men are either so arrogant, or just plain stupid, that they don't pay attention to how a woman is acting. But those aren't the ones you need to worry about. They're like your pretty boy last night. All you need to do is tell them nicely you're not an upstairs girl, and suggest one of the other chippies, and they'll usually leave you alone. It's the ones who decide to get mean and ugly that can be a problem."

Gabrielle tried not to think about those upstairs rooms without locks.

"With that kind," Sirena continued, twisting around to set down her empty glass, "you need something more than words to convince them you're serious. Your mama used a boob gun. I use this." She slipped up the flounced hem of her dress and multihued petticoats to display a bone-handled knife strapped in a beaded deerskin sheath to her calf.

Gabrielle's eyes widened as she watched Sirena slip out the knife and hold it with the comfort and familiarity another woman might display with a needle or embroidery hoop. The light from the desk lamp caught on the wicked edge of the blade, gleaming murderously. "You use *that*? But . . . how can you?"

"Most people think you need a lot of strength to use a knife, but you don't," said the other woman, misunderstanding the question. "You just need to know what you're doing. You don't want to go stabbing down on a man"—she illustrated with a violent overhanded slashing motion—"because you're likely to run into a rib that way, and what you're aiming for is his heart. You need to cut up, like this . . ." She flipped the knife in her fingers, and thrust it upward. "Just slip it in nice and easy."

Gabrielle lifted her gaze from that deadly blade to the face of the woman who held it. Something wild and terrible lurked in the woman's dark, fierce eyes.

"Who did you kill?" Gabrielle asked, her voice no more than a whisper. She was shocked when she realized she had spoken the question aloud, and she didn't expect an answer.

But Sirena's mouth parted in a wide, chilling smile, and she said, "My mother's husband."

It was only later it occurred to Gabrielle that the woman had said, *my mother's husband.* She hadn't said, *my father.*

Because Sirena's father had been an Apache warrior.

That evening Gabrielle wore another one of her mother's evening dresses, this one of white tulle and pink peau de soie, with puffed, off-the-shoulder sleeves and a low round Josephine waist. After she put it on, she stood in front of her dressing-table mirror and blatantly stared at her reflection, trying to see herself as a man might see her.

She curved her lips up into a smile, and wondered what a come-hither look was like. Somehow, she doubted she was achieving it, and she turned the caricature of a smile into a hideous grimace that made her chuckle.

Here was one of the deficiencies of a convent education, she decided, tucking a lace fichu into the gown's low neckline. Being raised by nuns, one had no opportunity to study the subtle interplay between men and women. It was a deficiency that three months in this house would doubtless remedy.

Her stomach roiled at the thought of facing the front parlor again. She banked the fire in her room, and forced herself to walk down the lamp-lit hall. Night had long ago fallen, and the house was crowded. She paused at the beaded archway to smooth her dress with an unsteady hand . . . and felt Jordan Hays watching her. She turned her head.

He leaned over one of the tables in the gaming room, one hand splayed on the green cloth, his head tilted back. Their gazes caught and held, and she saw something leap in his shadowed eyes. But she could never read him, this man who made a living out of keeping his face blank, this man who never let anyone know what he thought, what he felt.

She gave him a slight smile. It wasn't a come-hither smile, she knew. But then, she wasn't a come-hither type of woman, and she never would be.

He straightened up and walked toward her anyway. His gaze roved over her, from her bare shoulders to her waist, and she knew he was looking at her the way a man looks at a woman. That strange light glittered in his eyes. A light that made her breath hitch and her smile begin to slip.

He reached her side, just as a woman's scream, high-pitched and throbbing with terror, cut through the night.

CHAPTER
NINE

Jordan took the stairs two at a time.

The wide upper hall seemed filled with people. Women, naked, or in thin wrappers. Men in union suits, or hitching up their trousers, or just poking their heads and bare, hairy shoulders around doorways. One man, a skinny fellow with a gray tuft of hair on top and a long neck that made him look like an ostrich, squeaked, "This don't count as part of my fifteen minutes, you hear?"

The scream came again, from the third room on the left. Jordan slipped his Colt from its holster, and kicked open the door.

Naked and quivering with terror, she cowered against the far wall. Her name was Amy, and she appealed to the men who liked their women big-breasted and rounded. She had long, strawberry-blond hair that matched at both ends, and a pretty face. Only she didn't look pretty now. She sniveled incoherently, tears streaming down her face, her white skin gleaming pale and vulnerable in the dim light. She held one hand to her left breast, and Jordan could see the bright red blood that welled up between her fingers. More blood ran in a thin rivulet from another slash on her arm.

He took it all in with one, swift glance as he spun to face the man by the bed.

He was a giant of a man, a miner from the looks of him, with a red shirt and grease-splattered wool trousers and a long, thick black beard. He stood at least six-feet-six, his shoulders broad, his arms thick with muscle, his eyes glazed with a wild light. He held a long, ugly skinning knife gripped in one meaty fist, the blade naked and well-honed and bloody.

"Drop the knife," said Jordan quietly.

The man's lips curled back from his teeth in a snarl. "I paid for her, damn you."

"You paid to screw her. Not to cut her up."

The naked blade made a threatening pass through the air. "I paid for her. And you're interfering, mister."

"Drop the knife."

"You want it?" The man tilted his head, an eerie smile displaying tobacco-yellowed teeth and two, incongruous dimples. "I'll give it to you."

"Don't," said Jordan, but the miner was already lunging forward, his knife driving straight at Jordan's gut.

Jordan squeezed the trigger. An explosion of flame and smoke ripped through the room. The acrid stench of burned sulfur pinched at Jordan's nostrils. Some of the women in the hall screamed. Jordan thumbed the gun's safety and held it steady, still pointed at the miner.

The black-bearded man stumbled backward, weaving to and fro as if he were drunk. An ugly black hole had appeared in the middle of his chest, blooming a dark stain across his red wool shirt. He looked down at his chest, his eyes widening, as if in surprise. Then he lifted his head and stared at Jordan.

It seemed to Jordan that the man hovered there,

between life and death, for an eternity. His eyes were blue, Jordan noticed. The deep, vivid blue of a mountain lake. His lashes were long and thick, his eyebrows heavy, so that they almost met over the bridge of his nose. They stared at each other, Jordan and the man he had just killed, until the man pitched forward onto his face, and lay still.

"Here, let me through," said a deep, raspy voice.

A middle-aged man with a thinning head of gray-brown hair, a nose like an overripe tomato, and a sagging belly, pushed his way through the hushed crowd that had gathered at the door. Sheriff Baites must have been visiting one of the girls, because he wore nothing but a red wool union suit, a gun belt, and a tin star crookedly pinned to his half-fastened underwear.

His knees creaked, sounding an odd note of normalcy in the unnaturally silent room as he squatted down and rolled the fallen man over. One of the miner's big arms flapped out, lying awkwardly across the rug. Jordan stared at the man's callused, work-worn hand and thick, scarred, curled fingers.

"He'd dead enough," said the sheriff. "Looks like you plugged him right smack in the heart."

Jordan slipped his gun back into his holster. The air was thick and hot with gun smoke, his insides felt cold and dead. As dead as that miner on the floor.

He didn't realize that Gabrielle had followed him up the stairs and into the room until he turned and saw her standing there, her back pressed to the open door, her stricken gaze on the dead man. As he watched, she made a hasty sign of the cross, her lips moving in silent prayer.

She pushed away from the door, and he thought she meant to leave. Instead she lifted Amy's wrapper from the end of the brass bedstead and carried it over to the naked, sobbing woman huddled on the floor in the corner. He noticed she carefully avoided looking at the miner's body again, even though she had to walk right past him on her way.

"Are you badly hurt?" she asked, dropping the robe around Amy's shoulders and sinking down beside her. Amy pulled her hair over her face and shuddered, sobbing incoherently.

"Anyone know who this man was?" Jordan shifted his gaze to the slack-jawed men and white-faced women crowding around the doorway.

"His name's Cooper," said a deep-voiced miner. "He's been workin' a claim on the other side of Black Hawk since last summer. He goes crazy like this sometimes. Although I ain't never seen him this bad before."

The sheriff sighed and stretched to his feet. "Think some of you boys could give me a hand gettin' him outta here?"

Two men who looked like miners themselves stepped forward, while Jordan raised his voice and said, "No reason the rest of you'all can't get back to enjoyin' your-selves. And ladies, give them an extra fifteen minutes, and a drink of whatever they fancy. On the house."

Some of the men let out a ragged cheer, while the women swung back into action, coaxing, smiling, touch-ing, leading their customers away. The hall began to clear. Jordan glanced over to where Gabrielle was speak-ing in low, soothing tones to the terrified chippy.

"It's over," Gabrielle said gently. "Everything is all right now. That man can't hurt you. You're safe." She put her arm around Amy's shaking shoulders. "Here, let me help you stand up."

With an animal-like shriek, Amy flailed out with her arms, one elbow catching Gabrielle in the chest hard enough to knock her off her feet. She went sprawling backward, flinging her hands out at her sides to catch herself, her startled gaze fixed on the woman before her.

Amy threw off the wrapper and reared up, her head thrashing back and forth wildly, her tangled, strawberry-blond hair whipping through the air, her big bloodied breasts flapping, her teeth barred in a hideous grimace. Then, suddenly, she went rigid, her eyes rolling back in her head as a crescendo of eerie, mad laughter spewed out of her.

"What the hell—" said Jordan, starting forward.

"Stand back." Scrambling to her feet, Gabrielle seized the water pitcher from the washstand and dashed the contents in the face of the hysterical woman.

Water dripped from Amy's drenched hair and glistening wet body. A shudder wracked her naked frame. She sniffed, and her wild, crazy eyes gradually focused on the other woman. "Oh. He *hurt* me," she said with a sob, and fell forward into Gabrielle's arms. Gabrielle clutched the wet, naked, shivering woman to her.

Jordan picked up the wrapper, and draped it around Amy's shoulders again. Over the sobbing woman's head, his gaze met Gabrielle's. He could see the shock and fear lurking in the depths of her eyes, but she had herself well under control. She might be young and inexperienced, he thought, but she was one hell of a strong woman.

"Get her upstairs to her room, if you can," he told her. "I'll send Wing Tsue for the doctor. And, Gabrielle—" She had started to lead the now quietly crying Amy away, but she paused to throw a questioning glance at him over her shoulder. He gave her a lopsided smile. "Your mother couldn't have handled the situation any better than you did."

He meant it as a compliment.

But something in her face told him she didn't take it that way.

Jordan drew hard on his cigarette, sucking the smoke deep into his lungs. Tipping back his head, he stared up at the white, hard moon riding the star-sprinkled infinity arcing over the jagged mountaintops. The sky was a clear purple-black velvet, beautiful enough to make a man ache just looking at it. He exhaled sharply, and watched the blue-gray smoke drift slowly off across the night-darkened yard.

He shifted his hips against the low stone wall that ran along the side of the yard, in the shadow of the hay barn. Golden lamplight spilled out of the house windows to splash across the snow. A sudden eruption of laughter from the front parlor broke the gentle rhythm of the wind soughing through the pines and the creaking of a loose shutter on the old prospector's cabin up the hill. He took another pull on his cigarette, the tip glowing as red as the fires of hell in the blackness of the night.

The sound of the kitchen door opening brought his head around. He watched Gabrielle step out onto the back stoop, her slim frame silhouetted for a moment against the lamp-lit kitchen, before she shut the door behind her and walked down the shallow steps to the yard.

The wind caught the hem of her coat, billowing it around her as she stood in the yard. The wind was warm, adding the drip-drip of melting snow and ice to the other night sounds. But she hugged her arms across her chest as if she were cold. Cold from the inside out.

He took another drag on his cigarette, exhaled slow and easy, and saw her head lift as she caught the scent of his tobacco. It was too dark to see her face clearly, but he felt her eyes searching the darkness. He watched her suck in a breath deep enough to lift her chest, and he knew she was frightened, standing out here in the dark, windblown night.

He brought the cigarette to his lips, the red tip tracing a glowing arc through the shadows. She dropped her arms to her sides and walked toward him through the snow-filled yard, slipping some on the unfamiliar icy ruts. He watched her come at him, but he didn't say anything, even when she drew up some four feet in front of him.

Their gazes caught, and the warm, spring-scented wind gusted between them. Her hair was falling down; fine, moon-paled strands that curled against the graceful arc of her neck. He reached out and touched her there, lightly, just below the ear where the flesh was soft and sensitive. She shivered, but she didn't jerk away.

"Amy is sleeping," she said, as if needing to fill the silence between them. "The doctor gave her a sedative. He said she was more scared than hurt. The cuts weren't deep."

He didn't say anything, just stared at her, wondering why she was here. Wondering why she felt the need to come out here and be with him. And why he was glad she had come.

"I saw her little boy, Henry," Gabrielle continued. "Amy was crying so hard, she woke him up, and he got scared. He's only four. What would have happened to him if that miner had killed her?"

Jordan shrugged. "People die every day."

She shifted to look out over the silent, snow-shrouded

canyon below. "I saw a man killed once. He was knocked down by a beer wagon, in the street in front of the convent. He wasn't watching where he was going, and suddenly veered out into the street, just as the horses swung around the corner. It was an accident. But the man driving that wagon, he went to pieces."

She brought her gaze back to Jordan's face, as if looking for something he knew wasn't there. He could feel the blankness, the coldness of his features, like a betrayal of his humanity. Because in this instance, his face was an accurate mirror of his soul. Inside he felt . . . nothing. Not even mild surprise at his own lack of reaction. He had seen so many men die in the war, that after a while, it didn't matter if he had been the one who killed them or not. They were just . . . dead.

The girl beside him stirred, her feet in their thin-soled shoes moving restlessly in the crusted snow. "Sirena told me tonight that she killed a man once."

"I'd heard it was two." He took a final drag on his cigarette, and dropped it into the snow at his feet.

Gabrielle's gaze traveled over his face. Still searching. "She wasn't convicted, then?"

"No." He ground the glowing tip of his cigarette into ashes beneath the toe of his boot. "Although I understand she didn't deny it. Seems like they decided that the circumstances warranted whatever she'd done. But I'm not sure. It was a couple of years ago. Long before I got here."

"What did you do, before? Before you came here, I mean. To this house."

He gave her a deliberately rakish smile that showed his teeth. "Let's put it this way, there isn't much I didn't do."

She didn't return his smile. "It was the war that

affected you like this, wasn't it?" She gazed off across the darkened valley below. "I suppose in war, one would need to grow accustomed to seeing death. The alternative must surely be madness."

He looked down into her concerned, yet sweetly innocent face, with its softly parted lips and troubled eyes. Something stirred within him, something that was neither innocent nor sweet, but hot and wanting and explicitly carnal. Something that was all wrong for a man like him to be feeling for a woman like her. "Blamin' the war is easy," he said, the taste of his words bitter on his tongue. "But men have always gone to war. Most take no joy in it, and gladly leave the killing behind when they may."

"I see no joy in you," she said in a surprisingly raw, hurting voice, and he noticed the glint of wetness in the corners of her eyes, shining in the moonlight.

He knew he shouldn't touch her again, but he couldn't seem to help it. He ran his fingertips, lightly, along the crest of her cheekbone, brushing her lashes with his knuckles, catching her unshed tears. He rubbed his thumb along the wetness at the side of his finger. "But you see no remorse, either."

He heard her breath catch, then ease out again, like something painful. "What I see is a man who risked his own life to save a woman. To save a little boy's mother for him."

He tangled his fist in her hair, loosening the coil, drawing her closer, until she stood between his spread knees, almost but not quite touching him there. She let out a little mew of surprise, and curled her hand around his wrist. But she didn't hang back.

"What you see is a man who has *killed* boys," he said,

his voice cold and flat. "Boys not much older than Amy's Henry."

Her eyes widened, and she jerked her head sideways, as if in denial. "No."

"Yes." He tightened his grip on her hair, pulling her in until her face was just inches from his, her eyes staring deep into his. He wanted her to see the wasteland within him. He wanted her so scared of him, so repulsed by him, that she would stay the hell away from him. Far, far away.

"I was one of those men who didn't want to leave the killing of the war behind," he said. "I decided I liked death. I went looking for it." It was his own death he sought, his own death that eluded him, but he didn't tell her that. "After Appomattox, I rode south, joined up with a rag-tag group of Texas Rangers."

Her gaze dropped, as if she couldn't bear the desolation she saw in his eyes. She watched his lips, instead.

"One day," he told her, "I got into a shoot-out with three horse thieves I was trailing toward Mexico. They had holed up in some rocks, at the edge of an arroyo, and they shot my horse dead out from under me." He slid his thumb across the fine skin at the nape of her neck. She shuddered, but she still didn't pull away. "They kept me pinned down all afternoon, until eventually I picked them off, one at a time. It wasn't until I worked my way around behind them, to make real sure they were dead, that I realized two of them were only children."

A peculiar sound rose in her throat, but she choked it back down.

"I must have killed their daddy first," he said, "because he looked like he'd been dead for hours by the time I got to them. The older boy died next. I'd say he was eleven, maybe twelve. The little one was still dying when I found him. He couldn't have been more than eight."

"You didn't know," she whispered.

He shook his head. "No. I didn't. But those boys were still dead."

He had expected her to draw back from him in horror. That's why he had told her the story: to make her stay away from him, since he didn't trust himself to stay away from her. Instead she rested her hands on his shoulders. He went utterly still.

"What are you telling me?" she asked, her voice as gentle as a confessor's. "That you felt joy in their killing?"

She was trembling. He could feel it, feel the shudders passing through her slight frame. She had seen a man killed tonight, seen a naked woman left bloodied and hysterical from a knife attack. He should have been trying to comfort her, but he couldn't. He was dead inside. All he could do was keep the deadness within him from contaminating her.

"Joy?" He shook his head. "No. All I could feel was anger. Anger at that dead man, for taking his children out horse stealin', and putting guns in their hands. And anger at the boys themselves. For shooting at me, instead of just giving themselves up after I killed their daddy. And for not aiming well enough to kill me, before I could kill them."

He felt his breath build up in his chest, and expelled it in a harsh sound. His hands slipped down to her waist, drawing her in closer, settling her into the V of his thighs.

And she let him.

She did more than let him. She threaded her fingers through his hair, bracketing his face with her hands. Then she tipped her head, and kissed him.

She brushed his mouth with hers, her lips soft and dry, yet warm and yielding. It was a shy, hesitant, passionless kiss. A kiss that both offered comfort, and sought it. A child's kiss—the kiss of a young woman who had been kissed by a man only once before, and then as a threatening lesson.

He slanted his mouth against hers, returning the pressure, increasing it, sliding his hands up her back to ease her in closer, until her firm young breasts pressed against his chest. Her hands clenched in his hair, clutching him tighter. And a man's hunger surged through him, so powerful and primeval, he shuddered from it.

He wanted her. He wanted to kiss her deep and hot and long and lusty. He wanted to cover her breasts with his hands and feel her squirm with desire against him. He wanted to thrust her back against that damned stone wall and take her the way a man takes a woman he's desperate for—with her skirts rucked up and the wind warm on her naked thighs as he drove into her. Dear God, how he wanted her.

He closed his hands on her upper arms, and set her away from him.

They stared at each other. She was breathing heavily, her delicate nostrils flaring with each indrawn breath, her eyes wide with confusion and shock and something else. Something that looked very much like the glow of passion. Unwilling, perhaps; maybe even unrecognized by her. But Jordan saw it.

He had to splay his hands out flat against the cold stones of the wall behind him, to keep from reaching for her again. "You'd better go inside. Now."

She might have been an innocent, but whatever she

saw in his face was enough to send her scuttling backward. She held his gaze a moment longer, her hand fluttering up to press her fingers to her lips. Then she whirled and darted back toward the house, chasing her own trembling shadow across the snow-filled yard.

He watched her go. The wind gusted around him; a chinook, blowing out of the wild, empty deserts of the southwest. He heard the back door bang closed, heard the pines on the crest of the ridge thrashing back and forth in the turbulent night air.

After she left, he stayed where he was for a long time. Keeping company with a bleak moon, an infinity of distant stars, and a wild wind howling with loneliness and restlessness and an aching, almost unbearable kind of sadness.

Gabrielle heard the wind slam into the side of the house. A gust whistled down the chimney to eddy the fire and send formless, phantom shadows leaping across the carpeted floor and papered walls of her bedroom.

She lay in her bed, her eyes wide open, staring at the intricately tucked and folded satin lining of the canopy above her. He hadn't come in yet. She knew because he occupied the room between her bedroom and the gaming room. Last night she had heard him, when she lay still and he was moving around. She hadn't heard him tonight.

She imagined him out there in the yard right now, his hips resting on the edge of the low stone wall, his man's body a dark, lean silhouette against the snow-covered hillside. Her heart ached with the thought, ached for the loneliness she'd felt within him tonight.

She had thought him dangerously wicked and ungodly

and cold to the point of cruelty, and she knew he was all that and more. But it was the emptiness she had seen in his face, in his eyes, in his soul, that had frightened her more than anything. An emptiness she realized now was not an emptiness at all. Because there is no pain in emptiness, and she had caught an echo of his pain tonight. But only the echo.

It was as if the pain within him were so intense, so unbearable, that he had buried it deep, where he thought no one would ever see it, sense it, recognize it. So deep he must have forgotten it was there himself, for it was that very emptiness, that soullessness, that he had been berating himself for when she went to him.

It was the pain she had reached out to, sought to heal, when she kissed him. His pain and her own fears. And yet . . . and yet when his lips moved beneath hers, she had forgotten his pain, her fear. Forgotten everything but the unexpected wonder of that kiss.

She had always thought his mouth looked hard. But it wasn't hard, it was soft. Soft and warm, and the feel of it, the surprisingly sweet seductive pleasure of his lips opening to hers, stole her breath.

She remembered the heat of his body, pressed against hers, the strength of his hands roaming her back, the sound of her own blood rushing in her ears. And she felt it again, that strange inner clenching, as if something coiled tight, low in her belly. Something needy and wanting and surely sinful.

A week ago she probably wouldn't even have known what that feeling was. She tried to tell herself she might be wrong now, but she had seen too much, heard too much, since coming to this house.

She pressed her palm flat against her lower stomach, as

if she could somehow quell that unfamiliar trembling, stifle the wild, wanton desire that coursed through her. *"Thou art thy mother's glass . . ."* she thought, and she knew a panic that squeezed her chest.

She was the daughter of Celeste DuBois, a fallen woman all too obviously unable to resist the sins of the flesh. Gabrielle wondered if this was how it started, that long slide into carnality and wickedness. With a kiss, and a breathless wanting. A wanting . . .

Dear God. She rolled over and pressed her face into her pillow. Outside the wind moaned, restless and warm. But beneath her satin coverlet, Gabrielle shivered. Shivered with fear and confusion and an aching, seductively beckoning need.

The next day the gulch echoed with the sound of running water. Water poured off the edges of snow-covered roofs, dripped off the leafless branches of the aspens, trickled into tiny gurgling streams that cut across snow-filled clearings and gushed into the swelling creeks.

Jordan paused just inside the door of the livery stable near the base of Nevada Street, and tipped back his head to squint up at the puffs of insubstantial clouds scuttling across a deep blue sky. The warm wind curled around him, a wind pregnant with the secrets of the moist, dark earth and growing things, and sweet with the promise of spring.

Perhaps it was the wind that had stirred the old restlessness within him. The need to be gone, to be moving on. The wind, and memories of what he'd wanted to do last night to Gabrielle Antoine.

He thought about the way her hair had felt, sliding thick and heavy through his fingers. He remembered the sweet taste of her soft lips, moving so tentatively against his. The heady scent of her yielding young body, trembling in his arms.

She was so young, so innocent. And so dangerously ignorant of her own innately passionate nature. He'd seen the way she looked at him, the way she watched him. It would be too easy to tempt her, to charm her, to woo her, to seduce her.

To ruin her.

He let his breath out in a long hard sigh. He knew she thought he was a cold, hard bastard, but he wasn't that much of a bastard.

A gig flashed past, driven at a pace that sent mud spraying out from its wheels. Big globs of gumbo hit the side of the livery with a sodden splat. Thanks to the sudden thaw, the streets were already running a good twelve inches deep with muddy slush. If it kept up at this rate, Jordan thought, they were liable to have a flood.

He saw her then. She was coming down the hill from the house, taking tentative little steps that still had her slip-sliding every which way. She had the hood of her coat thrown back, letting the sunshine warm the golden hair she wore coiled in a neat braid high on the nape of her slender neck. Jordan let his gaze linger a moment too long on that sleek, sun-kissed plait.

She hadn't seen him yet. She had her head bowed, her chin tucked to her chest, her gaze carefully fastened on the slippery, icy slush that still covered the boardwalk at her feet. He noticed the side of her coat was caked with snow, and he figured she must have already fallen, at least once.

He leaned against the stable door and thumbed his hat back on his head, a slow smile tugging at his lips as he

waited to see what she was going to do when she suddenly ran out of boardwalk.

With her head bent like that, she didn't see the end of
the planks until she was right on top of the livery stable.
She slid to a halt, staring at the twelve feet of oozing,
foul-smelling muck that stretched between where she
stood, and where the boardwalk started up again on the
other side. Her gaze dropped to the tips of the thin-soled
city boots just visible beneath the hem of her gray Ulster
coat, and he saw her swallow as she tried to figure out
how the hell she was going to get across that sticky,
stinking morass without ruining her pretty shoes.

A door slammed on one of the houses up the hill
behind her. She twisted around to watch as a middle-aged
matron carrying a shopping basket let herself out her
garden gate and walked down the slope toward them.
When she reached the livery stable, the woman hitched
up her skirt and petticoats to expose a pair of serviceable
brown boots and an unappetizing expanse of fleshy calf
partially encased in long red flannel underwear. Shoul-
dering past Gabrielle, she waded unconcernedly through
the fifthly quagmire, then clambered up on the boardwalk
of the far side, dropped her skirts, and stomped off,
leaving little clumps of mud in her wake.

Gabrielle stared after the woman, then down at her own
skirts. Gingerly, she clutched fistfuls of coat, dress, and
petticoat, and eased them up. Jordan watched as a pair of
slim ankles and shapely calves, chastely encased in black
cotton stockings, came into view beneath a froth of ruffled,
lace-trimmed petticoats. But then she just stood there, her
skirts lifted high, her horrified gaze locked on the oozing,
freezing, stinking mud before her.

"That is, of course, one alternative," he said with an

easy drawl as he stepped out of the barn's shadowy interior, into the fitful sunlight. "Although I'm afraid it'll ruin your pretty black leather shoes."

She jerked and dropped her skirts, her gaze snapping to his laughing face. "Mr. Hays. I . . . I did not see you standing there."

He went up to her, his boots making sucking, plopping noises as he waded through the mire. He could see the stain of embarrassment that rode high on her cheeks, although he didn't know if it was the glimpse she'd just given him of her legs, or something else, that had put it there. The memory of what had happened last night hung in the air between them, charging the atmosphere with a subtle nuance that hadn't been there before.

"You need a sturdy pair of boots," he said, bracing the muck-covered sole of one of his own boots against the edge of the boardwalk beside her, so that he could rest his forearm on his bent knee. "That is, if you're still planning on stayin' here."

She lifted her eyes to his. "I am staying."

He held her gaze steadily. "Well, then," he said, after the briefest of pauses, "you ought to get yourself something like our sensible housewife there was wearing." He nodded toward the woman's receding broad rump. "And it wouldn't hurt to get yourself a warmer pair of gloves while you're at it. This thaw could last anywhere from a few hours to a week, but you can bet anything you want, we haven't seen the last of the snow and cold yet."

"It was my intention to purchase some more suitable footgear," she said. He watched an unexpected gleam of amusement light up her eyes. "Reaching the store to make my purchase appears to be the problem."

He let his breath out in a soft laugh, and she laughed

with him. Her laughter was a sweet, lighthearted sound that left him with a desire to hear it again, to see her smile again. "That problem's easy enough to solve." He straightened up, and clambered onto the walk beside her. "I'll carry you across."

"Oh, dear me, no. It would be most improper. I mean ..." Her voice trailed off as she glanced, once again, at the mire ahead of her.

He gathered her up in his arms before she had a chance to do more than yelp, and hopped off the boardwalk, his booted feet landing with a squelching *splat* in the oozing yellow mud.

CHAPTER TEN

"Mr. Hays!" Gabrielle felt a strong arm curl around her upper waist, and another catch her behind her knees. "Oh, my goodness." She clutched frantically at the lapels of his fine black coat as he swept her up into the air and stepped forward. "Put me down!"

Mud oozed up over the toes of his boots, making squishing noises with each step he took, and stirring up rank odors of damp hay and horse manure. "Now?" he said, his eyes alight with silent laughter. "Are you quite certain? Well, if you insist . . ." He stopped.

"Not here." She cast a quick glance at the golden-brown muck lapping against his ankles, and wrapped her arms around his neck.

He gave her a grin that caught strangely at something deep within her. "No?"

"No," she said, trying to frown at him. Only it was a struggle to try to look affronted, when she wanted so desperately to laugh. This was a side of him she'd only glimpsed before, a rascally, teasing side. A side she found she liked, even though she didn't want to.

He raised one eyebrow. "You're certain? Because if you really don't want me to carry you, I can put you down . . ." And he made as if to let her slide down his long body into the mud.

She squealed, and tightened her grip on his broad shoulders. "You wretched beast," she said with a gasp, laughing now in spite of herself. "Don't you dare put me down here."

"A wretched beast, is it?" he said, bouncing his eyebrows up and down lasciviously. "I should have warned you that if you start calling me names, the price doubles."

Her heartbeat gave a peculiar, kicking little *thump-bump*. "What price?"

"I did mention, didn't I, that I charge a slight cartage fee?"

"No, you did not. What kind of a fee?"

That teasing smile curled his lips, but the light in his eyes had changed from a simple gleam of amusement to something hotter, something that looked almost *hungry*. "A kiss," he said softly.

She sucked in a quick, startled breath, her gaze caught fast by his. She was suddenly, achingly conscious of the heat of his arms, pressing into her back, gripping her knees. She thought she had never been this aware of her own body before, of the swelling of her breasts against the bodice of her dress, and the easing of the cold mountain air in and out of her chest. "And if I don't pay?" she asked, her voice sounding oddly husky, unlike her own voice at all. "Will you put me down here?"

"Miss Antoine, how can you think so unhandsomely of me? Of course I'll take you back to where I found you." And he swung about, as if genuinely intent on leaving her marooned on that far boardwalk.

"Wait!"

He stopped.

She felt a tingling rush of fear and excitement. "This is blackmail."

"Yes."

"You are no gentleman," she said, half laughing, half in a panic.

His grin widened. "There you have it. My mama tried real hard to make me into a gentleman, but it just didn't stick. Now, do I get that kiss or not?"

She stared at his lips, just inches from hers, and that strange, warm ache bloomed again, deep within her. "Your cheek," she said, barely pushing the words out. "I'll kiss your cheek."

Their gazes met for one suspended moment. "Not what I had in mind, but I guess it'll have to do." He turned his head, presenting her with one lean, tanned cheek.

She gazed at his dark, cleanly shaved face. It looked surprisingly smooth. The wind gusted around them, warm and playful, ruffling the exposed flounces of her petticoats, and fluttering the silk tie around his strong throat. A Dougherty wagon rolled past, its heavy wheels plowing through the slushy street. From the depths of the livery came the *ping-ping* of a blacksmith's hammer.

"I don't mean to sound impatient," he said as she continued to stare at him. "But you aren't as light as a person might think, just lookin' at you. And if you mean to be all day about it, I can't guarantee I might not accidentally drop you. Not that I'd mean to, of course," he added, letting her slip a fraction of an inch.

Gabrielle tightened her hold on his neck, squeezed her eyes shut, and kissed him.

She discovered that his cheek was as smooth as it looked. Smooth and warm and undeniably pleasant against her lips. She let her breath out in a long, slow sigh, and opened her eyes.

She tried to tell herself it was nothing, just a quick, light kiss, a child's brushing of the lips. Only she was not a child, she was a woman. A woman who was learning that a kiss could be more than a chaste token of affection. That a kiss could be something sensual. Something disturbing. Something dangerous.

He turned his head and stared at her. His mouth was so close to hers that she could feel the moist warmth of his exhalation, caressing her lips. He had such deep green eyes, she thought; flecked with star bursts of black, radiating out from his pupils. Eyes that could look so cold, sometimes. But not now. Now they burned with a dark, compelling heat.

A shudder seemed to pass through him. He shifted her weight against his chest and churned through the last few feet of mud with long, swift strides. He set her down on the opposite boardwalk without climbing up onto it himself, and stepped back. He let her go so abruptly, she staggered, and had to fling out a hand to brace herself against the rough planks of the livery stable wall.

Their gazes locked, and it was as if something shimmered in the wind-warmed air between them. A tension, an awareness, a quickening that echoed the unfamiliar, nameless wants he stirred within her. She sucked in a deep breath. And then, because one wasn't enough, she took another. What he stirred within her was dangerous and frightening, sinful and fascinating. Like him.

"Th-thank you for your assistance, Mr. Hays." She gave him a trembling smile, trying to regain that light, teasing note that had started all this.

She thought he might smile back at her, but he didn't.

His face had gone blank, and cold. He jerked his head toward the darkened interior of the livery. "I'm having a shoe replaced on one of the horses. As soon as the smithy's finished, I'll get the shay and wait for you on Eureka Street."

"Thank you, but that won't be necessary."

"Oh, but it is," he drawled. "A rough mining town like this, you never can tell what kind of men a lady might run into."

"Oh? And do you think me incapable of dealing with insult?"

And then he did smile, a lifting of the corners of his mouth that deepened the creases in his cheeks and caused a peculiar, but faintly pleasant flutter in her chest. "I imagine you could handle an insult just fine, Miss Antoine. It's the misguided attempts at gallantry you need to learn to watch out for."

Doug Slaughter tilted back his chair and propped one booted foot up on the burgundy leather top of his desk at the Silver Spur. His hands moved slowly over the red silk-covered bottom of the hurdy-gurdy girl he held nestled against his crotch, but he kept his gaze fixed on the tall, lanky man with thin blond hair and watery blue eyes, who shifted nervously in the chair on the far side of the desk.

"You owe me a thousand dollars," Slaughter said around the unlit cigar he held clenched between his teeth. "And I'm tired of waiting for it."

A burst of music and laughter billowed up from downstairs. Frank Whitney's prominent Adam's apple bobbed up and down in his skinny neck as he swallowed hard, trying to find his voice. "Next week. I promise. I'll get it to you next week. Or at least some—"

"I don't think you heard me very clearly, Frank." Slaughter leaned forward to pluck a safety match from the tin on his desk. "I want it now."

"But I don't—I can't—"

"Frank." Slaughter made a sad *tssking* sound with his tongue. "I hope you're not trying to tell me you don't have it. And here I thought the dealers at Celeste's Place made such good money."

"We do. But coming up with a thousand dollars all at once . . ."

"You should have thought of that before you asked to play on credit." He struck the match and sucked on his cigar.

Frank Whitney's tongue flicked out to moisten his cracked lips. "If I could have just a bit more time."

"No." Slaughter tugged at the hurdy-gurdy girl's bodice until one of her ripe breasts tumbled out to fill his hand. "I want my money by this Friday, Frank. All of it. Or the consequences will be . . . nasty."

Frank's gaze had fastened onto Slaughter's hand, squeezing and undulating that big, blue-veined breast. Now, his pale, scared eyes jerked back to Slaughter's face. "But I can't come up with that kind of money by the end of the week."

"You could earn it."

Frank screwed his chin sideways and eased a finger beneath his celluloid collar, as if it suddenly felt too tight. "You mean, come work for you here?"

"Not exactly. You work for me. But not here."

"I don't understand."

"It's not that complicated." Slaughter used his tongue

to shift the tip of his cigar from one side of his mouth to the other. "Celeste's Place might have a reputation for clean play, but I've never met a dealer yet that didn't know how to cheat when he wanted to. You know how to cheat, don't you, Frank?"

Frank started to shake his head, then changed it to a nod.

"You don't have to be real good at cheating, Frank. In fact, you're going to be clumsy. So clumsy you get caught."

"I don't understand."

"You keep saying that, Frank. It's starting to get on my nerves." He swung his foot off the desk and brushed the half-naked girl off his lap, as if she were a cat he'd tired of scratching. "Do my back," he said, and she shifted behind his chair to massage his shoulders. She made a move as if to pull up her dress, but he said, "No, leave it."

He flicked the ash off his cigar, and pointed the smoking tip at the man across from him. "I'm gonna be real generous with you, Frank. Real generous. I'm gonna pay you fifteen hundred dollars just to keep doin' your job up at Celeste's Place. All you gotta do is cheat."

"But . . ." The dealer tugged at his collar again. "But a man can get himself shot if he's caught cheating."

"Men get shot for lots of things, Frank. Cheating is one. Not payin' their debts is another. Do I make myself clear?"

Frank nodded, his face a pasty white.

"Besides," said Slaughter, "the man you're going to cheat won't be shooting at you. That's not part of the plan." He reached around to grip the hurdy-gurdy girl's wrist. Pulling her in front of him again, he shoved her facedown across the desk before him.

Frank lurched nervously to his feet and began to edge toward the door.

Slaughter gave him a grin that showed his teeth. "Talk to Tucker downstairs. He'll explain exactly what I want from you, and give you five hundred now. The rest you get when the job's finished. Now, get out of here. I'm busy." He tossed up the woman's skirts and jerked down her drawers, then stood up, fumbling with his trouser buttons.

He heard the door click open, then slam shut again, but he didn't bother to look up. He was too busy enjoying the way the pink curve of the girl's bare bottom looked, stuck up in the air. He freed himself from his trousers with a grunt of satisfaction. And smiled as he drove into her.

That afternoon, before the house opened, Gabrielle took the back stairs from the kitchen to the third floor.

Until the shooting she had never ventured into this part of the house. She had expected it to be much like the first and second floors: dark, and oppressively luxurious, with a suffocating kind of sensual opulence. Instead she found it airy and comfortable and surprisingly homey.

But she still didn't like coming up here. It made her feel closer, somehow, to the wicked, carnal things that happened on the second floor. And for all her pious words about Christ and Mary Magdalen, for all the feelings of guilt and remorse that had driven her to move into this house, for all her desire to better understand the woman who had been her mother, Gabrielle still instinctively shrank back with a repressed kind of horror from the things that were done here, and the women who did them.

The door to Amy's room stood partly ajar. Gabrielle could hear voices, from the other side of the panel, and it was with a self-conscious sense of intruding that she shifted the small sack of penny candy she had bought to her left hand, and raised her fist to knock.

The voices broke off. "Come in," Amy called.

Gabrielle pushed open the door. Amy sat up in bed, the house's orange and white tabby cat curled up asleep beside her on the counterpane. In a slat-backed chair near the head of the bed, the petite, fair-haired woman called Jilly nursed a sleepy toddler. Jilly usually entertained in little more than a black and red corset and black stockings, and it occurred to Gabrielle that this was probably the first time she had seen the woman wearing a dress.

Both women's heads turned toward the door, their animated faces sliding into masks of wariness at the sight of Gabrielle. "Good afternoon," she said, embarrassed by the stilted formality of her voice, but unable to do anything about it. "I came to see how you were feeling today, Amy."

"Oh . . . I'm feelin' right faint," Amy said, sliding farther down in bed, as if suddenly overcome by weakness. "Real faint. Jordan, he says I don't got to go back to work for at least a week or two. I need to ree-coop-er-ate, he says." She stared at Gabrielle belligerently, as if she suspected Gabrielle might try to cut short her holiday.

"Why, yes. Of course," Gabrielle said hastily. Her gaze wandered around the room, to the child's truckle bed in the corner, and the untidy pile of blocks and carved wooden horses tumbling out of a wicker basket. She held up the paper sack of penny candy. "I brought something for Henry and the other children, but they don't seem to be around."

"They're probably still in the turret room," said Jilly, shifting the weight of the child in her lap. "Sirena tries to take them for a couple of hours every afternoon."

"Why?" asked Gabrielle, watching the tender smile that lifted the corners of Jilly's lips as she stared down at her sleeping son.

"For lessons," said Amy, stroking the tabby cat's back. "They used to go to school in town, but that closed last year. And even before that, the teacher and the other kids all give 'em such a hard time that Benjamin Franklin and Arabella wagged most days, and Jackson wasn't much better. So Sirena's been teachin' 'em herself for the better part of a year now."

"Sirena?" Gabrielle shook her head. She could not begin to imagine that fierce, frightening woman as a teacher.

From the other end of the hall came the sound of children's high-pitched voices, reciting the four times table. Gabrielle turned toward it. "Excuse me," she said.

She followed the voices to the front of the house. At the open door to the turret room, she paused, her hand on the jamb, and quietly watched for a moment.

Sunshine flooded through the big bay window that matched the one in the gaming room downstairs. The room was larger than most of the other rooms on the third floor, although it was only simply furnished, with a long pine table flanked by straight-backed chairs, and a shelf of books. Amy's little boy, Henry, sat cross-legged in a patch of sunlight on the floor. He held a slate balanced on his lap, and had his tongue pressed against his lower lip as he labored to copy something on his board. Gabrielle smiled. He was only four, and she suspected he came here largely because the other children did.

The older children were gathered around the table. Arabella and Benjamin Franklin and Jackson, the dusky-skinned son of Margot. One of the women was here, too: Youngmi, the Chinese girl.

She sat with her head bowed, a book gripped against the front of her *chang-fu*. " 'Mrs. Pepper saw what the children had done,' " she read in a halting, expressionless voice, " 'and flew into a rage.' " She paused, a frown wrinkling her nose. "Does this girl have that right, Sirena? It make no sense. How can this woman fly? And what is this rage she fly into?" She looked up, saw Gabrielle, and went, *"Oh."*

Sirena had been standing at Youngmi's shoulder. Now she turned, her expression unwelcoming.

"I didn't mean to interrupt," said Gabrielle, conscious of the silent, curious stares of the children.

Sirena lifted one shoulder in a casual shrug. "It was time to quit anyway." She nodded to the tensely expectant children. "You can pack up now." The children wiggled out of their seats and banged their books together, so that she had to raise her voice to be heard. "Jackson and Henry, you keep practicing those letters on your slates. And Arabella and Benjamin Franklin, I want you to learn those times tables. By Monday," she called after them as the children tore out the door.

Gabrielle looked at this woman, with her lightly painted cheeks and kohl-lined eyes, with her low-cut satin dress, and a child's ink-stained primer in her hand. And it was as if a part of Gabrielle's universe slipped, then realigned itself, although nothing was in quite the same place as it had been before.

"Race you down the stairs!" called Arabella from the hall.

"You cheated!" sputtered Benjamin Franklin. "You already started."

"Oh, dear," said Gabrielle, suddenly remembering the bag of penny candy she still clutched in her hand. "I forgot I brought this for the children." She held it out.

"Leave it, if you like," said Sirena, taking the bag from her. "I'll see they get it."

Youngmi slid out of her seat and bowed. "This girl go now," she said, and bolted out the door almost as fast as the children.

Gabrielle gazed after her. "Why is Youngmi here?"

Sirena reached to gather up the books left scattered on the table. "She wants to improve her English. She thinks maybe learning to read it will help."

"You mean, she wants to get a different job?" Gabrielle asked, encouraged.

Sirena gave her an enigmatic look. "No. She wants to speak English better."

Gabrielle wandered over to stare out the window at the snow-covered canyon, and the mountains beyond. "I don't understand why Youngmi is in this house at all," she said after a moment. "I mean, she didn't choose this life, and she had a chance to get out of it. So why is she still doing . . . what she is doing?"

"You mean whoring?"

"Yes," said Gabrielle, feeling her cheeks grow hot. *Someday,* she thought, *I am going to hear that word and not blush.*

Sirena stacked the books on the low shelf near the bay window, and stooped to pick up Henry's abandoned slate.

"Youngmi says she's no longer fit to be the wife of a decent man, so this must be her destiny."

"But—she doesn't seem to enjoy it."

Sirena paused, the slate in her hand, a hard smile curving her lips, glittering in her dark eyes. "You think the rest of us enjoy it?" Sirena swiped her hand through the air in a quick, angrily dismissive gesture. "Oh, I know it's what they teach—all those soft-handed, fat preachers, standing up in their flower-scented, white-painted churches, breathing fire and brimstone over their cream-fed, pinched-mouthed parishioners. They think we can't wait to get our hands on what the men who come here every night have dangling between their legs. That we never get enough of taking it between *our* legs. Well, let me tell you, the only difference between Youngmi and most of the other girls in this business is that she hasn't been doing it long enough to get over the shame of it, and she's not as good as the rest of us at pretending."

I will not ask if she enjoys it, Gabrielle thought. *It would be most improper.* She cleared her throat. "Don't you enjoy it?"

Sirena stared at her for so long, Gabrielle decided the woman wasn't going to answer. "Not in the way you think," she said at last. She turned away to collect some papers.

"But—if you don't enjoy it, why do any of you do it?"

Sirena swung around to lean against the low window-sill, her arms crossed at her chest, that hard smile twisting her lips again. "Do you have any idea how much money your average cowboy makes a month?"

Gabrielle shook her head.

"Thirty dollars. Thirty lousy dollars, which works out to about a dollar a day. Those miners out there"—she jerked her head toward the surrounding hills—"they make three dollars a day, and risk their lives every time they go down a shaft. Now, the laziest, sleaziest whore in the cheapest honky-tonk in town collects three dollars from every man she drops her drawers for, and she gets to keep at least a dollar and a half of that. Which means that if she entertains twenty men a night . . . Well, you figure it out."

Gabrielle felt the bile rise in her throat. Twenty men a night. *Twenty men.* She drew in a deep, shuddering breath, and turned away from the scorn she could read in the other woman's face. Away from the raw glimpse of reality the woman had given her. She forced herself to concentrate on this room, with its sturdy pine table and neat rows of chairs. "This is a good thing," she said, her voice oddly hoarse. "What you do for these children."

Sirena shrugged and pushed away from the windowsill. "They've got enough strikes against them in this life, just by being born in a whorehouse, poor little bastards. They don't need to be ignorant, too."

"I'd like to help," said Gabrielle. "It's what I did, before I left New Orleans." She started to say it was what she wanted to do with this house, once she owned it outright. But then she remembered she had promised Jordan Hays not to say anything about her plans until the three months were up, so she kept still about it.

Sirena shrugged again. "If you'd like."

Gabrielle smiled. "I'll enjoy it." She let her gaze drift, once again, around that makeshift schoolroom.

I could have been one of these children, she thought with a rush of painful emotions. She could have grown up in this house, rejected by the townspeople, forced to learn her lessons in a makeshift attic schoolroom.

There but for the grace of God, she thought humbly. There but for the grace of God . . .

The *bang* of the front-door knocker echoed through the house. Halfway down the wide, curving staircase, Gabrielle froze, her hand gripping the banister. She hadn't expected the house to be receiving customers this early, but she should have thought to use the back stairs anyway. A man coming into the parlor now to find her on the stairs could surely be forgiven for thinking she worked here.

Wing Tsue had already appeared from nowhere, gliding across the thick carpet in his white slippers to swing open the door. It always amazed her that such a big man could move so quietly. Gabrielle whirled about, ready to dart back up the stairs, then heard him say, "A desk? No, I don't know where it goes." He glanced at Gabrielle over his shoulders. "Miss Antoine?"

Reluctantly she came the rest of the way down the stairs and passed through the bead curtain into the hall. "What is it?" she asked.

Two men, one a big redhead with ruddy cheeks and a full mustache, the other man smaller, darker, waited on the porch, an elegant, cabriole-legged desk held between them. "Sure then, 'tes bought and paid for," said the red-headed man, his cheek distended by a wad of chewing tobacco. "All we're supposed to do is deliver it. But if you don't know where you want to put it, I'm thinking we can leave it right here." They made as if to set the desk down on the porch.

"No, wait." Gabrielle stared at the exquisitely worked piece of furniture. She could think of only one person who could have ordered such a thing. "Bring it this way," she said, and went ahead of them to open the door to Jordan Hays's room.

She had never been in his room before. It was similar to hers, although narrower. The walls were hung with champagne-and-burgundy-striped silk, the drapes a heavy burgundy brocade. It was simply furnished, with a brass-knobbed, black iron bedstead, a walnut armoire and wash-stand, and two round tables, one next to the wing chair beneath the window, the other beside the bed.

"Here?" asked the redheaded deliveryman, shifting his chew.

"Yes, that's fine," Gabrielle said as they dumped the desk near the fireplace. "Thank you."

She stood back to let them pass, but the man with the red hair and mustache stopped in front of her, and looked her up and down in a way that had Gabrielle plucking nervously at the high lace collar of her simple brown wool dress.

"My name is Sean O'Neal," he said, leaning in close enough that she could see the veins in his ruddy cheeks. "Are you a new upstairs girl here? Because if you are, I'm thinking I sure would like to be one of your first customers."

Gabrielle's hand itched to slap his face. But she had promised not to do anything to adversely effect Mr. Hays's profits for the next three months, so she forced herself to give the man a cool smile. "No, Mr. O'Neal, I do not work upstairs. But if you would like to come back later, I'm sure you could find someone who interested you."

"Damn," said O'Neal, shaking his head as he went out the door. "What a waste of prime woman flesh."

Her cheeks flaming with embarrassment, Gabrielle stayed where she was, her shoulders pressed against the silk-hung wall of Jordan Hays's bedroom, and listened to the stomping of the men's hobnailed boots as they trooped down the hall and out of the house. She waited until she heard the front door slam behind them, then pushed away from the wall. Only instead of turning around and walking out the way she should have, she went to stand in the middle of the floor.

She breathed in air pleasantly scented with leather and tobacco. It was a scent that went with the man, she thought. A manly scent. She told herself again that she should leave, but something drew her forward. Being in his room, she thought, was like catching a glimpse of the part of himself he always kept hidden. The part that seemed to intrigue her more and more each day.

She wandered over to the small, marble-topped table beside his bed. It held an oil lamp with an etched glass shade, and a stack of books. One of the books, a slim volume bound in blue leather, was charred on the edges, as if it had been left too close to a fire at some time.

Intrigued, she picked it up, and turned it over in her hands. It was a copy of Blake's *Songs of Experience*. She started to open it, and paused when she saw something written on the flyleaf. The ink had faded with time, but she could still make out the words someone had penned in an elegant, flowing copperplate. *To my husband on his twenty-second birthday. Happy birthday, Jordan. All my love forever, Sophie.*

Gabrielle's hands trembled so badly she almost dropped the book. She wished she hadn't seen it. It was too personal, too intimate. Too much a part of the painful shadows she had glimpsed behind the coldness in his hard green eyes.

She shut the book, but it was already too late. Even before she looked up, she knew he was there.

CHAPTER
ELEVEN

He stood in the open doorway, watching her. He must have only just come in, for he still wore his sheepskin jacket and his black Stetson, pulled low over his eyes. He had brought the crisp, wood-smoke and pine-scented air of the mountains in with him, and it hung about him now, making her shiver. His face looked cold, closed; it seemed difficult to believe this was the same man who had teased her and laughed with her just a few hours ago.

She set the book on the table. "I'm sorry," she said, lacing her fingers together before her. "It was wrong of me."

He didn't say anything, just stood in the doorway and stared at her.

"They delivered your desk. At least I assume you're the one who ordered it." She was talking too much, too fast, in a sudden need to fill that awful silence. "I had them put it by the fireplace. But if you'd like to move it, I'll ask Wing Tsue—"

"It's fine where it is."

Her chest felt tight, as if she were running out of air. She sucked in a deep breath. "I thought you used the desk in Celeste's office."

"I did. I decided it would be a good idea to get one of my own."

"Oh. I see." She wished he would move away from the door so that she could get out of the room without having to pass close to him. Only he didn't budge, so she had no choice but to walk toward him. She was almost abreast of him when he reached out his hand and caught her arm, just above the elbow. She went utterly still.

"You know why, don't you?"

Her head fell back, and she stared up into his face, at the arrogant flaring of his cheekbones and the almost frighteningly taut line of his mouth. "No," she said.

He framed her face with his hand, his thumb sliding across her lower lip as he spoke. "You think that because I know you are a virgin, and because I was your mother's friend, that you are safe with me. But you are not."

She quivered beneath his touch. "Why?" she asked, her voice only a whisper. "Because you are cold and hard and uncaring?" She shook her head. "I don't believe it."

He swayed toward her, his hand still cupping her cheek, his hard gaze fastened on her mouth. She thought he meant to kiss her, and she waited, tingling with fear and longing as she watched his lips move. "Believe it," he said. "And stay away from me." He dropped his hand, and shoved away from the door frame, moving past her into his room.

She whisked herself through the open doorway. The cool air of the deserted hall hit her in the face, bathing her heated cheeks. She sucked in a deep breath, and glanced back at him.

He stood beside the marble-topped table, the charred book in his hand. He wasn't looking at her, and she thought he had probably forgotten she even was there.

She watched him run his slim, gambler's fingers over the book's ruined spine, as if he could touch the past. As if he could touch the woman named Sophie. His wife.

Something wild and needy welled up within Gabrielle. Something wild and needy, and lonely and frightening. She brought her hand up to press it flat against her chest. But nothing could still the painful pounding of her heart.

That night Gabrielle wrote a long-overdue letter to Julia St. Etienne.

She curled up in the chair beside the fire in her room, a pad of paper in her lap, a bottle of ink on the table beside her. She dipped her pen, then let the ink dry as she stared unseeingly into the dancing golden flames. She ached with the need to confide in her friend, yet she found she balked at the thought of pouring out in a letter all that she had learned, all that had happened to her over the last few days.

So she told Julia that she had discovered her mother, but not that she herself was now living in a house of ill repute. She described for her friend the rugged beauty of the mountains, the raw roughness of the town, the sheer wonder of the snow. But she could not bring herself to talk about Jordan Hays, or the strange, frightening, sinful desires he stirred so deep within her.

She had expected that writing to Julia would make her feel better. But when she finished the letter, she found herself weighed down, almost suffocated by her sadness, and she sighed as she set the pages aside.

She could never go back to New Orleans, she realized with a sudden sense of despair. Not now. Not knowing what she knew. Everyone there would expect her to be the same person she had always been. The person she no longer was.

She leaned her head against the chair back and closed her eyes, letting her thoughts drift over the warm, honeysuckle-scented days of her childhood. Days filled with the sweet song of the mockingbird and the distant chug of paddle steamers, working their way up a mud-thick river beneath a sultry sky. She remembered the laughter of children echoing through a high-walled convent garden, and Julia's tremulous smile when she kissed Gabrielle's cheek, and said good-bye.

Then she dropped her face in her hands, and wept.

For three days the warm wind they called a chinook blew out of the southwest, melting the snow and swelling the creeks with runoff. And for three days Gabrielle stayed away from Jordan Hays, and he stayed away from her.

Her evenings at the piano in the front parlor grew no easier. She tried to concentrate on her music, tried to block out the scenes of licentious debauchery being enacted around her. But her imagination betrayed her. It seemed as if nothing could make her forget about what was happening upstairs on those wide, satin-draped beds. Nothing could stop her from picturing the flicker of the lamplight, the gleam of mirrors, the urgent, breathless wrestling of entwined bodies.

And nothing could diminish her awareness of Jordan Hays, her consciousness of his nearness, just across the hall, in the gaming room.

He never approached her, never came near her. But sometimes, she knew, he stood on the other side of the bead curtain, quietly watching her from the hall. She would feel his presence there, like a burning heat.

By the middle of the week, Gabrielle realized that her life at Celeste's Place was beginning to fall into a kind of pattern. Her world became the world of darkness, of candlelight. She sought her bed so late at night, that by the time she arose, the day was half gone. Most afternoons she spent in the turret room with Sirena and the children, although she tried to devote at least an hour or two to sorting through her mother's papers.

She had so many questions she was desperate to have answered. Questions about Celeste, about her family, about her earlier life. Yet as the days passed, Gabrielle knew a growing fear. A fear that she was never going to know any more than she knew now. That she would never know the name of the man who had fathered her simply because Celeste herself had never known.

Sighing, Gabrielle closed the box of letters she'd been reading, and set it back on the shelf. It was still early afternoon, but a shadowed hush had fallen over the room. Crossing to the window, she pulled back the lace panel, and found herself looking out onto a world of white. White clouds, white, thick-falling snowflakes, and a fresh layer of new-fallen snow that covered everything in sight.

"Oh," she whispered, pressing her fingertips to the cold glass. It looked so beautiful out there. A world of enchantment, of peace. She wanted to go stand in that white nebula and let the quiet majesty of the mountains in winter envelope her, soothe her.

The tick of the Louis XVI clock on the mantel intruded upon her. She glanced toward it, hoping to see that she had time. But she was already late for her lessons with the children.

She put out the brass desk lamp and hurried to climb the back stairs. She scooted past the second floor, unable, as always, to do more than cast a swift, guilty glance at that place of sinful decadence, of wickedness. She didn't even breathe until she reached the third floor hall.

She could already hear the children's voices, raised in a kind of collective, pleading whine, long before she arrived at the schoolroom.

"But it's probably the last real heavy snowfall we're gonna get," said Benjamin Franklin.

Henry's voice piped up. "I wanna make a snowm'n."

Gabrielle reached the open doorway in time to see Arabella lay a coaxing hand on Sirena's arm and flash a beguiling smile worthy of Crystal herself. "Oh, *please*, Miss Sirena. Can't we go?"

Sirena's head came up, her gaze catching Gabrielle's, a slow, rare smile softening her face. "What do you think?"

"Well . . ." Gabrielle hesitated, conscious herself of the pull of gently falling snow and clean white fields.

She felt a tug at her skirt, and looked down into Henry's big blue eyes. "Have you ever made a snowm'n, Miss Gabrielle?" he asked.

Gabrielle shook her head. "No, I never have. It doesn't snow where I grew up."

"I can show you how to do it. I'm real good at makin' snowm'n. 'Specially their heads." He shifted his intense gaze to Sirena.

"All right." Sirena threw up her hands. "Go on, then." The children whooped and ran laughing from the room, while Sirena sent Gabrielle a quizzical look and added, "After all, I wouldn't want to stand in the way of Miss Gabrielle's education."

* * *

Gabrielle was pulling on her coat when she heard the thud of a snowball, slamming into the side of the house just below her window. A shriek of childish delight rang out, followed by a man's throaty laugh.

Jordan's laugh.

She paused, her fist tightening around her mittens. Moving so that she stood in the shadows cast by the heavy bedroom drapes, she peered through the window.

It took her a moment to find him. He lay sprawled spread-eagle in the snow, his legs moving back and forth, his arms sweeping up and down in a strange motion she could not understand. Arabella lay head-to-head with him, her little arms and legs making the same peculiar strokes. As Gabrielle watched, man and child sat up. Carefully hoisting themselves to their feet, they twisted around to inspect the imprints they had left in the powder.

Squinting against the snow glare, Gabrielle could just make out the shadowy impressions, as if two angels, one long and lean, the other small and well padded, had lain down to rest in the snow. As she watched, the man and the little girl looked at each other, and Jordan laughed again, his light, easy smile disguising the hardness of his lips.

Gabrielle's hand tightened around the curtain, a painful rush of feelings swelling inside her. She saw him turn toward the house and throw one arm across Arabella's shoulders. The movement pulled at his sheepskin jacket, showing Gabrielle the gun on his hip.

It should have shocked her to realize that even when he played with the children, he wore his gun. Instead she thought what a contradiction this man was. He thought he cared for nothing and no one. Yet, as she watched him smile again at the fatherless child beside him, Gabrielle knew it was a lie. A lie he told himself.

Confused and suddenly, oddly afraid, she jerked away from the window and reached for her hat.

Outside she paused at the top of the front steps and drew in a deep breath of clear, fresh air. The day was cold, but not piercingly so. Perhaps spring really was on its way.

A ball of snow shattered at her feet to go skidding across the wooden planks of the porch. Startled, she jumped. Then her head fell back, and she found herself staring into Jordan Hays's laughing green eyes and dark, handsome face. He looked so big and strong, standing there in his black Stetson, silhouetted against the white, jagged peaks of the mountains, that he took her breath away.

"You missed," she said.

"Nope. That was just to wake you up."

She laughed lightly. She liked him best like this, when he wore his charming, rascal's smile, and buried the shadows and the danger so deep she could forget, at least for a while, that they were there. Except, when he was like this, she sometimes forgot to be afraid of him. Forgot that she *should* be afraid of him. Forgot to stay away from him.

She stooped down to scoop up a handful of fresh snow from the edge of the steps, and tapped it into a ball. He eyed these preparations with his arms crossed at his chest, his grin deepening. "You plannin' to throw that at someone?"

"You think I couldn't hit the broad side of a boxcar on a train going nowhere, don't you?"

"Did I say that?"

"You didn't need to." She packed the ball harder, searching the yard for a suitable target. "See that aspen? There, near the gate."

He swung around to eye the slender sapling. "I see it. But if you're lookin' for a target, that old pine tree might be a better bet." He nodded toward the enormous evergreen growing so close to the porch its lower bows scraped the roof.

"*Huh,*" she said under her breath. "You just keep your eye on that knot, right below the fork in the sapling." She swung back her arm with a confidence born of years of baseball played in the convent's gardens, and let fly. The snowball smacked into its target, and dissolved into powder.

He thumbed his hat back on his head. "Well, now, Miss Antoine, I am impressed."

Gabrielle dusted off her mittens and laughed out loud. "You ought to be. I might not have ever thrown a snowball before, but I was the champion pitcher at the academy for years. The Sisters of St. Agnes are great believers in the morally uplifting benefits of exercise for young ladies."

"That a fact?" he drawled. His voice took on a smoky edge as his gaze focused on her mouth. "What other hidden talents do you possess, I wonder?"

She moistened her suddenly dry lips with her tongue, aware of a growing heat within that owed itself to nothing more than the way he was looking at her. She suspected there might be a double meaning to his words, but she knew better than to ask what it was.

"Mr. Hays! Miss Antoine! Come help push!" called Jackson.

Jordan's head swiveled around, and she followed his gaze to where the two bigger boys were rolling an enormous snowball around the yard. "What in heaven's name is that?" she asked.

"That, Miss Antoine, is a snowman's nether regions.

Arabella there is in charge of his belly. And that lopsided creation of Henry's is supposed to be the head. Why don't you go help Arabella while I see what can be done about rounding out the poor fellow's noggin?"

He went to bend over little Henry, while Gabrielle waded through the fresh snow to where Arabella waited proudly beside a ball already almost as tall as her waist. Together they put their shoulders against it and pushed, their feet pumping and sliding, their chests heaving as they rolled the giant ball around and around the yard.

Gabrielle felt the kiss of moisture on her cheek, and looked up to catch the magical sight of big wet snow-flakes, floating lazily out of the white sky. She filled her lungs, experiencing again the invigorating bite of cold mountain air, tinged with the scent of wood smoke. The joyful sound of the children's laughter echoed off the jagged mountaintops above them, and she thought, *This is one of those precious, indelible moments.* One of those rare slices of life, when time seems to hang suspended, when one's awareness, when all of one's senses are suddenly heightened. And she knew—she truly *knew*—that this would be a memory she would keep forever sharp. Forever poignant.

She glanced over to where Jordan Hays was helping the boys settle the snowman's base into place, and found him watching her. Their gazes caught and held, and the moment stretched out and became something they shared. Swirls of snow drifted down around them and between them, and the cold wind sighed through the trees. And still they looked at each other.

"Mr. Hays," said Arabella. "Are you ready for mine now? Mr. Hays?"

There was a barely perceptible pause. Then his gaze

shifted to the little girl, and an easy smile put the creases in his cheeks. "Sure thing, darlin'," he said, exaggerating his drawl. "This snowman looks hungry to me, don't you think? We'd better get his belly and head on him real quick-like."

The children all giggled and scrambled to hoist the middle ball into position. But before he moved to help, Jordan brought his gaze back to Gabrielle's face, and his smile slowly faded, to be replaced by an expression that was so intense as to be almost frightening. "And then," he said, "I want to show you something."

The snow had wet his hair, so that it curled darkly against the strong curve of his neck. She knew a strange, inexplicable urge to reach out and touch him there, where the skin was smooth and sensitive. "What?" she asked, her voice barely more than a whisper.

"Something wondrous, frozen, and fairylike," he said with a crooked grin.

She shook her head. "I don't understand."

"You will."

They ran along the creek, the plum-colored sleigh a weightless, magical thing that skimmed across the surface of the frozen world, the runners scything through the snow to send twin fans of white powder flying up behind them.

Gabrielle turned to stare at the dark, silent man holding the reins beside her. "Where are you taking me?" she asked, putting up one hand to catch the stray wisps of hair tugged loose from her hat by the wind.

He looked at her, an enigmatic smile curling his lips. "I want you to see it first."

"You're being very mysterious," she said, returning his smile. But he only shook his head.

She gazed out over a strange, stark landscape. Beneath their heavy coating of wet, new-fallen snow, the dark green boughs of the stands of pines looked as black as the broken rock face of the canyon walls, towering over them. Even the swift, deep-flowing waters of the creek looked black, cutting through the pristine snowbanks. She could hear the rushing gurgle of the creek, and the muffled thud of the horse's hooves, the jingle of the sleigh bells, and the hiss of the flying snow, spraying out around them. But above it all hovered an awe-inspiring, resounding silence, so intense as to be almost palpable.

There was something about the harsh, frightening beauty of this rugged landscape—something wild and untamable, that called to a restlessness she hadn't even realized she had within her. A fierce, unexpected happiness welled within her, and she tipped back her head and laughed for the sheer joy of it. Then the laughter died on her lips, and she knew, even before she turned toward him, that she would find him watching her.

But she wasn't prepared for what she saw in his face. The look he gave her was as stark and wild and beautiful as the winter-seized landscape. Only not cold. Not cold at all.

She jerked her gaze back to the leaping, swollen creek beside them. He had warned her to stay away from him. Yet here she was, alone with him, miles from town or any sign of habitation. It was a thought that sent a quiver of fear coursing through her. Fear, and an undeniable, forbidden thrill of excitement.

"There it is," he said, reining in at the side of the track.

She looked around in surprise. The canyon was narrow here, and steep, hardly wide enough in some places for the road and the stone cribbing of the narrow-gauge Black

Hawk to Golden railroad tracks. Great jagged cliffs of basalt seemed to tower over them, blocking out the light, intensifying the roar of the creek as the icy waters cut through the snowbanks to leap and smash against the tumbled boulders and throw a glittering spray up into the frosty air.

"I don't see anything," she said, her boots sinking deep into the powder as she climbed out of the sleigh.

"You won't from there. Come around over here." He took her elbow to lead her out into the narrow, snow-filled clearing that ran between the road and the creek.

He released her almost at once. Yet she found herself unconsciously rubbing her arm, as if he had left the imprint of his fingers through the heavy layers of wool and serge. "I still don't—" she started to say, when her breath caught at the sight of something on the far side of the creek. Something so beautiful and strange as to appear almost otherworldly.

It glistened a glacial white, somewhere between translucent and opaque. Not one thing so much as a jumble of strange long shapes, like icy tentacles, interwoven and frozen together, clinging to the side of the rocky cliff face to end hanging suspended in air, as if afraid to touch the leaping, foaming waters of the creek rushing beneath.

It looked a thing of magic, the work of fairies, an object of wonder. It took a moment before she realized exactly what it was. It was a waterfall, frozen solid.

"But how can that be," she asked in awe, "when the creek itself is not frozen?"

He nodded to the icy black waters. "Clear Creek is faster, and deeper, than the little stream that makes that waterfall. It'll be at least a week yet before the stream itself starts to run again."

They gazed at it together, in silence. A few stray snow-flakes drifted down around them, but the sky had light-ened, and she knew the worst of the storm had passed.

Sighing, she leaned back against the smooth trunk of an aspen tree, and looked at the man who had brought her here. His attention was still fixed on the frozen waterfall, his face seeming to soften as he drank in its strange beauty. She let her gaze roam over him. He had his thumbs hooked in the pockets of his sheepskin jacket, his elbows spread wide in a way that emphasized his broad shoulders and long, lean back. As she watched, he braced one boot up on a snow-covered log beside him, so that the muscles of his leg showed, taut, beneath the fine cloth of his trousers.

And from somewhere, unbidden, came the thought that he had a magnificent body. And with that thought came a secret desire to see the man beneath the clothes—to see *him*. It was a scandalous thought, and a sinful desire, that left her feeling confused and ashamed, and yet tinglingly aware of her own body, buried beneath its layers of wool and whalebone and linen.

She should not have come. Not because she was afraid of him, but because she was afraid of herself. Afraid of all the forbidden, wicked things he made her feel. Made her want. She realized that now, with a swift rush of panic, just as he swung his head around and caught her watching him.

"Why did you bring me here?" she asked.

He let his boot slide off the log, and turned to face her. "It was your mother who first showed me this place. It was special to her. I thought you'd like to see it."

She nodded. But when she thought about her mother and this man, here, that awful suspicion she'd had before reared its ugly head, and she knew it was a nagging question that needed an answer. "Were you and my mother . . ." She hesitated, then somehow forced the word out, "Lovers?"

He studied her, his face that cold, blank gambler's face she hated. "No," he said. "Not lovers. But I like to think she and I came pretty close to being friends."

She didn't even realize she was holding her breath until she let it out in a long sigh. She turned away from him, to stare at the frozen waterfall across the creek. She couldn't look at him and ask the next question. "Did she have many lovers?"

"No. None when I knew her. Although I know she took them sometimes. The land she built Celeste's Place on came from one of them—a prospector who left her everything he had when he died. That's his cabin you can see still standing on the hill behind the house."

Gabrielle flattened her palms against the bark of the tree behind her. "But why would she continue doing . . . *that*, when she no longer needed to?"

There was a barely perceptible pause, before he said, a quiver of amusement in his voice, "I presume because she enjoyed it. There's a difference between sellin' it, and givin' it away for your own pleasure, after all."

Pleasure. Gabrielle stared at the twisted contortions of the ice floe across the creek. So Celeste *had* enjoyed the sinful things she'd done with the men in her life, despite what Sirena had said. She had looked at men and lusted after their bodies. She had admired their broad shoulders and lean hips and muscular thighs. She had admired, and she had wanted, and she had taken her pleasure. Gabrielle's fingers curled around the trunk of the aspen, gripping it tight.

"We can get closer, if you'd like," came Jordan's voice

from beside her. It took her a moment to realize he was talking about the ice floe.

She pushed away from the tree. "Yes, please. I'd like to."

"We'll need to get down that bank, first." He nodded to the steep slope in front of them, and held out his hand. "Here, let me take your arm."

"No," she said quickly, unwilling to let him put his lean, dangerous hands on her. Not because his touch repulsed her, but because she now knew that it did not. Because she now knew enough to be afraid of the things she felt when he touched her. "I can manage, thank you." She took two steps forward—

And her feet shot out from under her so fast, she didn't know what had happened. Her backside hit the top of the bank with a bone-rattling crack. But the hill was steep, and the snow made it as slippery as a slide. Instead of stopping where she landed, she flew down the slope, hit a bump, and was airborne.

She came to earth flat on her back in a snowdrift. The world was white. She had snow on her face and down her collar and in her mouth. She had snow up her drawers. It was wet and it was cold, and she was so disoriented she floundered about until she thought she might drown in the powdery stuff.

"You keep burrowin' in like that," said a familiar drawl, "and you're liable to end up so covered with snow we won't find you till the spring thaw."

She lay still, and sensed, rather than saw, him settle down on his haunches beside her.

"I take it you're more embarrassed than hurt, and that's why you're not answering," he said conversationally. "But don't let it ride you too hard. There's a definite knack to walkin' in snow. You just haven't managed to acquire it yet."

He was laughing at her. She felt winded and bruised, and he was laughing at her. A sense of moral indignation flooded through her. She wanted to scream at him that it was all his fault. That if she hadn't been so afraid of him—of the things he made her feel, the things he made her want to do—none of this would have happened. But she was a lady, and ladies did not scream at gentlemen, however great the provocation.

"I should maybe point out to you," he continued in that same conversational tone, "that your skirts are rucked up just about to your waist. And while you've got probably the finest pair of legs I've seen, and I'm enjoying the view, someone else might come along that track and—"

She sat up with a jerk, and gasped at the sight of her drawers and stocking-clad legs, so blatantly on display. "Jesus, Mary, Joseph, and all the saints," she hissed beneath her breath. She scrambled to shove her skirts down and yank her feet up underneath them, then used the side of her fist to wipe the snow from her stinging cheeks.

Her indignant gaze shifted to the man hunkered down in the snow some five feet from her. He had his hat with its strange silver band shoved back on his dark head, and his rascal's grin curving up the edges of his hard mouth. She wished she had something to throw at his handsome, laughing, hateful face. And then she realized she did. She scooped up a handful of snow from beside her, closed her fist to pack it, and lobbed it at him.

He saw it coming. His grin vanished beneath a look of almost ludicrous surprise as he ducked to one side. The snowball just grazed his neck. But she hadn't packed it very tight, so that it dissolved in a shower of powder that sprayed over his shoulder and fell down inside his open coat. He swiped his hand beneath his collar and shuddered. "Hell's bells, that's cold!"

"Awake, Mr. Hays?" she asked sweetly, scooping up another handful of snow. This time she hit him square in the chest. She crowed in triumph, but he was already lunging for her. She let out a squeal and tried to scramble up and run. Just as his big, hard body slammed into her.

The impact sent her flying back into the drift, his weight bearing her down into the snow. He caught her wrists, hauling her arms up over her head, as if he expected her to fight him. She went utterly still beneath him.

Never in her life had she been this close to another human being, touched someone so intimately. They lay together, chest pressed to chest, stomach to stomach, hip to hip, one of his thighs wedged up between her spread legs. Their faces were so close, the exhalation of their warm breath intermingled in the cold mountain air. She breathed, and her senses swam with the scent of pine and leather and him.

She looked into his dark, glittering eyes, and felt her heart pounding violently against her chest, sending the blood coursing through her body so hard she imagined she could hear it, thrumming in her ears. He held her trapped, beneath him, but she would not have moved if she could have.

He eased one hand down her arm to bracket her face with his palm and thumb. He rubbed the pad of his thumb back and forth against her neck. She swallowed, and felt his thumb press harder against her throat as her muscles worked.

"I did warn you to stay away from me," he said. "You

should have listened." The words were harsh, but the tone was a gentle, seductive whisper. He dipped his head until his lips almost touched hers. She watched his lids drift half closed, hiding the fearful, intense gleam of his eyes. Her heartbeat skittered with anticipation.

And his mouth took hers.

He *took* her. Took her, and filled her with fire. Fire and the sweet, unforgettable taste of him. She shuddered, opening her mouth to his, rising up to meet him, greedy for his warm, wet, incredibly soft lips and tongue and sharp, cruel teeth. His tongue slid between her lips, between her teeth, invading her mouth with its turgid heat. It was sinful. It was frightening. It was heady and intoxicating. But it wasn't enough.

Her fingers curled into the sheepskin coat pulled taut across his shoulders, drawing his body closer, closer to her. She was so hungry for him. And it came to her in a blinding flash that she now understood the hunger she had seen in his eyes. Because hunger, surely, was the only word to describe what she felt now. She ached with a hollowness, a clenching, burning need, deep within her that she didn't understand—yet knew instinctively only he could fill.

She squirmed beneath him, and heard him groan, low in his throat. His weight shifted, his hand slipping down between their bodies, tearing at the buttons of her coat, shoving the heavy cloth aside, to close over her breast. He groaned again, his hot breath washing over her face as tremors of desire shimmied through her. He kneaded her breast, filling his palm with her fullness, his fingers teasing her nipple through the layers of her dress and chemise. Her head fell back, and a strange, mewling cry of pleasure tore from her lips. What she felt, what he was *doing*, was wicked, sinful, wrong. She told herself she wanted him to stop. Only she could not bear to have him stop.

His mouth was all over her, pressed against her hair, her trembling eyelids, sucking at her neck. His palm slid down, to her waist, to her hip. Then, suddenly, she felt his hand clench tight, his fingers digging into her flesh through the stiff cloth of her skirt and petticoats as he stilled above her.

She felt a shudder rack his taut body, and he pressed his forehead against hers. She knew the rush of his exhalation against her ear, heard his hoarse, anguished whisper. *"Dear God, Gabrielle."*

He stayed like that for another moment, suspended above her, not moving. Then he sucked in a deep, ragged breath, and let it out in a trembling laugh. "Gabrielle," he said again. "We're lying in a *snowbank*."

He pushed up and off her, settling into a sitting position beside her. She sat up, shakily, and looked at him.

He had one leg bent, his forearm resting on his knee, his head bowed as he sucked in air, as if he were winded. She could see the tension within him, see the taut cords of his throat, the tight line of his back. The very air seemed to shimmer with potent male sexuality and frustration.

Hot shame washed over her. Shame for the sinful, forbidden things she had let this man do to her; shame for the wanton, abandoned way she had responded to him. But what shamed her even more was the realization that she would do it all again. That she *wanted* to do it all again. That she hadn't, really, wanted him to stop.

He lifted his head then, and they stared at each other, the air thick with things unsaid, and heavy with the memory of what had just happened between them—and what had almost happened. She watched his nostrils flare. "If I'd had you beneath me like that anywhere but in a snowdrift," he said, his chest rising and falling with each hard breath, "you wouldn't be a virgin anymore. You know that, don't you?"

She sucked in a quick gasp, and swung up her gloved hand to strike his cheek with her palm. Her fingers stung with the impact, and the sound of it cracked through the icy air. But he didn't move, didn't even flinch, just sat there, staring at her with those cold green eyes of his.

"I am not my mother!" she screamed. She drew back her hand to slap him again, but this time he grabbed her wrist. She tried to jerk her arm away. He tightened his grip, his strong fingers digging into her arm.

She turned her head to one side, and choked back a sob. *"Oh, God.* Please tell me I'm not like my mother."

He let her go. She drew her heels up to her thighs, wrapped her arms around her knees, and hugged herself into a tight ball.

"Gabrielle?"

She laid her forehead on her knees and squeezed her eyes shut, fighting desperately to hold back the tears.

"Gabrielle," he said again. "Do you know why your mother became a whore?"

She swiveled her head and looked at him.

His face was soft with a tenderness she hadn't expected. "Celeste told me once that her mother worked herself into an early grave trying to raise her five children after their father died. Your grandmother was a proud woman, you see—too proud to accept other people's charity and far too proud to sell her body in order to live better. She might have been cold and thin and worn-out and sick, but she always liked to say she still had her pride."

"You make it sound as if she were wrong."

"No. If that's the way she felt about it, then it was right for her. I'm just telling you the way Celeste saw it. Celeste was fifteen when your grandmother died. She'd grown up watching her mother waste away and grow old before her time, and she swore she wasn't going to spend her life slaving as a drudge for a pittance. So when a rich, handsome man she fancied offered her a warm house and nice clothes for doing something she wanted to do with him anyway, she took him up on the offer."

Gabrielle swallowed hard. "Why are you telling me this now?"

He reached out and ran his fingers over her cheek. She didn't realize until he touched her that her face was wet. She was crying. "Because you seem to think that your mother—and other women like her, end up in their profession because of some kind of moral weakness and innate disposition to sin. Maybe it is true in some cases— hell, I don't know. But for most I'd say it was just . . ." He shrugged. "Circumstance. And you haven't inherited your mother's circumstances."

She couldn't look at him anymore. She twisted her head to stare at the leaping, swirling waters of the creek below them. "Then, why did this happen?" she asked softly.

"Jesus Christ." She heard him lever up out of the snow beside her. She could see the toe of one black boot, just inches from her hip. Then he swooped down to wrap his hand around her upper arm and haul her up beside him.

She turned her face away from him, but he snagged his fist in the loose hair that had tumbled out from beneath her beaver hat, and forced her to look at him. "This happened, goddamn it, because this is what happens when a man and a woman are attracted to each other." He sighed, and his face gentled. "So don't you even think about blaming yourself for it, and adding another burden of guilt to the load you've already assumed. Because if anyone is guilty here, it's me. Teasing you, and provoking you, and trying to scare you into giving up this crazy scheme of yours, are one thing. But I had no business introducing an innocent, twenty-year-old, convent-bred virgin to the kind of hot, hungry, wanting kiss I just gave you."

She looked up into his fierce, frightening face, and felt an emotion swell within her that burned in her chest and clogged her throat. She swallowed hard, trying to remove it, but in the end she had to talk around it. "I am not a child," she said quietly.

The corners of his mouth lifted wryly, deepening the creases in his cheeks. "I know what you are. Better, perhaps, than you know yourself." He let go of her hair to trail the backs of his fingers, slowly, down her neck. Before she could stop herself, she shivered.

"You're cold," he said. "We'd better get back."

She wasn't cold. But she turned with him, to walk toward the sleigh. And when they reached it, she took his hand, and let him help her climb into the seat.

He slapped the reins against the horse's white rump. The sleigh jerked forward, the snow hissing up beside them as the runners sliced through the drifts, gathered speed.

Gabrielle lifted her face to the wind, feeling it snatch at her loose hair and billow it out behind her. She knew she should have tried to coil it back up into a chignon, but she found she liked the way it felt, blowing free. Once it fluttered against Jordan's cheek, and he caught it around his fist and gave it a playful tug. His lips curved into a teasing smile, but his eyes . . . his eyes glowed with something fierce and intent. And she found she liked that, too, in a way that clutched at something hot inside of her.

She kept thinking about the things he had told her about her mother, kept trying to reconcile them with what she had been brought up to believe about women and the sins of the flesh. Only it wasn't working. And it occurred to Gabrielle that the longer she lived at Celeste's Place, the more she was inclined to suspect the good Sisters of St. Agnes really hadn't known what they were talking about. After all, how could they, virginal brides of Christ that they were.

A sleek shadow cut across the sleigh. Tilting back her head, she squinted against the bright white sky, and saw a hawk, soaring high above the canyon. She watched it hover, her lips parting with awe at the sight of its stark, deadly beauty. Then it swooped, its wings back, its claws outstretched, and dropped from her sight.

Oddly moved, she let her gaze fall to the dark, predatory man beside her. And she felt it again, that stirring of something within her. Some wild part of her that thrilled to the feel of the wind, and the sight of a hawk, and the gentle touch of a dangerous man.

That evening Gabrielle decided to wear the wine-red velvet dress with the satin-trimmed, shoulder-strap sleeves. The gown had a basque bodice that ended in a low V, with buttons down the front and fan seams that made it fit like a corset. The square neckline was cut shockingly low, revealing the upper swelling of her breasts. But she resisted the urge to tuck a lace fichu in the cleavage, and tied a velvet ribbon with one satin rose around her neck, instead. She crimped the front of her hair and caught it up in a spray of red satin rosebuds; the rest she coiled into ringlets and let fall over one bare shoulder.

Jordan Hays was standing in the hall, watching the play in the gaming room, when she walked up to him. He propped his shoulder against the doorjamb, his weight on one hip, and looked her up and down with an expression she couldn't begin to read.

"Care to explain why you're wearing that dress tonight?"

"What's wrong with this dress?" she asked, pausing beside him.

He held her gaze for one quizzical moment, then shifted his attention back to the gaming room.

There was an aura of tension about him tonight, of anticipation, that was like a hum in the air. She noticed he had the right side of his coat folded back, away from his gun.

"Is there trouble?" she asked.

"Not yet."

She studied the darkly paneled gaming room, with its brass oil lamps and moss-green velvet curtains, its roulette wheel and green baize-covered tables and white-shirted dealers with darting eyes and flashing hands. The customers tonight were the usual assortment of miners and businessmen. Except for one.

He played twenty-one at a table being run by the tall, lanky dealer named Frank Whitney. He had gold-shot brown hair that hung in long curls over his collar, and a drooping mustache that combined with his slightly protuberant teeth to make him look like a walrus. His clothes were fine to the point of being flashy, and he wore a pair of pearl-handled guns, strapped low on his hips.

"Is he a professional gambler?" Gabrielle asked, leaning in close to Jordan and dropping her voice.

"Sporting that kind of rig?" Jordan shook his head. "No. His name is Warren McLeon, and he fancies himself a shootist."

"You know him?" she asked in surprise.

"I've met him. He's not the problem."

"Then, what is?"

"Whitney. I think he's—" Jordan broke off, then swore softly beneath his breath, *"Son of a bitch."*

He pushed away from the doorjamb, just as Warren McLeon snatched one of his pearl-handled guns from its tooled holster, grabbed Frank Whitney by the shirtfront, and flattened the dealer's nose with the blue-black muzzle of his deadly looking pistol.

CHAPTER
TWELVE

Gabrielle started forward, but Jordan's strong fingers closed around her wrist, jerking her behind him. "No," he said quietly. "Let them play it out."

She watched McLeon's lips curl away from his large front teeth in a caricature of a smile. "The way I see it," he told the dealer, "you should get yer cards from the top of the deck, jist like everybody else."

Frank Whitney's eyes rolled inward as he stared down at the shiny gun barrel shoved in his face. "I—I don't know what you're talking about, mister."

"Show 'em." McLeon drew back the gun's hammer with a click loud enough to echo around the suddenly hushed room. "I want you to show everybody here just what you've got up your sleeve, boy."

There was a scramble and a thud of falling chairs as the other men in the room dove out of the way.

"Up—up my sleeve?" stammered Frank. The lamplight gleamed on the beads of sweat forming on his brow, and Gabrielle saw a quiver of fear run through his body.

The muzzle of McLeon's gun dug into the fleshy tip of the dealer's nose, distorting his face hideously. "Show 'em. Now. Or you're gonna be sportin' a third nostril, boy."

"I'll show them." Frank's voice broke on a sob. "I'll show them. Only, for God's sake, don't shoot me. Look. Here it is." He thrust out his arm, palm up. A king of diamonds winked in his palm. "See? Now, for God's sake, let me go. You're not supposed to shoot me!"

McLeon drew back his right arm, and Gabrielle thought he meant to put the gun away. Instead he brought it smashing down on the side of the dealer's head. Frank's legs buckled beneath him. He slumped over the table, slipped to the floor.

That's when Jordan Hays stepped forward. "You having a problem with one of my dealers, McLeon?" he asked, his voice smooth and deadly.

Gabrielle felt a tug on her arm, and turned to see Wing Tsue, trying to pull her away. She shook her head.

"Your dealer?" McLeon's teeth flashed again. "Naw. I reckon the boy's jist doin' his job. It's the lyin', cheatin', no good son of a bitch who owns this joint that I've got a problem with." Warren McLeon eased the gun's safety into place, and slipped his Colt back into its holster. Gabrielle noticed he kept his hand hanging loose at his side.

Jordan flexed and unflexed his own right hand, as if limbering it up. "If Frank Whitney was cheating," he said, "then it was without the knowledge or approval of this house. I assure you, you'll be well compensated for any losses."

McLeon shook his head, still smiling. "I don't want compensation. I want satisfaction."

As Gabrielle watched, McLeon's entire body seemed to tense. His right hand flashed toward his hip. A scream of warning rose in her throat, but before she could push it out, Jordan's gun had appeared in his hand, and Wing Tsue lunged at her, his big body knocking her off her feet. She crashed to the floor, just as an explosion shattered the room.

Gabrielle flung up her head. Through swirling skeins of gun smoke, she saw Jordan standing spraddle-legged, his Colt trained on the man who now writhed at his feet. Thick red blood welled up from between McLeon's fingers as he clutched at his shoulder. He had his head tipped back, his eyes squeezed shut in agony. Hays held his gun steady, and pulled back the hammer to fire again.

"No! Don't." Gabrielle shoved herself up off the floor. "Don't kill him."

She saw Jordan's hand tighten around the handle of his gun. Saw the chilling coldness of his eyes. The bitter stench of powder burned her nostrils as her fingers twisted in the velvet of her skirt. She saw a muscle tighten in his jaw, then relax.

He eased the safety back in place. "Wing Tsue," he said curtly. "Get his guns—and don't forget the derringer he's probably got under his coat. Then get Miss Antoine out of here, and send for the doctor."

"Shall I get Sheriff Baites, too?"

Jordan shook his head, and a wintry smile curled his lips. "I think not yet."

She didn't see him again until much later that night, when the house was nearly deserted.

She came upon him in the dining room, selecting a plate of hors d'oeuvres from the feast Celeste's Place provided for its customers. He glanced up at her as she entered the room, then went back to choosing a slice of roast beef from the silver meat platter.

There was a savage edge of barely controlled ferocity about him tonight that she'd never seen before. It was different from the cold inner pain she'd sensed within him the night he'd killed the miner. This was like an intense anger, directed outward, and it made her almost nervous to approach him.

"Will that man, McLeon, live?" she asked him, curling her fingers around the edge of the white damask-covered table.

"He'll live. But you ought to know that Frank Whitney's dead."

"What?"

He glanced up at her, then down again. "Not by my hand, if that's what you think. Someone got him in the back with a hatchet, down by Dostal Alley."

"But . . . why?"

"I found out tonight that he lost a lot of money in one of Doug Slaughter's hells a while back, and ended up owing him a thousand dollars. It seems they struck a deal whereby Frank was to let himself get caught cheating."

"To ruin the house's reputation, you mean?"

"Maybe." He reached for a thinly sliced ham roll, bulging with a creamy filling. "Or maybe the idea was to give McLeon an excuse to draw me into a fight, and kill me."

The memory of the way Jordan's gun had appeared in his hand, like a phantom spouting fire, flashed through Gabrielle's memory. If Warren McLeon had a reputation as a shootist, what did that make Hays? She turned away from him and went to stand by the fire. But the logs on the hearth had been reduced to a glowing pile of coals, and she ran one hand along her other arm, shivering.

"Cold?" He set aside his plate and came up to her, and she felt it again, the brittle iciness of his barely controlled violence. He reached out his hand, and she tensed, but he stretched past her to pick up the poker. "Or afraid?" He held her gaze for one, heart-thudding moment, then hunkered down to stir the sluggish fire.

The glowing coals cast harsh planes of light and shadow across the angular features of his face. "Both," she admitted.

"So why don't you let Slaughter have what he wants, Gabrielle?" He swiveled on his haunches and reached to toss another log on top of the glowing red coals. "Sell him the house, and go back to New Orleans. Now. Before there's any more trouble." He reached for another log, the strong muscles of his back and shoulders bunching and flexing beneath the fine cloth of his coat as he worked.

"You know why I can't do that," she said quietly. "I'm going to see this through, Mr. Hays. For the sake of my mother, who fought to keep that man from getting his hands on this place. And for the sake of the people in this house, who don't deserve to suddenly be given a choice between losing their jobs or working for someone so evil. And for my own sake, too. Because I could never do such a thing and walk away with a clear conscience."

He braced his hands on his spread thighs and tilted his head to look at her. "Then, you ought to know Slaughter has someone else in this house on his payroll."

Gabrielle sucked in her breath. "Good heavens. Who?"

He shrugged his shoulders. "Whitney didn't know for sure, but he thought it was one of the girls."

Gabrielle stared at the quietly violent man beside her as a terrible suspicion formed in her brain. "What did you do to Frank Whitney, to make him tell you all this?"

Instead of looking at her, he picked up the poker again and began to shift the smoldering logs. They erupted, suddenly, into flames. "Are you sure you want it on your tender conscience?" he asked, keeping his attention focused on the fire.

A burst of sparks shot up the chimney, sending an eerie red light over his half-averted profile and making him look hard, almost cruel. She found she couldn't answer.

He made a harsh sound that might have been a low laugh. "I'm going to warn you one last time, Gabrielle. If you're not tough enough to do what it takes to fight a man like Slaughter, then you'd better do what I said. Sell the house and get out before this gets any uglier. Because believe me, it will."

"I won't sell to him."

Hays stood up in one easy motion that brought him so close to her that his thighs crushed her red velvet skirts. "Then, he'll try something else."

She forced herself to meet his hard stare. "If you are afraid, you can leave now. I'll run the house by myself until the end of June, and send you the profits."

She waited for his response, barely daring to breathe.

An unexpected gleam of amusement lit up his eyes. "I didn't know they taught ladies how to run a bluff in convents."

"This is no bluff."

"No? It would be something to see, then, I must admit. A virgin runnin' a whorehouse and gamin' room." He turned away to pick up his glass of wine. "But I think I'd rather stay and protect my investment. No offense, of course."

He raised the glass to his mouth. She watched the wine wet his lips, watched the muscles work in his strong throat as he swallowed. Then she glanced away quickly, conscious of a confusing, frightening tumult of emotions, deep within.

She told herself she was relieved she wouldn't need to face the prospect of running this place alone. But that was only part of the truth.

The other part—the part she didn't want to admit—was that she desperately, shamelessly could not bear the thought of this man walking out of her life. Not now. Not even—she realized with a sudden sense of panic—when the end of June finally did come.

As the days passed, Gabrielle continued to divide her time in the afternoons between helping Sirena with the children, and going through her mother's papers. But it wasn't until the Saturday after Jordan shot Warren McLeon, that she pulled out the last drawer on the right-hand side of the desk, and discovered a stack of thick files.

Picking one at random, she flipped it open and found herself staring at a list of dates, times, and names, briefly annotated. Her gaze focused on the page before her.

Monday, 23 November, 1873
   5:20 P.M.: Nathanial Tate, with Amy, straight.
   5:30 P.M.: Lester Snipe, with Vanessa, French Trick.
   5:35 P.M.: Ernie Snodgrass, with Tierney, bondage and spanking, including . . .

Gabrielle slammed the folder closed and stared at the far wall, her heart thumping painfully. Then, slowly, cautiously, pulled by a curiosity she could not deny, she opened the file again and read more.

Celeste had kept notes, Gabrielle discovered, on the

men in Central City who were her regular customers. The dates and times they visited the house, the girls they preferred, the peculiar, sometimes perverse direction of their sexual preferences—all were carefully recorded. Reading that list, Gabrielle felt herself burn with hot shame and painful embarrassment. It amazed her that she could live in this house the way she did, play the piano in the front room every night, and still remain so ignorant of the kinds of things that went on upstairs.

Closing the file, she slipped it back in the drawer, planning to quit for the afternoon. It was getting late, and she still needed to dress for the evening to come. But then the next file caught her attention, and she lifted it out and opened it on the leather desktop.

It contained yellowed parchments, official documents of some sort. Gabrielle selected one and held it up to the lamplight. It was a mineral claim. She set it down and leafed through the contents of the file. They were all claim forms.

She leaned back in her chair and stared at the file, remembering something Jordan Hays had said to her about Celeste DuBois selling her jewelry to invest in mining ventures.

Gabrielle scooped up the file, and went to knock on his door.

"Come in," he called.

Tucking the file under her arm, she turned the handle and walked in.

He stood in front of the washstand, splashing water on his face. He was naked to the waist. Light from the lamp on the marble-topped table bronzed the skin of his bare back with a golden glow, highlighting the ridges of his muscled shoulders, the hollow shadows thrown by his backbone. He looked so big and strong and manly, standing there, that her breath left her chest in a startled, peculiar little huff.

He swung around, reaching for his towel, scrubbing it over his glistening face, running it behind his neck, his dark green eyes focusing on her as she stood riveted in the doorway, her fascinated gaze roaming over his naked torso.

His back had been smooth, but he had fine dark hair that curled across his upper chest and narrowed down across his flat, taut belly. His belt hung unbuckled, and he had the top two or three buttons of his trousers undone, in a way that looked sinfully inviting and left her feeling oddly breathless and hot.

"You want something?" he asked.

Her gaze snapped to his face. She could see the amusement there. Amusement, and something else that made her look away again in embarrassed confusion. "I—I wanted to talk to you about these." She waved the clutch of claim papers through the air.

"What about them?"

"I . . ." She swallowed hard. "I'll come back later."

He shrugged. "Might as well come in now." He sauntered over to shut the door behind her, and gestured toward the burgundy leather chair near the window. "Have a seat."

She stayed where she was, her hands tightening around the papers until they crackled.

"I thought I told you Celeste had invested in some mining ventures." He pulled a fresh shirt from his drawer.

Gabrielle watched the sleek muscles of his arms and chest flex as he pulled on his shirt, and knew a sudden shiver of forbidden pleasure. "I didn't realize she was involved in this many mines."

"She wasn't. Those claims you have there are all old."

"Then why did she keep them? From what I've come to understand about Celeste, she never kept anything without a good reason."

"She had a reason all right. If you'll take a look at them," he said, turning his back on her, "you'll see that they're not in her name."

Merciful heavens, Gabrielle thought, as she watched Jordan casually shove his trousers down low on his hips. *He's tucking in his shirt.* She jerked her gaze away, and went to perch on the edge of the chair near the window, her attention firmly fixed on the old forms. "Who—" Her voice cracked, and she had to start again. "Who are Archibald Johnson and Isaiah Flinders?"

"Prospectors. From Central City's early days. They were partners, although why anyone would want to be partners with Archibald Johnson is hard to figure. They used to call him Old Squint Eyes, and from what I hear, he must have been about as crazy as a peyote-eatin' coyote."

Gabrielle looked up and let out a startled laugh. "How crazy is that?"

His lips curled into a delicious smile. "Pretty crazy."

She watched him open the door of his wardrobe and reach for a vest. "And Isaiah Flinders? Was he the same?"

"Isaiah? Oh, no. Isaiah was . . ." He paused for a moment, the vest still in his hand. "Well, let's put it this way. Your mother took him as her lover."

Gabrielle knew a rush of some peculiar emotion she could not name. "Is he the one you were telling me about the other day? The one who built the cabin out back?"

"That's right." She watched him pull on his vest. "He left your mother everything he had when he was killed."

"Killed? How?"

"Old Squint Eyes stabbed him."

"Oh." Gabrielle let her gaze rove over the room's high ceiling, with its intricate plaster moldings, the silk-hung walls, the marble mantelpiece. "He must have left my mother a fair amount of money."

"That he did. Those two partners discovered what was supposed to be the richest lode in this county."

"So my mother built this house on the proceeds from the sale of that mine?"

Jordan raised his chin to button his collar. "Nope. Isaiah had enough gold in the bank to pay for the house. The mine itself was lost. It's known around here as the Lost Letty Mine."

"Lost? How can something as big as a mine get lost?"

Jordan slipped a silk tie around his neck. "Well, first of all, it wouldn't have been much of a mine at that stage. So it wouldn't have looked any different from the thousands of other diggings that have been started around here in the last fifteen years, but never panned out. And it's lost because Isaiah Flinders died without telling anyone where it was."

"But his partner—Old Squint Eyes. Wouldn't he have known where the mine was?"

"He knew all right. Only he wouldn't tell anyone. You see, it was because of the mine that the two partners got in a fight in the first place. They got snowed in in that cabin out there for something like two weeks, and spent the entire time drinking rotgut and playing poker. By the time the storm let up, Old Squint Eyes had lost his half of every single claim—including the Letty—to Isaiah."

"And so Old Squint Eyes killed him."

Jordan shrugged his shoulders into his coat. "They said it was manslaughter, but he still got seven and a half years in prison for it. Before he was sent up, your mother offered to give Old Squint Eyes back his half of the mine, if he'd just tell her where it was. He wouldn't do it. Said he'd only tell her if she married him."

"*Married* him?"

"She refused, of course. Said he was crazy. Besides, I guess she figured that as long as she had those claim papers and knew where all their old diggings were, she'd eventually find the mine."

Gabrielle glanced down at the yellowed papers on the table. "But she didn't."

Jordan shook his head. "She grubstaked a lot of prospectors over the years, to go back into the different sites and see what panned out. But having those old claim forms is like having a treasure map without a key." He came to stand beside the table. "You could hunt forever."

She tipped back her head to stare up into his face. The brass oil lamp on the table picked out the chestnut highlights in his dark hair, and cast a shadow on his neck, where his skin showed smooth and dark above the collar of his shirt.

They looked at each other, and she became aware of the stillness of the early evening falling around them. Aware of their solitude, and all its implications, and the way their bodies had touched and kissed in the past. She felt a tightness in her chest, constricting her lungs, squeezing the breath out of her in a long sigh. Her lips parted, and she saw a tautness in his face, a sharpening that she had come to recognize. They stared at each other for a long, dangerous moment. Then he turned away.

She stood up and began to gather together the papers.

"About six months or so ago," he said, lifting his watch and chain from the top of the dresser, and slipping it into his vest pocket, "a stranger came through town. He bragged all over about how he'd shared a cell with Old Squint Eyes in prison one time when the old prospector was delirious with fever. Claimed he knew where the mine was."

She looked at him over her shoulder. "But he didn't?"

Jordan shrugged. "He left town before your mother had a chance to talk to him. She'd pretty much given up looking by that point, and was just hoping that when Old Squint Eyes got out of prison, he'd reconsider her offer."

"You mean, he's still alive?"

"Last I heard. In fact, he's due out soon."

She glanced down at the old yellowed papers. "So one of these claims actually might be worth something?" An unexpected thrill of excitement coursed through her, heating her blood, quickening her breath.

She heard Jordan laugh softly. "You've got gold fever sparkling in your eyes, Miss Gabrielle Antoine. Now, what would a woman like you do with all the money something like the Lost Letty Mine would bring?"

She looked up at him, and smiled sheepishly. "I'd start a girls' school, of course. It's what I've always wanted to do. I'd make it as good as any boys' school anywhere. Good enough to educate women not just to be wives and mothers, but doctors and lawyers and—oh, anything they want to be." She saw the lift of his eyebrows, but pushed on. "Anything at all. And I'd offer scholarships to girls like Arabella. To keep them from following their mothers into . . . this profession."

There was a strange light in his eyes she'd never seen before. "You wouldn't spend any of it on yourself?"

"Well . . . I'd keep enough to build a house for myself." She smiled, remembering long-ago, lazy summer afternoons spent hidden in the fork of the big old moss-draped live oak at the bottom of the convent gardens. There, safely hugged by its spreading branches, the little girl who had neither a home nor a family of her own used to dream about one day having both.

"When I was little," she said, "I used to spend hours dreaming about the house I'd have someday. Imagining what it would look like, figuring out whether I wanted it to be brick or frame, in the city, or in the country. I finally decided it would have two stories, with double galleries, all around." She smiled at the memory. "And thirteen bedrooms."

"Thirteen?" His smile broadened enough to show a flash of his white teeth. "My, you were an ambitious little girl, weren't you?"

"Oh, I didn't see it as a sign of ostentation or wealth. I wanted thirteen bedrooms so that each of the twelve children I planned to have would get a room of her own. In the convent, you see, I never had a room of my own."

Her voice trailed off as she watched the laughter die out of his eyes, to be replaced by that coldness she hated so much. She wondered what she had said to cause such a change in him, and she searched desperately for something to say, some way to grab back that pleasant interlude of warmth and friendship she'd just destroyed. "What—what would you do with that much money?" she asked.

He shrugged and turned away. "Live."

"I suppose you could live very well on the proceeds

from the richest mine in this county," she said, keeping her voice light.

He twisted off the oil lamp on the bedside table, and she watched his gaze focus on the charred blue leather book beside it. "There's something you need to understand about me, Gabrielle. I don't want a two-story house in the country. I don't dream about having children, and I'm not looking for the woman who will someday give them to me. If there's anything I dream about . . ." He swung his eyes back to her, and she saw that they were as blank and empty as his face. "It's death."

"You mustn't say such a thing." She felt a chill, as if the depths of desolation and soullessness she had seen in his eyes, had somehow touched her. "It's a sin."

A humorless smile twisted his lips. "I didn't say I was plannin' to do myself in. I'm just not as anxious to avoid death as most men. And I don't fear it."

" 'I will be a bridegroom in my death, and run into it as to a lover's bed,' " she quoted softly.

She saw a muscle tick in his cheek. *"Antony and Cleopatra?"*

"Yes."

He turned away from her again. She pushed on, before her courage failed her. "What happened to your wife?"

He stiffened, as if he were bracing himself against pain.

"Her name was Sophie, wasn't it?" Gabrielle walked toward him until she could have touched his hard, broad back, if she had dared. "Did she die?"

For a minute she thought he wasn't going to answer her. Then he said, "Yes."

"She must have been very young. I . . . I'm sorry."

She saw his shoulders lift as he sucked in a deep, shuddering breath. "She was twenty."

"Did you love her very much?"

He swung slowly around. And if she ever thought his face gave nothing away, she was wrong. The pain in his face now was an agony to see. "I loved her my whole life."

He pushed past her and went to stand beside the fire roaring on the hearth, his head bent, one arm braced against the mantel, his thoughts in the past. Gabrielle let her eyes roam over his dark head, the taut line of his broad shoulders. She ached to take him in her arms and soothe away the pain she saw.

"We grew up together. She was barely seventeen when I married her. I wasn't much older, but I was old enough to go to war, and she said she wouldn't let me go unless I made her my wife first. She was afraid I'd get myself killed, you see." He flung back his head, his eyes shut, and Gabrielle saw the muscles in his throat work.

"How did she die?"

His head snapped around, his gaze slamming into her. But he had himself under control now, and his eyes were blank. "She was killed by Union soldiers. It was near the end of the war. They took over our house and used it as some kind of headquarters. Only, one night, they broke into my father's wine cellar and got drunk. And then they went crazy. Smashing things. Killing anything that moved. They grabbed Sophie and . . ." He swallowed. "My father tried to stop them, so they killed him."

"Jordan, you don't need to tell me—"

"They took turns at her. One after the other. She was with child at the time, and what they did to her made her lose the baby. She bled to death as they burned down the house, and everything around it."

His voice was flat, dead. He dropped his arm from the

mantel, and walked up to her, not stopping until he was almost on top of her. "So you see, Gabrielle, I've already had what you want out of life. I've had it, and I've lost it, and I don't ever want it in my life again."

He tangled his hand in her hair, pulling her head back until she was forced to look up into his hard face. "I want you, Gabrielle. I want you the way a man wants a woman. I want to feel your body warm and willing beneath mine. I want you to wrap your bare legs around me and pull me inside you."

He brought his mouth down over hers in a kiss that was brutally raw and on fire with naked passion. He kissed her long and deep and deliberately, sliding his tongue around her lips, as if marking her before he left her.

Then, still holding her head captive by her hair, he said into her open, trembling mouth, "I want you in my bed, Gabrielle, but I don't want you in my life. So don't ever get to thinkin' you might like to have those things you want—that house, and all those children—with me, because it won't happen. I'll take your virginity, and I'll take my pleasure from your sweet young body. But I have nothing to give you, and in the end, I will ride away and leave you with less than what you had before."

His hand spasmed in her hair, tightening enough to hurt, then he let her go and turned away. He walked to the door and jerked it open, going out and leaving her there in his room.

His hand had loosed her hair, so that a lock of it fell against her cheek. She reached up to tuck her hair behind her ear, but her hand shook so badly she turned it into a fist and pressed it against her parted lips. Pressed and pressed, as she realized that, somehow, he had guessed the awful truth she had refused to admit, even to herself.

That she did want him in her life—not just now, but forever. She wanted to take his weight in bed, and bear his children, and grow old bringing the teasing laughter back into his eyes and chasing away all the cold, dark shadows the tragedies of his past had left there.

But he didn't want her in that way.

And that was the most awful truth of all.

CHAPTER
THIRTEEN

When she was a little girl, Sirena's mother taught her to write by scratching letters in the dust. At first Sirena had seen no sense in this strange compulsion that obsessed her fair-haired, sad-eyed mother. But Sirena had loved her mother, and so she had paid attention and practiced. Just as she practiced reading the often meaningless sentences in the thick books that her mother seemed to value above all other worldly objects. Sometimes the books had to be left behind when the family moved with the seasons. But Sirena's father always managed to find new ones for the wife he had loved, even if he had never entirely understood her.

The lessons Sirena liked best, though, were the ones her father taught her. It was her father who showed her how to read the surface of a stream to find the fattest fish. Who showed her how to track a deer, and ride a horse with only the pressure of her legs to guide it. It was her father who taught her to live in harmony with the changing length of the days, and the direction of the wind.

She thought about him now, as she sat on the house's wide, sun-warmed porch and looked out over the melting snow and greening slopes of the gulch. Spring had finally

come to the high mountains, filling Sirena with a restlessness rooted in her childhood, and in the Apache blood
that flowed through her veins. The idle chatter of the
other women around her annoyed her. She had come out
here to be alone, to listen to the mating calls of the robins
and the gurgle of the stream rushing past the edge of the
stand of tamaracks. Yet, one by one, the others had
drifted out to join her.

"I wish that boy of mine would stop growin' so much,"
said Jilly, setting quick, neat stitches in the shirt she was
making for little George. "I seem to do nothin' these
days, 'cept let out his clothes."

Amy came to settle beside Jilly on the house's wide
front steps. "Not me," she said. "I wonder when Henry's
going to *start* growing. I don't know who his daddy was,
but he musta been a shrimp. Look at that—" She nodded
to where the two little boys were panning for gold in a
big puddle left by the melting snow. "Here's Henry, four
already, yet he's hardly bigger than your two-year-old
George."

She leaned over to peer at Jilly's handiwork. "Land
sakes, you sure can sew. You ever thought about taking it
up for a living?"

Jilly lowered her sewing and stared at the other
woman. "Now, why in tarnation would I want to quit
whorin', jist to ruin my eyes and get a hunched back
from bendin' over a needle all day? You musta been
talkin' to Gabrielle. Before she came, we used to dream
about the man who was gonna walk in that door someday and start out buyin' us for a fifteen-minute poke, but
end up by takin' us away from all this to keep his bed
warm every night, and have his babies. Now, suddenly,

Vanessa's talkin' about learnin' how to make hats, and you're sayin' I ought to take up sewin'."

"Me, I'd like to own me one of those fancy dress shops," said Crystal, shifting her awkwardly pregnant body on the wicker chaise Wing Tsue had recently treated to a fresh coat of white paint. "You know the kind, like you see in places like San Francisco?"

"Ged on wid you, girl," said Margot, poking her with her elbow. "When you ever been to San Francisco? You answer me dat?"

"I might not have ever been there, but I seen pictures. And I know just the kind of place I'd have. Everything I sold would be gen-u-ine im-ported from Paris, France." She glanced at the black woman beside her. "What about you, Margot? What would you do?"

"Me? I'd buy me a restaurant, I would."

"Serving what?" asked Tierney. "Collard greens and black-eyed peas and hominy grits?"

Margot turned her head to give the British girl a long, cool look. "Meybe."

"My parents had a dairy farm, back in Ohio," said Amy, a dreamy expression coming over her face. "I used to think I hated it. But lately, I've been remembering what it's like to breathe air not tainted with tobacco smoke and whiskey fumes. The world looks so nice and pretty early in the morning, when the cows are lowing to be milked and the dew is still on the grass and the birds are singing and the whole day is fresh and new—"

"Sure then," sneered Tierney. "And do you remember the sweet, fragrant smell of cow shit? What's Youngmi going to do, then? Open a Chinese laundry? And I suppose Sirena here could always go back to the reservation and open a school for all the little squaws and braves."

She gave a brittle laugh. "Listen to the lot of you. You're nothing but a bunch of whores. You always have been, and you always will be."

"I haven't always been a whore," said Jilly, setting down her sewing again. "And I don't want to be one for the rest of my life, neither. The day Jeff Hogan asks me, I'll be outta here so fast—"

Tierney threw back her head and laughed. "What's he waiting for, then? Till he strikes it rich? You're going to be one decrepit, ever-hopeful whore."

"Among the Crow," said Sirena quietly, "there is a tale of a wily old coyote who coveted his own daughter. He was a thief, they say, who taught his daughter everything she knew. Including how to spread her legs for a man. Tell me, Tierney, do they have a story like that where you come from?"

Tierney's hands turned into two, intent claws. "Shut up, you stinking half-breed—"

"Come on," said Sirena, smiling as she whipped her knife out fast enough to stop the British girl before she was half out of her chair. "It's been a while since I enjoyed cutting white flesh."

Tierney sank back against the high wicker of her chair. "You are sick. You hear me? Sick! I don't know why Celeste took you in here. They should have hanged you when they had the chance. Because sure then, you were born to swing. Just like my da."

"You talk too much." Sirena eased her knife back in its sheath and pushed away from the house wall to walk down the steps and across the yard. But she no longer heard the dancing wind whispering to her from the tamaracks. And the greening of the trees and meadows around her brought her no joy. Because her mother and father were dead, and her brother lost to her. Her soul was destroyed, and her life was dark, and bleak, and empty.

"Now, you all remember," said Jordan, handing over apples and cookies and canteens of water to the three little boys who stood in a semicircle in front of him in the middle of the kitchen floor. "Whatever you all find, twenty percent is mine."

"Yes, Mr. Jordan," they chorused.

Gabrielle paused near the foot of the back stairs and watched as Jordan looped the canteen strap over Jackson's shoulder. She felt a bittersweet kind of ache deep inside her, a warm seizing of her heart.

She had grown up in a closed world of women, of cloistered nuns and sequestered schoolgirls. Her later friendship with Julia had given her glimpses of another world, a world that included fathers and brothers and male family friends. But this was something she had never seen—this rough, male way of dealing with young children.

It was different from the kind of protective nurturing a woman gave a child, she thought. This was a gruffer way of guiding children to adulthood, of helping them to grow and learn to rely on themselves.

She let her gaze travel over the three, gap-toothed, fatherless boys, and it occurred to her, suddenly, that these children were also growing up in a woman's world. Because this house of sin was a woman's world. A place where men came and went, but rarely stayed long, and certainly never long enough to notice the needy, neglected, half-lost children growing up in the shadows.

But this man . . . this man was different. This man who wanted no children of his own was willing to take the time to try to give these children what they would need to understand themselves and others as they prepared to deal with the world. Gabrielle looked at Jordan and felt her heart swell with so much love for him, it hurt.

The boys stooped to assemble shovels and basins, and she took the last few steps down into the kitchen. "Where are you all going?" she asked as they trooped past her on their way to the back door. "Digging for worms?"

"Worms!" echoed Jackson, his voice rich with scorn for the ignorance of females. "We're diggin' for *gold*. And Mr. Jordan here is grubstakin' us."

"Ah, prospectors," said Gabrielle, trying to hide her smile.

"We're going to find the Lost Letty Mine," whispered Henry, his young face solemn.

Jackson poked him in the ribs. "Shhh. It's a secret."

"I won't tell anyone," Gabrielle promised, bending to bring herself down to Henry's height. "Do you know where to look?"

" 'Course," said Henry with a slight swagger. "Everybody knows it was Old Squint Eyes and Isaiah Flinders what 'scovered the Lost Letty Mine in the first place, and since Jackson found out that the prospectors' cabin out back used to belong to them two, we figured the best place to start looking would be along the creek beside it. We gots to find it quick, though, 'cause Mr. Jordan, he says Old Squint Eyes is due outa prison any day now, and if he comes back here—"

"Henry," said Ben, his voice low and menacing. "You talk more'n a girl. If we'd awanted a chatterbox along, we'd be takin' Arabella with us."

Henry hung his head and looked so abashed that Gabrielle regretted having asked. "Don't worry," she said, ruffling his blond hair. "I already promised I wouldn't tell, remember?" But Ben and Jackson looked at her skeptically, and although they didn't say it, Gabrielle could tell they were thinking that she, too, was only a girl.

"You men," she said, standing beside Jordan as they watched the three boys run, laughing, down the back steps and across the yard. "By the age of five, you already think you're superior to every female alive on this earth, just by virtue of having been born male."

A light of amusement kindled his eyes. "You think so, do you? The way I see it, we all think we're *supposed* to be so much better than you females, but each one of us knows, deep down where it counts, that he's not. That's why we're always trying so hard to convince not only ourselves, but you, too, that it's so."

Gabrielle laughed. "Maybe some of you. But I think there's more than enough of you out there who actually do believe it." By now the boys had disappeared around the corner of the miner's cabin. Gabrielle turned away from the window. "What's in that old cabin now?"

He shrugged. "I understand it's used mainly as a storeroom."

"You mean, you've never actually been in there?"

She watched the ends of his lips curl up in a delicious smile. "What do you think? That you might find some clue to the location of the Lost Letty Mine in there?"

"No, of course not," she said, feeling herself flush with embarrassment. How could she explain that it wasn't the tale of the lost gold mine that drew her, but curiosity about the man who had been her mother's lover. "It's just that . . . Well, I thought . . ."

He laughed, and lifted the oil lamp from its hook

by the door. "Come on, then," he said. "Let's go look, shall we?"

She glanced at him in surprise. In the week that had passed since the incident in his room, he had avoided being alone with her again. Even now she could tell that he was deliberately keeping his tone light and friendly.

Only, between them, things could never really be easy. Not when the simplest of accidental touches was enough to make her breath catch, and her entire body leap in reaction.

Jordan lifted the latch and pushed in the door of the old prospectors' cabin. Stale, musty air, tinged with the odors of damp earth and rotting wood, wafted out. The hinges screeched, and he heard a rustling noise in a far corner as something ducked for cover.

"What was that?" Gabrielle asked, her hand held flat against her chest.

He grinned. "If it's a rat, then we're in trouble. He's liable to have eaten all the important bits of the treasure map before we even find it."

"Huh," she said, flustered prettily by his teasing. "We already have the treasure map, remember? What we need is the key."

Laughing softly, he set the lamp down on the plank table in the middle of the floor and struck a safety match, while she wandered around the single room. The wick caught, flared, then steadied, its soft glow filling the small cabin.

It was crudely built of logs, except for the back wall, which had been dug into the side of the steep slope and faced with rough stones. The prospectors' old bunks were still there, along with a few pieces of furniture, fashioned mainly from packing crates and kegs, jumbled together with a broken carriage wheel, some tack, and a pile of worn-out mattresses.

He watched Gabrielle tip back her head, her neck arching gracefully as she stared up at the chinks of daylight visible through the weathered old roof. He thought about what it would be like to run the tips of his fingers down her slim white throat. To slip the pins from her hair and let it rain down around them both like liquid gold. To kiss her lips, to taste the muskiness of her breasts, to ease her down on that pile of mattresses and slide his body deep inside her. And at the thought, the hunger surged through him so strong he almost shuddered.

He was all wrong for her. She was sweetness and goodness, innocence and honesty and hope. A man like him could only contaminate her, destroy her. Yet she was vulnerable to him. He excited her and intrigued her and called to the wild, restless woman she didn't even know lurked within her. He knew, though. And so he tried, he really tried, to stay away from her. But there were times— like now—when he couldn't seem to help himself.

"It was pretty rough, wasn't it," she said, glancing around the cabin, taking in the packed earth floor, the rusty iron frying pan left abandoned on the ash-filled hearth.

"One must admit it doesn't look like the home of a couple of men who had just struck it rich."

She brought her head around to look at him. "Do you really think Old Squint Eyes will come back here when he gets out of prison?"

Jordan picked up a battered tin candlestick from the crude hutch that leaned against the back wall, then set it down again and wiped the dust from his fingers. "Who knows? Although the man did say he'd be back." He went to stand in front of her. "What are you really lookin' for here?"

She blew out a sigh through those full, ripe lips of hers that tormented him so. "I'm not sure. I've been living in the house for weeks now. And while, in some ways it seems as if I've learned a great deal about my mother, in other ways, I'm beginning to think I'll never really understand her."

He watched the gentle rise and fall of her chest as she breathed. "Maybe," he said. "But then, how many people do we ever really know well in our lives? Even among those we seem close to?"

She brought her gaze to meet his. She had such unusual gray eyes. The color of schist, shining warm and full of fire in the sun. "Perhaps not many," she said. "It's just that . . . I don't know. I guess I always hoped finding out about my mother and father would do more than just help fill this sense of aloneness I've always had within me. I also thought it would help explain things about *me*. Things I've never understood."

"Maybe the problem is that you've been so horrified by *what* Celeste was that you haven't been able to look past that, to see *who* she was." Somehow she had acquired a smudge of dirt on her cheek, and he reached out to rub it off with the pad of his thumb.

"Besides," he added, his hand hovering beside her face. "I think you've come to know Celeste better than you realize. When you brought those old claims to me the other day, you wondered why she had kept them, because you knew her well enough to be sure it wasn't for sentimental reasons, or because she'd been too disorganized to throw them out."

She stood still, looking at him with a wide, fathomless gaze that caught at something inside him. "Perhaps you are right," she said.

"Gabrielle." Her name tasted smooth and mellow on his tongue, and suddenly the need to hold her, to taste her, was too much. His fingers slid down and closed about her upper arm. He braced his legs wide, drawing her into the cradle of his hips. She made no move to resist him, but settled against his body as if it were where she longed to be. Her hands came up, shyly, to rest against his chest. He dipped his head, and she lifted her face for his kiss.

He molded his mouth to hers, gently, tenderly, rubbing his lips against hers, lips that were wondrously warm and soft and yielding. He let out a soft sigh, his hands sliding across her shoulders, down her back, to ease her slim young body in closer to him, until her breasts were pressed against his chest and his senses filled with the sweetly feminine scent of her.

She made a little mewing sound and strained against him, and all his desire for this woman, all his need, surged through him. He slanted his mouth urgently back and forth against hers, and the kiss became something hot and wet and raw. A searing kiss of tongues and teeth and shuddering, gasping longing.

He tangled his fist in her hair, and her head fell back. He kissed her neck, the tender flesh beneath her ear, the wildly throbbing pulse by her collarbone, and felt her tremble, heard her husky murmur of incoherent wanting. She clung to him, her fingers digging into his shoulders as he filled his hands with her, kneaded her breasts, taunted her nipples, slid his fingers with aching slowness down over her quivering belly.

He bunched up her skirts and petticoats, seeking the bare flesh. He heard the hiss of her indrawn breath as his fingers found the slit in her drawers and ran up the inside of her thigh. He wanted to touch her—*needed* to touch her, there, where they would join.

"Sweetheart," he whispered in her ear and heard a low, keening moan escape her lips. She squirmed against him, clutching him to her, her breath sucking in and out, the mindless, unstoppable heat of all-consuming passion glowing in the molten silver pools of her eyes. He saw it, and felt her unspoken surrender to it. And he knew that if he didn't somehow find the strength to stop this now, she wouldn't.

"Gabrielle . . ." He shuddered, burying his forehead in the curve of her neck, and let her skirts escape from his grasp. He tightened his arms around her as he fought the urgent, almost overwhelming need to lay this woman down and bury himself deep inside her. "God, Gabrielle. I'm so sorry."

She went utterly still in his embrace. He felt her stiffen, and he closed his hands around her arms and forced himself to put her away from him.

She pressed her palms to her flaming cheeks. Her lips were swollen and wet from his kisses, her breath coming hard and fast. "Mother of God," she whispered. "What must you think of me?"

She spun around, but before she could pull away, he put one hand on her shoulder and drew her back until she was leaning against his chest. He thought she might resist him, but she didn't. He could feel the length of her body against his, feel her shaking with shame and fear and the aftershocks of newly discovered arousal.

"Don't be ashamed of what just happened," he said quietly. "You're a beautiful, desirable, passionate woman, Gabrielle." His breath stirred the stray wisps of hair beside her ear. "A woman who deserves far more than I can give her."

"I don't want more." Her voice cracked, and he turned her in his arms to see her eyes swimming with the tears he knew she was trying hard not to let fall.

"Yes, you do," he said gently, fighting the urge to tighten his arms around her again and kiss her tears away. "You want that house you were telling me about, and all those children to fill it. And you want a husband beside you, to give you those things and to lie down to sleep beside you every night and still be there when you wake up in the morning."

"I . . ." She drew in a deep ragged breath that was more of a sob as her eyes slid away from his probing, knowing stare. "I don't need those things."

He cupped her chin, tilting her head up. "Look at me," he commanded, and she lifted her eyes to his. Her beautiful eyes glowed with a deep, wondrous, heartbreaking emotion he knew only too well. An emotion he never intended to feel again.

"I don't need those things," she said again, her chin jerking defiantly.

"Liar," he said softly, a sad smile tugging at his lips. "What you want is shining in your eyes, Gabrielle. Once I could have given it to you—I would have given *myself* to you. Joyously and wholeheartedly. But I've lost too much in my life. Inside I'm dead."

She pressed her fingers against his lips. "You don't have to be like that," she whispered.

"Maybe not," he said, his lips moving against her hand. "But that's the way I like it."

Her fingers curled into a fist that she drew back to press against her chest, as if she had a pain there. She turned away from him, and this time he let her go.

"Gabrielle . . . I never meant to hurt you. God knows, I've tried to stay away from you. But it's just too damn hard, living in this house together, rubbing up against each other every day. I . . . aw, Jesus, I ought to leave here. Before I finally go ahead and do something we'll both regret."

"No." She spun around, her eyes wide with panic. "No. You said you wouldn't leave. That you would stay and protect your investment."

"And you said I could go, and you'd run the place yourself for the next couple of months."

"I was bluffing." A draft from the back of the cabin fanned his cheek, flattened her skirts.

He pushed out a sigh. "I know you were. And the bitch of it is, I can't go off and leave you. Not as long as you've got Slaughter giving you trouble. I could never square it with my conscience."

"Then, you'll stay to the end of June?"

He wanted to groan. "I'm no saint, Gabrielle."

Her lips curved up in a sad smile that tugged at his heart. "No. You remind me of that line from *Hamlet*— 'Though I am not splenitive and rash, yet have I in me something dangerous, which let thy wisdom fear.' " Her smile faded. "I fear, Jordan."

Because he couldn't stop himself, he reached out and let his fingers trail lightly over her soft cheek. "But not for the right reason."

Doug Slaughter poured a generous measure of fine Kentucky bourbon into a cut-lead glass, and held it out to the man in the black frock coat and white collar. The Reverend Reginald Parkes scooted to the edge of the horsehair-covered sofa in the richly paneled study of Slaughter's Black Hawk mansion, then cast a furtive glance over his thin, stooped shoulder, as if afraid he might find one of his parishioners hiding behind the heavy damask drapes, ready to leap out and censure him.

"Come on, Reverend," coaxed Slaughter, giving the parson a smile that showed his teeth. "It'll be our little secret."

It was a secret they had shared at least once a week for months now, and the details of what went on when the Reverend Parkes visited Doug Slaughter in his enormous Black Hawk mansion had never become known. Sometimes Slaughter plied the good parson with whiskey and the illicit thrill of a discreet poker game that the reverend always seemed to win. But there were times when Slaughter brought some girls from one of his houses, and the activities were frenzied and debauched. The reverend, he had discovered, was a man of twisted and insatiable sexual appetites.

The Reverend Parkes had arrived in Central City earlier that winter, and it hadn't taken Slaughter long to spot the man's corruptibility. Years of self-indulgence and self-pity might have blurred Parkes's fine, New England features, and his coat might be shiny with age and his collar yellow with sweat, but it was obvious that Reginald Parkes had been raised to expect better things than a mining-town ministry.

At first Slaughter hadn't even known how he intended to use the man. He only knew that a self-righteous, Bible-thumping, but morally weak parson could be very useful to a man in his position. Now, however, Slaughter knew exactly what he wanted the good reverend to do.

"Well, I suppose one drink wouldn't hurt," said the reverend, licking his loose, wet lips. He grasped the glass quickly, as if afraid Slaughter might suddenly decide to withdraw the offered spirits, and gulped half of it in one quick, greedy swallow. "Ah," he sighed, smacking his lips with satisfaction. "Excellent. Excellent."

Slaughter took a sip of his own whiskey and watched the parson through narrowed eyes. "I wonder, Reverend, if you've heard of the recent, distressing occurrences at Celeste's Place, up in Nevada Gulch?"

"Indeed I have, sir. Indeed I have," said the reverend, draining his glass. "Two men shot in a matter of weeks. And one fatally."

Slaughter moved, discreetly, to refill the parson's glass. "And one of the men guilty of nothing more than an aversion to being cheated of his hard-earned cash. I understand some people are suggesting that a house of that kind should no longer be allowed to operate in an area like Nevada Gulch. After all, the city has spread in the last ten years. There are a lot of good, decent people living up there now."

"Very true," said Parkes, his voice muffled by his raised glass. "How shocking to think of pure-minded ladies and even children constantly being exposed to scenes of unbridled lust and passion. It's intolerable. Quite intolerable."

"I agree, Reverend," said Slaughter smoothly. "I think what we need is for one of the better educated, more refined pillars of the community to organize the high-minded, concerned citizens of this town to do something about it."

Over the edge of his glass, Parkes's watery eyes met Slaughter's determined stare. "Organize?"

"That's right. Something like a petition drive. To force Celeste's Place to close down."

"A petition?"

"I'm convinced we can count on a man of your background and erudition to know exactly how to go about it."

"Why, yes. Yes, of course."

"And when it's all over, you'll have to find the time to look at the plans my architect has drawn up for the proposed extensions to the parsonage." Doug Slaughter flipped open the lid of a sandalwood humidor and turned it toward his guest. "Have a cigar, Reverend."

CHAPTER
FOURTEEN

The letter from Julia St. Etienne arrived two days later.

It had been brought up to the house during the afternoon, when Gabrielle was with the children, and left on her desk. But she didn't hear of it until that evening when she was taking a break from the piano. Wing Tsue stopped her in the hall with one of his slow smiles and said, "You get good news from home?"

"What news?" she asked.

In the weeks since she had moved into the house, Gabrielle had come to both like and respect the house's big, soft-spoken doorman. He had been born in San Francisco, he once told her, to a Chinese joy girl and some black-skinned miner who had paid a dollar or two for the chance to ease the tension in his loins, and then gone on his way.

Wing Tsue's enormous size and exotic appearance made him usefully intimidating to the house's customers. But Gabrielle had gradually come to realize that the man was actually a gentle giant. A gentle giant, and a lonely, hurting soul, with no home and no family, and not even a clearly defined race or nation.

Lately it had occurred to Gabrielle that Wing Tsue was only one of several victims of life's vagaries who had found a refuge of sorts at Celeste's Place. Like Youngmi, sold into slavery and a life of hideous exploitation. And Sirena, with her mysterious past and dark, wild eyes.

"He that diggeth a pit shall fall into it." Or so Gabrielle had been taught. Except that, Youngmi and Wing Tsue hadn't dug their own pits, and Gabrielle doubted that Sirena was totally responsible for her own, either. Yet the world condemned them anyway, labeling them as fallen, degenerate creatures, lost to all shame and decency, abandoned to eke out a meager existence on the fringes of society.

That their lives were not utterly, wretchedly miserable was entirely due to a woman named Celeste DuBois. A *fallen* woman, who might have been cold and hard, but who obviously could have taught the good people of Central City something about compassion. And decency.

The thought brought Gabrielle a swift, unexpected surge of pride in the strong, redoubtable woman who had been her mother. Pride, followed by a twinge of guilt when she remembered the horror and mortification with which she had first reacted to the knowledge that Celeste was her mother.

Now she watched Wing Tsue's smile slide into consternation. "You didn't see the letter? I put it on your desk and asked Arabella to tell you it was there."

"She must have forgotten," said Gabrielle, her hand closing over the cream lace and satin of her skirt to lift the gown's demi-train clear of her feet. "I'll go read it now. Thank you."

She almost ran down the hall to the office, she was that anxious for news of the world she had left behind. She had been gone from New Orleans only a month, but it seemed like a lifetime.

She snatched the travel-worn envelope from where she found it, propped against the brass base of the oil lamp. In the dim light of the banked fire, she could just make out the name Julia St. Etienne in the return address. Her heart leapt in anticipation.

She set the letter down again and tried to calm her impatience while she fumbled for a match from the safe, and lit the lamp. She adjusted the wick, then curled into the leather desk chair and ripped open the envelope, unfolding the stiff sheets with hands that were suddenly not quite steady.

"My dearest Gabrielle," she read, hearing Julia's husky contralto forming the words in her mind. "I have had no news from you since you left, but doubtless you have by this time reached Colorado and learned what I, too, now know. That Celeste DuBois is your mother, and that we are cousins."

Gabrielle's hands spasmed around the papers as her breath caught in her throat. She leaned forward in the chair, lowering the pages slightly so that the light fell directly on them.

"Cousins! Imagine that. It's wonderful, isn't it?" wrote Julia. "Or rather, it would be wonderful, except that my parents are now forbidding me to see you, or even write to you again, and they say that any letter you send to me here will be destroyed. I have had to beg and plead and threaten and bribe Louis into agreeing to send this letter for me, but he warns he'll do it only this once. I had no idea he could be so unreasonable and obstinate. But even he agreed it was only fair that I should write and tell you what has occurred.

"After you left New Orleans, I stayed with my sister

and her husband for a few more days, then went home to Beaulieu. I chose the dinner table that night to tell my parents about the unexpected letter and mysterious inheritance you had received. Up to that point, you see, I hadn't mentioned the woman's name. But when I said Celeste DuBois— *Mon Dieu!* If the consequences had not been so unfortunate, it would have been comical. My father knocked over his wineglass, and my mother dumped her soup bowl in her lap.

"How much have you learned, my dear, lost friend, in those cold, faraway mountains? Have you learned that your mysterious benefactor was really your mother? I have no way of knowing, so I will tell you what I can. You see, it *was* a tragedy, Gabrielle, although not exactly as we envisioned it that day before you left.

"I wonder if you ever heard me talk about my uncle, Beauregard St. Etienne, who died before I was born. I have always been told he was a wild and wicked one, although no one would ever tell me exactly what he did that was so scandalous. Young ladies aren't supposed to hear of such things, I suppose. He probably did other things I still haven't been told, but I know now that when he was in his late twenties, he took Celeste DuBois as his mistress.

"She was young at the time, not more than eighteen or nineteen, although Beau was not, my parents insist, the first man to have her in keeping. He set her up in a house of her own in Prytania Street, which I suppose was bad enough, although a thing that wild young men did. But evidently what truly outraged the family is that he eventually fell in love with her, and when he discovered she was to bear his child, he planned to marry her.

"Only, before the marriage could take place, he

became involved in a quarrel with some man who had insulted her, and there was a duel. The other man was killed outright, and Beau died a few days later. Before he died, he begged my family—my father, his brother—to care for Celeste and his unborn child. But my family refused to have anything to do with either Celeste or the baby—that is you, my dear friend.

"So Celeste did what must have seemed, to her, the only option. She took other women—loose women—into her house in Prytania Street, and turned it into a brothel, with Celeste herself as the madam. And that is where you lived until you were five years old, and someone succeeded in forcing your mother to leave town.

"It seems at that point that she swallowed her pride and contacted my family, asking them to take care of you. But they again refused to have anything to do with you, so I suppose she must have gone to Monsieur Longchamps, whom I have learned was once Beau's lawyer. He did help her, by getting you admitted to St. Agnes, and keeping the secret of who you were all those years. Since your name was different, and none of the family had ever seen the child of Celeste DuBois and Beau, they never realized that you and that child were one and the same. Indeed, we don't look like cousins, do we?"

Julia's writing now became more slanted, rushed. "*Mon amie—ma cousine,* I must close quickly or Louis says he won't send this letter for me. My thoughts and love are with you. Do not forget me, and someday we will find each other again. I promise. Your friend always, Julia."

Gabrielle sat, unmoving, staring down at the letter. She didn't even know she was crying until she saw the wet splashes darkening the paper, falling on her cream satin skirt. She rubbed absently at the spots with the heel of her fist. Rubbed and rubbed. And still the tears fell, coursing silently down her cheeks.

Beauregard St. Etienne. Her father had been a St. Etienne. *She* was a St. Etienne. All her life, she had dreamed of finding her family. Now she had found them, and they didn't want her.

They had never wanted her.

The door to the office stood partially ajar. Jordan hesitated, then tapped his knuckles lightly against the upper panel. "Gabrielle?" he called.

The door creaked inward another foot, then stopped. The room beyond lay cold and dark, the hearth a pile of glowing coals, the only light from the flickering fire just visible through the open archway to her bedroom.

He pushed open the door and walked in. One satin slipper rested on the floor near the desk, the other a few feet away, as if she'd kicked them off. A flash of white caught his eyes. He bent over and picked up a torn envelope, then stood in the middle of the room, tapping the envelope thoughtfully against his thigh. Wing Tsue had told him she'd had a letter from home, and had disappeared into the office to read it. But that had been hours ago. Whatever was in that letter, it couldn't be good news.

He started toward the entrance to the firelit bedroom. He knew she was there even before he reached the curtained arch. The cream satin and lace dress she'd been wearing had been abandoned over the arm of one of the wing chairs near the window. Dainty, feminine things lay strewn across the Belgian carpet.

He followed the trail to her bed, and found her, sprawled facedown on the coverlet, her arms curled up around her head, her legs bent awkwardly beneath her. She wore only her chemise and petticoat, with the lace-trimmed edge of her drawers just visible beneath the rucked-up flounce. The bare skin of her shoulders and arms shown pale and oddly fragile-looking in the fire's glow. He saw her fingers twitch, sending some of the pages of the letter she held drifting to the floor. Then she lifted her head, and saw him.

Her eyes were wide and still and bruised, her face a strained, unnatural white. He watched her suck in a deep breath that shuddered her chest, lifting the eyelet-trimmed edge of her chemise where it lay against the swell of her full young breasts.

For a long moment they looked at each other, neither saying anything. He was in her bedroom, and she wasn't wearing much of any significance, but she didn't look the least bit flustered or embarrassed by it.

He stripped off his coat and dropped it around her shoulders. "You must be cold."

She didn't say anything, but she grasped the coat's lapels with one hand and pushed herself up further. He turned away to walk over to the hearth, where the fire burned sluggishly.

"Sometimes," he said, stirring the coals with the poker, "it helps to talk." He waited a moment, and when she didn't say anything, added, "I'm willing to listen."

He hunkered down to grasp a log and throw it on the fire. When he looked at her over his shoulder, she was sitting up, her bare feet swung over the side of the bed. Her hair was coming down; the leaping flames caught and turned the fine golden curls into molten fire. He jerked his gaze away, and reached for another log.

"I found out who my father was," she said, her voice scratchy.

He tossed the second log on the fire, sending a shower of sparks up the chimney, then reached for the poker to reposition it, letting her get out whatever she wanted to tell him in her own time.

"I'd thought I never would, you know. I'd decided I was like Arabella, Henry . . . all of them. The result of a ten- or fifteen-minute trick with a man forgotten before he was even out the door." He heard her sigh, and looked over to see her throat working as she struggled to get the words out. "It's funny, isn't it? All these weeks of going through Celeste's rooms, and I never found anything to tell me who my father might have been. And then I get a letter from my best friend . . ."

She reached to assemble the crumpled pages scattered half on the bed, half on the floor. "Her name is Julia St. Etienne. Her parents have a plantation on the River Road, outside of New Orleans, and they sent her to the academy when she was thirteen, as a boarder. She became like the sister I never had. And her family, they were like the family I never had. I used to go home with her at Christmas, during the summer. I loved it. I loved *them*. They were always so vibrant, and fun-loving. Sometimes I used to pretend they were my family."

He settled the poker back in its stand and stretched to his feet. She wasn't looking at him. She had her head bent, her hands moving over and over the folded letter.

"And now you've found out they are?"

She lifted her head, her gaze meeting his across the room. "Yes. Only it seems they never wanted anything to do with the illegitimate child of the family's black sheep and his mistress. And now that they've found out Celeste was my mother, they don't want to have anything to do with me."

Her voice broke on a sob, and he moved toward her, gathering her up into his arms. He only meant to hold her, to comfort her. But her hair was softer than silk running through his fingers, her body yielding as she pressed against him. Her sweet scent rose up to envelop him, seduce him. He looked down into eyes shiny with tears, dusky with passion. His hand tightened in her hair, his head lowered. Her lips parted, as if in surprise. He tipped his head and fit his mouth to hers.

She tasted salty from her tears. She opened her mouth beneath his, slanting her head to deepen the kiss, her tongue meeting his shyly, but willingly. He felt his coat slide from her shoulders as he drew her trembling body closer to his. Her flesh was warm and smooth beneath the thin linen of her chemise, and he let his hands run over her shoulders, down her back, up again, loving the feel of her, wanting to feel more.

He tore his mouth away from hers to kiss her eyes, her cheeks, her hair. "Gabrielle," he said, his voice a raw whisper, "I never meant . . . Ah, Jesus." He closed his hands around her shoulders, meaning to put her away from him.

She threaded her fingers through his hair, holding his head so that they stared into each others' eyes. They were both breathing hard, their chests heaving, their lips parted and almost touching. "Don't stop," she said, her face taut with passion and need. "I don't want you to stop."

"Gabrielle . . ." He slid his thumbs over her high, wet cheekbones. "I'm not the man for you."

"You're the man I want now."

"Now, maybe. But in a couple of months, when I ride away, you'll hate me if I let this happen."

The fire on the hearth crackled and flared, filling the room with golden light and swelling heat. "I'm hurting, Jordan. In here." She took his hand in hers and laid it on her breast, pushing down the low neck of her chemise, so that his fingers rested against her bare flesh. "I've been alone my whole life, but I never felt as alone as I do right now. Please."

"Don't do this, Gabrielle. Jesus Christ." She moved so that his palm slid over the swell of her breast. His breath hitched as he felt the hard peak of her nipple, and his hand closed over her fullness. "Gabrielle," he said again, although it was more of a groan. She raised herself on her tiptoes, leaning into him as she lifted her face to his.

His mouth came down on hers again, and this time he let his tongue delve deep, turning the kiss into something hot and lusty. He growled, low in his throat, his hands coursing down to close over her bottom, to draw her up against him and let her know the hardness of his man's body, let her know what she would be getting.

He felt her quiver, but she didn't draw back. He bent and swept her into his arms, carrying her the two steps to the bed. He knelt on one knee, the mattress giving beneath him as he eased her down. She kept her arms locked around his neck, pulling him down with her.

He caught his weight on his elbows, so that he could gaze at her beautiful face. " 'Behold, thou art fair,' " he whispered, smoothing her hair back from her face with gentle fingers. " 'Thine eyes are as doves behind thy veil. Thy lips are like a thread of scarlet, and thy mouth' "— he ran the pad of his finger across her lower lip—" 'is comely.' "

"The Canticles," she said breathily.

He nodded. *"The Song of Songs."*

She stared up at him with wide, solemn eyes as he let his fingers trail down her throat, slowly, tenderly, to her white chest. He was aware of her watching him as he unbuttoned her chemise and peeled back the sides to reveal her breasts, riding full and high and perfect. "God," he said on an expulsion of breath. "You are so beautiful."

He settled back on his haunches and jerked off his tie. Her fingers went to work on the buttons of his vest, his shirt. He pulled them off together and sent them flying into the darkness, his eyes never leaving the woman who lay beneath him.

Naked from the waist up, he leaned over her again. He saw her pupils dilate as she stared up at him, her hands moving over his shoulders, his back, down around his sides. He watched her chest rise and fall with her rapid breathing. He could see a pulse beat, pounding tempestuously, at the base of her neck.

He touched her there, and heard her make a hoarse moan, low in her throat, as he skimmed the backs of his fingers down the outer swell of her breast, along the lower curve, before spreading his hand and bringing it up to cup her fullness. " 'Thy two breasts are like two fawns that are twins of a gazelle, which feed among the lilies,' " he quoted, easing himself down until they lay, bare chest pressed to naked breasts, his mouth hovering just above hers.

She shifted her hips, settling her thighs around him as she slid her hands up his back, caressing him, touching his bare skin as he'd ached to have her touch him for far too long. " 'Until the day break and the shadows flee away,' " she whispered, " 'I will get me to the mountain of myrrh, and to the hill of frankincense.' "

He tipped his head and kissed her, lightly, sweetly at first. Tender kisses that quickly intensified, became desperate and needy and gasping, as their breath soughed in and out, and their hands roamed, caressed, aroused, seeking the flesh that burned and quivered.

If she hadn't been a virgin, he'd have taken her right then, hard and fast, because the need was that urgent, that intense, in both of them. But she was a virgin, so he forced himself to slow down, to initiate her carefully into the wondrous joys of the flesh.

He nibbled at the sensitive area behind her ear, and heard her whimper. He trailed kisses down her neck, up over the swell of her breasts. He closed his lips over a nipple, and she arched her back and moaned as he licked and sucked and let his warm breath wash over her. He felt her fingers tangling in his hair, holding his head to her as his mouth made love to first one breast, then the other.

Reaching between them, he worked at the tapes of her petticoat, the buttons of her drawers. Then he let his lips drift to her belly, his fingers easing the linen down over her hips, baring her before him. She lifted her bottom for him, and he slid the clothes from her slim, naked body.

He stared down at her, the hunger raging through him with so much force now that he was shaking. Kneeling between her spread thighs, he slid his hands from her knees, ever so slowly, up her legs, to their juncture. He touched her there, softly, lightly, and she jerked, her eyes widening, her lips parting on a gasp. Her fingers closed around his wrists. He let his hands lie still.

"Do you trust me?" he asked.

She nodded solemnly.

"Then relax," he said, his voice a husky whisper. "Relax and let me show you the pleasure your body can give to you." Her hands fell away from his, and he touched her there again, loving the look of rapture it brought to her face. Her head tipped back, her eyes closed. She lost herself in his touch as he slowly, carefully explored her, delighted her.

When he thought the time had come, he eased one finger inside her, and found her wet and ready for him. She writhed beneath his touch as his fingers initiated her to the feeling of something inside her. With his other hand he jerked at his belt buckle, fumbled with the buttons of his trousers, shoved them down.

He slipped his hands beneath her bottom, gathering her to him, positioning her beneath him as he lowered himself over her again. " 'Open to me, my sister, my love, my dove, my undefiled,' " he said, letting his hardness rest against her, where she could feel him. " 'For my head is filled with dew, and my locks with the drops of the night.' "

She bracketed his face with her palms, and gave the poem back to him. " 'I rose up to open to my beloved, and my hands dropped with myrrh, and my fingers, flowing myrrh, upon the handles of the lock. I opened to my beloved.' " Her mouth was wet and trembling and parted in a shy smile, her eyes huge. "Come to me, Jordan," she whispered. "I want you. I burn for you. And I'm not afraid of what will happen next."

"Ah, Gabrielle." He took her mouth in a gentle kiss, and eased himself inside her. She was so damned tight. He heard her breath hitch as he stretched her, wider and wider. But she didn't struggle, didn't fight him, just watched his face, her eyes open and glazed with passion as he took her.

When he was part way in, he stopped, his chest heaving with the need for restraint. "Does it hurt?" he asked.

"A little." Her fingers clutched at his naked shoulders, holding him to her. "But don't stop. It's a—a pleasant hurt, if you know what I mean?"

He let his breath out in a low laugh. "I do know." He smoothed her hair back off her damp cheek, and kissed her. "But I need to warn you, it might hurt more, for a moment. Then the worst of the pain should go away."

He felt her hips squirm beneath him. "Jordan, please." She swallowed hard, her throat working convulsively. "I want . . . I need . . ."

She didn't know what she needed, what she was asking for. But he did. He plunged into her, sighing with ecstasy as he buried himself inside her moist, tight heat. He felt her tense momentarily beneath him, and he immediately began to move gently within her, taking her beyond the pain to the slow thrust and drag of exquisite pleasure.

She arched up against him, calling his name, her legs wrapping around his naked hips, clutching him to her as she moved with him. He gripped her hips, thrusting into her, taking her, giving himself to her, joining himself to her.

And then they soared, together, beyond pleasure, beyond the gasping, heart-pounding, frantic plunges of need, and into a free-floating, astral glimpse of the sublime.

Gabrielle felt the tears well up within her, clogging her throat, burning the backs of her eyes. It was a spontaneous outpouring of emotion she didn't understand and couldn't control. Caught unawares, embarrassed by this unexpected weakness, she buried her face in the warm curve of his neck.

He loomed over her, a tall, dark, naked man, his hard body slick with sweat beneath her hands. Against her breasts she could feel his muscled chest heaving with the aftershocks of what they had just done together. He still lay between her legs, turgid and heavy and wet.

She tightened her arms around his neck, hugging him to her, not wanting this moment of closeness, of rapturous union, to end. She drew in a deep breath, her senses exalting in the musky male scent of him. She felt filled up by her love for him; completed and uplifted and somehow enhanced. But then he splayed his hands on the bed, flattening the pillow beside her head as he raised himself above her. Their bodies sucked apart, and the cold air hit her sweat-dampened skin, chilling her.

He braced himself on his outstretched arms and stared down at her, his brows drawing together in a frown. Shifting his weight sideways, he caught a tear as it slipped traitorously from beneath her lashes and rolled toward her ear. "You're crying," he said.

She tried to twist her face away, but he caught her chin, forcing her to meet his gaze. She didn't expect the understanding and compassion she saw softening his face. "It happens sometimes," he said.

She knew he meant his words to comfort her, but instead they hurt, because they reminded her, in a sudden, unpleasant way, that while this event had been unique and special for her, his own experience was far more vast. She felt her own naïveté, her own innocence, weighing heavily upon her.

He kissed her eyes, licked away her tears. "Did I hurt you?" he murmured, nuzzling her temple.

She shook her head. "Only for a moment." She ran her hand over the smooth flesh of his chest as he eased himself, half propped on one elbow, beside her. She loved the way he felt to her touch—hard muscle beneath soft skin. His body was a wonder to her. She wanted to touch him everywhere, explore the lean length of his thigh, the tight curve of his buttocks, the rocklike ridges of his stomach. But she suddenly felt shy, unsure of herself. "Did I satisfy you?"

He gave her his devil's grin, the one that never failed to pull at her heart and send shivers down her spine. " 'O wonderful, wonderful, and most wonderful wonderful, and yet again wonderful, and after that, out of all hoping.' "

A gurgle of laughter bubbled up from inside her. "What is *that* from?"

He grinned. "*As You Like It.* What else?"

She laughed again and pressed her forehead against his. He caught her behind the neck and pulled her against him for a kiss that drew out and became something more than she had expected it to be. "I'm going to want you again," he said, his voice husky with what she recognized as renewed arousal.

She stared up into his eyes and saw the hungry need there, and she reached out to rest her hand on his bare hip in a shyly intimate gesture that left her trembling. He took her hand in his and slid it lower, until she was touching the hard length of him.

"See how much I want you," he said.

She looked at that part of him, although she trembled at her boldness. He was so beautiful, so long and hard. She loved him so much in that moment that she ached with it.

"I want you again." He cupped her chin in his palm so that she looked him in the face. "And I'm going to keep wanting you until the day I leave here. Only you need to understand, Gabrielle. What happened between us tonight has changed a lot of things, but it won't change that. At the end of June, I'm still going to be leaving."

She felt as if something were tearing inside of her, something precious and painful. It was only with an enormous effort of will that she managed to keep her voice steady as she said, "I know. I told you before, I understand."

It was the truth, but only as far as it went. She might know he planned to leave, but that didn't stop her from loving him. Didn't stop her from wishing she could keep him in her life, forever. It only filled her with an urgent, desperate need to have as much of him now as she could.

Their gazes met and held, and she thought they probably both knew what her tears had been for earlier, although neither was willing to say it. He leaned forward to touch his lips to hers. She entwined her arms around his neck and snuggled up against him, slanting her mouth against his with a soft sigh. She felt his warm palm slide down to the small of her back, nestle her against his hips.

"This time," he said, his lips not even leaving hers. "This time, we're going to take it nice and slow. I'm going to touch you all over. With my hands. With my tongue. And then, you're going to do the same with me."

"I'd like that." She gave him a saucy smile. " 'Come, let's have one other gaudy night: call to me all my sad captains; fill our bowls once more; let's mock the midnight bell.' "

He rolled her onto her back, laughing. "I think," he said, "those nuns didn't do as careful a job as they should have in supervising your reading." He caught her laugh with his kiss. And her laugh turned into a sigh, which rose in an ardent moan that was lost in the rush of the spring wind, wrapping its warmth around the house.

CHAPTER
FIFTEEN

When she awoke to the light of morning, he was already up.

She ran her hand over the cold, empty space beside her, breathing in his lingering elusive fragrance, finding curious delight in the indentation left by his body. Then she rolled over, and the movement made her aware of a faint, unfamiliar soreness between her legs. She knew immediately what it was.

What she was.

She was no longer a virgin. All her life she had been taught that chastity was a young woman's most beautiful ornament, the talisman a bride presented to her husband on her wedding night. Yet Gabrielle had given her innocence away, freely, to a man she knew had no intention of ever marrying again. A man who had repeatedly warned that he would be riding out of her life in just a few months' time.

She flopped onto her back, her elbow coming up to shadow her eyes. She sucked in a ragged breath that seemed to catch in her chest, before she let it out in a long sigh. She had not planned what happened last night. He had come to her out of the cold and darkness, when she had felt lost and bereft. He had given her his warmth, his strength, and his compassion, and although she knew she should feel covered with remorse and stricken by sin, she could not find it within herself to regret what had happened between them. She loved him, and she had given herself to him, and their union had been an unexpected wonder. For one suspended moment, that terrible aloneness she had always carried within her had been filled. She had joined with another human being in a way that transcended their physical union; in every way that mattered, they had been one. And she knew—she was certain—that the pain he always carried so deep within him had been eased. At least for a time.

She moved from beneath the covers, feeling them slide over her bare skin. She had never slept naked before, never even moved around without at least her underclothes. She swung her feet to the floor and stood up, experiencing a forbidden thrill of sensuality and freedom that surprised her.

The air that hit her body was warm, and she saw that before he left, Jordan must have fed the fire, for it blazed and crackled cheerfully on the hearth, chasing the spring chill from the room. She started to reach for her wrapper, then stopped, and went instead to stand before the ornately carved rosewood cheval mirror that occupied the corner near the fireplace.

She had never looked at herself naked before. But she looked now, looked at this woman with the wantonly tumbled hair and pale flesh. This unmarried woman who was no longer a virgin.

She brought up one hand and tentatively touched her breasts, as he had touched her, and felt an echo of pleasure ripple through her body. He had loved her breasts, praising them, lavishing attention on them with his hands, his lips, his tongue. She had never imagined that a man's touch could bring such pleasure. She let her hand slide down across her belly, to that other part of her that he had touched, and kissed. Never had she dreamed that a man and woman could do such things together. She remembered the ways she had touched him, and her body began to heat, just at the thought.

"Beautiful, I agree," said a deep, Virginia drawl behind her.

She spun around. He stood hip shot in the archway from the office, one thumb stuck beneath the cartridge belt he wore slung low. He was fully clothed, wearing a black coat and trousers, the whiteness of his shirt emphasizing the dark masculinity of the features above. She faced him, her arms hanging loosely at her sides.

"For some reason," she said, "I thought I should look . . . different."

He strolled forward, until he was close enough that she had to look up at him. He reached out his finger and brushed it across her shoulder, just beneath the collarbone. "I see no scarlet 'A' branded into your young flesh."

It was the simplest of touches, but it made her want to shudder with reaction. To be standing here, naked before him . . . She should feel shame, but all she felt was . . . heat.

"I don't see it, either," she said, her lips curling up into a smile.

Firelight leapt, flashing, in his aroused eyes, glazed the taut line of his cheek. They moved toward each other at the same time, her arms coming up to curl around his neck, his hands closing on her waist, drawing her naked body against the long, lean length of him. She felt his warm palms ease down over her bottom to cup her cheeks and pull her in against him. She was intimately aware of his fingers curling around her, almost touching her secret women's flesh. Of the edge of the buckle on his gun belt, digging into her bare stomach.

He took her mouth in one of those long, hot kisses she loved, that left her trembling and aching. For his mouth, for *him*. "Jordan . . ." she began hesitantly, then gasped as his strong arms caught her up, carried her toward the bed. She grasped the lapels of his coat, laughing. "But we can't. In the middle of the day—Surely it's not . . . decent?"

He laid her on the bed before him and began stripping off his clothes, his gaze never leaving her as she sprawled naked before him. "Do you want to be decent and frustrated, Miss Gabrielle Antoine?" He gave her one of his devil's grins. "Or wicked and satiated?"

She reached up to draw him down to her. "I've decided I like being wicked."

Afterward, as they lay in each other's arms, she felt him stir restlessly beside her. "Gabrielle . . ." His palm traveled down her ribs, to her waist, up over the curve of her hip, then hovered, uncertainly. "I think you need to talk to one of the girls—Sirena, probably. About preventing . . ."

She raised herself up on her elbow, propping her chin on her fist so that she could gaze down at his face. He wasn't looking at her. "About preventing a baby, you mean?"

He glanced at her, then away. "Yes."

She eased back down, burrowing into the curve of his shoulder, so that she didn't have to see the cold, distant look that had crept back into his face. She'd always hated that blankness he could assume. Now she found it disturbed her in a new and far more threatening way.

"You should do it soon," he said, when she didn't answer him. "In fact, you probably should have done it before now. If—"

"You don't need to worry," she said quickly, before he could say anything more, because what he'd already said had hurt badly enough. She supposed it was a measure of her innocence and naïveté that she hadn't even given the possibility of a baby a thought. Now she felt a ripple of uneasiness that she knew could easily bloom into something like full-grown panic, if she let it. She had to resist the urge to press her palm against the flat of her stomach, as if to reassure herself that no child grew there. "You don't need to worry," she said again. "There will be nothing to hold you here to me when the time comes for you to leave."

It didn't come out sounding quite as brave and nonchalant as she'd meant it to, because knowing he was going to leave her, and liking it, were two very different things. She felt his head turn against the pillow. She knew he was looking down at her, but she kept her head tucked in the curve of his arm, so that all he could see was the top of her hair.

"Gabrielle," he said, expelling his breath in a very masculine-sounding, exasperated sigh.

And a new uneasiness rose up within her as it occurred to her that he might not wait until June to leave Central City. He could ride out now, or tomorrow, or whenever he felt her beginning to cling too tightly to him, whenever he felt she might make it hard for him to leave.

So she forced herself to lift her head, forced herself to gaze down at him, forced herself to keep her face as blank as his. "I don't want a baby from what we've done here any more than you do, Jordan. You forget, I'm illegitimate myself. I wouldn't wish that on a child of mine."

It was the truth, as far as it went. His face softened, and he caught her around the neck with the crook of his elbow, dragging her until she lay half on top of him. "You never told me what happened to your father."

"He was killed," she said simply, letting her hands roam over the hard, strong chest beneath her. "In a duel, before I was born."

"I'm sorry."

She thought he probably was. After all, he knew better than anyone how much her search for her parents had come to mean to her. She nodded. "It means I'll never know either one of them."

"At least now you know who they both were."

"Yes," she said. And it occurred to her, as he drew her down for his kiss, that the truths she'd learned about her parents probably went a long way to explaining why she was here now doing what she was doing.

There was a place, where the swaying tops of the pines and tamaracks seemed to brush the wide, free sky. Where the spreading branches shut out the ugly gouges the white men had made in the sides of the mountain, and where the jutting rocks hid the strings of wooden buildings, clinging to the gulches like river-washed barnacles in the crevices of a boulder. There was a place where the wind whispered through the high grass, and water laughed over the tumbling stones in its course, almost drowning out the *tap-tamp* of the stamp mill down in Black Hawk.

Sirena hitched up her skirts and petticoats, letting the

sun caress her bare legs and feet as she stretched out on the big, flat-topped granite rock beside the mountain stream. This was her place, high on the slope behind the house. She came here when she wanted to be alone with the person she used to be, before.

But she wasn't alone today. Today she could see Gabrielle, climbing up through the trees toward her. Sirena stayed where she was, watching the other woman wend her way through the slim trunks and low underbrush, until she reached the far bank of the creek, where she stopped short.

Sirena hid a smile as Gabrielle eyed the rapid-flowing, snow-fed stream at her feet, then lifted her gaze to where Sirena sat, silently watching her.

"How do you get across?"

"You take off your shoes and stockings, and wade."

"Oh."

Sirena watched the other girl hesitate a moment, before flipping up her skirts and petticoats to untie her garters and roll down her stockings. She unbuttoned and pulled off her high-top shoes, stuffed the stockings inside them. Then, her skirts held high, she stepped gingerly into the stream.

Sirena waited expectantly for the half second or so it took Gabrielle's feet to notify her brain of the temperature of that water. Then Gabrielle let out a shriek, and splashed across so fast she almost dropped her shoes.

"Merciful heavens!" she said with a gasp. "That water is as cold as ice."

"Ice is exactly what it was, up until a few minutes ago. It's snow runoff, remember?"

Gabrielle collapsed beside her, and began to use the flounce of her petticoat to dry her wet red feet.

Sirena crossed her arms beneath her head. "How did you find me?"

"Youngmi told me you come here sometimes."

"When I want to be alone."

Gabrielle's head came up, and she met Sirena's unwelcoming stare. "I'm sorry for intruding, but I needed to ask you a question."

Sirena propped her weight up on her elbows. "Oh? What's that?"

As she watched, a slow tide of embarrassment crept up the other girl's neck to darken her cheeks. Gabrielle didn't blush so often these days. How could she, after weeks of living in a whorehouse? Curious, Sirena sat up.

Gabrielle didn't meet her eyes, but looked off down the hill to where a clump of white bulbs bloomed in a clear patch left by the melting snow. "I need to know about . . ." Her throat worked hard as she struggled to force the words out. "Female preventatives."

Something that wasn't surprise caught at Sirena sharply, robbing her momentarily of speech. She thought perhaps it was compassion, mixed with a healthy dose of anger directed at Jordan Hays. She sucked in a deep breath that came out as a sigh. "So he took you to bed, did he?"

The other girl's head swung around. Her unusual gray eyes were luminous and troubled and . . . knowing. Sirena thought that if she had looked in the other girl's eyes, before, she'd have known even without being told that Gabrielle was no longer a virgin.

"Well, hell," said Sirena, bending one knee to hook her elbow around it. "You should have done something about it before now. But there's a douche I can make up for you that might help. Then there's cones you'll have to use if it happens again. I assume it'll be happening again?"

Gabrielle nodded, her gaze dropping to her fingers, which were busy pleating and unpleating a line in the hem of her skirt. Sirena stared at the girl's bowed head, and suddenly felt old, older by far than her eighteen years. "You love him, don't you?" she said quietly.

Gabrielle's eyes lifted. "I wouldn't have done it, otherwise."

Sirena's mouth twisted into a hard smile. "No, I don't suppose you would have."

Gabrielle held her gaze. "Did you love the first man you were with?"

Sirena jerked violently. It was as if she could feel the blood draining from her face.

Looking stricken, Gabrielle reached out to touch her sleeve. "I'm sorry. It was wrong of me to ask. Forgive me."

"No," said Sirena, forcing herself to relax. "I don't mind telling you. After all, it's no big secret." She tucked her knees up against her chest, and wrapped her arms around them. "The first man who took me was my stepfather." She heard Gabrielle's incoherent expression of shock, but went on anyway. "His name was Silas Priestly, and I was fifteen when the cavalry handed my little brother and me over to him. My mother was dead by that time, but since she'd been married to Silas Priestly when she'd been taken captive by the Apache, they figured he was the one we belonged to."

Sirena tilted back her head and stared up at the brilliant blue sky, remembering the painful confusion of those heart-rending days, when she'd been torn from the only world she'd known and thrust into something alien. And dangerous. "My little brother was thirteen. Silas sent him off to my mother's family in Boston, but he kept me. The very night after he put my brother on the stage, he came into my room and raped me. He did it again the next night, and the night after that, and the night after that."

She stared at Gabrielle, as if daring the other girl to try to sympathize with her. Instead Gabrielle said, "Why didn't someone stop it?"

Sirena shrugged. "Who would bother? To my stepfather and men like him, I was just a *breed*. At first he was the only one using me. But then he started letting other men pay to have me, too. He kept me locked in a lean-to at the back of the house, like some kind of an animal. He kept me like that for almost a year. Until one night I managed to steal a knife from one of the men he let in to have me. I killed that man. And when Silas came to let him out, I killed Silas, too."

There was a long silence, filled only with the sighing of the wind and the gurgling of the stream. Sometimes the sound of that stream reminded Sirena of the noise Silas had made, deep in his throat, the night she had killed him.

She expected Gabrielle to draw back from her in horror. But she only stared at Sirena with wide, solemn eyes, and said, "How brave you were."

"Brave?" Sirena shook her head. "Oh, no. If I had been brave, I'd have killed him that very first night." *If I had been more my father's daughter,* she thought, *and less the daughter of that gently bred, Boston-reared woman, who had taught her children, over and over, thou shalt not kill . . .*

"So you see," she said briskly, swinging her legs over the edge of the rock and standing up. "In a way, I envy you. Because I've never known pleasure with a man. Just pain. And then . . . numbness."

Sirena stooped to pick up her shoes and stockings,

but Gabrielle stayed where she was, looking at Sirena with eyes that had seen so little of the ugly side of life. So little of the ugly side of people. "But how did you come to be here?" she asked, her forehead puckering in confusion.

Sirena shrugged. "They meant to hang me. They probably would have, too, if it hadn't been for the cavalry lieutenant who had turned me over to Silas in the first place. He somehow found out what had been done to me, and managed to put a stop to it all. Problem was, after they let me out of jail, I had nowhere to go. I was a killer breed, and no one would have anything to do with me. Except your mother. She offered me a place to stay for a while. That was all—just a place to stay. It was my decision to start working here."

"But *why*? Why this?"

Sirena shrugged again, and turned away to wade through the snow-fed creek. She heard Gabrielle splashing behind her, but Sirena didn't turn around, and she didn't try to answer her question. Because she knew she'd never be able to find the words to explain to this innocent, sheltered girl, the ritual of self-humiliation and revenge in which she was caught.

Ten days later the Reverend Parkes's petition was printed in the newspaper, along with columns and columns of the names of the people who supported it.

Gabrielle was in the kitchen, eating a slice of toasted bread with preserves, when Jordan dropped the open newspaper beside her plate. "Trouble," he said.

She twisted her head to look up at him. Since they'd left her bed an hour or so ago, he had washed and shaved. But he hadn't put on his coat and tie yet, and his white shirt hung half open, revealing a swath of dark, hard chest that immediately caught her eye.

He had been her lover for over a week now. Yet she never tired of looking at him, never tired of touching him, never tired of what they did together in her sinfully wide bed. If anything, she was becoming more fascinated by his body, more enraptured by his lovemaking . . . and falling ever more dangerously in love with him as time went on.

She had to jerk her gaze away from him, and force herself to concentrate on the paper he'd set on the table. "What is it?" she asked, quickly scanning the page.

"It's a move to close us down. And it seems to have attracted a hell of a lot of support. At least a quarter of the names on that list are our goddamn customers."

"Hypocrites," she murmured, reading the petition's polemic attack on Celeste's Place. "How can someone frequent gambling establishments and houses of sin, then turn around and sign a petition objecting to them?"

"If you read it carefully, you'll see that they don't object to gambling establishments and bawdy houses in general." He poured himself a cup of coffee and pulled out the chair opposite her to straddle it backward. "It's only gambling establishments and bawdy houses in Nevada Gulch that they want to get rid of. We're in a respectable neighborhood. I guess they figure we belong down on Main Street with all the other gambling houses and hurdy-gurdy halls. Or else in Dostal Alley with the Chinese opium dens and Doug Slaughter's stews."

"Do you think he's behind it?" she asked, lifting her gaze to his.

"Slaughter? Maybe. Except that it doesn't figure. He might be able to drive us out of business by exciting the moral fervor of the citizens of Central City against us, but what good does it do him? If they don't want us operating a house up here, they won't want him, either." Jordan reached out his slim hand to point to a name near the middle of the list. "Evidently he's even signed the petition himself."

Gabrielle sighed, and glanced at the polemic again. "Who is this Reverend Parkes, anyway?"

"Wing Tsue is down in the town right now, finding out everything he can about the man. All we know at the moment is that he came to Central City some six months ago to take over the living at St. James church, and that the evils of King Faro, Prince Stud Poker, Bacchus, and the Depraved Females of the Gutter are his favorite sermon topics."

She lifted her troubled gaze to his. "What are we going to do?"

He shrugged. "I don't know." A crooked smile unexpectedly lifted one end of his lips. "Look at it this way, though. If Reverend Parkes succeeds in what he wants to do, at least you'll be getting your school building a lot sooner than you figured."

She tried to summon up a smile to give back to him, but dismay clutched at her stomach, and tore savagely at her heart. Because once the house ceased to function in its present capacity, then there would be nothing to keep him here. He would leave.

And she would lose him.

It was Wing Tsue who told Jordan about Parkes's regular visits to Doug Slaughter's Black Hawk mansion.

"Do you think this Reverend knows what kind of man Slaughter is?" Gabrielle asked, watching the office fire beside her crackle and pop. Spring might finally have arrived, but the nights could still be ferociously cold.

She sat on the Belgian carpet at Jordan's feet, leaning against his knees. They often relaxed like this at night, alone, before they went to bed. He would take off his coat and waistcoat and undo his tie, and she would put on her nightdress and curl up at his feet while he brushed her hair.

She loved the feeling of his strong, agile hands moving through her hair. Sometimes he'd whisper love poems in her ear as he gently stroked the brush over her shoulders, and down her back, and they'd end up making love in front of the fire. But not tonight. Tonight they could talk of nothing but this new danger that seemed to have come out of nowhere to threaten them.

Jordan gathered her hair up in one hand, then let it slip through his fingers. "I suppose our good parson could be gullible, but I doubt it. Greedy is more likely."

Gabrielle rested her cheek against his hard knee, and let her hand drift slowly up and down his leg. "I have the most criminal, sinful urges," she admitted. "Ranging from blackmail to murder."

"A good convent-bred girl like you? I am shocked, Miss Antoine." She could hear the amusement in his voice. "I can think of several candidates for murder, but exactly whom were you planning to blackmail?"

"I wasn't really. I was just remembering this file that my mother kept on all of her customers. Some of the men who signed that petition are probably in there."

He stopped brushing her hair. "What file?"

"It has names, dates . . . other things."

He wrapped her hair around his fist and used it to draw

her head back until she was looking at him upside down. "What other things?"

She only had to think about the things written in that file, and she blushed. Still, after all she had seen. All she had done. "I'll get it for you, if you like."

He let go of her hair. She pushed off from the floor and went to the desk to pull the file from the lower drawer. "This is it."

He strolled over to take the file from her and flip through it. At one point he stopped and threw her a penetrating look. "You've read this?"

"I . . . glanced through it." She felt the color in her cheeks deepening. "I never imagined people did those kinds of things."

Jordan grunted, his attention focused on the file again.

She studied his still, intent figure. "You're not actually thinking of blackmailing those men?"

He shook his head. "No. Not that I've any moral objection to it, of course. It's just that even if we could get some of the men who added their names to that petition to withdraw their support, I doubt it would stop our good reverend."

"Is he married?" Gabrielle asked, settling back against the desktop.

"A widower, according to Wing Tsue. It seems to be one of Slaughter's holds on him. In the pulpit the Reverend Parkes comes across as a regular modern Tertullian, telling women they should all walk around draped in sackcloth and ashes in repentance for the Fall of mankind and the murder of the Son of God. But in private, he likes to— Well, let's put it this way. He has unusual tastes."

"He sounds like a thoroughly disgusting character."

Jordan tossed the file onto the desktop. "He reminds me of a fellow my parents once hired to tutor my brothers and me. He used to give us thundering lectures in which he blamed women for everything from the decline of the Roman empire, to the French Revolution. But he also had a habit of pinching and fondling the female house servants whenever he thought no one was looking."

Gabrielle stared at the man beside her. He so seldom spoke of the life he had lived before coming to Central City. Until now she hadn't even known he'd had brothers. She found herself wondering if what had happened to those brothers had something to do with the immense pain he carried within him. A pain she suspected went beyond what had happened to his father and Sophie, as terrible as that had been. It was as if everything this man had ever believed in, everything he'd ever loved, had been destroyed.

"My brothers and I hated the old codger," Jordan was saying, and he smiled at the memory, although it was a sad, haunted smile. "We finally got rid of him by bribing one of the housemaids to hide in his bed, and then telling my mother about it before the old goat could get the wench out."

She loved the gentle, almost youthful look the thoughts of his childhood had brought to his face. But then, as she watched, that look faded, to be replaced by something cold and bleak and hurting.

"Are you suggesting we slip one of the whores into Reverend Parkes's bed?" she asked, trying to keep her voice light.

He walked away from her, to hunker down before the fireplace and stir the smoldering coals. "Since he doesn't

have a mother or a wife, I don't see how it would do
much good. Unless . . ."

"Unless what?"

He looked up at her, an unexpected gleam of mischief
shining through the painful void in his eyes. "All we
really need is witnesses, right? Some of the leading lights
of his congregation would do. If we could convince them
he was a sinner, we wouldn't need to take care of Parkes.
They'd get rid of him for us."

"But how?"

He straightened up and came toward her. "Here. Let
me see that file again."

Sirena watched in silent amusement as the man across
the desk from her squirmed. That was the only word for
it. Mr. Finley Sinclair, the vice president of the Rocky
Mountain Bank, was literally squirming in his oak swivel
chair.

He wasn't an unattractive man. Of medium height, still
trim, with a full head of cinnamon-colored hair and even,
if unremarkable, features. He hadn't recognized her
when he invited her into his private office in the classi-
cally fronted, ostentatiously proper bank that was one of
the fixtures on Eureka Street. She had worn a heavy veil,
and a most discreet green wool dress, and it wasn't until
he had solicitously pulled out a chair for her and smil-
ingly said, "How may I help you?" that she had put back
her veil.

"Sirena!" Beneath his neatly waxed mustache and jutting side-whiskers, Finley's jaw dropped. "What are you
doing here?" he demanded in a panicked undervoice, his
gaze darting nervously around.

"Relax, Finley. No one recognized me."

"But why are you here? If anyone sees me talking to you—if my wife—"

She fixed him with a cold, steady stare. "I thought you liked Celeste's Place, Finley. I thought you enjoyed your visits with me."

"Yes, but you shouldn't be *here*. If my wife—"

"The reason I asked, Finley, is that your name is on this petition." She unfolded a copy of the newspaper and laid it on his desk.

Finley stared down at the paper, a tick jumping beside his eye. He raised his head slowly, and the beat of the tick intensified. Most of Sirena's customers were a little afraid of her, she knew that. It was the knife she kept strapped to her calf, and the stories of the men she had killed, that fascinated them, and added an irresistible element of danger to their couplings with her.

"I had to sign it." His voice was pleading, almost a whine, because Finley Sinclair was a basically weak man. It was why she had selected him, when Gabrielle had approached her for help. "It was my wife, you see. She was there and . . ." He swallowed hard, his Adam's apple bulging against his starched collar.

Sirena pulled back her lips in a cold smile. "Finley, I hope you don't think I came here to try to pressure you into withdrawing your name from that petition. Celeste's Place has always believed its customers need to be assured of complete anonymity in their dealings with our establishment . . . however unusual or interesting other people might find the details of their visits."

She watched a bead of sweat form on his high forehead and trickle down his pale cheek. "I am relieved to hear that, Sirena," he said, eyeing her closely.

She broadened her smile. "What I would like is to

request that you take your wife to visit the Reverend Parkes at his home for tea this afternoon. At three o'clock."

"But he hasn't invited us."

Sirena stood up and carefully lowered the veil over her face. "Yes, he has, Finley. Do I have your assurance you will go?"

"Yes, if you like. That is— But I don't see why—"

"You will." She turned to leave, then stopped with her hand on the knob of his office door. "Oh, I almost forgot. Come up and see me sometime this week, Finley. It'll be . . . *on the house*."

CHAPTER
SIXTEEN

The Reverend Parkes pulled a heavy gold watch from his vest pocket and looked at it with annoyance. It was five minutes past three.

He was a man of habit, the Reverend Parkes. It was one of the things upon which he prided himself. Habit was a sign of self-regulation. Control. Discipline. It gave order to an otherwise unruly existence. From the moment he arose every morning at six o'clock sharp, the events of his day ticked away with the careful, inevitable precision of a Swiss timepiece. And at three o'clock every afternoon, his tea was supposed to be served to him in the parlor he liked to call his library.

Mrs. Bateman was late.

The Reverend Parkes sighed. *Frailty, thy name is woman.* It was a pity that men could not, in the final analysis, do without those wretchedly inferior beings, females. But, he supposed, someone had to cook the meals and clean the house and keep a man's clothes neat. It was, after all, why women had been created: to take care of men, to be their helpmates, and to bear and raise the next generation of males. Only sometimes the Reverend Parkes couldn't help but wonder why the good

Lord had seen fit to inflict men with such unarguably tire-some creatures.

He closed the ornate case of his watch with a loud snap, and slipped it back inside his vest pocket. He would have to ring his bell. Picking up the little silver handbell he habitually kept at his side, Mr. Parkes shook it back and forth rigorously. Its rich, metallic sound traveled easily through the house's four principle rooms.

The parsonage of St. James was small, and rather beneath the dignity of a man of Mr. Parkes's stature. When he'd first come to Central City and seen the place where he was expected to live, Mr. Parkes had hovered on the brink of resigning his appointment. But that was before he met Doug Slaughter.

Doug Slaughter was a man of vision and insight. At their first meeting Mr. Slaughter had been flatteringly impressed with the Reverend Parkes's scholarship and breeding. He had rapidly developed into the reverend's secular arm, metaphorically slaying both the unrighteous and the merely obstreperous, and (in the most discreet way, of course) generously supplementing the grossly inadequate recompense the reverend received for his position. True, Mr. Slaughter's business interests were not exactly above reproach (which is why Mr. Parkes preferred to keep their friendship a secret). But the reverend liked to think he could be a charitable soul, on occasion, and a man had to be forgiven some faults, after all.

But certain faults, such as tardiness, were insufferable. Mr. Parkes rang his bell again. He was about to get up and go look for that godforsaken female himself, when the door of the library opened.

"There you are," he grumbled. "You know very well I—"

The reverend's voice ended in a kind of horrified, strangled squeak. The face that peeped impishly around the partially opened door did not belong to the errant Mrs. Bateman. In place of the housekeeper's severe, iron-gray bun tumbled a wanton head of golden locks. And whereas Mrs. Bateman's face was tired and worn with age and adversity, this girl was young and pretty, with sparkling blue eyes and two very improper dimples.

"Howdy, Reverend," drawled a silken voice with a heavy Alabama accent. "Was you lookin' fer somethin' to drink? I got jist the thing fer you, right here."

The Reverend Parkes started to stand up, then collapsed back into his chair as the girl pushed the door open wide and walked into the room.

She was so close to being naked that his mouth began to water and the blood to surge through him, his body reacting even as his mind screamed out a warning. Two, red-tipped breasts jutted provocatively above a tightly laced corset profusely trimmed with red satin ribbons. The ribbons matched the garters that held up her black stockings, and also matched the red high-heeled shoes that clicked across his library floor. But except for the corset, stockings, and shoes, she wore nothing. Nothing at all.

"What—what are you doing here?" he said with a gasp, rising shakily to his feet.

"I brought you somethin' to drink," said the girl brightly, waving a bottle of cheap gin and two glasses.

"You must be mad!" He moved toward her, suspicion and anger rapidly replacing his initial shock and titillation. "Who sent you? Why are you here? You must leave. Leave at once, I say!"

"Aw, come on, now, Reverend. We ain't even had us a

good time yet." With a hand that was far from steady, she poured a hearty measure of gin into one of the glasses and held it out to him.

"I don't want your— Watch what you're doing, you fool woman! You're going to spill that drink all over me." Even as he spoke, the glass tipped, and a cold wetness sluiced down his front, filling the air with the sharp smell of alcohol.

"Aw, I am right sorry, Reverend," crooned the girl. "Look what I've gone and done. I got your coat and shirt all wet. Let me help you."

Before he knew what she was about, she had managed to relieve him of his coat and to loosen his collar, too.

"Here, don't do that! I don't need you to—"

Clang.

At the sound of the front door knocker, Mr. Parkes froze, and the girl took advantage of his immobility to pull his shirt front half open. "What are you *doing*!" He grasped her slim wrists and tried to pry her off him, but for such a tiny thing, she was amazingly tenacious.

To his horror, he became aware of the sound of footsteps, tapping down the hall toward his front door. Then he heard the front door open, and an unfamiliar voice with a pronounced New Orleans accent said, "Mr. and Mrs. Sinclair, and Mr. and Mrs. Tate. How good to see you. And you, too, Mrs. Turner. Your husband couldn't come?"

"You must be new," said a voice he recognized as belonging to one of his most influential parishioners. "I do hope nothing has happened to Mrs. Bateman?"

"Oh, no. Mrs. Bateman simply . . . had a better offer, as they say," crooned that mysterious voice. "I'm filling in for her until the good reverend can find someone else.

He is waiting for you all in the library now, I believe. Won't you come this way?"

"No." The Reverend Parkes tried to move, to avert the doom that was about to befall him, but the girl clung to him with almost supernatural powers. That was when he recognized her for what she was. She might look like an angel, but he now knew her for a demon; she was the devil's daughter, sent by the forces of evil to be his undoing.

"Get thee behind me, Satan!" he bellowed. "I'll not— Oh, no. What have you done now?"

Mr. Parkes felt his suspenders give way, along with the buttons that held up his pants. He made a grab for them, but before he could stop them, his pants slid heavily to the floor.

"Aw, Reverend. Look what's happened," purred the girl. "Here, let me help you."

"Please don't help me anymore! I—"

How she did it, Mr. Parkes could never afterward explain as anything other than the workings of the ungodly. She reached down, ostensibly to help him pull up his pants, but instead, she gave them such a mighty tug that he was knocked off his feet. She went down with him, tangled in his arms, just as an attractive young woman with unusual gray eyes, threw open his library door and announced, "Mr. and Mrs. Finley Sinclair. Mr. and Mrs. Robert Tate, and Mrs. Turner."

Thus it was that the Reverend Parkes was discovered by the leading lights of his congregation, with his pants quite literally down, reeking of cheap gin and in the arms of a naked woman.

* * *

"Jilly's performance was truly virtuoso," said Gabrielle that night as she lay beside Jordan. They had turned out the lamps, leaving the room lit only by the dancing flames of the fire, and one bedside candle. "I wish you could have been there to see Mr. Parkes's face when all those people walked in on him."

Jordan wrapped his arm around her and drew her close. "I doubt we'll hear anything more about that petition of his."

She ran her fingers lightly over the bulges and hollows of his bare, muscled chest. "Do you think I ought to feel guilty about what we did to him?"

Jordan laughed softly. "If he was an honest, decent man, then I'd say yes. But he isn't, Gabrielle. He's greedy and deceitful and corrupt. On top of being a hypocrite."

She propped herself up on her elbows so that she could look into his face. "Did you ever feel guilty about what you and your brothers did to that old tutor of yours?"

"Me? No," murmured Jordan. He pulled her down to nestle in the crook of his shoulder, so that he could rest his chin against the top of her head. "But one of my brothers did. His conscience tormented him so that he finally confessed his sin to our father." She heard the smile in his voice. "None of us could comfortably sit a horse for a week after that."

She lay silent for a few minutes, then said, "Jordan?"

"Mmm?"

"What happened to them? Your brothers, I mean."

She felt him stiffen, and thought for a moment that he wasn't going to answer her. Then he said, in a matter-of-fact tone, "They were killed in the war. Sam, my older brother, died in my arms after Gettysburg. Matt was the youngest. He died in a Yankee prisoner-of-war camp just a few months before the war ended. I was told they beat him to death for trying to escape."

She felt a great ache in her chest that made it difficult to breathe. "And your mother?"

She heard him suck in a ragged breath, and almost regretted having asked. Except, she had to know. She had to know what it was that made him so ... so *afraid*. Because he was afraid. Not of death, but of love. He was terrified of letting himself love anything or anyone ever again, and she had to know why.

"My mother died when I was seventeen. It was right before Christmas. She'd caught a cold, but instead of taking care of it, she just laughed in that way she had and kept doing all the things she was always doing. It turned into inflammation of the lungs. She was dead within a week."

He paused, but Gabrielle could sense that he wanted to talk ... needed to talk about the past. "What was she like?" Gabrielle prompted. "Your mother?"

His voice became gentle. "She was a beautiful woman, Gabrielle. Beautiful and good and kind. She was always so full of life and laughter and love, that I never believed she could die. Not like that. Not for no reason. Seventeen is such a naive, idealistic age. Seventeen believes that everything always happens for a *reason*—that life is good, that love is something beautiful, that people only fight for noble causes, and that the good always win."

Gabrielle lay beside him silently, listening to the fire crackle on the hearth. She should have said something, but she couldn't think of anything that didn't sound either banal or trite. What could she say, really? He was right. The good often don't win. People fight for many reasons, but few of them are as noble as they would have others believe. Life is often cruel and senseless. And love . . . love can break your heart.

"The funny thing is, she was the lucky one, really," he went on. "She died happy. She didn't have to go on living and see what happened to us. To the South. To the plantation. To Matt and Sam. To my father." He tilted his head back on the pillow and stared with agonizingly dry eyes at the ceiling above them. "Or to Sophie."

Gabrielle was the one who was crying. Great, silent tears that drenched her cheeks and rolled down her bare shoulders to leave them glistening wet in the moonlight. She cried for a gay, loving woman who went to an early grave, leaving a once happy family to mourn her. She cried for two young men, laying down their lives for a cause that was lost before it began. For an old man, watching everything he'd built, destroyed. And for a beautiful, pregnant woman, brutally abused and left to die in a pool of her own blood.

But most of all, she cried for the man beside her. A man who hadn't been able to cry for the last nine years.

Jordan caught her warm tears with his fingertips. "Don't cry for me, Gabrielle."

She wrapped her hand around his wrist to turn her tear-streaked face into his palm, and he sucked in a quick breath as she kissed him there in one of those naturally sensual gestures of hers that so often took him by surprise.

She might have been raised in a convent, but he'd discovered her to be an innately sexual woman, a woman who loved to touch and taste and feel. A woman with strong physical desires, who found immense joy in the giving and receiving of pleasure. She'd been sometimes shy, but always willing as he initiated her into the myriad

ways a man and a woman could make love to each
other's bodies. It was so easy—too easy—to forget that
she had been a virgin when he'd taken her.

He wasn't proud of what he'd done. The weeks she
had spent living in Celeste's Place might have gone a
long way toward corrupting the innocence of the young
woman she had once been, but she had still been a virgin.
And although she never said it, he knew she still wanted
the same things all women like her wanted—a home,
children, a man who would promise to stay and love her
forever.

The wind outside gusted around the house, causing the
flame of the bedside candle to flicker in a sudden draft.
The golden light wavered, casting a warm glow over her
fall of thick, wavy hair. She closed her eyes, and he let
his fingers drift over the beautiful features of her face.

He'd bedded his share of women in the last nine years,
but never one like Gabrielle. Until now his lovin' had
been easy, and always involved the kind of women who
could take a man between their legs without thinking
about things like tomorrow, and growing old together.
The kind of women he didn't need to worry might ask
him to stay when the time came for him to ride on.

But this one was different, and it wasn't just because
she had been a virgin when he'd taken her. When he
finally rode away from her, he was going to carry with
him a hundred different memories, a hundred haunting
images. Of Gabrielle, troubled and confused, staring at
the portrait of the mother she had lost so long ago; of her
shyly proud smile as she looked at herself in her first evening gown; of her joyous laughter as she sent a snowball
hurtling through the air to smack against its target; of the

way she gasped, her neck arching, her eyelids sliding closed, when he entered her.

He ran the pad of his thumb across her full lower lip. This time, he thought, when he rode away, it wasn't going to be easy. It was going to hurt. Hurt her and, damn it, hurt him.

He watched her tongue flick out to lick at his thumb. She made love to his hand, tickling his palm with her soft lips, drawing each of his fingers, one by one, into her mouth in an erotic parody of what he had taught her to do with his erection.

"Gabrielle," he said.

Her eyes met his, and she must have seen something of his thoughts in his expression, because all the fun drained out of her face, and she said with low urgency, "Dear God. You're thinking about leaving."

He speared his fingers through her loose golden hair, and slipped his hand around to cup the back of her neck. "I'm hurting you, Gabrielle. I'm not the man for you, and we both know it. You need someone younger. Someone who is good and kind. Someone who hasn't seen the things I've seen, done the things I've done. It would be better if I left now and let you get on with your life— your plans to turn this house into a school."

He watched her breasts rise and fall with her quick breathing. Her face was pale, her eyes huge, as she stared at him. "You said you'd stay until the end of June. We had a deal."

He shook his head. "You don't need to give me the profits from the next couple of months. The money from the sale of the jewelry is more than enough." Hell, he'd let her have his share of the house for nothing, but he knew she'd never take it.

"This house is worth more than that, and you know it."

"I don't need the money."

She pushed away from him, and sat up, holding the covers against her breasts with one splayed hand. "If you leave, I'll keep the whorehouse going for another two months, and send you the profits." Her chin jerked up. "And this time, I'm not bluffing."

He knew she wasn't. If she could make herself say *whorehouse*, after pussyfooting around it for all these weeks, she could undoubtedly find the strength within her to run the place until she felt her obligation had been fulfilled.

He blew out his breath in a long, slow sigh. "Damn it, Gabrielle. You know it's wrong for me to be treating you like this. As if you were nothing but a—"

"Whore?" she said.

He met her gaze squarely. "All right, damn it. As if you were a whore. You deserve better. I'm just not the man to give it to you."

"If I don't care, why should you?"

He touched her tearstained cheek. "Because I'm not so sure you don't care," he said softly. His hand slipped down to her shoulder, coaxing her to come close to him again. "Aw, Gabrielle. I don't want to fight with you."

She held back a moment, then came to him. He wrapped his arms around her, hauling her up so that she lay along the length of his body. "Hell, I couldn't leave you now anyway," he said, kissing the top of her hair. "Not with Slaughter giving you trouble like this."

She lifted her head to look at him. "You still think he was behind Mr. Parkes's move to shut the house down?"

"Everything Wing Tsue found out seems to point to it."

Gabrielle sighed. "I can't seem to quit thinking about

what Frank Whitney told you, about one of the girls in the house working for Slaughter. I find myself looking at them and thinking, which one? I don't like suspecting the people I live with."

He pushed his fingers through her hair, lifting it gently from her bare shoulders. "You trust people far too easily."

She met his gaze, her eyes dark and troubled. "You trusted Jilly and Sirena to help us deal with Parkes."

He shrugged. "Of all the women, I figured they were the least likely to be mixed up with Slaughter. Jilly, because she's so simple and open. And Sirena, because she's—well, because she's Sirena."

"I don't understand Sirena," Gabrielle said slowly. "I wish I knew her better but . . . she frightens me sometimes."

He grinned. "Only sometimes? She scares the hell out of me *all the time*."

She laughed softly. Then, as he watched, the smile faded, to be replaced by a troubled, thoughtful frown. "Maybe Slaughter didn't have anything to do with the Reverend Parkes's petition. I mean, what good would it have done him?"

"I don't know. Revenge, maybe. Men like Slaughter don't like to be crossed. Don't like to lose."

She stared at him, her eyes still and wide. She knew him too well, he thought, could read too much into a face that for years he thought he'd succeeded in keeping blank. "You think he'll try something else, don't you?"

"Yes," he said, letting his hands drift down her slim sides, then up her back. "Yes, I do." He caught his fingers in her hair, pulling her down for his kiss.

He should leave, he thought vaguely, as her lips moved sweetly against his. He should kill Doug Slaughter and leave, before it was too late. Before he lost himself forever in this woman's kisses. Lost himself, or ... He groaned as she hugged his hips with her thighs and slipped him inside her.

Or found himself.

Spring came to the Rockies with a sudden intensity that startled Gabrielle, who until now had known only the limited seasonal changes of the Deep South, where most trees and bushes kept their green leaves through the winter months, and flowers bloomed all year long.

She'd thought of Colorado as a land of harsh contrasts: white snow, black rocks, stark, bare branches, empty skies. But now a surprisingly warm sun poured its golden strength upon what had seemed a dead land. Overnight the trees turned green, winter-yellowed grass sprang up fresh and new, and the earth rang with the sweet songs of robins and meadowlarks and jays, newly arrived from the south. Snow still lay in the shadows of the gullies, or deep in the darkest recesses beneath the pines and firs. But every day the creeks swelled with the runoff, and it was as if the whole world had been reborn.

The warmer temperatures and lengthening days made the children restless at their lessons, and brought a booming business to Celeste's Place. "I suppose it's all for the same reason," said Sirena one evening as she leaned against Gabrielle's piano and sipped a glass of champagne. "It's like the sap rising in the trees."

There had been a time, not so very long ago, when the allusion would have passed Gabrielle by. Now she laughed, even as she felt her cheeks heat in an inevitable blush.

She watched Sirena lift her drink to her lips, watched

her eyes dart around the room, assessing the customers. No matter how hard Gabrielle tried, she could never reconcile this Sirena of the front parlor—this loose woman who rouged her cheeks and flaunted her bare body and did unspeakable things with strange men—with the other Sirena she knew. The gently spoken, quietly giving Sirena, who spent her afternoons selflessly teaching other women's children in an attempt to give them a better future than the one they would otherwise have had. It seemed to Gabrielle, at times, as if there were two different, separate Sirenas. She even suspected Sirena saw herself that way, although she could never be sure.

In many ways, she thought, Sirena was like Jordan. Both had been soured on life, and both could seem cold and uncaring to the point of intimidation. But whereas Jordan had buried his pain deep within, behind his teasing smile and dead eyes and devil-take-the-world attitude, Sirena's devils rode her, like a wild sadness that was close to madness.

"Now, that," said Sirena, eyeing the tall young miner who had just pushed his way through the bead curtain, "is worth going back to work for." She drained her glass with a practiced flick of her wrist, and pushed away from the piano. Watching her, Gabrielle remembered Jordan telling her, once, that Celeste used to discourage the girls from drinking while they worked. The only one who did it anyway was Sirena.

Gabrielle saw the big, blond-haired man's face break into a wide, innocent smile as Sirena strolled up to him. He looked like a kind, gentle man, and Gabrielle thought fleetingly it was too bad he hadn't ended up with someone like Amy or Jilly, whom Gabrielle had slowly realized possessed a completely different attitude than

Sirena toward what they did. It sometimes seemed to Gabrielle that Sirena saw the men who came to the house not so much as customers, but as victims.

Yet the big blond miner was still smiling when he came downstairs some half an hour later, and Gabrielle decided Sirena must have been nicer to him than usual. He was just leaving when a commotion that had been going on for several minutes in the hall suddenly grew louder, drawing Gabrielle's attention.

"Goddamn it. No, I ain't got ten dollars," said a querulous, whiny voice. "But then, I ain't here to buy no whore, neither. I'm here to see Celeste." The voice rose to an angry bellow. "Celeste!"

Gabrielle could see him now. A raggedy old prospector with a tangled gray beard, a big, shiny bald head, and wild, squinting eyes.

"*Celeste—*" He broke off to slap at Wing Tsue's restraining hand. "Goddamn it, git yer paws off me."

He stood in the middle of the gilt-and-burgundy-tasseled hall, an outlandish figure in hobnail boots, gray flannel trousers, and an old-fashioned, sourdough coat caked with mud. As Gabrielle watched, he threw back his head and let rip with a mighty roar. "Celeste! It's Archibald Johnson here. Come tell this hell-begotten gatekeeper of yers to let me pass. Celeste? Celeste!"

"Celeste isn't here."

Jordan's voice, low and quiet, came from the entrance to the gaming room. Gabrielle glanced at him. He looked relaxed, his left shoulder propped against the doorjamb, his right hand hanging loose and limber by his gun-slung hip. But she knew him too well; she could see the expectant, watchful tension in him.

She slipped off the piano bench and went to the crystal-bead curtain as Archibald Johnson whirled around to face Jordan. "Who are you?" the prospector demanded.

"I'm Celeste's partner."

It seemed to Gabrielle that she could feel the air crackle between the two men. "Where's Celeste?" Archibald demanded.

Jordan's cold eyes never left the other man's face. "She's dead."

As Gabrielle watched, the old prospector seemed to collapse in on himself. "Dead? Celeste is dead?"

Jordan pushed away from the door frame, his face unreadable, his voice surprisingly gentle. "There's brandy, if you'd like some."

Archibald swiped at his nose with the back of one hand. "I prefer whiskey."

"Whiskey it is," said Jordan.

Gabrielle followed the two men down the hall to the office. All of Archibald Johnson's belligerence seemed to have leeched out of him. He stood before the office hearth, his two gnarled hands wrapped around the glass of whiskey Jordan handed him. Every once in a while, he would let loose of a gusty sigh, shake his head, and say, "Dead. Celeste, dead. Who'd have thought it?"

Jordan hooked one hip on the edge of the desk, crossed his arms over his chest, and watched the man through narrowed eyes. Gabrielle went to stand beside Jordan, almost but not quite close enough to touch him.

A log fell on the fire, sending flames shooting up, casting an orange glow over the old prospector's craggy features. Wind and sun had dug deep grooves beside the man's lips, etched fans at the outer corners of his eyes. But his skin had a faded look, as if he hadn't seen the sun for a long, long time. Gabrielle knew a sudden rush of compassion so intense, she had to blink back tears and turn away.

"You're Gabrielle, ain't ya? All growed up now."

Her head snapped around in surprise. Until now he had seemed barely aware of her presence. Yet he had noticed her resemblance to her mother, which was so elusive that most people missed it entirely.

"Why, yes. Yes, I am. How did you know?"

"Me and yer mama, we go way back." He sighed again. "Lord knows, I musta asked that woman to marry me twenty times, even though she kept turnin' me down. Said I was crazy, she did. But I told her, I said, I'll be back. Told her I'm not the kinda man to take no for an answer. I been waitin' more'n seven years to ask that woman again. Now you tell me she's dead."

"I'm sorry," said Gabrielle. "It must be a shock to you."

The old man's eyes glowed. He had the most peculiar eyes she'd ever seen. Even in the dim light of evening, they were no more than two thin slits, his brow perpetually lowered as if in frowning concentration. She couldn't begin to decide what color they were. It was as if they burned with a fire that went beyond color, to pure madness.

His fierce gaze narrowed even more in sudden, unexpected truculence. "You probably think there's not much chance she'd have accepted me, don't you?" He swung one arm through the air in an unsteady, all-encompassing arc. "I gotta admit, it looks like she done right well for herself without me. Christ Almighty, look at this place. Never woulda thought there was this much money in whorin'. Unless maybe—"

His head reared back, his nostrils flaring wildly above

his stained mustache. "She found it. Is that what yer tellin' me? That she found the Letty?"

Jordan shook his head. Gabrielle noticed his gaze never wavered from the man beside the fire. "No. She didn't. Although I must say, it wasn't for want of lookin'."

Archibald Johnson's lips peeled back from his teeth in an eerie grin. "Ha. Knew she wouldn't. Told her she could look till this whole damned town shriveled up and blew away, and she still wouldn't find it. She shoulda married me."

Gabrielle cleared her throat of the strange obstruction that seemed to have formed there. "Mr. Johnson . . ." She cleared her throat again. "I'm willing to make you the same offer my mother made you. To give you back your half of the mine."

He stared at her, hard, his eyes glowing with that strange, inner turmoil. "If I tell you where it is, is that what you mean?"

She was intensely aware of Jordan, standing silent and unmoving beside her. Slowly she nodded.

Old Squint Eyes raked his fingers through his beard, and stared up at the ornately plastered ceiling. "We-ll," he said, drawing out the syllable. "I might do that. It might be a good deal. Then again, it might not."

"Sleep on it, why don't you," Jordan suggested. "Where are you staying?"

"I'm beddin' down at the livery, with my mule. But I'll be doin' my drinking at the Dusty Sombrero. You know it?"

"I know it."

Archibald winced, and touched his arm, where Gabrielle noticed a jagged, stained tear in his coat sleeve. When he brought his hand away, it was smeared with blood. "Damn," he said. "I guess meybe I oughta go see the doc."

"What's the matter?" she asked, starting forward. "Are you hurt?"

"Naw, just winged. Some son of a bitch bushwhacked me when I was comin' up the canyon. Knocked me right off my mule, he did. But I fooled him. I jist layed there on the trail real still like, and played possum. And when he come up to make sure I was dead, I gutted him. Gutted him good, from his privates to his gullet. And then I took this as a little memento." He held up a pelt of what looked like curly, sun-shot brown hair. "Recognize him?"

"What is it?" asked Gabrielle, her stomach clenching sickeningly.

Old Squint Eyes didn't say anything. Just kept fingering the curls, and grinning.

It was Jordan who answered her. "It's a man's scalp. Warren McLeon's scalp."

CHAPTER
SEVENTEEN

A faint glow of dawn shown through the break in the curtains. Gabrielle stood in the office, her toes curling into the thick Brussels carpet, one hand clutching the ends of a blanket together across her naked shoulders. In the dim light the portrait of her mother was barely visible, more like a shadow, a faint suggestion of flaring cheekbones and almond-shaped eyes and delicately curving lips.

She had been such a beautiful woman, Gabrielle thought. Beautiful, strong, and untouchable. Looking at her mother's portrait, Gabrielle sighed, and forced herself to confront a painful but unavoidable truth. That for her, Celeste would never be more than a dim memory, a painting on a wall, an enigma she was never really going to understand.

A whisper of movement brought her head around. Jordan stood in the doorway from the bedroom, his man's body naked and powerful. The light of the rising sun slanted over the taut muscles of his chest, the ridges of his stomach. He was so tall and lean and masculine. She let her eyes rove over him, savoring his dark beauty, feeling again the bittersweet ache that surged through her every time she saw him. An ache that was equally composed of fierce love and an instinctive fear of coming pain.

"What is it?" he asked.

She shook her head. "Nothing, really. I was just thinking about Old Squint Eyes and Isaiah and my mother. I was thinking how much I—" She swung to glance back at the painting. "No. It's silly."

He came up behind her to wrap his arms around her waist and draw her against the hard length of his body. "Tell me."

She rested her hands on the strong forearm pressing warmly beneath her breasts, and let her head fall back against his shoulder. "I was thinking how jealous I am of people like you and Sirena—even that crazy old prospector. People who knew my mother. Who shared her life. Who can remember her when I cannot."

He laid his cheek against the top of her head, nuzzled her hair. "I'm sorry," he said softly.

She let the blanket slip from her shoulders, so that she could feel the bare flesh of her back nestled against the heat of his naked chest and belly. "Do you think Archibald Johnson will agree to my proposal?"

"I don't see why not. Once the man has a chance to think about it, get used to the idea of Celeste being dead. He might be crazy, but I don't think he's stupid. We'll see what happens when I talk to him tomorrow."

She knew a sudden, uncomfortable sensation, as if time were passing too quickly, hurtling her forward into a future she was unprepared for, and didn't want. She wished she could reach out and stop it, hold onto this moment forever.

"It would change things, wouldn't it?" she said. "If he agrees."

"What? If you become a rich woman?" He let his hands slide down her sides to her hips, pulling her back against him. She could feel his arousal riding hard against her bottom. "Are you saying I won't be able to afford you anymore?"

She let out a huff of laughter that ended on a hitch as one of his hands slipped down over her belly to the juncture of her thighs. "Are you saying I won't be able to do this?" he whispered, his lips beside her ear, his breath warm against her neck, his fingers softly insistent.

She would have turned to him, but he tightened his arms around her, holding her back pressed flat against him. "Stay like this," he said, his voice low and urgent. "Just open your legs for me a little more, darlin'."

She shifted her feet, and felt his fingers part the folds between her thighs. He touched her there, where she was moist and needy, and she let out a low, keening moan that she only ended by sinking her teeth into her lower lip.

"Gabrielle," he whispered, her name a harsh, guttural groan.

She surrendered herself to his touch. He had such wonderful hands. Sensitive, skillful hands, so adept and selfless in the giving of pleasure. Her eyes drifted closed, her nails digging unconsciously into the tense muscles of his arms as he whirled her away in a warm spiral of exquisite sensation. She heard their rapid breaths, soughing in and out as one. Felt his heart pounding beneath the hardness of his hot, sweat-slicked chest against her back. Knew the pressure of his own need, hard and insistent against her.

"Please," she whispered, twisting her head toward her shoulder.

He bent over her, his hair sliding across her cheek, his

mouth catching hers in a hot, sucking, demanding kiss that was all tongues and desperate longing. Never had she wanted him like this. There was something different, something savagely physical, something almost frantic about this coming together. It was as if the reappearance of Archibald Johnson had brought the future suddenly looming before them. A future neither of them was ready to face.

"Lean against the desk," he said into her mouth.

"What?" she asked, too dazed to understand.

He took her hands and braced them against the desktop in front of her. She felt his palms cupping her bottom. Felt his sex, smooth and hard, thrusting against her. Easing into her.

She gasped, arching back against him. His hands gripped her hips, holding her steady as he sheathed himself inside her. He stilled for a moment, a shudder racking his body. Then he began to move, slowly at first, filling her, filling her so deeply, it was as if he completed her.

"Feel me," he said. "Feel me inside you." He flattened his palm against her belly, down low, so that the heel pressed against her, pressed until she was writhing, panting, spiraling out of control. "Feel me, a part of you."

She flung back her head, her mouth seeking his again, her tongue tangling with his, her body moving with his as he thrust into her, deeper and deeper, faster and faster. It was primitive, decadent, deliciously, sinfully carnal. She was soaring with pleasure. Soaring, straining, gasping, peaking. She heard his hoarse moan. Felt his last, powerful thrust that ended with a climactic throbbing deep within her. She cried out, his name a hosanna. Then they collapsed together, chests heaving, breath shuddering in and out.

He cradled her in his arms, swung around so that his hips took their weight on the edge of the desk. His breath felt hot against her damp flesh as he buried his face in the curve of her neck, his lips warm and trembling as he rubbed his open mouth against her hair.

She turned to him, her fingers tangling in his hair, her head coming up, her mouth finding his. He smelled of sex, tasted of sex, all hot and musky. His hard body was wet with sweat, trembling with the aftershocks of spent arousal. He kissed her long and deeply, his palms stroking up and down her back, holding her close against him.

"Why?" she asked, her words slurring as her lips moved against his. "Why like this? Why now?"

He leaned his forehead against hers. "I don't know. Did you mind?"

"No." A wry smile tugged at her lips. "I'm not exactly the innocent virgin I was two months ago, when I first came to this house."

She saw the flare of reaction in his eyes, saw the effect her words had on him, and if she could have called them back, she would have done it. She knew it never sat well with his conscience, that he had taken her virginity, that he still took her every night, yet would not, could not marry her.

"Hell, Gabrielle." He cupped the back of her skull with his palm, drawing her head down until it rested on his shoulder.

That was all he said, but it was enough to send a cold dread sluicing through her.

She became aware of the tick of the mantel clock, marking the minutes, the passing of her time with Jordan.

And she knew again that urge to seize time, to stop it, to put off forever the approaching day when the prickings of his conscience and the restlessness of his soul were going to combine to take him away from her.

She wrapped her arms around his strong back, hugged him close. Yet she couldn't really hold him. Not hold him in her life. Because he had never truly given himself to her, not in the same sense that she had surrendered herself to him. He was not hers. She could hold him in her arms, take him in her body, but he was not hers. He would never be hers. It was as if, in his own way, he remained for her as remote and illusive as the woman whose portrait hung on the office wall.

A tinny rendition of "Buffalo Gals" filled the cool, wood-smoke-tinged night air, mingled with the indistinguishable rumble of voices, hoots, and laughter billowing up from the tall, narrow buildings facing each other across the unpaved street.

Jordan worked his way downhill, past knots of half-drunk miners, his boot heels scraping on the rough wooden planks of the uneven boardwalk. It was far enough into May that most of the saloons and dance halls had taken off their winter doors. Golden lamplight spilled out from above and below the swinging panels, and shone hazily through grimy windows. One or two of the newer buildings were of brick. But in this part of town, most were old firetraps, made of unpainted, rough-hewn planks, weathered gray with age, or of logs, chinked with mud.

He paused outside one of the oldest, a squat log cabin that looked as if it had probably been here since the first boom days. The Dusty Sombrero boasted a single, square-cut, small-paned window, and bat-wing doors so battered by time that they sagged on their hinges. Inside, beer-soaked sawdust covered the puncheon floor. The air was thick with the smells of whiskey and tobacco slops and the sour stench of sweaty wool and unwashed human bodies.

His eyes narrowed as he peered through the thick cigarette smoke. The rough bar sported a sparse line of hip-shot men and two hovering, tawdry women. In a gloomy corner near the back, a poker game was in progress. Jordan's gaze flicked over the half-empty, ring-marked tables, the crooked, mismatched chairs, to settle on the solitary man in a filthy sourdough coat, talking to himself at a table beside the black, pot-bellied stove. A bottle of rotgut sat at his elbow, only a finger's worth of murky liquor ringing the base.

Heading for the bar, Jordan tossed a gold coin on the sticky, battered counter. He rested one boot on the brass rail and swiveled to survey the tonk from beneath his hat brim while he waited for the skinny, narrow-shouldered bartender to mosey up to him. "Give me a bottle of red-eye and two glasses," he said.

The barkeep had a shock of white hair and a near-nonexistent chin that he kept drawn up in a perpetual pout. Flicking the gray, tattered cloth off his shoulder, he took a swipe at the bar, then bent down to pull a bottle out from beneath the counter. He plunked the bottle down on the board and scooped up the coin, all in the same motion, then reached to pluck a couple of glasses off the pile behind him.

"Thank you," Jordan said.

The man sniffed and turned away.

Jordan picked up the bottle and glasses, and wandered

over to where Old Squint Eyes sat, still mumbling to himself.

"Buy you a drink?" Jordan asked, holding up the red-eye.

Archibald tipped back his head and fixed his crazy stare on Jordan. "Whiskey?" He seized his own bottle of rotgut by the neck and upended what was left of it into his open mouth, swallowing hard. "Whiskey sounds good."

Pulling out a chair, Jordan sat down and poured himself a shot, then pushed the whiskey and remaining glass toward Archibald. Archibald shoved the glass aside, and drank straight out of the bottle.

Jordan let his gaze drift over the old man's weathered features, his stained, tangled beard, the tattered, mud and straw-caked clothes. "So. You been thinkin'?"

Archibald lowered the bottle and wiped his mouth with the back of his hand. "Yeh, I been thinkin'. You wanna know what I been thinkin'?" He leaned forward, his fetid breath washing over Jordan's face. "I been thinkin', it was a sorry day when Isaiah and me found that mother lode, that's what I been thinkin'. We was jist gettin' ready to head on over to Nevada for the winter, we were. Then we stumbles on the Lost Letty, and Isaiah, he says, 'No, we ain't gonna sell this one quick. We're gonna do this one right.' Baahh."

He took another swig, and shook his head. "Do this one right. Ha! It were already startin' to snow, and the whole damn mountain was about to disappear under ten feet of the damn stuff. But Isaiah, he says, no, we're not gonna sell. We're gonna build us a cabin here and sit on things till spring."

Jordan watched Archibald stare moodily down at the

bottle he held gripped fast in his gnarled old hand. "Oh, we sat on things, all right," he said after a moment. "Sat around with next to nothin' to do but play cards to pass the time. Least ways, I had nothin' else to do. Isaiah, though, he spent a good part of that winter in Celeste's bed."

"That's what you two fought over, wasn't it?" said Jordan softly. "It wasn't the mine at all. It was Celeste."

Archibald squinted sideways at him, the whiskey and madness running wild in his eyes. "She tell you that?"

Jordan shook his head. "No."

Archibald sighed. "She shoulda married me. I thought as long as I knew where the Lost Letty was, she'd wind up havin' to give in to me in the end. Now I'm gonna have to settle."

Jordan eased his thumb and forefinger up and down the outside of his whiskey glass. "Most people wouldn't consider settling for half of the richest find in the country too much of a hardship."

The old man's bushy gray brows drew together. "Naw, that weren't what I meant. I meant, settle for less than Celeste. You tell that little girl, that Gabrielle. You tell her, if she wants her mama's mine, she's gonna have to marry the man her mama shoulda married."

Jordan sat very still. "I'm afraid that won't be possible."

Archibald reared back, his hand tightening around the whiskey bottle as something hot and wild leapt in his eyes. "What you tellin' me? You tellin' me she's already married, is that what you're tellin' me? You know somethin', mister? I ain't liked the looks of you from the start. You remind me of somebody, and I jist figured out who. Goddamned if you don't remind me of Isaiah. And, now, you gonna sit there and tell me you're married to Celeste's daughter?"

"No." Jordan flexed and unflexed his right hand, his eyes on that whiskey bottle and the unstable man who held it. "We're not married."

"Well, then, what's the problem? Unless you're thinkin' of trying to convince me she's plannin' on becomin' a nun." Archibald's eyes danced with crazy lights. "A nun! Think about that. Celeste's daughter, a nun." He threw back his head and laughed.

He was still laughing when the crack of a Winchester, followed almost instantaneously by the *pop-pop* of half a dozen six-shooters, sent a hail of bullets smacking into the thick log walls.

Jordan flattened himself on the beer-soaked, sawdust-covered floor. Flying lead tore through tables, shattered windowpanes and glasses and bottles, filled the air with shards of glass and wood splinters and the pungent tang of spilled liquor. From outside came the pounding of hooves as a bunch of drunks on a spree sent their horses galloping down the street, splitting the night with their caroling whoops and indiscriminate wild shots.

Jordan waited until he heard the riders reach the bottom of the hill, then raised his head. A moan from the far side of the room told him someone near the bar had been hit. But his attention focused on Archibald Johnson.

Old Squint Eyes lay stretched out flat on his back beside the overturned table. A red stain spread across his chest until it looked almost like a bib.

"Christ Almighty," swore Jordan, easing himself down beside the dying man.

He was still conscious, but the wildness had faded from his narrow eyes. Eyes that Jordan realized were a golden-brown, now clouded, and dim. "I'm done for," Archibald said, trying to lift his head. But the movement set him to coughing, and he choked on the blood it brought up.

"Don't talk. I'll get you a doctor," Jordan said, although he'd seen too many dying men, during the war and since, not to know when death was near.

Archibald clutched at his sleeve with gnarled, scarred fingers. "No time. Got to tell you about ... Letty's grave."

"Letty?"

"Only female ... never let me down. The mine ..." His face twisted with pain. "You'll find it two hundred and fifty yards downhill from Letty's grave. Celeste's little girl ..."

Jordan leaned closer to hear.

"Her Gabrielle ... want her to have it. Even though her mama ... never would look at me." He gave a ragged laugh. "Said I was crazy. Said I'd end up gettin' shot one day." He laughed again, which brought up more blood and made him cough again. By the time he quit coughing, he was dead.

"He was shot by a Winchester," Jordan said the next day, as Gabrielle knelt to place a bunch of wildflowers on the freshly turned earth of Archibald Johnson's grave.

It was early afternoon, on one of those glorious, sunny May days that can come in the Rockies, when the colors are so vivid, and the air seems so clear, it hurts. She had already visited her mother's grave. Now, at his words, she tipped back her head to look up at him, and he knew by the tightening of her lips and the flare of fear in her eyes, what she was thinking. That a shot from a rifle had killed her mother.

"You're certain?" she said.

He held her gaze and nodded. "I talked to Doc Collins a little while ago. Sheriff Baites had him dig the bullet out before Archibald was buried."

She straightened up. "But those men riding through town, shooting at signs . . ."

He turned away from her, to stare down at the bottom of the canyon, where the black, foam-flecked waters of Clear Creek swirled around the cliff face and rushed out of sight. This was the first real chance he'd had to talk to her since the shooting. And he knew she wasn't going to like what he had to tell her.

He blew his breath out in a long sigh. "The first shot I heard was a Winchester, and that's the one that killed him. As for what came after . . ."

He stooped to pick up a twig, and began snapping it between his fingers, over and over, into smaller and smaller pieces. "If this were Abilene or some other rail-head, no one would be surprised if some drunken cowboys decided to go on a rampage through town, letting off steam at the end of a long drive. But this isn't Abilene."

He tossed the broken sticks away, and they turned together, to walk downhill toward the wrought-iron gates. The warm wind gusted around them, fresh with the scents of new grass and fragrant pine. From a nearby stand of aspen came the sweet trill of a meadowlark. He watched her head lift as she glanced toward it.

"You're saying they were paid to shoot up the town like that so that Archibald Johnson's death would look like an accident?"

"Not paid. More like . . . led into it."

She stopped, and swung around to face him. "But why? Why kill that crazy old man?"

Jordan peered at her from beneath his black hat brim. "How did King John put it? 'Bell, book, and candle shall not drive me back when gold and silver becks me to come on.' "

He knew by the stillness that came over her that she recognized the quote, and understood its implications. "You think it's because of that mine, don't you? The Lost Letty Mine. Someone knows where it is, and they killed Old Squint Eyes to make sure he wouldn't tell us."

"That's right."

He watched her throat work as she swallowed. "It's Slaughter, isn't it?"

He paused outside the cemetery gates and turned to look down into her troubled gray eyes. "It seems likely, doesn't it? Given that it was McLeon who tried to bushwhack Archibald Johnson when he was coming up Clear Creek Canyon. Slaughter probably got the location of the mine out of that drifter who came through town last year. I wouldn't be surprised if the fool ended up dumped in some shaft up in the mountains, with his neck broken."

"But if it is the mine he wants, why has be been trying to get the house?"

Jordan shrugged. "Maybe his plan was to get your mother—and now you—to sell the house and leave town. The idea being that he could then offer to take all those old mining ventures off your hands, at the same time."

He watched the color drain from Gabrielle's face as she worked the whole sordid tale through. "That means he won't stop, doesn't it? That even if I turn Celeste's Place into a school, he's not going to leave me alone."

Jordan thumbed his hat back on his head. "The way I

figure it, we have two options. The most obvious one is to find the mine ourselves."

"Find the—" She let out an unexpected trill of laughter that clutched oddly at something inside him. "Shall we outfit ourselves in grease-stained trousers and hobnail boots, and go prospecting?"

He let his gaze drift deliberately down to the swell of her hips as his mouth curved up into a slow, suggestive smile. "You, in trousers? Now, that would be a sight."

"Huh." She ducked her head, but not before he caught the sparkle in her beautiful eyes. He loved teasing her, loved that flustered but pleased flush it brought to her cheeks.

"Gabrielle . . ."

Her gaze came back to his face, her expression thoughtful, alerted by the renewed note of seriousness in his voice.

"Before Archibald died, he told me something. I suspect the man was three-quarters crazy, so it's hard to decide if he knew what he was talking about or not. But he said we'd find the mine two hundred and fifty yards downhill from the grave of someone named Letty."

The silence stretched out between them as she assessed what he'd said. "I wouldn't think a dying man would make something like that up."

"Maybe. Maybe not. The thing is . . ." The breeze caught a loose strand of her hair and sent it fluttering across her face. He reached out to catch it between his thumb and forefinger, and tucked it behind her ear before letting his hand drift down her throat, to the delicate arch of her neck. "You've got to understand this, Gabrielle. Finding the Lost Letty Mine might be the best way to protect you from Doug Slaughter in the long run. But if he knows we're looking for it . . ."

"He'll probably try to kill us before we find it," she said, meeting his gaze unflinchingly.

"That's right. And if he's got someone in the house working for him, he'll know our every move before we make it."

He watched her brow wrinkle at the thought. He knew how much she hated suspecting the women, and wasn't surprised when she veered away from the subject. "Do you have any idea who this Letty was?" Gabrielle asked. "Where she might be buried?"

"No. I've asked Wing Tsue to make a few discreet inquiries among the older residents in the area, and I thought I'd try checking back issues of the local papers. But it could take a while . . . and that's assuming she even existed in the first place."

Gabrielle twisted to glance back up the hill, at the lonely, windswept cemetery behind them. "Just how careful were they about burying people in graveyards, anyway?" she asked. "I mean, back in the days of the first strikes?"

"More careful than you might think. They had to be, in the towns and camps. But if someone died while working a claim up some high canyon . . ." He shrugged, and nodded toward the peaks still glistening white with snow in the distance. "Hell, this Letty could be buried anywhere in this whole damned mountain range—if she existed at all."

Gabrielle stood very still, staring at those wild, jagged mountaintops, and he knew the implications of what he was saying weren't lost on her. She swung her solemn gaze back to his face.

"You said we had two options. Finding the mine is the first. What's the second?"

"I can kill him," said Jordan, his voice flat and weary. "I can kill Doug Slaughter, before he has a chance to kill us."

Her lips parted, her eyes widening. "No, you mustn't." She clutched at his arm, her fingertips digging through the cloth of his coat. "For your own sake, for the sake of your soul. He's not worth it."

Jordan's lips quirked up in a sad travesty of a smile. He lifted his hand, nuzzled her cheek with his knuckles. She trembled, but whether it was because of his touch, or because of what she saw in his eyes, he didn't know. "My soul was damned long ago."

"No." Her grip on his arm tightened. "You mustn't say that."

" 'Have not to do with him, beware of him,' " he quoted wryly. " 'Sin, death, and hell have set their marks upon him.' "

He saw the shock in her face, although he couldn't begin to fathom its meaning. "Don't say that," she repeated, her eyes huge and dark in a white face. "You're not that way. You're not."

"But I am," he said simply.

Doug Slaughter bit off the end of his cigar and shot it in the general direction of the spit box.

He wasn't the only man who'd missed. The sawdust-strewn plank floor of the cheap tonk was stained with streaks of brownish slime. The tang of tobacco juice mingled with the sour smell of whiskey and unwashed bodies, and the faint, musky scent of frequent, hurried sex that wafted periodically from the back room. The Blue Blazes was not one of his high-class establishments.

"They're planning to ride up to Payetteville on Monday," he said to the small, slim man resting his elbows on the ring-marked bar.

"Payetteville?" Bart Tucker pushed his hat back on his forehead with one finger. "What the hell they want to go up there for?"

"It doesn't matter." Slaughter gripped the cigar between his teeth and searched his waistcoat pockets for a match. "Your job is to make sure neither one of them comes down again. Neither one, hear?"

"I can handle it."

Slaughter struck the match, and met the gunman's gaze over the flaring light. It was Tucker who looked away first. "Make sure you do," said Slaughter, sucking on his cigar. "As of tonight, you will be officially and very publicly fired. If you get caught, my ass is covered, and I won't do a damned thing to help you."

Tucker's hand caressed the well-worn stock of the Winchester that never left his side. "I won't get caught."

Slaughter pursed his lips to expel a stream of blue-gray smoke. "Hays used to be a Texas Ranger, remember. And before that, he rode with Lee himself. He won't be that easy to take."

"A bullet in the back is always easy." Tucker's lips curled up into a tight smile. "Mind if I have a bit of fun with the woman, though, before I kill her?"

Slaughter bit down hard on his cigar, his eyes narrowing as he thought about Gabrielle Antoine's long legs and high young breasts. He'd like to have had a chance to try her himself. He especially liked the idea of personally making her regret the day she'd decided to cause him trouble. But at the moment, getting her and Hays out of the way was more important.

"Shit," he muttered, pushing away from the bar. "You can bugger her for a week if you want. Just make sure you kill her when you're through with her."

CHAPTER
EIGHTEEN

Youngmi's quiet sobs were lost in the gurgle of the brook and the sighing of the wind through the pine boughs. She huddled in the soft grass beside the snow-fed creek that ran near the house, her dark head bowed, her red *chang-fu* a splash of exotic color among the cool greens and browns of the woods.

Gabrielle had gone for a walk, seeking some kind of elusive comfort in the brilliant golden warmth of the noonday sun and the chirping happiness of the birds. But the sight of the Chinese girl, her shoulders hunched and shuddering, brought Gabrielle up short. One of her high-topped boots came down on a small twig, breaking it with a crack that sounded unnaturally loud in the stillness of the mountains. Youngmi's head shot up, and she jumped to her feet with a startled gasp.

"Please don't go." Gabrielle stretched out her hand as if to stop the girl when she looked ready to bolt. "I didn't mean to disturb you, but . . . Are you all right, Youngmi? Are you ill? Or are you—" Her gaze dropped unconsciously to the Chinese girl's flat stomach. *Are you with child?*

Youngmi shook her head. "This girl all right," she said

in her awkward, liltingly accented English. "I sorry to worry you."

"Youngmi, wait," said Gabrielle as the girl turned to go. "If you're upset because you don't like working in the house, I can help you find something else to do. Maybe you would like—"

"*No.*" Youngmi swung around. Gabrielle was surprised by the vehemence in the girl's voice, by the flash of some emotion in her dark eyes before she quickly lowered them. "No," she said again. "You are like Wing Tsue."

"Wing Tsue?"

Youngmi gripped her hands together so tightly, her fingers turned white. "He wish to marry me."

Gabrielle sucked in a startled breath. She had seen the two of them together often, and noticed the gentle smile that lit up Wing Tsue's face whenever his gaze rested on the young girl. But for some reason, it had never occurred to Gabrielle that his interest lay in the direction of marriage. They seemed such an unlikely pair—the giant of a man, and this tiny slip of a girl.

"Congratulations," she said cautiously. "That's wonderful."

"No!" Youngmi's small hands slashed through the air. "You are like Wing Tsue. You not understand. I can marry no man. I am not fit to be wife. I am now what I have become. This is my destiny." She turned and ran down the hill toward the house. She ran stiffly, her arms splayed out at her sides, her hair streaming out behind her.

"Jesus, Mary, Joseph, and all the saints," whispered Gabrielle. She watched Youngmi until the girl disappeared among the trees. Then she swung around, and followed the stream uphill, to where the tamaracks and pines grew thick and tall, and the stream tumbled rapidly down its stone-filled course, filling the air with a soothing, laughing rush.

She found Sirena stretched out on her rock, one arm bent up to shade her eyes. She might have been asleep, but Gabrielle knew she was not.

"If you want me to go away, I will," Gabrielle said, halting on the near side of the stream.

Sirena shifted her elbow behind her head. Her eyes were open. "No."

Stripping off her shoes and stockings, Gabrielle splashed through the icy water to perch on the edge of Sirena's rock.

"I thought you were going to Payetteville today," said Sirena, her gaze fixed on the floating white clouds above them.

Gabrielle looked at her in surprise. "No, tomorrow. How did you know?"

The other woman shrugged. "Nothing stays a secret in a house like this."

Gabrielle swiped at her wet legs with the flounce of her petticoat. "Then, maybe you can explain to me why I just found Youngmi crying because Wing Tsue asked her to marry him."

At that Sirena turned her head. "He did, did he?" A faint smile curled her lips. "It's about time. He's been hopelessly in love with her ever since your mother first took her into the house."

Gabrielle looked at the woman beside her. "I always thought she liked him—at least as a friend. But she won't have anything to do with marrying him. Why?"

Sirena sat up. "Because she thinks she's unworthy. As far as she's concerned, she's a prostitute, not a wife."

"That's ridiculous."

Sirena shrugged. "It's the way she sees it. The ironic part of it all is that he put off asking her for so long because *he* thinks he's unworthy of *her*. Because he's only half Chinese."

Beside them the stream purled and sang. Gabrielle breathed in the sunbaked, earthy scent of the mountain. A jay darted past, a flash of blue quickly lost in the piney shadows. The golden May sun beat down warm on her back, but she felt cold and wrapped her skirts around her wet feet. "Does Youngmi love him, do you think?"

"She adores him."

Gabrielle squinted against the glint of sunshine off the water. "Then, this should be an easy problem to solve."

Sirena lifted her chin, her gaze focused on the ragged peaks of the mountains thrusting up behind them. "You think so? My father used to say that the only truly insurmountable obstacles we face in our lives are the ones we put there ourselves."

Gabrielle stared at the fiercely beautiful young woman beside her. The sun bronzed the skin of her cheeks, shadowed her dark, exotic eyes. "Your father sounds like a very wise man," she said quietly.

"He was." A flicker of emotion passed across Sirena's features, then was gone.

"Isn't he still alive?" Gabrielle asked.

Sirena shook her head. "He was killed with my mother when the cavalry attacked our camp."

Gabrielle sucked in a quick, startled breath. "The cavalry killed your mother? But she was white."

"Yes."

"Were you there?"

"Yes."

Gabrielle sat silently watching the stream ripple around

the base of the rock. She tried to imagine what it must have been like for a fifteen-year-old girl to watch her parents killed before her eyes. To be yanked out of the only life she'd ever known, and thrust into a frightening, alien world. A world with men like Silas Priestly and lean-to rooms with locks on their doors. "You told me once that you had a brother. Whatever happened to him?"

Sirena arched her neck, her eyes sliding closed as she lifted her face to the sun's caress. "He lives in Boston now, with my mother's family."

"Does he know? I mean, does he know what happened to you? Where you are now?"

Sirena lowered her head and opened her eyes. "No." She nodded toward the wind-tossed, spirelike tips of the pines, swaying back and forth against the blue sky. "His Apache name is Wind Dancer. Whenever I hear the trees moving in a wild breeze, I think of him." She splayed her palm against the flat gray rock, and levered herself gracefully to her feet. "But we will never meet again." Then she stepped off the rock and walked away, without her shoes, without another word or even a backward glance.

Gabrielle sat very still, her fingers curling around her bare toes as she watched the other woman disappear into the shadows of the trees. She felt a swell of sorrow crush her chest, burn the backs of her eyes with unshed tears. Above her, the pine boughs rustled in the warming breeze. It was such a lonely sound, she thought, a restless, sad sound.

Gabrielle closed her eyes, shutting out the sight, but not the sound of the dancing wind.

Their attempts to trace the woman named Letty hadn't proved very successful.

No one who had been in Central City back in the sixties seemed to be able to remember her, and whatever newspaper records might once have existed had been destroyed in a fire that burned down most of the town back in 'sixty-seven.

It was Gabrielle who suggested they try exploring the areas around the more promising of the old prospectors' claims. And so they decided to start with Payetteville, an abandoned mining camp so deep in the mountains that they were up with the dawn on Monday morning, in order to get there and back in one day.

They rode through woods of pine and aspen, fir and spruce. The golden rays of the rising sun sparkled on the lingering mist caught in the dark green boughs of the trees until the very air shimmered like a river of gold. Gabrielle rested the reins of her horse against her thigh, and sighed with wonder.

To experience the beauty of the mountains in the morning was to be given a special gift, she decided. A gift, like life, and love. But like all precious gifts, she thought as she watched the mist dissipate on the warming breeze, it needed to be savored quickly because nothing . . . nothing lasts forever.

She filled her lungs with the fresh, pine-scented air, and let her gaze rove over the man beside her. He rode so tall and easy in the saddle. She loved looking at him. At his hard thighs gripping the horse beneath him. At his fine-boned hands with the reins threaded through his fingers. At the lean length of his toned body, moving naturally with the rhythm of the horse. Her love for him swelled inside her, until it became a sweet, agonizing ache.

There had been a time, not too long ago, when she'd

have said that if she could only have what she had at this
moment—the man she loved, beside her—then she
would be happy. But it occurred to her now that happiness is ephemeral, like a morning mist. You think you
can see it, sometimes you can even feel it, but you can
never reach out and touch it. You can never grab it and
hold onto it and stop it from slipping away.

A rabbit scampered across the path in front of her, startling her horse, so that he snorted and tossed his head. A
light breeze rustled the branches of the trees overhead,
filled the air with the warm scent of damp earth and sun-
warmed grass. The path turned, erupted suddenly into an
open meadow filled with pink phlox and fairy slippers,
columbines and bachelor buttons, and a riot of other
flowers in a splash of blue and white and yellow and
purple and red, that reminded her of one of those new
Impressionists' canvases, vibrating with color.

"Beautiful, isn't it?" Jordan said softly, reining in
beside her.

She looked at him, at the gentle curve of his lips, at the
clear, strong lines of his face.

And even though it hurt, even though she knew it
would have to end one day soon, she let herself fall in
love with him all over again.

Jordan leaned forward and rested his wrist on the
saddle horn, his gaze on the scene spread out before them.

Once it had probably been pretty here, a gentle clearing cut by a swift-flowing stream. But miners had
dredged most of the creek bed, piling its grassy banks
with great, ugly heaps of gravel. The surrounding hillsides were bare, scarred slopes of raw earth and weath-

ering stumps, their timber gone to shore up the miles of tunnels dug deep in the mountain's bowels, or to fuel the fires of the mills that had once worked the ore.

He twisted his head, and saw his own pain reflected in Gabrielle's face as she stared at the eroded hillsides, the piles of rusting tin cans, the tattered pieces of canvas, flapping forlornly in the warm breeze, the remnants of crude log huts, fallen in from the weight of too many winters' heavy snows.

He swung out of the saddle, and reached up to lift her down. " 'What a piece of work is man,' " he said with heavy irony. " 'How noble in reason.' "

She put her hands on his shoulders, and slid into his arms. For a moment they held each other, with the sun beating down and the wind gusting around them, dusty and forlorn. Even the birds had abandoned this place. All was silent, dead.

"I don't like it here," she said, her face pale.

He didn't like it, either. "We won't stay longer than we have to." He released her to hook his stirrup over the horn and loosen the cinch. He worked quickly, stripping the saddles from their horses and tethering them where they could graze, while she stood with her hands cupping her elbows, her gaze searching the surrounding ridges.

He came up behind her, and eased his arm around her waist. She glanced at him and smiled, but her face was still pale. "That looks like the cemetery up there." She nodded toward a knoll on the far end of town. "Shall we take a look there first?"

He stared into her dark, troubled eyes. "If you really don't like it here, we can go."

"No, I'm just being silly." She linked her arm through his. "Come on."

It was a steep climb to the top of the hill, where a scattering of weed-choked, weathered wooden crosses baked in the afternoon sun. He watched Gabrielle pause to stare down at a pathetically small depression in the stony ground. "Most of these graves aren't even marked," she said.

"Letty could be here." He unfolded the crude map he had made, laying out the locations of the old claims in the area, and squinted against the glare of the bright light as he tried to get his bearings. "It looks to me as if one of the claims was down there." He nodded toward the rocky ravine that dropped away to their right.

She peered down into the shadowed coulee. A dank, musty breeze wafted up on the sound of trickling water. "What exactly are we looking for, anyway?"

He gave her a slow smile. "Don't you know? I'm expecting a big tunnel entrance, with a rusted ore car abandoned out front, and a weathered sign stuck overhead that says, 'Lost Letty Mine.' " He drew his hand through the air, sketching the image as he spoke. "Didn't you ever read any dime novels?"

"Huh." She stripped off her chip straw hat so she could use it to fan her face. "What a fraud you are, Jordan Hays. And here I thought you were the kind of man who read only Shakespeare and the Roman poets."

He watched as the afternoon sun caught the warm highlights in her hair, and made it glow like gold. There was a sheen of perspiration on her skin, and her nose was a bit sunburned. Her lips parted in a teasing smile, and she looked so young and lovely and full of life that his breath caught in his throat.

"Gabrielle," he said, his voice low and urgent with an

unexpected surge of desire and another emotion he didn't want to name. An emotion that was more than simple liking and admiration, more than just lust. An emotion that was nonetheless real for being unwanted, and unacknowledged.

He reached for her, but she whirled playfully away from him, toward the rocky path leading to the ravine. " 'Oh mistress mine, where are you roaming?' " he called after her. " 'Stay and hear, your—' " he paused, his lips curving up into a bittersweet smile as he said the next line. " 'Your true love's coming.' "

She spun around, laughing, the hand that held her hat slowly coming up to shade her eyes, the fullness of her skirt billowing around her in the breeze. He caught a glimpse of a dark, shifting shape, a shadow that was not quite right for a tree or boulder on the far side of the ravine behind her. Sunlight glinted in his eyes, as if glancing off the barrel of a gun.

"Look out!" he shouted, his hand slashing to the gun at his side, just as she veered between him and the man who rose up with a Winchester in his hands.

The crack of a rifle shot echoed through the ravine. He saw her jerk, pitch forward. "Gabrielle!" he screamed. His gun leapt into his hand. The rifle cracked again. He felt the wind from the bullet kiss his cheek, but he was already firing.

Jordan's first bullet clipped Bart Tucker's shoulder. The second caught him square in the chest.

He tottered on the edge of the ravine, his small, lithe body jerking again and again as Jordan coldly pumped four more bullets into the man who had just shot

Gabrielle. Only when Jordan's gun was empty, did the rifleman tumble forward in a shower of pebbles and dirt.

The heavy thump of his body bouncing against the rocks echoed through the ravine. Jordan flipped open the Colt, emptied the spent cartridges, reloaded. He was hideously, agonizingly, heart-wrenchingly aware of Gabrielle lying motionless beside him, the breeze fluttering her bloodied golden hair where it spilled across the grass. His entire being screamed with the need to go to her, to assure himself that she still lived, to touch her, hold her, comfort her. Yet he forced himself to stay crouched where he was while he scanned the rocks, searched carefully for a second gunman, listened to the slow return of silence.

He could hear the distant trickle of water flowing through the bottom of the coulee, and the harsh cry of a hawk, circling up near a stand of yellow pine on the ridge. He caught a movement out of the corner of his eye, and his finger tightened on the trigger. But it was only a lizard, scuttling quickly across a hot rock and disturbing a white butterfly that wafted upward on the breeze.

They were alone.

He eased the Colt back into his holster. Straightening stiffly, he walked the few feet to where she lay, facedown in the dusty grass. He dropped to his knees beside her, his breath soughing painfully in and out, his hands shaking with fear as he reached for her.

He lifted her gently, turned her face upward. His gut twisted horribly as the right side of her face came into view. *Oh, God ... Gabrielle.* She was covered with so much blood and dust that he couldn't see where the bullet had struck. Her body hung limply in his arms, her eyes closed, and for one, horrible, heart-stopping, mind-numbing, unbearable moment of agony, he thought she must be dead. Then he found a faint but steady pulse in her neck, and his own heart started beating again, slamming against his chest so hard that he gasped.

He gathered her into his arms, cradled her against his chest, breathed in her sweet scent, tinged now with a mixture of blood and dust. A sob shuddered up from someplace deep inside him, and for a moment he simply held her to him, rocking back and forth with her in his arms, his eyes squeezed shut, while he found the strength to force himself to look at her beautiful, beloved, bloodied face again.

Shaking with the effort, he opened his eyes. With tender, loving hands, he stroked her hair away from her forehead, his breath whistling through his clenched teeth in a painful hiss.

The bullet had clipped the side of her skull, leaving a jagged, ugly wound that looked deep. Dangerously deep. Dark red blood surged up, ran down her face and neck to soak the sleeve of his coat, stain the front of his vest.

"Gabrielle," he whispered, his voice cracking with anguish as he fumbled for his handkerchief, folded it into a thick pad, tied it tightly in place with a strip torn from her petticoat. She was bleeding so badly, and they were so very far from home. "Gabrielle." He tried to swallow his tears, but they were already running down his cheeks. "Please don't die. Not you, too. Not you."

He lifted his head and stared down the hill, to where the tethered horses grazed peacefully beside the ruined stream. A sigh shuddered through him, and he stumbled to his feet, Gabrielle clutched desperately in his arms.

"Not you," he said again, and started to walk.

* * *

She awoke to a darkened room.

It was still daytime—early afternoon, probably, judging by the muted shafts of light she could see slanting in around the heavy, dusky blue velvet drapes. It confused her that she should be in bed at this time of day, with the curtains closed. She tried to think, tried to remember, but her head ached almost unbearably, and her memories were blurred, unreal. She shifted against the pillow, and fire arced across her forehead. Before she could stop it, a groan slipped from her lips.

She heard a sudden movement beside her, and realized that Jordan had pulled a balloon-backed chair up to the side of the bed, and had been resting there. Now he shifted forward, his hand groping to touch hers where it lay against the satin counterpane.

He looked terrible, haggard. He hadn't shaved in days, and there was a strange glitter in his eyes that in anyone else she would have taken for tears.

"You're awake," he said softly.

She wanted to smile, to reassure him that she was all right, but she felt so weak. When she tried to speak, all that came out was a whisper. "What happened?"

"You were shot." His voice was rough, scratchy. She'd never heard him sound like that before. "The doc says you're lucky you made it. You lost a lot of blood."

She twisted her hand beneath his. "You didn't get hurt?"

"No."

She saw it then. The cold emptiness in his face, the stiffness in the set of his shoulders. And she knew, without being told, that the man who had shot her was dead. Jordan had killed him.

She ached for him, for the numbness she knew he felt inside, for the pain he kept hidden. "Who . . ."

He pressed his fingertips to her lips. "No. Don't talk anymore. You need to rest."

Her mouth moved against his fingers. "But I—"

"Shhh." He stilled her lips. "Go to sleep."

Against her will her eyelids slid shut. She sensed herself drifting into sleep, felt his lips brush her cheek in a tender kiss that faded as if it were only part of a dream.

When she awoke again, he was no longer there.

Jordan watched Tierney dance, her hands moving in sensuous, suggestive circles, her near-naked hips and breasts thrusting seductively against the filmlike gossamer of her gown. From the circle around her came a low murmur of male voices roughened by whiskey and raw lust, and punctuated with staccato bursts of feminine laughter and high-pitched squeals. Jordan raised his brandy to his lips, took a slow sip, then knocked back the rest with a shudder.

He was tired. Tired of it all. The late nights, the loose, easy women, the atmosphere of joyless, hopeless, soulless pleasure-seeking. Yet when he thought about leaving . . .

Setting his jaw, he started to raise his glass again, before he remembered it was already empty. He shoved away from the wall, intent on getting another drink, but paused when he heard a door open at the end of the hall.

Turning, he saw Sirena let herself out of Gabrielle's room and come down the hall toward him. Tonight Sirena wore a black velvet dress trimmed with black satin, which might have looked somber if it hadn't been strapless and cut so low as to expose a good percentage of her high, round breasts. Instead of being mournful, the effect was almost macabre, and decidedly theatrical. Which was probably appropriate, he thought, since it often seemed to him as if Sirena spent a good portion of her life playing a part. She should have gone on the stage, he decided, watching her walk up to him, rather than into a whorehouse.

She stopped beside him, her sharp, uncompromising gaze taking in the empty glass and the restless, dangerous glitter that too many brandies always kindled in his eyes. "How many of those have you had?"

"Not enough," he said, giving her a slow, cynical smile she didn't return.

"What exactly are you doing? Drinking to get up the courage to leave? Or are you drinking to keep from finding the courage to stay?"

He drew his brows together in a dark frown that seemed to have no effect on the damned woman whatsoever. He thought about asking Sirena what the hell made her think she knew what he was planning to do, when he hadn't figured it out himself yet. He thought about telling her she sounded more like a dried-up, prudish schoolteacher than a fun-loving whore. He thought about suggesting she mind her own damned business. But in the end he simply shrugged his shoulders, and said, "Maybe a bit of both."

A shadow of some emotion he couldn't name flickered across her face, then was gone. "You need to talk to Gabrielle."

Jordan pursed his lips and let his breath out in a long sigh. He hadn't been near Gabrielle for almost a week now. He had sat at her bedside, night and day, until he had known for certain that she was out of danger. Then he had stood up and forced himself to walk away from her, and he had stayed away from her ever since.

He stared down at his empty glass. "Did she ask for me?"

Sirena shook her head. "She won't ask for you. But she'd be a fool not to know what you're thinking. And that girl is no fool."

He raised his tormented gaze to Sirena's hard, unforgiving eyes. He could have told her that he knew who the fool was. He could have told her that the worst of our hells are usually of our own making. But then, he figured she already knew that. So he set his glass on the marble-topped hall table, and walked out the front door into the restless, storm-tossed night.

CHAPTER
NINETEEN

A wild, angry wind buffeted Gabrielle's cheeks, snatched at her hair, roared through the thrashing pines on the ridge. Overhead, heavy gray clouds piled up thick and ugly.

It had rained only a little, earlier that morning. But the new grass covering her mother's grave was still damp with it. Gabrielle sank to her knees anyway, her eyes squeezing shut, her hands coming up to cover her face as a sob shuddered through her.

She had never felt so alone. Not even during all those long years growing up in the convent, had she felt this alone. Or this afraid. "Oh, Mama," she whispered. "What am I going to do?"

It had been a week now since she had awakened to find Jordan gone from her bedside. A week of hearing his voice in the distance, a week of wondering why he stayed away, a week of confusion that turned slowly to worry, and hurt that slid first into fear, then into a growing certainty.

He was leaving her. She wasn't sure if he knew it himself yet. But she knew it.

Ever since the night she had first given herself to him, she had known that someday he was going to leave her. Every time she opened her mouth beneath his kiss, every time she held his dark head to her breast, every time she took his hard man's body deep within her own, she had known that the day would eventually come when he would realize he was getting too close to her, too vulnerable to her. When he would grow restless and troubled, and force himself to leave.

But knowing this time would come, and bearing it now, were two very different things.

She opened her eyes as a sudden flurry of wind brought a sprinkling of raindrops that mingled with the tears on her upturned face and battered the flowers she had placed on her mother's grave. It seemed such a lonely place for a woman like Celeste DuBois to have come to rest, Gabrielle thought. So far from the sultry, magnolia-scented air of New Orleans. So far from the man she had loved.

It was only the night before that Sirena had told Gabrielle what she knew about Beauregard St. Etienne and Celeste. Gabrielle had been sitting at her dressing table, absently toying with her mother's pearl necklace, when Sirena unexpectedly said, "Your mother told me once that there were times when she went without eating, rather than sell that necklace."

Gabrielle turned slowly from the dressing table to stare at the woman beside her. "Why? Why did it mean so much to her?"

Sirena stared back, her face inscrutable, her eyes hooded. "Your father gave it to her the night before he was shot. The night he asked her to marry him."

Gabrielle fingered the warm pearls that lay in her palm, thoughtful for a moment. "Did she love him, do you think?"

An enigmatic smile curved Sirena's mouth. "More than life itself."

Gabrielle sucked in a quick breath. "Why didn't you tell me this before?"

Sirena shrugged. "I'm telling you now."

Gabrielle thought about Sirena's words again as the wind dried the rain on her cheeks and whipped her skirt about her legs. The air was cold, cold enough to make her shiver. She pushed against the grass-covered earth, and stood up. Thunder rumbled down the mountain. She turned, and saw Jordan's tall, solitary figure, silhouetted against a gray, stormy sky.

She knew a sudden, intense need just to look at him. At the broad shoulders that had loomed, naked and sweat-slicked, above her in the night. At the firm mouth that had kissed her with such tender hunger. At the sensitive hands that had touched her with fire and given her a glimpse of eternity. She thought she could look at him forever, and still find him a wonder.

Yet soon he would be gone.

Her heart pounded loud and painfully in her chest as she walked toward him. The smell of rain-dampened dust hung heavy in the air. Her skirts made gentle swishing sounds as she pushed her way through the rank grass that grew between the rows of neglected graves.

Jordan waited for her, his hands resting on his slim, gun-slung hips, his intense gaze fastened on her face. Her steps faltered when she was still some five feet away from him. She could not make herself draw any closer.

They stared at each other across the storm-charged distance that separated them. Lightening ripped through the dark afternoon gloom, illuminating his hard face. Yet it showed her nothing. He was so much better at hiding his feelings than she.

"Why?" she asked, a terrible fear that was close to panic surging up from deep within her. "Why did you come here?"

"You shouldn't have walked this far. You don't have your strength back yet."

She didn't realize she'd been holding her breath until she let it out in a long sigh. "I'm stronger than you think," she said, and pushed past him toward the shay he had drawn up at the side of the road.

"I know how strong you are." He came up behind her, his hands closing on her waist to help her up. But instead of lifting her, he held her against him. "There's a private party in the house tonight. A mine owner named Harry Appleby. He lives in Denver, now, but he made his fortune here in Central City, and every year he comes up to Celeste's Place to celebrate his birthday."

"I know." Gabrielle's hands closed over Jordan's, where they bracketed her waist. She couldn't stop herself from leaning against him so that she could feel his chest, warm and solid against her back. "Sirena told me."

"Did she tell you Doug Slaughter is one of the guests?"

Something in his voice made her spin around to face him. "Dear God," she whispered. "You're thinking about killing him. You said once that you couldn't leave as long as he was a threat to me. So now you've decided to kill him."

He didn't say anything, just stared down at her in that calm, terrible way he had.

"I'll go away." Fear and pain tangled together to

thread her voice with dread. "I'll sell the house and go away. Only, please don't do this. It's a sin. A terrible sin."

He ran the pads of two fingers across her lower lip. Then his hand shifted, gently lifting her hair from the bandage that still covered her wound, and she saw his jaw tighten with a cold, quiet anger. "Whether you stay in the house or not, doesn't make any difference, Gabrielle. This is something I must do."

She gazed up into his dark, taut face. "Because you're leaving."

"Because I am who I am."

"But you are leaving. Aren't you?"

He turned away from her to stare out over the canyon below, one foot propped on a deadfall, his hand resting negligently on the handle of his Colt.

She looked at him. At his lean, hip-shot stance and coiled, wary way of holding himself. He was as wild as the mountains around him, she thought. As wild and frightening and, ultimately, untamable.

He stood there for so long, his gaze fixed on the roiling clouds, that she didn't think he was going to answer her. Then she heard him draw in a breath. "I didn't say I was leaving."

The wind gusted around them, tearing her hair loose from her hat, and stealing her breath. "You didn't say you're staying, either."

He brought one hand up to pinch the bridge of his nose between his thumb and forefinger. "There are things that aren't easy for a man to say, Gabrielle. I don't know if I can make you understand, or if I even understand it myself. It's just that . . ." His hand dropped, his gaze swinging around to the lonesome mountains behind them, as if he could see beyond them, to the person he used to be before. "Ever since the war, I've been like an empty husk, a . . . a walking shell of a man. Hollowed out inside, just waiting to die. Then you came here, and . . ."

She watched his throat work as he swallowed. "That day, up at Payetteville. I thought you were going to die." He turned to face her, and she saw the shadows that haunted his dark green eyes and tormented his soul. "It almost destroyed me, Gabrielle. I'm not sure I can live with that—with the fear that I could suddenly lose you."

Her love for him rose up within her, hot and painful, until it seemed she could no longer breathe. She went to him. She expected him to hold himself stiff, aloof. Instead, he opened his arms to her and she walked into them, her breath catching on a sob as he clasped her to him. Her throat felt so raw, it was hard to talk. "All my life," she said, her face buried against his strong, broad chest, "I've wanted someone to love, someone to love me. I can't understand how anyone could be so *afraid* of love."

"Everyone's afraid of something, Gabrielle." He combed his fingers through her loose hair. "Some people fear death, disease. Other people can't stand the thought of simply being alone."

"But love?" She tilted back her head so that she could look up into his face. "For heaven's sake, Jordan, how many people are afraid of love?"

He gave her a wry smile that broke her heart. "Only the smart ones."

The wind slammed against the side of the house, flickering candle flames and howling loud enough to be heard over the roar of voices and laughter generated by Harry Appleby's birthday party.

Harry Appleby stood in the middle of a circle of his guests in the parlor, the cigar in his right hand waving in an arc through the air as he told some tale about a mule that had saved a miner from a rattlesnake. Harry was a small man, still thin and wiry despite the sixty years that had grayed his handlebar mustache and thinned the hair on the top of his head. And he knew how to tell a story. Only Jordan was barely listening. He was concentrating on Gabrielle, who sat at the piano nearby, playing a sad piece by Handel.

She wore blue satin and pearls, and her fair hair gleamed a warm gold in the lamplight. But her cheeks were still disturbingly pale, Jordan thought. Far too pale for her to insist on playing the piano all night.

His gaze shifted to Doug Slaughter, who was sitting on one of the burgundy sofas, and being hand-fed grapes by Amy. Jordan felt his jaw tighten, and he turned away.

"And then," Harry was saying, "just when Isaiah was about to light into Letty for practically trampling him in his sleep, he looked down and saw that rattler. Letty had smashed it when it was only inches from where Isaiah's head had been. Saved his life, he reckoned. But Old Squint Eyes, he was for bashing her anyway—for waking them up." Harry laughed so hard at the memory that he had to stop and wipe his streaming eyes. "Yep," he said after a moment, shaking his head. "That Letty was some mule. Archibald always used to say she was the only female that never let him down."

Gabrielle's hands stilled at the keyboard, and Jordan realized she must have been listening as she played. She twisted on the bench, her startled gaze meeting his.

He gave Harry Appleby an easy smile. "A mule, you

say? I always thought the Lost Letty Mine was named after a woman."

The old man guffawed. "Hell, no. Letty was a mule, all right. Most people also think they call it the Lost Letty Mine because Isaiah died without telling anyone where it was. But the fact is, it's always been the Lost Letty, because it was Letty that discovered it, one day when she got lost. She strayed away from their camp, and when Isaiah and Old Squint Eyes finally found her, her hoof was caught so bad in a crevice between some rocks that they had to dig to get her out. That's when they struck pay dirt."

Jordan reached for a bottle of champagne, and poured the mine owner another glass. "I trust Letty was properly recompensed for her lucrative ordeal. After that, she should have been turned out into a nice green pasture."

Appleby took a sip of the champagne and sighed. "I reckon they would have, 'cept poor Letty had got her leg so mangled by those rocks that they finally had to shoot her. Just about broke Isaiah's and Old Squint Eyes's hearts, I can tell you. They gave her a grand funeral, though. Got some of the girls from Celeste's old house to sing a hymn, and a real preacher to say a few words over her. Everybody in town turned out for it. It was the biggest event since Four Finger Jack had been strung up the year before."

Gabrielle pushed up from the bench and walked over to stand at Jordan's elbow, her eyes huge in her white face. "Where—where exactly did they bury her?"

"Not too far from here, as a matter of fact. In an old shaft about two or three hundred yards up the hill there, I'd say." Harry took another sip of champagne, and belched loudly. "It was right after the funeral they built that cabin out back, to see 'em through the winter." He shook his head sadly. " 'Course, we all know what happened then."

Jordan watched as a distant, thoughtful expression stilled Gabrielle's features. He knew she was remembering that day in the old prospectors' cabin, when he had first talked about leaving her. When they had stood beside the rugged hutch that rested against the back wall, and felt a damp breath of air waft through the cabin, stir the fine tendrils of hair beside her cheek, ruffle the hem of her dress. A damp wind that came, not from the open door behind them, but from the back of the cabin, as if from a cellar. Or a mine.

Her gaze met his for one, pregnant moment. Then she linked her arm through Jordan's, and gave the surrounding circle of men a dazzling smile that made her look startlingly like Celeste DuBois. "Excuse us for a moment, gentlemen?"

Gruff male voices chorused, "Of course," as they turned away and slipped down the hall.

In the kitchen Jordan lifted the coal oil lantern from its hook near the back door, and turned to face her. A white flash of lightning lit up the room, followed almost immediately by a clap of thunder that seemed to shake the house around them. "I suppose I'd be wasting my breath if I were to suggest you stay inside," he said, striking a match to light the lantern.

He saw the flare of pain in her soft gray eyes, and knew he had hurt her, even though he hadn't meant to. He dropped his gaze to the lantern, and adjusted the wick. "We could be wrong." He closed the lantern, and reached out gently to touch her hair where it lay against her shoulder. "You do know that, don't you?"

He felt her quiver beneath his touch, then still. "We could be," she said, "but I doubt it." She tilted her head as she looked up at him, her expression solemn, intent. "And will it make any difference if we do find Isaiah's mine? Will you still ride out of here?"

He found he could not continue to meet her gaze. Turning, he stared out the window at the pines on the ridge, their boughs thrashing dark and wild against the storm-tossed sky. He knew she was waiting for his answer, but he didn't seem to have an answer to give her. He thrust open the back door. The wind took it and slammed it against the side of the house with a *bang*.

"Let's go," he said.

The atmosphere in the cabin was thick with fetid odors. Damp, musty earth. Decaying wood. Gabrielle hesitated with one hand braced against the rough plank door, aware of an unexpected frisson of fear as she watched Jordan enter ahead of her, and set the lantern on the edge of the old table.

Great thunderheads rumbled overhead, but there had been no more rain since the scattered showers that afternoon. The air was full of the smell of dust and the crackle of electricity. The golden flame of the lantern flickered and threatened to go out, before flaring up again. Shadows danced over the beaten earth floor and log walls, turning the piles of mattresses and old furniture into mysterious masses that seemed to loom out of the darkness. A loose shutter banged in the wind, and the boughs of the big old spruce outside scraped against the roof. A stale breath of air slid over Gabrielle's cheeks, making her shiver.

"It seems odd, doesn't it?" she said, her voice sounding

hollow, hushed. "That no one ever noticed the dampness and the draft in here before."

Jordan swung around, letting his gaze rove over the crude chinked logs, the stone wall. "I don't know about that. We noticed it. We just didn't think anything of it. The way the cabin's built into the side of the mountain, it would be damp in here in any case." He gripped the edge of the hutch that stood against the back wall. "And the air currents could just as easily be caused by some gap between the wall and hill outside, as by a mine." He shoved the hutch to one side. "Who knows, maybe—"

He broke off as the hutch scraped dully across the dirt floor, revealing a break in the stone courses of the cabin's back wall. A break that formed the entrance to a small hole.

Gabrielle gasped and picked up the lantern to bring the light closer. It shone on a tunnel so small it looked like little more than an animal burrow. "That's it? That little hole?"

Jordan laughed. "What were you expecting? Ali Baba's cave? Here, give me that lantern."

She passed it to him, but he had to shimmy through the opening on his belly, pulling himself through with his elbows. The light bounced around the narrow tunnel, illuminating damp walls sheared up with crude timbers.

He twisted around to throw a cocky grin back at her. "This little hole," he said, "has enough gold in it right here to make anyone very, very rich. And God knows how far back the vein runs."

Gabrielle stared at him. The glow of the lantern highlighted the flaring bones of his cheeks, threw the hollows beneath into shadow, and hid his eyes. But then, she thought, his eyes never told her anything anyway.

Heedless of her satin skirts, Gabrielle sank to her

knees on the cabin's dirt floor. Her gaze fastened on that dark, shadowy hole with something very much like hatred as she realized exactly how much this mine had cost her. "This is why Slaughter wanted the house," she said softly. "He knew. He knew this cabin was built in front of the mine entrance, and so he killed my mother, and he tried to kill me. For this—this hole in the ground."

Jordan wiggled back into the room, until he was crouched beside her. "Looks like it." He set down the lantern to dust off his hands. "Slaughter has been here since the early sixties. Which means that if Archibald's old cell mate told Slaughter about Letty's grave, he'd have known right away where the mine was."

Gabrielle felt suddenly cold, and wrapped her arms around herself, trying to keep herself warm. "So my mother died just for *gold*," she said, a sour taste in her mouth.

"No." He picked up the lantern and straightened, wrapping one hand around her upper arm to haul her up beside him. "Your mother fought and died for the same things you've been fighting for, Gabrielle. For the house she built, and the future of the people she felt responsible for, and the conviction that evil shouldn't be allowed to triumph just because decent people are afraid to stand up and fight against it."

She looked into his fierce, beautiful face, and felt her love for him swell within her until it was something painful, something that stopped her breath and choked her throat. She felt a desperate need to reach out and hold him in her life, hold him with her, forever. She took a step toward him and rested her cheek against his strong, broad chest.

She expected him to pull away from her, but he didn't.

She closed her eyes, listened to the heavy drumbeat of his heart. "I love you, Jordan," she whispered. She felt him stiffen, but pushed on. "I never said it before because I knew you didn't want me to love you. But I do. It hurts, and I'm scared. Yet you'll never convince me it's not worth it. Pain and fear may be the price we pay for love, but love . . . Love is what gives meaning to life."

"God." She felt his hand spasm in her hair, crushing it. "I love you, Gabrielle," he said, his voice an agonized whisper against her ear. He let out a ragged laugh. "It's ironic, in a way, because if I didn't love you, I'd find it a lot easier to stay with you. But as it is . . ."

His voice trailed off, but she knew what he was trying to say. All at once the wind outside seemed to die. The cabin was so quiet, she could hear the faint drip of moisture from the mine.

The drip of moisture and the rasping of her own breath, and the sound of a shotgun being cocked as Doug Slaughter's clipped voice said, "Just keep your hands in sight and away from that gun on your hip, Hays."

CHAPTER
TWENTY

Doug Slaughter stood inside the open doorway, his thumbs hooked in the pockets of his silk vest, an unlit cigar clenched between his teeth. He wasn't armed, but then, he never was. He didn't need to be. He had Skeeter McCoy, who clutched the stock of a shotgun to his shoulder. And the sallow-faced man Jordan recognized from the Silver Spur, who calmly levered a cartridge into the breech of his Winchester with an expert's economy and surety of motion.

Then, slowly, the man raised the barrel until it pointed right between Jordan's eyes.

Jordan's gaze shifted from the Winchester, to Slaughter. The edges of Slaughter's mustache lifted, and he smiled. "You see why you should have talked her into selling when you had the chance, Hays."

"You think so?" Jordan shook his head, answering the big man's smile with one of his own. "I think I should have killed you when I had the chance." He tightened his left hand around the lantern he still held, ready to throw it. A flash of bright green satin caught his eye, stopping him.

A woman slid into the cabin. A woman with titian hair and brown eyes that flashed contemptuously as she wrapped her arm around Slaughter's waist and leaned into him. Slaughter didn't even look at her.

Jordan heard Gabrielle gasp and whisper, *"Tierney."* He flung out his hand, the hand without the lantern, his gun hand, and caught her arm when she would have rushed forward.

"Now, why am I not surprised to see you here, Tierney?" said Jordan, his voice a lazy drawl, the pressure of his fingers tightening on Gabrielle's arm in a warning squeeze. Her head jerked around. She stared at him, wide-eyed, alert.

"You didn't know I worked for him." Tierney's brows drew together. "You couldn't have known."

"No. But I knew Sirena never liked you or trusted you, and that was enough," Jordan said. Then he whispered to Gabrielle, *"Get down,"* and shoved her out of the line of fire at the same time as he swung the lantern up and threw it, straight at the door.

The lantern sailed through the air, the flame dimming, almost going out. The lanky man with the Winchester flung up his arm to protect his face, just as Jordan's Colt leapt into his hand and spit fire.

In the near darkness he could only shoot by memory, by instinct. He heard Tierney scream. Then the lantern landed with a dull thud on the pile of old mattresses, and burning oil spilled out onto the rotten ticking.

"Goddamn it, get him," snarled Slaughter as Jordan fired, again and again. Flames rushed across the dry, worn bedding, filling the cabin with a hellish, damning glow. Skeeter's gun boomed. Jordan felt the shot tear painfully along his scalp, just as something that was both hot and cold at the same time slammed into his shoulder, knocking him backward.

He heard a crack of thunder. The wind rushed oddly in his ears, confusing him. He tried to bring his Colt up, to fire again, but his arm was too heavy. So heavy, it seemed to be dragging him down.

The musty, damp earth floor of the cabin rose up to meet him. He felt a warm wetness trickle into his eyes, spread across his chest. And he realized that it wasn't the sound of the wind in his ears that he could hear at all. It was the coursing of his life's blood, ebbing away.

"Let's get out of here before the whole place goes up," a man cried.

Someone else snarled, "No, leave her. There's no time."

"No," Gabrielle screamed. Jordan tried one last time to lift his head, but he could not. Then the light dimmed and darkness settled over him, warm and welcoming and total.

"Let me go!" Gabrielle sobbed, trying to hang back. "My God. You can't leave him in there."

Hard fingers dug cruelly into her arm, yanked her forward, away from the crackling heat of the burning cabin. Away from Jordan.

"No." She twisted her head around, her agonized eyes widening as she saw the flames already leaping through the unshuttered windows of the cabin behind them. "No. Please, I'll do anything if you'll just—"

Whiskey-soured breath washed over her. "Shut up," spat the tall, sallow-faced man. She noticed he kept one bloody hand clutched to his side as he leaned into her. "Hays is dead. Do you hear? He's as dead as that whore. Come on."

"No!" She stumbled as the wind whipped her hair

across her face, blinded her, carried her shouts away into the darkness, where they were lost in the boom of thunder and the fury of the storm moving through the trees. *"No,"* she screamed again. *"Someone help me. Fire!"*

"For God's sake," said Slaughter, spitting the words out around his cigar. "Shut the bitch up."

"She won't shut up."

"Then, I'll shut her up," said Slaughter. And he sent his fist smashing into her face.

She awoke in a cold, narrow room, containing only a simple iron bed frame with a bare, dirty mattress, a small dresser, and a straight-backed chair. The air smelled vilely of filth and sweat and cheap sex. Her jaw ached, and at first she could not imagine where she was or how she had come to be here. Then she remembered.

Dear God. Jordan.

Her mind slammed shut against a scream of agony too terrible to be borne. He could not be dead. She refused to believe that he was dead. Surely if she could get to him, she could save him.

She struggled to her feet, staggering against the end of the bed as a giddy rush of dizziness overwhelmed her. She flung out her hands, gasped the iron rails, clung to them until her head cleared. Then she groped her way to the door and twisted the handle.

It was locked.

"Let me out!" she yelled, rattling the handle, banging on the panels. "Someone, please!" She clawed at the crack between the door and the frame, breaking her nails, tearing her skin on the rough wood. She beat on the crude planks until her fists were bruised, and screamed until she was hoarse. But it was useless. Worse than useless.

Exhausted, breathing heavily, she collapsed against the

door, her eyes squeezing shut against the waves of grief and panic that threatened to wash over her. He could not be dead. Someone had seen the fire. Someone had saved him. He was not dead.

A muffled blend of sounds from the room beside her brought her head up. She recognized those sounds. The creak of bedsprings. The labored breathing of human mating reduced to an animal level. And she knew, in a hideous rush of horror, where she must be. She was in one of Doug Slaughter's cribs in Dostal Alley.

I'll see you naked and trembling at my feet.

Nausea rose up in her throat, burning, until she had to set her jaw to keep from being sick. Remembered snatches of conversations returned, unbidden, to terrorize her. Tales of women kept naked and drugged, beaten and locked in these cribs, forced to prostitute themselves to a never-ending stream of brutal, vicious men.

"No," she whispered. "Dear God. Please, please, no."

She twisted around to flatten her spine against the door, her hands splayed out at her sides as if to bar the door to whatever was going to happen. Only, it wasn't that easy, of course. When Slaughter was ready, he would come to her, and she had no way to stop him. So she laced her fingers together instead, and brought her entwined hands up to press them against her trembling lips.

"Our Father, who art in heaven," she prayed, then stopped, frozen, as her straining ears caught the grating sound of a key, turning in the lock.

He had expected death to be cold, not hot. But he could feel the heat of death enveloping him, welcoming him.

Life was pain. Pain and loss and fear. While death . . . death was oblivion. He'd prayed for it—sought it even—

for nine long years. If he wanted it, he could have it now. Except that something . . . *someone* held him back.

Gabrielle.

Jordan opened his eyes to find the cabin engulfed in flames, the air thick with roiling smoke and falling debris, the heat so intense it seemed to wick the moisture out of his body.

He lifted his head, his gaze focusing on the storm-tossed night sky, visible through the distant open door. Blood trickled into his eyes, soaked his side. His right arm hung limp, useless. Sucking in a deep breath, he heaved himself over onto his left side, then had to squeeze his eyes shut as the smoke-tainted air seared his lungs, and waves of sickening pain radiated out from his shoulder.

Gritting his teeth, he propped himself up on his elbow and hip. By jackknifing his legs, he managed to propel himself forward half a foot, and almost passed out again as a white agony engulfed him. It took all his determination to force his body to move again, and again, and again. The fire crackled and roared in his ears, the fierce light and choking black smoke burned his eyes and throat and lungs. A cold, trembling sweat glazed his skin, and with every movement, his head swam dangerously and his shoulder shrieked.

He wanted desperately to lie down on the dirt floor and simply let death take him. But he couldn't. Couldn't leave Gabrielle . . .

"Gabrielle," he said, or thought he said. All around him, red-hot flames danced and roared. A burning log crashed down beside him, showering him with sparks, blistering his skin. "Gabrielle," he said again, his parched lips cracking. And shoved himself forward another foot.

He was almost to the door when his raw, reaching hand touched flesh. Soft female flesh. For one wild moment, he thought it was Gabrielle, that he'd found her. He edged closer, and found himself staring into unseeing brown eyes.

"Tierney," he whispered hoarsely. He pressed his fingers to her neck, even though he knew she must be dead. The hellish light of the shooting flames glimmered on a slick black pool of blood soaking her chest.

He stared at the dead woman, his sides heaving with the need for oxygen. Every breath he took filled his body with smoke instead of air, until he was racked with endless coughing fits that threatened to steal the last of his strength. He forced himself to lift his head, push on. He was so close to the door. So close.

An eddy of cool, fresh air hit him in the face. He struggled to his feet, staggered out into the night, dizzy, swaying. He took two steps away from the burning building, and the roof of the cabin collapsed behind him with a mighty roar that sucked in more air to feed the flames and send a shower of sparks shooting up into the night sky.

His legs buckled beneath him, and he fell. Fell through the clean night air. Rolled across the cool grass of the hillside.

He flopped onto his back and lay watching as a thousand tiny pieces of flaming wood were picked up by the wind and borne off down the gulch toward the houses below. He saw them dancing through the trees like a horde of fireflies, and he thought vaguely that he should do something. Only by now the fireflies had turned into stars, which was strange, since he wouldn't have expected stars on such a stormy night.

And then, one by one, the stars went out, and the night became dark and quiet.

With a smothered moan Gabrielle spun away from the door, her wide-eyed, terrified gaze searching desperately for some kind of weapon in that stark, wretched room.

Fear swelled within her, thick and innervating, until she couldn't think, couldn't move, could barely even breathe. She was aware of her own breath, soughing painfully in and out, almost drowning out the screech of the hinges as the door swung slowly inward.

Doug Slaughter's big, brawny body filled the doorway. He carried a coal oil lantern in one hand. A lantern he set on the dresser with a faint *thump* before he turned to shut the door.

The fear within her surged into a powerful burst of energy. She lunged toward the open door. She felt a gust of wind, fresh in her face. Saw a flash of lightning fork across the stormy night sky. Then a powerful arm wrapped around her waist, jerked her back, flung her spinning across the room.

"Oh, no, you don't," he said.

She smashed into the far wall, bruising her hip, throwing up her arm to protect her face, wincing as the crude planks scraped her bare skin. Tears stung her eyes, but she blinked them back, swinging around in time to see Doug Slaughter close the door and twist the key in the lock before dropping it into his pocket.

She watched him walk toward her. She was shaking as if from a chill, but she could feel a bead of sweat form and run down between her breasts.

"So." He hooked his thumbs in his vest pockets and gave her a smile that lifted the ends of his mustache and showed a flash of yellow teeth. "How do you like your room? Not quite up to your usual standards, I know. But you'd better get used to it. You're going to be here for a long, long time."

Gabrielle swallowed her fear and set her jaw, forcing herself to remain rigid and silent.

She saw his eyes narrow, his lips tighten in annoyance. "You're a proud one, aren't you? Too proud to beg and plead with me to let you go." He leaned into her, and her nostrils filled with the smell of him. The smell of expensive cologne and cigars, and something else she thought might be the essence of evil. "Or maybe you don't know yet where you are."

"I know," she whispered hoarsely, because she didn't want to have to listen to him telling her where she was, she didn't want to hear him say what he planned to do to her.

He told her anyway. "You're in one of my cribs." His smile widened as he reached out one of his great hands to twist his fingers in her hair, and jerk her head cruelly to one side. "And I'm going to make you whore for me."

His hold on her hair tightened, and although she hated herself for it, she couldn't stop the whimper that eased out of her parted lips.

He laughed. "Hear that, Miss Gabrielle Antoine? You're going to be a *whore*. And not a high-priced, choosy harlot like your mother was, but a cheap, Dostal Alley slut who spends her days cringing naked in a crib and spreading her legs for any man who has the dollar to pay for her. By the time I'm through with you, you'll be begging me to kill you."

His words seemed to wash over Gabrielle as if they were coming from a long way off. She heard a roaring in her ears, and for one dreadful moment, she thought she might faint.

He released her hair and let his fingers drift down along the length of her neck in a crude parody of a lover's caress that made her stomach heave. "But first," he said, touching her breast, "you and I are going to have us a bit of fun."

She could not bear to have him touch her. She slapped at his hands, a moan of horrified revulsion rising up from within her.

He laughed. "Going to fight, are you?" His big hands closed over hers, swallowing them, squeezing until it hurt. "Good. I like a woman who fights. It gives me a chance to rough her up a bit, and make sure she knows who's boss."

Gabrielle stared into his broad, arrogant, cruel face, and felt something snap inside her. Lunging forward, she sank her teeth into the fleshy part of his nearest hand, deep enough to draw blood. He howled and jumped back, letting her go.

"You *bitch*." He cradled his injured hand against him, the pupils of his nasty yellow eyes dilating with fury. She saw his jaw set, saw him draw back his arm to slap her with the full force of his open hand.

Her head snapped around, pain exploding in her cheek and jaw and neck. Then he slapped her again, hard enough to send her flying sideways.

She landed in an ungainly sprawl on the filthy floor. Panting, she pushed herself up onto her hands and knees. But before she could stand, his fist closed cruelly around her wrist, jerking her to her feet.

"Bloody bitch," he snarled, pressing his face so close that he sent spittle spraying over her. "Come here."

She tried to twist away, but he dragged her, stumbling, across the room and threw her down on the bed.

She landed flat on her back on the bare, stained mattress, the cheap bed swaying and creaking beneath her. She flung out her hands, levering herself up. "Stay away from me," she said through gritted teeth, fighting to hold back the hysteria that threatened to swamp her. "Stay away."

"You'd better get used to me touching you." He stood beside her, his face slick with sweat, his strange, feral eyes glimmering with excitement. "Because pretty soon I'm not only going to be touching you, I'm going to be inside you."

"Stay away!" She slashed up at him with her nails, aiming for those terrible yellow eyes. His big hands flashed out, catching both her wrists easily, his heavy body pressing her back down onto the creaking bed.

"Goddamn you," he snarled, his breath washing over her, his hands hot and sweaty on the skin of her arms. "Enough of this."

He yanked her arms over her head, wrenching her shoulder so hard she screamed. Holding both wrists easily in one hand, he jerked a fine linen handkerchief out of his pocket and swiftly tied her to the ornate swirls of the cheap iron bed frame.

"There." He stood up and backed away from her, breathing heavily in the stale atmosphere of the airless room. She watched in wide-eyed horror as he shrugged out of his coat and hung it carefully across the straight-backed chair, then removed his neck cloth and collar and undid the top buttons of his shirt. She caught sight of a broad expanse of white chest, thickly matted with coarse dark hair. She thought of that chest, looming over her, crushing her down into the depths of that vile mattress, and the bile rose in her throat until she had to swallow, hard.

Turning away from her, he stooped to retrieve something from the pocket of his coat. When he stood up, she saw that he held a flask of brandy, which he uncorked and raised to his lips. She watched his thick lips moving, wet and greedy, and she clenched her eyes closed, shutting out the sight of him.

She heard him drink long and deep. Then he brought the flask over to hold it to her lips. "Here. Drink."

She opened her eyes and stared mutely up at him. He dug his fingers into her hair, pulling her head back until her mouth parted in a gasp.

"I said, *drink*." He poured the brandy into her opened mouth. She choked and retched as the fiery liquid burned its way down her throat and splashed over her face and chest.

He recapped the flask and tossed it to one side. "You should be more careful, Gabrielle," he said, tsking as if he were scolding a child. "Look what you did. You got your pretty dress all wet." Reaching out his hand, he ran his finger across the bodice of her dress, where the brandy had left a dark stain on the blue satin.

She tried to squirm out of his reach, and felt one of the ornate swirls of the headboard dig painfully into her back. "I guess you'll just have to take it off." His fingers closed around the neckline, and he jerked his hand downward, ripping the dress open to the waistband.

Her camisole and the upper part of her chemise ripped with it, leaving her chest bare to the fetid air and his hungry gaze. Her naked breasts pressed up above the confines of her low-cut corset, and Slaughter let his eyes travel insolently over them, before reaching out to cup them in his hands. While he touched her, he brought his gaze back to her face, as if enjoying the torment he saw there. Before she could stop herself, she squirmed and choked on a sob.

"You're right," he said, pressing one of her nipples between his thumb and index finger, until it hurt. "Brandy was the wrong choice. So crude." He stood up and turned toward his coat. "What would you prefer instead? Opium? Or hashish?" He gave her a smile that showed his teeth. "Or shall we have both?"

The cloth on his forehead was cool. Cool and wet. Jordan opened his eyes and discovered that he lay on his back in the grass, with Wing Tsue kneeling beside him. The air around them was hot. Hot and heavy with smoke and the acrid stench of fire. Although it must still be night, Jordan could see the features of Wing Tsue's impassive face as clearly as if they were bathed in the red and gold light of a fiery dawn.

The light hurt his eyes and made his head ache. The light and the noise. The wind thrashed the trees, and there was a roaring sound, as loud as a steam engine in a tunnel. He wondered if it was the noise that was frightening Jilly. She seemed to be crying, and Jeff Hogan had one of his brawny arms around her, trying to comfort her. There was nothing unusual in that. Except why was Hogan also holding little two-year-old George, and what were they all doing out here on the hillside?

There must be an explanation, but at the moment, it seemed to Jordan too much of an effort to think about it. So he simply turned his head and closed his eyes. The last thing he remembered seeing was the figure of Sirena, standing pale and gaunt against the eerie night sky. A rosy-orange glow highlighted the objects she clutched to her: a gilt Louis XVI clock, and a portrait of a woman with pale blond hair and eyes that shone like silver in the fire's light.

Gabrielle's mind whirled away from her body, and she was in a dream. She was running through the cold night air. The crust on the surface of the snow broke beneath her every step. She stumbled, but she had to keep running.

She was running away from a man. A man whose evil laugh and harsh voice seemed to reverberate through her body. She shivered, only it wasn't cold, it was warm. Warm and stuffy, and she was gasping for breath. There was a sickly sweet smell in the room. And then the man laughed again, and she knew she wasn't running away from him. He had her. He had her, and Jordan . . . Dear God, Jordan could not be dead.

The bed creaked beneath the weight of Doug Slaughter's body as he sat down beside her. Gabrielle tried to draw away from him, but she had nowhere to go, and her body felt heavy, weighed down by the drugs he had forced on her. She could only lie there as he ran his hand up her thigh, pushed up her skirt and petticoat until they bunched around her waist. As hard as she tried, she could not stop herself from flinching, and that made him laugh more.

"What's the matter, Gabrielle? Don't you like it? Maybe you should have some more opium." He snagged his fingers in the waistband of her drawers, and tugged them down, baring her private woman's parts to his hot gaze. "But then again, maybe not. I don't want you to enjoy yourself too much."

His eyes were glinting like shards of yellow flint. He laid hold of what was left of her dress with both of his hands, and ripped the last shreds of her dignity away from her. "You still have too many clothes on, Gabrielle," he said, unbuttoning her corset. "I can't see you properly."

The humiliation was almost overwhelming. The humiliation and the sense of utter helplessness and, on top of it all, the crushing, mind-numbing grip of fear and unutterable grief. She tried to lose herself again in some drug-induced dream, but even that eluded her. And so she prayed.

Holy Mary, mother of God, pray for us sinners—

Doug Slaughter stood up. Her eyes widened, then squeezed shut as he began to unbutton his pants.

Central City was on fire.

To Jordan, Main Street looked like a tunnel through hell. Flames leapt from the roofs of buildings, danced along the length of the wooden sidewalks. The rutted streets shone orange in the firelight. There were people everywhere, shouting, crying, trying to beat back the flames with rugs, hastily pulling whatever they could from buildings rapidly turning into death traps. The noise was deafening. The din of the people. The roar of the fire. The unrelenting buffeting of the wind, and the continuous, frantic *clang-clang* of the fire bell.

And somewhere in this surging, frightened mass of humanity was Gabrielle. Gabrielle and Doug Slaughter.

The street was so crowded, and Jordan so weak from loss of blood and smoke inhalation, that if it hadn't been for Wing Tsue, he would never have been able to push his way through. But the big, quiet doorman had insisted on coming with him, and with every step, Jordan found he was more and more grateful for his presence.

Yet, even with Wing Tsue's help, the chances of finding Gabrielle were so slim that Jordan wouldn't have bet a dime on them. Doug Slaughter owned two gambling houses on Main Street and several more in Lawrence Street. Gabrielle could be in any one of them. Or in none of them.

Finding out was going to take time, and time was one thing Gabrielle didn't have. Jordan knew Slaughter, and he had no illusions as to what Slaughter was probably doing to her at that very moment. The thought of it made his stomach heave so violently that he almost retched.

A blast of hot air hit him in the face as the roof of a nearby building collapsed with a mighty roar. Jordan looked up and realized that this flaming skeleton was all that was left of the Silver Spur. In the street in front of the building, a score of people had gathered, each upturned face harshly illuminated by the shooting red flames. And there, at the edge of the crowd, stood Skeeter McCoy.

Jordan touched Wing Tsue's arm. After a moment's whispered consultation, they worked their way behind the hired thug. Skeeter didn't even realize they were beside him until Wing Tsue's slim knife pricked him in the ribs and Jordan's voice sounded in his ear, saying, "Don't move."

Skeeter froze. Only his eyes moved as he rolled them from one side to the other. At the sight of Jordan, his big, craggy face paled.

"Where is she?" Jordan asked, his lips pulling back from his teeth.

Skeeter's jaw hung open, slack. Wing Tsue prodded him with the stiletto, and the man let out a squeal like a stuck pig.

"Where is she, damn it?" hissed Jordan.

"I . . . I dunno!" Skeeter stammered. "We dumped her in Slaughter's cribs. But whether she's still there, or if Slaughter's with her, I—"

Jordan didn't wait to hear more. He had already turned away, running toward Dostal Alley, when he heard Skeeter let out a small sigh and sink quietly to the ground.

"I figured he might take it into his head that maybe he outta warn somebody," said Wing Tsue as he caught up with Jordan.

The fire hadn't spread that far yet, but the smoke was already as thick as a gray foul fog at the entrance to Dostal Alley. It stung Jordan's eyes and set him to coughing until he had to lean on Wing Tsue's arm for support. The cribs were easy to find. To anyone who knew what they looked like, they were unmistakable. Just two long lines of doors facing each other across the alley, each door leading to a narrow room barely large enough to hold a bed.

"You take the ones on this side," suggested Wing Tsue, shouting over the roar of the wind and the fire. "I'll check the other ones."

Jordan nodded grimly. The doors to four or five of the cribs stood open, their inhabitants already having fled the approaching flames. But a good half of the doors were still closed, and from behind them Jordan could hear the frantic screams of those women who, lacking customers, were locked inside alone.

Until that moment Jordan had only half believed the stories he'd heard, of women locked in cribs, kept drugged and forced to whore in a state of virtual slavery. But as he battered down the door of the first crib and saw the half-naked, half-starved creature who came stumbling out, he realized it was all too horribly true.

The second room was empty. He kicked in a third door, but after one look at the wild-eyed woman with matted dark hair who cowered away from him, he moved on.

By now his head was spinning dizzily, and a growing patch of wetness on his shirt told him the wound in his shoulder was bleeding again. He had to kick at the last door twice before the flimsy, rotten wood finally gave way.

A gust of wind from the open door sent the flame of the lantern on the cheap dresser shooting high. By the flaring light Jordan could see the pale skin of a woman, lying naked on the bed. She had her head thrown back as she struggled frantically with the bonds that held her tied to the bed frame. But he didn't need to see her face or the silken hair that spilled around her to know it was Gabrielle.

And in the middle of the room, bare-chested, hastily pulling on his trousers, stood Doug Slaughter.

CHAPTER
TWENTY-ONE

Doug Slaughter was no opium eater. He was only too familiar with what the drug could do to a man, or a woman. But he wasn't above the occasional use of hashish, which he found mildly erotic.

It had taken some time before it occurred to his drug-numbed mind that the continued clanging of the alarm bell was excessive for a small fire in an old prospector's cabin. He had supposed, at first, that the flames must have spread to Celeste's house, or perhaps even to some of the other houses up the gulch. But it wasn't until much later that he realized the sweet smell of burning hemp left by the drug had been overlaid with the heavier, acrid smoke of burning wood, and that the roar he could hear in the distance was more than just the wind rushing through the gulches and the thunder rolling over the mountains. It was the sound of an entire city going up in flames.

"Son of a bitch," he swore, rolling reluctantly off Gabrielle Antoine's soft body. She had fought him for a long time, but now she lay acquiescent, accepting. He'd been just on the verge of entering her when he heard the crackle of the flames.

Staggering to his feet, he reached for his trousers. He

had them half buttoned when the splintering of the door brought him spinning around.

"Son of a bitch," he swore again, diving for the clothes he had piled on the straight-backed chair. He might not like to handle guns, but he never went anywhere without a knife.

The mingling lamp and firelight danced along the length of the naked blade as he held the knife up, and laughed. He expected the gambler to lunge at him. Instead Jordan Hays lashed out with his booted foot, and the knife went spinning across the floor. With a growl Slaughter lowered his head, and charged.

The sheer momentum of his attack sent the bastard flying backward. He smashed against the wall behind him and slumped down, his eyelids fluttering as if in a faint. On the rough planks behind him, a smear of blood shone almost black in the fire's light.

Slaughter smiled, and closed his big hands around Jordan Hays's throat.

All the while Doug Slaughter touched her body and whispered his vile obscenities in her ear, Gabrielle had been working her hands back and forth, trying to loosen the cloth that bound her to the bed. It had given her something to concentrate on, something to think about besides what he was doing to her body.

But when he rolled hastily away from her, and then Jordan came crashing through the door, she struggled openly.

The pungent smell of wood smoke filled her nostrils. Through the open door she saw naked flames licking up the dry walls of the building across the alley, heard the roar of the approaching fire. One of her hands came loose. She clawed frantically to free the other, her nails tearing into her own skin.

The knot gave. She threw the handkerchief aside, flung herself off the mattress. She meant to seize the cheap chair and bring it down on Slaughter's head. Then she saw the red glow of the shooting flames reflected on the steel blade of Slaughter's knife, lying discarded near the door. She snatched it up, the ivory handle heavy and unfamiliar in her palm.

A film of sweat glazed Slaughter's naked back, glistened in the firelight, matted the dark hair that curled thickly across his naked shoulders as he tightened his hold on Jordan's throat. Gabrielle sucked in a deep breath, and thrust the knife into him.

She felt the blade slide into his flesh. Her stomach heaved violently, but she forced herself to push harder. Not slashing downward, as she might once have done. But cutting up, as Sirena had taught her. Driving straight for the heart.

"What happened to her?" Sirena asked as Wing Tsue eased Gabrielle down into the thick, soft grass that grew beside the hay barn. The girl lay motionless, her eyes closed, her face pale, her body limp and naked except for Celeste's pearls and Jordan's torn, bloody shirt.

"She fainted." Jordan leaned against the barn wall, his own face gray with pain. "Probably the effect of the drugs Slaughter fed her."

"I'll go get the doctor," said Wing Tsue, rising quickly to his feet.

"He's not going to be easy to find in this mess," warned Sirena. "I already sent one of the dealers after him. Amy tried going back into the house, and ended up burning herself pretty badly."

"I'll find him." Wing Tsue set off down the hill at a lope.

Sirena knelt beside the unconscious girl and took one of Gabrielle's slim hands in her own. She stared at it a moment, then lifted her gaze to Jordan. "She has dried blood all over her. And I don't think it's from your shirt."

Jordan pressed his palm to the blood-soaked bandage on his shoulder. "She killed him. Stabbed him with his own knife."

Sirena felt the shock of his words as if it were something physical. She gazed down at the pale, still girl. "Slaughter? Gabrielle killed Doug Slaughter?"

Jordan nodded. He was practically weaving with fatigue and blood loss.

"You need a doctor yourself," she told him.

He tightened his jaw. "I'll be all right."

"Don't be a fool." The words were harsh, the tone gentle. "I'll take care of her, Jordan. She'd probably rather have another woman with her right now, anyway. You go rest until the doctor gets here. Go on," she said again when he hesitated. "Or do you want to be unconscious when she finally wakes up? And ask Youngmi to come help me," she called after him as he reluctantly turned toward the stables.

The stables, like the hay barn, had been upwind from the cabin and had escaped the fire. They now provided shelter not only for the men, women, and children of Celeste's Place, but for many of the other burned-out inhabitants of the gulch. Sirena could hear the thin, reedy wail of a newborn baby, and the hacking cough of a man who'd swallowed too much smoke. Beside her on the grass, Gabrielle stirred and opened her eyes.

As Sirena watched, the girl's pupils dilated with sudden fear, then relaxed. "Oh, Sirena. It's you." Her gaze lifted to the storm-tossed night sky above her, and she blinked in confusion. "Why am I out here?"

Sirena sucked in a quick breath. "You don't know, do you? The house—it burned."

"The house?" Gabrielle twisted her head, and stared down on the smoking hulk of what had been Celeste's Place. "Oh, dear God." She swallowed hard. "Is everyone safe?"

Sirena shrugged. "One of the girls got burned a bit, trying to go back for her dresses, of all things. But she'll be all right. Most people are more concerned about what they're going to do in the future, than about what they lost. They liked working in Celeste's Place. They didn't know you were planning on trying to turn it into a school."

Gabrielle lifted her head to stare at her. "How did you know that?"

"I knew."

Gabrielle's head dropped back. She swallowed hard. "I want to help the women find new jobs. Respectable jobs."

Sirena smiled. "I suppose you can try."

The girl lay silent for a moment, staring up at the restless sky. "I killed him, Sirena."

Sirena tightened her grip on the bloodstained hand she still held. "Jordan told me."

Gabrielle's fingers clutched at hers. "I killed him, and I don't even feel guilty about it."

"Why should you?"

Their gazes met, and held, as the wind gusted around them, thick with smoke and billowing ash and the wild fury of the night. "You're right," said Gabrielle slowly. "Why should I? Why should either of us?"

A gentle footfall on the grass brought Sirena's head around. Youngmi came toward them, carrying something over her arm. "Woman from house down gulch have bundle of clothes with her. I get her to lend me these," she said, and held up a simple cotton dress and petticoat.

Gabrielle laughed softly, and sat up, clutching Jordan's torn shirt together over her breasts. "Thank God."

By the time Wing Tsue came back with the doctor, Gabrielle had washed at the backyard pump, and dressed. "No, I'm all right," she insisted. "But Mr. Hays has been shot, and I understand one of the girls is burned. They're in here." And she led the way to the stables.

Wing Tsue hesitated beside Sirena, his throat working as if he had something to say, but couldn't quite push the words out.

"Youngmi is over there, looking at what's left of the house," said Sirena. "I think you ought to go to her."

He stared down at the ruins of the house, where Youngmi's red *chang-fu* made a bright splash against the flame-darkened timbers. The longing in his face was painful to see, but he shook his head, and sighed. "She told me to stay away from her."

Sirena felt a spurt of exasperation. But then she noticed the lines of strain beside his gentle, hooded eyes, and she ended up feeling sorry for him, instead. She shook her finger under his nose, as if she were fussing at one of the children. "You listen to me, Wing Tsue. This house has served as some sort of a sanctuary for that girl for over a year. Someplace she could hide, where she could just let life flow past her without having to find the strength to take a stand and say, yes, this was done to me in the past, but I'm going to move on from it and make my own future. Well, she can't hide anymore. Celeste is gone, and now the house is gone, too. She needs you, Wing Tsue."

Wing Tsue shook his head. "But I'm not worthy of her. Now, more so than ever. With the house gone, I no longer even have a job."

"Yeh? Well, neither does Youngmi." Sirena's voice was cold and hard, but she softened the effect by reaching out and touching his arm. "Go to her, Wing Tsue. And this time, don't take no for an answer."

Feeling suddenly old and tired, Sirena sank down on the low stone wall that jutted out from the barn, and watched him walk away, down the hill. She saw Youngmi turn and look up, startled, at his approach. The little Chinese girl hovered on the balls of her feet, as if poised for flight. But she had no place to run.

They were too far away for Sirena to hear their words. But she could see Youngmi's hands flashing through the air, see her head shaking back and forth in vehement denial. Wing Tsue just stood there, letting her talk herself out. And when she was finished, he drew her into his arms and kissed her.

Watching them, Sirena felt a foolishly sentimental smile tug at her lips. A smile that slowly faded as she forced herself to confront an uncomfortable but inescapable truth: Youngmi wasn't the only one who had been hiding in the house. Only, unlike Youngmi, Sirena had no gentle giant to help save her.

She was going to have to save herself.

* * *

The bark of the pine felt cool and rough and solid against his back.

Jordan shifted his weight against the tree trunk, trying to ease the strain on his newly rebandaged shoulder. Below him the smoldering ruins of the burned city still glowed red in the murky light of early dawn. The scent of charred wood hung heavy in the air, acrid and sharp, mingling with the tang of pine needles and the sweet scent of clover-laden grass.

"You should be lying down," said Gabrielle, settling beside him, an anxious frown marring the smooth line of her forehead. "You might not think your wound is serious, but Doc Collins said you lost a lot of blood, and if an infection sets in—"

He lifted his left hand, pressed his fingers to her full lips. "I'll rest in a minute, Gabrielle, so you can stop fussing. I just want to see the sunrise."

She caught his hand between both of hers, and cradled it against her cheek. "I thought you were dead," she said, her voice rough with emotion. "I couldn't bear to go through that again."

He traced the curve of her face with his fingertips. "Someone told me once that fear and pain are the price we pay for love."

She stared at him, her eyes as deep and still as a mountain lake. Her lips parted, but she said nothing.

He tangled his fist in the thick golden hair that fell loose around her shoulders, and lifted the heavy mass back so that he could cup the nape of her neck. He felt his love for this woman swell in his chest like a warm, sweet ache. An ache that was never going to go away—an ache he now knew he didn't want to go away. It seemed ironic that he had spent the last nine years avoiding love, welcoming his own death. Yet when he had come face-to-face with death in that fire last night, he had realized just how desperately he wanted to live. To live, and grow old loving this woman.

But he had no illusions about the kind of man he was, and his allegiance to an ancient, inbred code of honor forced him to say, "Did I ever tell you that you deserve to marry some nice, dull young man?"

Her mouth quirked up in a funny smile. "Why you thought I *deserved* such a miserable fate, I'll never know. But yes, you did tell me."

"Good. Then, I don't need to repeat myself, and can just go right ahead and ask you to marry me."

He watched the smile fade slowly from her lips, and felt a piercing stab of fear as he waited for her answer. "And will you stay with me, Jordan?" she asked. "Always?"

He didn't realize he was holding his breath until it came gushing out in a long sigh. "Always," he said hoarsely. "Dear God, always." He tightened his fingers in her hair, drawing her forward until she was so close his mouth brushed hers when he spoke. " 'Set me as a seal upon thine heart, As a seal upon thine arm, For love is as strong as death.' "

"The Song of Songs," she said quietly.

"Yes. The part I would never quote before."

She held his gaze a moment longer, then tilted her head and kissed him.

He let his hand slide down her back, to her waist, and eased her in beside him as the kiss lengthened into something raw and desperate. She bracketed his cheeks with her palms, and drew back. "Your shoulder," she said breathlessly.

"To hell with my shoulder," he growled, trying to pull her down again.

She shook her head, and settled back on her heels. "Look. The sun is coming up."

The clear, sweet call of a meadowlark cut through the morning air. She turned toward the sound, then went very still as her gaze fell on the blackened, smoking husk of the house her mother had built. He saw her hand flutter up to touch the strand of pearls she still wore clasped around her neck.

"Perhaps," she said quietly, "in some ways it's for the best." She twisted around to face him. "I was thinking . . . I'd like to give each of the girls a small percentage of the mine. Something they could use to make a new start. Margot's been talking about opening a restaurant, and Vanessa says she always wanted to be a milliner, and—"

"And Crystal will probably use anything you give her to build her own whorehouse."

A glimmer of amusement lit up Gabrielle's eyes. "She says she wants a dress shop, but . . ." She shrugged. "Their lives are their own, after all. I can only try to help."

He laced his fingers through hers. "And what will you do with your percentage? Build that girls' school you always wanted?"

"Yes," she admitted almost shyly.

"Where? New Orleans?"

She shook her head, and the smile turned into something wistful. "No. Not now. Not knowing . . . what I know."

"Where then?"

"I don't know. Where would you want to go?"

"Me?" He tugged her back down beside him, just as

the sun erupted over the edge of the ridge, caught the snow-crowned peaks above the town, and touched them with shades of rose and vermilion that turned first to gold and then, finally, to a dazzling white.

"What's wrong with right here, in Colorado?" he said at last.

She laid her head on his good shoulder. "Nothing. Nothing at all."

He pressed his lips against her hair, and they sat together, quietly, marveling at the beauty of the sun-washed heights. "It's a gift, you know," he said softly. "The sight of the mountains in the morning. A gift, like life, and love."

EPILOGUE

A mountain-cooled breeze wafted in through the partially shuttered windows, lending the scents of pine and sun-warmed grass to the darkened room. Gabrielle paused in the open doorway, a smile tugging her lips at the sight of her two sleeping children.

Both children had their own bedrooms, yet Gabrielle often found them like this, asleep in each other's arms. She let her gaze linger on their beloved faces. Two-year-old Alyssa, with her golden curls and flushed cheeks, was the image of Gabrielle herself. But three-year-old Matt was his father's son, a dark angel with finely drawn features, and a long body tanned brown from the hours he spent at Jordan's side, learning to work with the horses.

A door slammed in the distance, and Gabrielle's head swung around as Jordan's quick tread sounded in the downstairs hall. She watched him climb the steps toward her, his black Stetson pulled low to shadow his handsome face, the sleeves of his white shirt rolled up to reveal muscled forearms. Her heart lurched, and a pleasant warmth spread through her body, filling her with love and happiness. Even after four years of marriage, the sight of him still had that effect on her. She supposed it always would.

He gave her a lazy smile as he came up behind her and wrapped one arm around her waist, drawing her back against the hard line of his man's body.

"Shhh," she whispered, twisting around to press a finger against his lips. "They're sleeping."

She saw his features soften as his gaze slid past her to their children. His lips moved against her finger. "Come outside where we can talk," he said quietly. "I have a surprise for you."

"What?"

"You'll see."

He linked his fingers through hers, and she let him draw her down the wide hall to the French doors that opened onto the upstairs gallery. They had built the house of her dreams, two stories tall, with double wraparound porches and—over Gabrielle's laughing protest—thirteen bedrooms.

Crossing the plank porch floor, Gabrielle leaned her arms on the gallery railing, and lifted her face to the July sun. She loved this place, loved the sight, the smell, the *feel* of it. They had chosen to settle near Golden, where the grass grew thick and sweet, and the Arabians Jordan raised could race like the wind through the foothills. From here, she could see the white rail fences of the lower pasture, and a herd of some twenty or more sleek, graceful brown and black mares grazing peacefully beside their playful foals.

From here, too, she could see the red brick buildings of her school, empty now in the summer heat. Most of her students came from the mining towns of the Rockies, or from the growing city of Denver, to the east. But the reputation of Gabrielle's Academy was spreading, and it now attracted boarders from as far away as Wyoming Territory, and New Mexico . . .

Gabrielle let her gaze drift toward the jagged, snow-covered peaks of the south, and felt a swift sadness grip her heart. Somewhere in that wild, empty, dangerous land, Sirena had taken refuge. She never wrote, never sent word. Gabrielle knew only that she had returned to her father's people, and that she was determined to mend the wounds she had carried for so long, hidden from herself.

The unexpected sound of feminine laughter drew Gabrielle's attention to the gravel sweep in front of the house, where a chestnut-haired girl of about fifteen was flapping a straw hat in front of her pretty face with an ostentatiously languid gesture. "Why, I do declare, Benjamin Franklin," Gabrielle heard the girl say. "Your feet have gotten to be the size of a couple of buffalo robes. I bet if you tried to run, you'd trip right over those big ol' things."

"You think so, do you, Arabella?" said Benjamin Franklin, who now stood six feet tall and worked for Jordan. "Watch me."

He lunged forward. With a squeal Arabella took off, her heels kicking up the flounces of her skirt to reveal enticing glimpses of a red silk petticoat. She wasn't running very fast, and hardly had the two disappeared around the side of the house when Arabella's shrieks ended abruptly.

Gabrielle swung about to throw a questioning look at Jordan. "Care to tell me what Arabella is doing here—besides trying to seduce Benjamin Franklin?"

Jordan thumbed back his hat and gave her a slow

smile. "I told you I had a surprise." He pulled a white envelope out of his pocket. "She brought you this."

"From California?" Gabrielle reached eagerly for the letter. "Youngmi's baby was due soon."

"It's not from Youngmi and Wing Tsue," said Jordan, and something in his voice made Gabrielle look more closely at the return address. "It's from New Orleans."

"Julia," said Gabrielle on an awed expulsion of breath. "Dear God. It's from Julia St. Etienne."

Gabrielle sank onto the seat of the wooden porch swing. For four long years, she had never stopped thinking of her friend, never stopped looking for a letter. She ripped open the envelope with trembling hands and tore out a thick sheaf of folded papers.

"Hell, it's a book," said Jordan, leaning his shoulders against the wall, and folding his arms across his chest as Gabrielle quickly scanned the pages.

"Her father—my uncle—is dead," Gabrielle said, her voice breaking.

Jordan's warm, comforting fingers closed over her shoulder, and Gabrielle gratefully pressed her cheek to the back of his hand. A hot wetness stung her eyes, and she had to swallow hard. "I don't think I'd realized, until now, that a part of me was still hoping he would relent someday and welcome me into the family."

"So that's why she's writing to you now," Jordan said softly. "Because he's dead?"

Gabrielle nodded. "Julia would never have gone against her father's wishes, as long as he was alive. She's like that. Always so rebellious in some ways, yet when it comes to her family . . ."

Gabrielle folded the letter and slipped it back into the envelope, her gaze lifting to the jagged peaks of the

Rockies. "She says she'd like to come out to Colorado to visit me, and to see this mysterious house and business I inherited."

Jordan ducked his head so that his hat hid most of his face. "Well ... I guess you could always show her Crystal's Place."

"Huh." Gabrielle reached up to give the brim of his hat a tug. "Don't you dare say I told you so."

"OK. I won't," said Jordan solemnly, then spoiled it by giving her a big, fat, know-it-all grin.

After the fire, Crystal, Margot, and Vanessa had pooled their share of the money from the mine to buy one of the new brick buildings being erected on Lawrence Street. But while Margot's restaurant and Vanessa's millinery were both still going concerns, Crystal had quickly tired of her dress shop—despite refusing to carry anything that wasn't a gen-u-ine import from Paris, France. Within a year she had sold out to Jilly, whose husband, Jeff Hogan, was now the superintendent of the Lost Letty Mine.

Crystal then opened her own brothel, and it wasn't long before Amy joined her. Crystal's Place made no attempt to imitate Celeste's Place in either reputation or decor. But Gabrielle understood that the chippies all enjoyed daily fresh milk from the dairy cows Amy insisted on keeping in the barn behind the house.

Arabella's voice sounded again, from the direction of the hay barn. Gabrielle turned toward the sound, a sudden sense of heaviness that was like a defeat, weighing her down. "I wish Arabella would have accepted that scholarship to the academy I offered her."

Jordan slid his hand down to her wrist and pulled her up into his arms. "You can't take care of the whole world, single-handedly, darlin'," he said, his gentle laughter warm against her ear.

Smiling, she leaned into him, and felt his hands begin to stroke her hair. His fine-boned, sensitive hands, that knew how to hold a gun and cut a deck of cards, but also how to touch a woman, guide a little girl's first steps, and teach a boy to ride a horse.

The sun poured down, rich and golden, around them. She rested her cheek against his strong chest, and sighed contentedly. "I suppose it's because life has given me so much . . . you, the children, our home. I feel as if I need to give something back to the world. Not as payment, exactly. Maybe as a thank-you."

"Are you happy, Gabrielle?"

She looked up and found his eyes dark and intense with a deep, joyful emotion that mirrored the tender ardor within her. "Yes," she said, holding his gaze solemnly. "Oh, yes."

He cradled the sides of her face in his hands, his features gentling as he brought his lips down to hers. "God, I love you," he whispered, his voice as soft and caressing as a mountain breeze. *"I love you, love you, love you . . ."*

AUTHOR'S NOTE

Although the characters and major events portrayed in this novel are fictional, one significant event is not.

Central City did indeed suffer a devastating fire on May 21, 1874. By the time the flames had burned themselves out, little of the original town remained standing. But the town was rebuilt on an even more lavish scale, using fire-resistant stone and brick. It is this town that can still be seen in the foothills above Denver today, little altered from the days of its golden glory.

THE BRIDE FINDER
by Susan Carroll

Susan Carroll has written a novel of emotion, passion, and mystery that will captivate every reader. Just look at what these nationally bestselling and award-winning authors have to say about THE BRIDE FINDER:

"Charming and delightful . . . Susan Carroll weaves an intriguing tale that proves the wounds of the heart can be healed by the magic of true love."
—NORA ROBERTS

"A spellbinding combination of magic, passion, and destiny . . . Like Disney's *Beauty and the Beast*, THE BRIDE FINDER is an irresistible fairy tale."
—KRISTIN HANNAH

"A truly delightful story to make you believe in the magic and power of love."
—ELAINE COFFMAN

"THE BRIDE FINDER was absolute perfection from start to finish."
—TERESA MEDEIROS

"THE BRIDE FINDER is the most beautiful love story I have ever read. Susan Carroll is another name for 'magic.'"
—KIMBERLY CATES

"THE BRIDE FINDER is a perfect romance. I can't praise this book enough."
—MAGGIE OSBORNE

Published in hardcover by Fawcett Books.
Look for THE BRIDE FINDER wherever books are sold.

If you enjoyed THE BEQUEST,
you won't want to miss
Candice Proctor's acclaimed debut,
NIGHT IN EDEN*!*

Sentenced to a life of servitude in New South Wales for a crime she did not commit, Bryony Wentworth is ready to fight for her life. Wanting no part of the man who would save her, the rugged and enigmatic Captain Hayden St. John, Bryony suppresses the passion that threatens to overwhelm her.

Set against the panorama of a harsh, gorgeous, and unforgiving land, this passionate pair learns to trust, to love, and to triumph over the danger that shadows their lives until destiny and desire become one.

NIGHT IN EDEN
by Candice Proctor

Published by Ivy Books.
Available wherever books are sold.